SECRETS OF
THE ISLAND

PAMELA M. PIMLOTT

Secrets of the Island
© Pamela M. Pimlott 2023

Typeset by SPD

Badger Moon Books
2023

*To Keira and Shannon,
my wonderful granddaughters.
Thank you for your patience.*

SECRETS OF
THE ISLAND

CONTENTS

1	The New Neighbour	1
2	Old Mill Cottage	10
3	The Mahogany Chest	20
4	The Professor's Letter	30
5	Petra's Night Adventure	37
6	The Cellar	42
7	Discoveries	49
8	Holiday Plans	55
9	Missing	61
10	Relics	70
11	Discoveries at the Cottage	78
12	An Afternoon of Study	87
13	The Girl	96
14	A Mystery	104
15	Secrets of the Cliffs	112
16	Another Castle	119
17	Emily Jane	127
18	Rock Pools	135
19	Who is on the Island?	144
20	Intruders	155
21	Close Encounter	164
22	Underground Ruins	170
23	The Letter	178
24	The Shrine	187
25	Secrets	195
26	Ursula's Story	206
27	The Rival	219
28	Kidnap	227
29	The Cage	234
30	Investigation	247
31	Worrying Thoughts	257

32	Lucas	266
33	The Cave Bears	276
34	Tragedy	289
35	Confession	302
36	In Plain Sight	317
37	The Body	326
38	Revelations	334
39	Departure	344
40	A Stranger	355
41	Disturbance	369
42	Bonding	381
43	The Last Sunset and a Final Secret	393
44	Rest in Peace	406
45	Panic in the Village	417
46	One Last Trip	426

1
THE NEW NEIGHBOUR

"Hey, Mum, have you seen that strange man who is moving into that old cottage in the lane?" Petra asked her mother as she dumped her school bag in the hall.

"I did hear Sir Lawrence Mortimer was going to occupy the Old Mill Cottage at the bottom of Mill Lane," replied her mother. "Why are you so interested?"

"One of our teachers told us today in our history lesson."

"And she said he used to be famous on TV in the 1980's." Rosie arrived home and dumped her bag down too. "It's exciting. Can we go and introduce ourselves?"

Their mother gave a big sigh. "I do wish you wouldn't drop your bags in the hallway. And no, you cannot go and visit our new neighbour. Poor man, at least let him have a few days to settle in."

"OK," Rosie looked disappointed. "If we do our homework now, can we go and see him later?"

"We'll see," replied their mother. "Have you much homework to do, Petra?"

"Not much. I did some in my break."

"Go and help Rosie with hers," said their mother, as she picked the two school bags off the hall floor.

"No, Mum, I'll do that!" exclaimed Petra much to her mother's surprise.

"Right then, I'll make dinner. Mali and your Dad will be home from work soon."

"How do you know this Lawrence Mortimer, Mum?" asked her daughter. "Did you watch any of his programs?"

"No, I didn't," said their mother. "I just remember your Nan mentioned him once. Nan was interested in archaeology, especially old castles in Wales, and he worked on the excavation of the old, ruined castle on Swallows Island."

"Wow!" exclaimed Rosie, "Will it be OK to go and welcome him to the village later?" said Rosie, looking out of the window, where she has a good view of the road. "Look, Mum, the furniture lorry is driving away. Please can we go and see him, Mum?"

"All right then, but when you have finished all your homework and eaten all your dinner. And stay on the doorstep. He won't want visitors poking around inside."

"Thanks, Mum. We will be very polite and just say, welcome to Swallows Village Mr Mortimer, and our Mum has sent you a cake," Petra said impishly, with a big smile on her lovely face.

Their Mum smiled too. "Well, actually you could take him one. I made one last night and Nan has made one too, so we do have too many cakes."

"Thanks Mum, we'll say you sent it for him."

"Oh, go on then!" and their mother waved them out of the kitchen.

So, it was settled that was the plan. The two girls finished their homework and ate their dinner.

"I'll go and tell BB," Rosie proceeded to run up the stairs to the bedroom she shared with her sister. Brown Bear or BB, as the children called him, was fast asleep at the bottom of Rosie's bunk bed, and Rosie didn't want to disturb him. 'A bear needs his sleep,' she thought as she found her hoodie.

"Mum," said Petra. "We are going now. We won't be long. Come on, hurry up, Rosie."

"Yes, I'm ready," Rosie replied as she ran down the stairs.

Their mother was just about to remind them to take the cake when the front door banged behind them and the house shook. She let out a huge sigh and carried on tidying the kitchen.

It was early July and the girls were looking forward to the long summer holiday.

"What did Miss Lawson tell you about this archaeologist?" Rosie asked her sister as they left Swallows Village and turned left into Mill Lane.

"Not a lot," replied Petra. "Only that we were privileged to have an eminent archaeologist as our new neighbour."

"Yes, it is exciting!" exclaimed Rosie. "I think you have to be old like Nan to remember him."

As they approached Old Mill Cottage the leaves in the high hedgerow began to rustle and the wind caught the branches of a nearby oak making the boughs creak, as if a great weight was suddenly thrust upon them.

"I like this part of the village, do you, Rosie?"

"Yes, I do. Do you remember the den we used to have down at the bottom of the dingle?"

"Yes, it was great fun. I think Mali found it first." Mali was their older brother. Petra grasped hold of her sister's hand and urged her to hurry and then she remembered. "Oh no! We forgot the cake!"

"Shall I run back for it?" Rosie volunteered.

"No, we are here now. It all looks very quiet though. Perhaps the professor has gone to bed early, tired after his journey."

Old Mill Cottage stood before the two sisters, and Petra thought it had echoes of the past whispering around in the scented summer air. She imagined she could see the old mill wheel turning, moving the water in the stream below.

"Look, Petra! The front door is open. What shall we do?" cried Rosie.

"Knock on it, of course," Petra replied.

Rosie stood up on tiptoes to reach the old brass knocker, she lifted it and let it drop with a loud bang, but there was no reply from inside, only silence.

"Sir Mortimer," Rosie called into the cottage, but still there was no sound. "He can't have gone out leaving his front door open."

"Maybe he has." replied her sister. "I think we had better go inside and call him. Perhaps he is in the garden at the back."

The stout oak door creaked on its hinges as both girls pushed it ajar. There was a step down into the oak panelled sitting room but there was no sign of the famous archaeologist.

"It smells damp," remarked Rosie.

"Well, it was built next to a stream."

"Yes, I know! Perhaps I mean musty."

"This house has been empty for years," Petra informed her sister. She called out again but was again met with silence.

The sitting room was filled with unopened packing trunks and an old mahogany chest in one corner. There were heavy velvet curtains at the window; one was only half opened, letting in a beam of midsummer evening sunshine that scattered across the room.

"This is odd!" exclaimed Petra. "I wonder where he is?"

"It's a bit creepy in here," whispered Rosie. "Let's just look in the garden and then we can go home."

The door that led out of the sitting room opened on a small study with lots more unpacked boxes. This room was dark and smelt musty. There was a muffled thud in the room beyond and Petra caught hold of Rosie's arm startling the little girl. Both girls stood still.

"We shouldn't be here. Come on! We'll come back tomorrow.

Our new neighbour might be at home then."

"Yes, you're right, it is a bit creepy in here. We should go." The girls turned and just as they reached the sitting room door, they heard a loud groaning sound.

"Help! Is anyone there?" came a troubled voice.

"Yes, we're here," said the girls, following the sound of the voice to the kitchen. There lying twisted on the stone floor was Sir Lawrence B Mortimer, the famous archaeologist.

"Who are you? How did you get in?"

"Your door was open. I am Petra and this is my sister Rosie. Our family lives in the village."

"We wanted to meet you," gushed Rosie. "Our history teacher mentioned you had moved into our village and we should feel privileged to have you as a neighbour."

"Well, that was very kind of your teacher and lucky for me you came this evening."

"What is the matter? Why are you lying on the floor?" Petra asked, bending towards this stranger. "Are you hurt?"

"Not as much as my pride, my dear, but yes. I've twisted my ankle coming down that wretched step," he grimaced in pain. "Here fetch me my stick from over there." Sir Mortimer pointed to the AGA that was fitted in a recess. After his fall the walking stick had ended up over by his wood-burning stove.

Petra retrieved the stick and both girls attempted to help this old gentleman to his feet. As he tried to put his weight on his ankle, he let out an excruciating yell and collapsed onto the floor once again.

"I'm sorry, Mr, Urrr. Sorry I mean, Sir Mortimer, but I think you have broken your ankle," Petra was dismayed. "I will telephone an ambulance to take you to hospital." She deftly used her mobile phone to call the emergency number.

"It can't be a fracture," said the Professor. "I have so much work to do on the island."

"Do you mean Swallows Island?" asked Rosie.

"Yes, of course!" he exclaimed. "That is why I have moved back to live here again in this community. I lived here and last worked on the island twenty-seven years ago, excavating parts of the castle."

There was a sharp gasp from Rosie, "How exciting."

But Professor Mortimer didn't answer, as he was overcome with pain. The girls comforted him as best they could. Rosie found a glass and the cold-water tap she filled it and passed him a drink of water.

After a while there was a loud noise in the lane outside and a blue flashing light whirled round outside the front room window.

"Is it alright to come in?" A burly paramedic stood in the open doorway.

"Yes," called back Petra. "Your patient is in here."

The two paramedics lifted the professor onto a stretcher and carried him out to the waiting ambulance. The archaeologist was protesting all the way and he almost cried in dismay, when one of the ambulance men informed him that it wasn't just one break in his ankle, but it was broken in two places.

Inside the ambulance was well lit, and instruments lined parts of the walls and the two medics did their best to make their patient comfortable. The girls stood by the open rear door peering in. When they were ready to leave, and just as the driver was about to close the vehicle doors, Sir Mortimer raised his head off the pillow and beckoned to the girls.

"I need to talk to you both," his voice was low and urgent.

Petra and Rosie were allowed in the ambulance to say their goodbyes, but the old archaeologist reached out for their hands.

"I need your help," he whispered. "I did some special work on the island many years ago. I found that the island held secrets. Now that I am going to be incapacitated for a good few weeks, I want you two to go to the island and find those secrets. You were very kind to come to visit, and goodness knows how long I would have lain on that floor if you hadn't."

'Lain?' thought Petra. 'That's an old-fashioned word but why am I surprised? He is an old-fashioned man.'

Petra joined Rosie at Sir Mortimer's side. He wore a very smart suit with a watch pinned to his top pocket. 'But then he is an archaeologist!' She had many thoughts about this man they had just rescued.

"Come nearer, young ladies. I presume you are sisters. Now please listen closely." Both girls took a step closer to the patient. The ambulance driver was preoccupied with resetting his satnav and was out of earshot.

"Listen carefully to what I have to say. Now one of you take my keys out of my pocket, one is for the front door to my cottage and the other the back door. Can you see this small one?" Petra and Rosie nodded to their new neighbour.

"Now, this one unlocks a mahogany chest in my study. When I lived here years ago, I had two chests, but the whereabouts of the other eludes me now." The professor grimaced in pain once again.

At that moment the paramedic came back to see that his patient was comfortable, he checked he was securely strapped onto the stretcher.

"Be quick, take my keys and lock up my house. Please, girls." The gentleman handed them three keys on a ring. Two were obviously house keys but the third was a small shiny silver key.

"But how will we know what to look for on the island?"

"Clues will be in a mahogany chest!" said the Professor.

"Yes of course, we saw it in your study!"

"You will find what you need in there! I think you are as bright as you look. Now off you go and don't let me down. And do not say a word to anyone."

The ambulance man started to usher the girls out of his vehicle when Rosie went back to Mr Mortimer's side.

"But we have to tell BB. We couldn't go to Swallows Island without our very best friend."

"And who is this BB?" Mr Mortimer raised his head from his pillow.

Rosie answered quickly as the driver was now getting a little impatient. "He's my huge teddy Bear who sleeps at the bottom of my bed every night and he is wonderful and wise, and he has taken us to the island before," Rosie gushed her words, as the driver started the engine.

"Well, mind he takes good care of you on the island." The Professor gave them a wave.

The girls waved back, "Yes, he will!" Rosie called to the invalid.

"BB always does!" said Petra, as she helped her sister down from the step of the vehicle.

Then the assistant medic secured the doors at the back of the ambulance and joined the driver in the passenger's seat. The girls stood by the cottage gate for a minute or two, watching the vehicle making its way down the lane to the main road.

"I will just go and lock both doors of the cottage, and then we must get home and tell Mum what has happened!" Petra secured the back door and then joined Rosie at the front.

"Shall we go and look in that chest now?" The young girl was anxious to start finding the secrets.

"No! Rosie it's too late. We have his keys and we'll look in the chest tomorrow."

"Why not now?"

But Petra had made her decision. She took her sister's hand and started to walk back along the lane in the direction of their home.

"We will come back after school tomorrow."

"Good idea, I am very tired, but we will have to tell BB," Rosie yawned.

"Listen, Rosie, not a word to anyone else and tomorrow we will bring BB to open the chest."

"OK," said a very reluctant Rosie, but she was far too tired to argue.

2
OLD MILL COTTAGE

Although Petra and Rosie were very tired as they prepared for bed. The night of excitement culminating with meeting their new neighbour and all that had happened came flooding back into their thoughts. As they were putting on their pyjamas and then cleaning their teeth all the activity seemed to wake them both up. Their Mum had been in their room to say goodnight and put out the bedroom light but the minute they heard her footsteps on the stairs both girls sat up in the darkness and woke Brown Bear.

"BB! Guess what happened earlier?" Rosie put on the torch on her phone and prodded Brown Bear, all though very gently making their furry pal sit up and blink his large brown eyes in the sudden light.

"Whatever is going on?" he whispered. "You should be asleep by now."

"Yes, we know," said Petra.

"Hey that's bright!" Brown Bear exclaimed. "Rosie please don't shine it into my eyes."

"Oops sorry, BB, but we have something important to tell you."

"Won't it wait until morning?"

"No, not really, we… err well, to be honest, BB, we have to go to the island again."

"Oh no! Not again. Last time we were nearly taken into deepest space far away across the universe and I need a rest and you girls are far too adventurous for me at my age."

"BB, you are not old and anyway it was your idea in the first place, to take Rosie to the island a couple of years ago," said Petra with a slight hint of indignation.

"O…kay." Brown Bear relented. "Tell me what's happened."

Quite a lot of time was spent whispering. No one wanted Mum and Dad to know what these three pals were planning in the dead of night.

"So, it was your history teacher who told you about this archaeologist moving into the village?" Brown Bear was beginning to see why the girls were excited.

"Yes!" replied the girls together.

"And he knows of a secret hidden on the island and he has entrusted us to find it." Brown Bear yawned with a loud growly noise.

"Shush, BB! Do keep quiet, it is very late. Mum and Dad will hear us."

"Umm… you are right. We must go to sleep now before we wake the whole household. Put that light off now please." Brown Bear settled down in his place at the bottom of Rosie's bed but he couldn't sleep with all the excitement.

Rosie snuggled down under the duvet in the bottom bunk feeling safe that her beloved bear was nearby, but she couldn't sleep either. Petra, who had to climb the wooden ladder onto the top of their bunk beds every night, tried to sleep but suddenly remembered the injured professor.

"I wonder how Sir Mortimer is now?" There was a great deal of concern in her voice.

"He will be fine! There is a good hospital twenty miles away, and I'm sure his ankle will be in plaster by now," Brown Bear assured them.

Rosie pulled up her duvet and snuggled down for the rest of the night.

"We will ask Mum to ring tomorrow. I do hope he is alright," said Petra, in rather a loud voice

"Girls!" Their Dad's voice boomed from the next room. "Why aren't you asleep?"

Well, that was it and silence was the only sound that came from the girl's room for the rest of the night.

The next morning was a bit of a scramble to get ready for school. Brown Bear decided to stay in bed, as he hadn't had much sleep mulling over the girl's news. He had spent the night thinking about Hobgoblins and black aliens with silver eyes. 'Oh dear!' he thought. 'Must we really go back to the island once again?'

It was four o'clock and the girls were home from school and Brown Bear's peace was shattered.

They dumped their bags on the floor, kicked off their outdoor shoes and made a beeline for the food cupboard in the kitchen. At the same moment their mother entered the room through the garden door carrying a basket of dry laundry.

"Hi. You will be pleased to know I rang the hospital this afternoon to ask how Professor Mortimer is today."

"What did they say?" Petra asked, and then suddenly remembered their Mum didn't really like their school bags and shoes 'decorating' the hallway. Rosie twigged too and before their Mum could answer they both retrieved the obstacles and put them in a neat pile in a corner of the kitchen.

Their Mum began to fold the washing into a neat pile ready to go upstairs to the airing cupboard. She had heard Petra's question but was working out the best way to give her daughters the news.

"Mum, what did they say at the hospital? Will Sir Mortimer be home soon?"

"I'm afraid not, his ankle has a bad break, and he is having an operation tomorrow, to insert some special pins to strengthen the bones. Then hopefully it won't take too long to mend." Their mother looked concerned.

"What's the matter, Mum?" asked Rosie, looking quite

perplexed.

"I asked the person I talked to and she said there were complications."

"Oh! Mum, why?"

"Well," replied her Mum. "The receptionist put me through to one of the doctors in charge, and he said Mr Mortimer had already broken his ankle in the same place once before."

"Oh, the poor man!" exclaimed Petra.

"It's alright girls, the doctor told me that Sir Lawrence Mortimer will be well taken care of, and he has already been taken to the Orthopaedic hospital on the Welsh border, not too far away."

"Mum!" Petra was looking questioningly at her mother. "Did you ask where he was when he broke his ankle before?"

"I did! because I knew you would ask, Petra," her mother answered with a twinkle in her eye.

"Where?"

"Well, the first time was when he was excavating part of Hadrian's Wall up on the Scottish border."

"Please say he hasn't broken his ankle twice before. Mum, that's awful."

"Yes Petra, I know!" she replied.

"And the second time?" Rosie felt quite upset.

"He really is very eminent in his field, you know, girls. When he was young he spent three years in China working for a television company."

"On the Great Wall?" Petra was very interested

"Yes, he was in charge of one of the digs," replied her mother. "A load of rubble fell on his foot."

"Poor man!" Rosie looked as if she was going to cry.

"Oh! Petra, you had better have these," said her mother. "I had a spare set of keys cut when I was in town, just in case you lose Professor Mortimer's."

"Thank you, Mum. You are so thoughtful."

"Where's China?" Rosie asked.

"A long way away in the Far East," answered Petra.

"Wow! How exciting! I want to be an archaeologist when I grow up," said Rosie.

"I think I definitely want to be an archaeologist," agreed Petra while deep in thought.

"A great profession!" remarked their mother. "But I won't hold my breath because Rosie tells me she is destined for a cashier's job at Tesco's, and Petra, you will probably open your own Beauty Salon."

Both girls laughed and their mother picked up the washing basket and carried it into the hallway.

"Mum, can we go and check on Old Mill Cottage after tea?"

"Yes! You can but don't be late home."

The evening turned into a very wet one, but it didn't deter Brown Bear and the girls from keeping their promise to the professor. They were on their way to Old Mill Cottage and were getting soaked. The rain was persistent, a low grey cloud was hanging over the village and an eerie mist was lingering above the treetops. Soon they were outside the cottage, being enchanted by the picturesque building, and the stationary water wheel that had once been a vital part of this old mill in bygone times.

"Come on, quickly girls, let's get out of the rain," Brown Bear hurried the girls under the shelter of the front porch. "Now who has the key?"

Petra stepped forward, "I do!" she smiled. "And it is ours to keep."

"How come?" Brown Bear was a bit puzzled, as they had given the bunch of keys that Professor Mortimer let them take from his waistcoat pocket to their Mum for safekeeping.

"Mum had a spare set cut for us to keep, she is looking after the original ones," announced Petra, as she turned the key in the lock of the stout oak door.

The door creaked open and there inside on the doormat was a pile of letters addressed to Sir Lawrence B. Mortimer. Rosie stooped down to pick them all up and was about to hand them to her sister when she noticed a postcard with a view of the sea.

"Look, you two, this card is from another professor at a university in Devon," Rosie proceeded to read the message aloud.

> Hi, good luck with your next project, and I bet it feels good to be home after twenty-seven years away. If I can be of any assistance let me know. I am staying with my daughter in Plymouth for the summer.
> Regards Eustace.

"Oh!" exclaimed Rosie. "He hasn't given a phone number or an address."

Brown Bear held out his paw for the mail. "I don't think we should be reading the professor's personal mail, do you?"

"Suppose not." Rosie passed him all the letters.

"Tell you what is interesting." Petra remarked as her young fingers brushed strands of her wet hair from her face.

"What?" Brown Bear and Rosie said in unison.

"The fact that Sir Mortimer lived here twenty-seven years ago!"

"We will have to ask around among the older inhabitants of the village. To see if they can remember him living here in the past." Brown Bear gave his head a quick scratch, his usual action when he was puzzled.

Petra wanted to go and see the unpacked boxes in the study, but Brown Bear thought he had better check out upstairs to make sure windows were secured, and that nothing else needed their attention. The girls were close behind him and proceeded to look into the two bedrooms above.

"This is really interesting because the window in this room looks down onto the top of the mill wheel," commented Rosie, as she leaned out of the window a little too far for Brown Bear's liking.

"Come in and make sure you lock that window tight, Rosie," he said in a curt voice.

'It's OK,' replied Rosie.

Petra had wandered along the landing and had been surprised at what she saw.

"Come here quick!" Petra called with urgency from the next room. "Come and see what is on the wall of this room."

"Why are you yelling, Petra, what is so important?" Rosie and Brown Bear came to Petra at once.

"It's this picture on the wall! Look. It's the Island," said Petra, her voice hushed.

"Why are you whispering?" Rosie ran to see what Petra thought so important.

"Look closer, it is really old fashioned. Brownish like all old photos."

"Umm!" mused Brown Bear. "I see what you mean."

At that moment all three jumped in fright. There was a noise downstairs.

"Shush, keep quiet. I'll go and see what's down there," said Brown Bear, in his quietest voice. "Go and hide behind that bed."

It seemed ages before Brown Bear returned to the girls. He had made it to the kitchen without being seen but to his surprise, he saw a middle-aged woman taking a vacuum cleaner out of a cupboard that was set in the wall over by the AGA.

Then it twigged. 'Oh no!' he thought. 'He's got a cleaning woman to come in. Now how are we going to search for clues?'

Brown Bear returned to the bedroom and explained the situation to the girls. "We've got to get out of here without this charlady seeing us," he pulled Rosie over to the window. "Do you think you could climb down from here onto that old mill wheel?"

Rosie shivered but said, "Yes!"

"Good girl. Now Petra you go first and help your sister jump down from the wheel, it is rather high up from the ground."

"Why can't we just meet the cleaning lady?"

"No, we can't," said Brown Bear in earnest. "She might change the locks if she knows we have a key. Then we won't be able to come back to search in that chest for the secret clues the professor wants us to find!"

After a bit of a scramble Petra was soon out of the window and stood on top of the disused waterwheel.

"Come on Rosie! It's quite wide. We won't fall," Petra helped her sister down. "What about you, BB?"

"Don't worry about me. I have been practising climbing in and out of Mali's window often enough. If your cats can do it, so can I," Brown Bear was soon on top of the wheel and the girls breathed a big sigh of relief.

Petra had already pulled a branch of an overhanging willow tree to within reach for the three escapees to descend onto the millwheel. A few minutes later they were all down on the lawn in the back garden of the cottage.

"Hey, look, you two!" exclaimed Rosie. "It's getting dark and the cleaning lady has put a light on. Shall we go and see what she's doing?"

"Why not!" remarked Brown Bear, making a clearing in the bushes.

Soon all three were peering into the study window, unobserved by the woman inside.

"That's not right!" Petra gasped. "Look, she is rooting through the drawers in that old sideboard."

"What's going on?" Rosie pushed to the front to get a closer look.

Suddenly the woman stopped what she was doing and grabbed

her coat and made for the front room in a great hurry.

"What…" Brown Bear was just about to speak, when they heard a car tooting its horn loudly outside the front gate. By the time the girls and Brown Bear reached the front of the cottage the car had gone.

"That was a black BMW," said Brown Bear, scratching his head.

"She must be a rich cleaning lady to have someone pick her up in a car like that." remarked Petra, puzzled.

"I don't think she is a real cleaning lady," said Rosie.

"Nor do I. She was having a good search of those drawers," Petra caught hold of Brown Bear's arm. "Quick, we have to go back in and check the old chest, remember we have the key."

The front door opened easily this time and Brown Bear made his way to where they had last seen the old mahogany chest. They stepped down into the sitting room and there was the wooden box in the corner of the room.

"Here, Petra, take hold of the other end and let us see if we can carry it between us."

"I'm surprised it isn't as heavy as I thought it was going to be." Petra remarked, as she and Brown Bear placed the box on an old oak table."

"Are we going to open it now?" Rosie remarked,

"No!" said Brown Bear in a very positive voice. "We are going to take it home and hide it in Mali's room. He told me he is away till the weekend."

"BB, you are right. It won't be safe leaving it here in case that cleaning lady comes back and finds the secret of the island," said Rosie.

"Come on quickly!" Petra and Brown Bear were on their way to the front door. "Right, Rosie, you lock the door after us and let's get home before it rains again."

Outside the night air felt cool and damp. The rain had cleared but as the wind stirred, the overhanging trees were still dripping large raindrops.

"Ouch! Water has just gone down the back of my neck," complained Rosie in a loud voice.

"Shush! Rosie," warned Brown Bear. "We must be quiet and hide this treasure, as soon as we get in."

"We have promised the professor that we will find the secrets of the island and that is what we intend to do," said Petra as they arrived home.

Luckily their Mum and Dad were watching TV in the lounge and weren't disturbed as the children carried the chest upstairs and hid it in Mali's bedroom cupboard.

"Come on, you two, let's go to the kitchen and have a hot drink before we go to bed. I'm really cold," Petra shivered. "And after school tomorrow we will open the chest and find the secret of the island."

3
THE MAHOGANY CHEST

It was two weeks later when Petra and Rosie found time to open the mahogany chest. It had been very frustrating to know the casket was hidden in Mali's cupboard and not have a quiet moment to find out what was inside Sir Lawrence Mortimer's private chest. It was now the school holidays and on the last day of term the six weeks of the summer holidays seems to stretch on endlessly, with delightful thoughts of how they would spend their valuable time.

The first week had flown by, they had both been taken to the south of the country by their parents for a seaside break and the second week was spent at home having school friends to stay over. They even erected a tent one evening and they had enjoyed a very cosy night under canvas out in their back garden.

Brown Bear had been feeling a bit disgruntled, well a bit left out really, but as he lay at the bottom of Rosie's bed the next night, he had a positive thought.

"Girls, wake up! I have an idea," he got up and opened the bedroom curtains.

"What is it?" Petra woke first. "BB, why have you opened the curtains?"

"What's going on?" Rosie soon woke up with the disturbance. She sat up on the bottom bunk and rubbed her sleepy eyes.

"It's BB, he's saying he has an idea," said Petra.

"What is it, BB? Is it morning?" Rosie was a little confused.

"No, it is a full moon shining as bright as day," Brown Bear replied. "It is the moon that has given me the idea."

"What idea?" Petra was getting a bit annoyed, as she was very tired. "Oh! BB! It is two o'clock in the morning! This better be good."

"I want us to go back to the cottage. I am worried that if that supposed cleaning woman returns and realises the chest is missing…"

"She might change the locks," interrupted Petra.

"OK, let's go now!" exclaimed Rosie. "It will be easy in this moonlight to see what we are doing. You know without putting lights on in the cottage," Rosie was now very willing to join in.

"How are we going to get out without Mum and Dad hearing us?" Petra was already putting on her day clothes.

"We will be very quiet and not step on the fifth stair down," said Brown Bear, in a whisper. He had obviously been caught out before.

Rosie put on leggings and a hooded jacket and was ready to go first.

"Wait Rosie, I'll lead and remind you of the creaking stair."

They crept out onto the landing and Brown Bear descended the steps down into the hall, showing the girls the stair to be avoided at all costs.

The house was very quiet as they all made their way through the kitchen into the conservatory hoping the key would be in the lock, as usual.

"We have three hours at the most," whispered Petra. "Dad always gets up very early for work."

"So, we must get a move on. Have you got the cottage key, Petra?"

"Yes, I have BB," she opened the outside door and stepped into their back garden.

The moon really was as bright as day. It seemed to be sailing along above the dark blue sky. They crept round the house to the front and made their way through the village. There was no movement in any of the houses they passed as they made their way to Mill Lane. It was a warm night with only a very light breeze stirring the leaves in the treetops. An owl hooted and gave Rosie a fright; she reached out for Brown Bear's paw.

After a while they stopped outside the low gate of Old Mill Cottage and listened intently. "Come on. All clear! We will walk all round the cottage to be on the safe side."

"What are you worried about, BB?"

"Rosie! I am worried. It has been over two weeks since we were last here. A lot could have happened in that time," he sounded anxious.

"Like what?"

"I'm not sure." replied Brown Bear. "But as Professor Mortimer is still in hospital, I feel it is time to follow his wishes and find out why he wants us to go to the island."

"I just think we should have opened the chest before now," said Petra. "It is still in Mali's cupboard."

"I know!" exclaimed Brown Bear. "But you girls have been so busy with your holiday and camping."

"It wasn't real camping," remarked Rosie. "It was just in our garden."

"Well!" exclaimed Brown Bear. "Camping is camping so long as you have a tent!"

Suddenly Petra stopped just as they were nearing the kitchen door, at the back of the cottage. The moon had gone behind a cloud leaving an eerie shimmering light, just like the gloaming. Petra reached out to touch the dark wooden door and gave a low-pitched squeal.

"Whatever's the matter, Petra?" Brown Bear stepped towards her.

"It's open!" she exclaimed, in her lowest tone.

"Shush," warned Brown Bear, and took charge by pushing the

door open a little more.

"Be careful! BB, please be careful!" Rosie caught hold of her sister's hand.

"Yes! Please be careful, BB," said Petra. "This door was locked, I locked it myself."

"Stop worrying girls! We are going in!"

Well, that was it! The two sisters followed their very best friend into the back door of Old Mill Cottage, and within seconds they all stood in the long kitchen with the AGA and what looked like a cupboard door at the other end.

"This is a creepy kitchen," said Petra.

"I agree!" Rosie exclaimed. "Very old fashioned. Don't you think, BB?"

"To be honest I haven't had much to do with kitchens in my humble life."

Suddenly they stood still, frozen to the spot. They could hear a creaking door swinging to and frow on its hinges! They all turned and saw the door they had just come though swing open, and BB swore he had closed it behind them. The girls were terrified and Brown Bear couldn't believe his eyes to see the door move unaided.

"Oooo!" Rosie ran to hide behind Brown Bear. "Ghosts?"

"No! Don't be silly Rosie!" he reassured the little girl. "It will be the wind."

"But there wasn't one," Rosie was adamant. "There was only a very gentle breeze as we walked from the village."

"It's OK!" Petra closed the door tight. "We mustn't let anything unnerve us. Now, let us look around everywhere, see what we can find."

"We should have opened the chest, then we would know what we are looking for," said Brown Bear.

"But we haven't had time!" Rosie exclaimed, with a little frustration in her voice.

The three chums slowly made their way through the kitchen and were quite aware that this was where they found Professor Mortimer lying helpless, on the cold quarry: tiled floor.

The full moon was giving them enough light inside the cottage to see everywhere quite clearly. Rosie ran her hand along the worktop and exclaimed in an excited voice.

"Look at all this dust! That proves that the woman wasn't a real cleaning lady. Do you agree, BB?"

"Yes, I agree with your logic, Rosie, but it isn't really proof," Brown Bear stopped suddenly as they reached the steps into the study. "Look, that door has moved since we were here last."

They all went over to the corner near the AGA. Brown Bear stopped and examined another door. By Jove, I can feel a strong draught coming from here, there could be a corridor."

"Or another room behind there." Petra stepped forward to examine the door. As she pushed it a little it gave way and swung to one side.

"What is it?" asked Rosie, in astonishment. "Could it be a very long pantry behind here?"

"Yes!" Brown Bear reached for his torch. Since he had met these adventurous sisters, he always carried one. "This one and only door serves both the kitchen, and the pantry, just by swinging on its hinges."

"Wow!" said Rosie. "That is the loudest creak I have ever heard."

"Me too!" agreed Petra. "I think this is exciting! Let's explore."

Behind this double door was a strange surprise. Our trio found themselves in a long narrow room about four metres long and one and a half metres wide. At the far end set high in the white painted brick wall, was a window. The full moon was shining its silvery beams through the opening in long tenacious fingers of light, illuminating the red and grey quarry tiles on the floor.

"This is a strange room just as creepy as the others. Don't you think so, BB?" Petra stood still by the strange double door.

"Do you think it is a pantry?" Rose pulled at Brown Bear's arm.

"I do indeed!" he replied. "Just look at all this shelving made of beechwood."

"How do you know that?" Petra looked straight into Brown Bear's big brown eyes.

"I grew up in a forest, I know every tree there is in Northern Europe!" he exclaimed.

"Oh! BB, you are so clever." Rosie opened the double door and to her surprise found the pantry continued in the direction away from the window and ended up with a very low sloping ceiling under the stairs.

"Hey! What's that?" She picked up a strange object from the very back of the room.

"It looks like a mask but what is that rubber tubing used for?" Petra examined their find very closely.

"It is a gas mask," remarked Brown Bear. "They were used to save civilians from a gas attack by the German armies in the Second World War."

Suddenly the double door creaked once again without anyone being near, and all three shivered in fright.

"BB, I think we should go home now!" Petra exclaimed in a less than calm voice. "It is nearly half past three."

"Yes, you are right, one last look around for anything unusual and then we will go," said Brown Bear in his most positive voice.

"What are we really looking for, BB?"

"Anything Rosie! Well, anything that proves Sir Lawrence Mortimer lived here twenty-seven years ago.'"

"OK! You two look high on those shelves and I will search these low ones. See what we can find. And then we must go, or Dad will be up and we'll get caught."

"That's a deal, Rosie. Now be quick."

For many years the pantry had been left idle but suddenly it became alive with activity. The torch was switched off and the convenient moonlight aided the search. Brown Bear and Petra scoured the high shelves, sometimes with Brown Bear lifting Petra up high, so she could reach the back of the beechwood shelves.

But it was Rosie who made a discovery and let out a yell in the dead of night.

"Shush! Rosie, we must be quiet."

"Sorry, BB, but I have found something that looks very important," she thrust an attaché case into Brown Bear's arms.

"Hey! Whoa! Careful, Rosie, that hurt!" Brown Bear exclaimed, rubbing his chest. "Where did you find it exactly?"

"It was right at the back of the very bottom shelf; I think it is a briefcase." replied Rosie.

"Is it unlocked?" Petra examined the find. "Good! Yes, it is!"

"Well, that's a stroke of luck. I wonder what it contains." Brown Bear examined the brown leather case with interest.

"Is it the professor's?" asked Rosie,

"Yes, I am certain! But I think we must go now; the moonlight is not so good; the moon is going down below the western horizon. Come on, girls, it is Saturday. And we must make time to unlock the Professor's mahogany chest sometime today. Thanks to Rosie we have more intrigue."

"I think you thrive on intrigue, BB," said Rosie, squeezing her friend's paw.

"You know I do, little one!"

Rosie was just about to answer when all three stopped talking and listened intently.

"What's that?" exclaimed Petra.

"Shush, we must get out of here now." Brown Bear ushered them along the pantry back to the double door and the house beyond. The kitchen was cold and dark, as they approached the back door of the cottage.

"I hear a car's engine running outside the front gate," whispered

Rosie.

"Ooo! I'll quickly take a look out of the sitting room window," said Petra, in an excited voice.

"No! you won't, I will! You girls go and wait in the back garden."

"OK, BB! Come on Rosie. And don't talk, your voice is deeper than mine, even when you whisper."

"No, it isn't." Rosie was about to protest some more when Petra pushed her out into the garden.

Then Brown Bear came back to them rushing through the kitchen, and out into the garden. He was panicking and worried about his girls.

"Right now, we must hide! Then as quickly as we can, we must get away from here. That car is none other than the black BMW."

"Ummm. Why would a cleaning lady come this time of the night or morning, for that matter?" Petra remarked. "Well, of course she's not a real cleaning lady, is she, BB?"

"No, I don't believe she is." Brown Bear scratched his head. "What time is it, Rosie? Shield the light of your phone. I think we will have to stay put in this garden until the car departs, because I don't know a way back home other than the lane."

Rosie shielded the light of her iPhone with her cupped hands. "It's nearly three thirty," she gasped.

"It must be! Look, dawn is beginning to break. Now listen, girls. I am going to peer in the ground floor windows and see what is happening. See that old shed at the bottom of the garden, go and hide in there and I will come to you," he paused for breath. "Stay there whatever happens! Shush! I hear voices. The woman is not alone."

Both girls nodded and made their way to a small rustic building in the corner of the garden, near an overgrown hedge. Brown Bear started his detective work by peering into the study window.

Petra and Rosie sat on a low bench very quietly straining their ears listening for Brown Bear to return. The scent of honeysuckle wafted on the night air, and Rosie was about to fall asleep, with her head on Petra's shoulder, when raised voices could be heard coming from inside the cottage. After a while they heard the car drive away going very slowly down the lane and Brown Bear returned carrying the briefcase.

The girls were very pleased to see him, but he gave them a warning sign to keep quiet.

"We must go home before the sun rises any higher," he whispered, with his growly voice. "Thank goodness it is Saturday and we can have a lie in."

There was no sound or sign of the black BMW when they reached the gate, but Brown Bear hesitated. "I want a quick look in the sitting room before we go. Give me the key Petra."

"What for?"

"I'll tell you everything later. Just wait here." That was it, they had no choice but to wait.

The girls felt Brown Bear was taking a long time. Rosie began to feel nervous, as some of the local owls took up a chorus of "Twit a woos."

"Oh! That sound scares me!" she said, getting closer to her sister.

"It's alright they are just calling to their mates to hurry up to bed," said Petra. "You never hear owls in the daytime, do you, Rosie?"

"Suppose not!" Rosie sounded very tired by now.

Eventually Brown Bear returned, "Oh! There you are BB! what kept you?" Petra sounded worried.

"BB, you have been ages!" yawned Rosie.

Brown Bear caught hold of the girl's hands. "You won't believe this!" he panted. "But every box the furniture removers placed in the study," he took a deep breath. "Remember, we saw them unopened on my first visit here."

"Yes, of course we did," responded the girls together.

"Well, they have been ransacked, opened and scattered all over the study floor!"

"Oh no!" Rosie exclaimed in horror.

"Not only that! I found a letter on the front doormat addressed to us from the professor. He obviously didn't know our address, so he knew we would be taking care of things for him here. So, he wrote to us care of his own address. We will read it tomorrow, but we must get to bed. Look, the sun is up already."

Swallows Village was suddenly flooded in sunshine and the birds were singing high in the trees.

"Quick as you can, girls. We mustn't get caught."

They all ran as quickly as they could and thankfully got back into bed before anyone in the household was up.

Petra lay awake listening to Rosie's soft breathing and Brown Bear's familiar growly snore. She was puzzled.

'Why hadn't the intruders found the letter by the front door?' She made up her mind there and then, that she would go alone to search the cottage one night. 'I'm sure there must be another entrance that the woman and the driver are using. Probably because they don't want to be seen using the front door. I wonder who they are? People obviously up to no good!'

Suddenly she heard her dad getting up for work. Petra closed her eyes as she was so tired; she immediately fell asleep and soon she was dreaming about the island and its secrets.

4
THE PROFESSOR'S LETTER

When the girls woke the next morning Petra thought they ought to report the mess they had discovered in the Professor's cottage. But when BB reminded her that they would have to explain why they had all been inside the property in the middle of the night, she thought better of it.

So, after a late breakfast they decided to open the mahogany chest. They located the small shiny key that had been given to them in the ambulance, on the evening the girls rescued their injured neighbour. The three pals met in the girl's bedroom.

"Is the door locked?" Brown Bear asked, in a solemn voice.

"Of course not! We have never locked our bedroom door, have we, Rosie?"

"No never!" Rosie replied.

"Well, we will get on with it then," said Brown Bear. He proceeded to open the mahogany chest but unfortunately, he was having trouble inserting the small key into the lock.

After what seemed an age to Petra and Rosie, he eventually proclaimed "It doesn't fit!"

"Oh, BB, let me try," said Rosie. The key went in at last, but she tried to turn the key in the lock, but for some reason it wouldn't turn. "It is stuck! "She was dismayed.

"Here let me try," Petra turned the key, but she couldn't get it to unlock the chest either. "Not to worry, I will go and get some of that oil Dad uses in his garage."

While she was gone Rosie and Brown Bear sat looking at this

mysterious casket frustrated because now that they had time to discover the contents of the chest, they had yet another setback.

"Look! Rosie this is the most beautiful wood I have ever seen," Brown Bear was caressing the chest with his paws. "Just look at the grain of the wood and this highly polished surface."

"Yes, I can see," Rosie stroked the fine smooth wood. "Is it really made of mahogany?"

"Yes, it is! It is an excellent finish!"

"Where does mahogany wood come from, BB?" Rosie sat on the floor and looked deep into Brown Bear's eyes. She thought how wise he was.

"Well, mainly mahogany comes from West Africa," Brown Bear was deep in thought. "Countries like Senegal and Ghana produce a great deal of it. There are five different genera of mahogany trees in Africa, including one called Khaya."

"Oh! That was the show name of Nan's Siamese cats she used to breed, a long time ago."

"Ummm, you are right Rosie. There is a place called Kayah in Thailand. Very appropriate as your Nan's kittens were of the Siamese breed."

Rosie was pleased she remembered that snippet of information, as BB, always knew such a lot of interesting facts. "I wonder why Petra is taking so long?"

"She's on the way I can hear her on the stairs," Brown Bear looked hopeful, as Petra returned with a tin of WD40.

"Good girl! Now let me try that key."

A little poke around the lock with the end of the nozzle at the top of the can of oil, and in went the key. And then the chest was opened.

"Now let us see this great secret that the Professor wants us to find," remarked Brown Bear. All three crowded over their prize.

"Oh, BB!" Petra exclaimed. "The chest is empty!"

Rosie wanted to cry but thought better of it. "What shall we do now, BB?"

Brown Bear gave his head a quick scratch and began turning the chest upside down and pressing it all over.

"You think it might have a secret compartment?" Petra asked Brown Bear thoughtfully.

"Umm, it could have, but I've no idea where to look for it," Brown Bear looked very concerned now.

Then Petra remembered something, "Where is that letter you picked up in the cottage, the night Rosie and I hid in the garden shed?" Petra looked at Brown Bear. She felt a bit annoyed with herself, not to have mentioned the correspondence before now.

"Yes! Where is that letter?"

"It's okay! Now don't you worry girls. I have the letter in a safe place."

"BB!" said Petra, with an element of annoyance in her voice. "Go and get it, please."

"Right, okay," Brown Bear left the room and returned almost immediately.

"BB, we are very worried," said Rosie. "Come on, please read it to us."

"Is the door locked?" he sat on the rug with the letter clasped between his paws.

"No! BB, it isn't. We never lock doors in this house," sighed Petra impatiently. "Come on, please read that letter to us now."

It took a few minutes for Brown Bear to read the letter to himself. The girls watched his face closely and soon they realised that BB was struggling to see the contents.

"What is it? Please tell us quickly!" The girls sat back on the rug in anticipation.

"It is a long letter, so please girls concentrate," he said, looking at the postmark. "I'll read it out loud for you both. Sir Lawrence Mortimer is now in the West Country staying with a colleague."

Dear all,

> I am so sorry to have burdened you with my problems concerning the Island. I did live in your village for a while, over 27 years ago, but my work has taken me all over the world since then. An old friend of mine told me last summer that Old Mill Cottage was up for sale, and I jumped at the chance to purchase the property once again.
>
> It was so unfortunate that I was clumsy enough to fall within hours of moving in. After a rather painful time in hospital, I have been offered hospitality with my dear friend Eustace, who lives and works in Devon.
>
> I thought it rather a good idea to employ a housekeeper while I am away. So, do not worry yourselves regarding the cottage. My only worry is that you will, as I instructed, look after my mahogany chests until I get back.

Petra gave a deep sigh, "This is all very interesting! So, the professor knows about the cleaning lady!"

"Don't stop reading, BB." said Rosie, anxious to hear what else is to come.

Brown Bear carried on reading the letter.

> If you have opened the chests, I think you have found a certain amount of disappointment, as the contents are well hidden. You young ladies looked very intelligent on our first and last meeting, so I feel you can work out from my papers enough for you to find the secrets of the island. As soon as I recover completely, I will find a way to meet up with you all.
>
> I know you must be thinking, 'Whatever is this old scholar bumbling on about?' but if you find some clues, especially regarding the castle, you will be able to find the island's secrets, and all will be revealed in due course.
>
> I don't believe I have underestimated your intelligence,

but you will find answers within the island documents in my chests, and some more hidden in my pantry at Old Mill Cottage. I believe you haven't left any stone unturned even at this stage of helping me, and you surely will find the secrets of the island before very long.

I realise I owe you a great deal, because if you hadn't shown an interest in a new neighbour, I may well be still on that cold kitchen floor. I am extremely grateful for your friendship and do thank your dear mother for her telephone calls to the hospital. I look forward to meeting you all.

If you need help getting to the island, do seek out my old friend Lucas; he will be able to conquer those perilous rocks that surround the island. You will find him on the Quay.

Yours sincerely,

Lawrence B. Mortimer.

"Wow!" said both girls simultaneously, and Brown Bear sighed, because he found the letter a very long one to read out loud.

"Quick Rosie go and fetch the briefcase you found in the pantry at Old Mill Cottage!"

"On it, BB!" Rosie replied, as she pulled out her find from under her bed.

Brown Bear took hold of the leather case; it seemed to be stuffed with papers of all sizes.

"What exactly are we looking for?" Petra began to pore over some of the documents, as she knelt on the rug.

After a while, Rosie stood up and looked down at her sister and her beloved BB, still crouched over the briefcase. She didn't often tell them what to do, but at this moment in time she had an idea.

"I know what we should be looking for."

"What?" Brown Bear and Petra demanded together.

"A map! Yes, of course, a map," the little girl looked pleased with herself.

"Of course! Rosie, you are right. I think that is what the Professor means. Come on you two, let us find it now." Petra was very excited with the realisation that the Professor would at least give them clues as to what they would be looking for when they arrive on the island.

The next few minutes were spent emptying the whole contents of the briefcase and spreading them all over the floor.

"What a mess." Rosie remarked. "Hope Mum doesn't come upstairs now!"

Suddenly Petra gasped and held up an old piece of parchment. Brown Bear and Rosie yelled in delight.

"BB, I think this is what we are looking for," Petra had the biggest smile on her pretty face.

"Yes, it is!" cried Rosie in delight. There was a great deal of noisy excitement.

"Oh! Listen! Mum is coming upstairs," Petra began to bundle all the papers including the map, back into the case and pushed everything under their bed.

"Girls, get changed into something nice!" Their mother entered the bedroom, just as Rosie pushed the last piece of paper under her bed, alongside the rest of the contents of the Professor's briefcase.

"Why? Where are we going?" Petra asked.

"Do we have to go out? Rosie looked a bit glum.

"Yes, we do! Dad is taking us to the Chinese restaurant for an all we can eat buffet. So, do hurry!"

"Yippee!" yelled Rosie, in excitement. "Can BB come too?"

"Certainly not!" replied their mother. "Sometimes I think you girls believe that bear is real," she sighed.

"But he…." Petra interrupted, but then decided not to argue. "That's great Mum, we'll be there in a minute."

So, that was it! No chance of exploring anything more that day. Instead, they were whisked away to the nearest town for a Saturday night supper.

It was past eleven thirty by the time they were tucked up in bed. Petra couldn't sleep. She lay for a while listening to Rosie's soft breathing and Brown Bear's growly snoring, somethings she had grown accustomed to.

'We still haven't found anything in the chest, only the map amongst the papers from in the briefcase. This is no easy task the Professor has given us!'

Then a plan was taking shape in her mind. She was wide awake tonight and she decided she would go alone as soon as she could and find the answer to a new idea that was forming in her mind. In the Professor's letter she had been quick to notice he had written chests, not chest and that means there is another chest hidden somewhere in Old Mill Cottage!

'It's Sunday tomorrow, we might be going to a car boot sale,' she thought. 'I will have to wait till tomorrow night.' And with those plans clear in her head Petra drifted off to sleep, dreaming of what they might find on the island.

5
PETRA'S NIGHT ADVENTURE

The next night Petra made her way through the sleeping village, along the lane encroached by the late summer's growth of the hedgerow. Leaves rustled above her head, as gusts of wind played with the topmost branches. Suddenly she stopped and froze to the spot as a loud screech disturbed the night air. She could feel her heart pounding deep in her chest.

'Come on! Don't be stupid,' she sighed. 'It is only screech owls, calling to one another,' she told herself, and carried on towards Old Mill Cottage.

Petra caught her breath, as she listened to the strange noises of the night.

Far down the hill she could hear animals, fighting with vicious squeals, she thought it could be foxes down in the dell where her brother Mali had once made a den for them all to play, when they were much younger. There were other noises further away and some much nearer. Heckles rose on the back of her neck creating shivers down her spine. The night was full of strange eerie sounds. In that moment Petra thought of her cosy bed and how she should be in it, but no she mustn't falter. She had a mission to fulfil tonight.

Petra looked at the time on her phone; it was 12.35 am. 'Oh! I had better hurry.'

She had thought of nothing else all day than her plan to find another entrance into the cottage. Petra had been very puzzled because BB had found the letter from the professor with

'The Children' written on the envelope for them to find. Brown Bear said he found it lying on the mat inside the cottage. Yet, the woman and her driver, whoever they might be, did not find it. Surely, they must have seen the envelope lying there when they entered the front door. But obviously they had not seen the correspondence at all, because it was when BB had gone back into the house, he found the study had been ransacked. It was only then that Brown Bear had discovered the letter.

She and Rosie had been waiting in the garden shed for his return, and of course that is when he brought the letter to show them. The main door opened directly into the sitting room and the study lay beyond. Petra was now convinced that there is a secret entrance to the cottage, an entrance the intruders had used last night.

So, she remembered that they had entered the cottage through the kitchen door, and they all must have been in the pantry, when the woman and her companion had entered the house. The young girl shivered at the thought of being caught.

She was now outside Old Mill Cottage. She pushed open the gate and walked to the front door. She pushed it, but it was locked. It stood solid and she noticed it was a very old-fashioned door made of solid oak. The moon was doing its best to give her light, but wispy clouds were hovering over its face, distorting the moonbeams, and only now and again could she see her surroundings clearly. She didn't want to use the torch on her iPhone, but luckily at that very moment the moon broke free of clouds and gave her a soft silvery light so she could see the path that led to the back of the cottage. She examined the path for footprints.

'Umm! That's what I expected,' Petra thought. Her footprints were the only ones she could see. There must have been a stony path here at one time, but now after years of neglect the soil and weeds had encroached upon the driveway. The dew was heavy tonight and she felt sure her footprints were the only impressions to be seen. There was no sign of any constant use of foot traffic near this doorway, of that she was sure.

Petra decided to walk all round the cottage to check on her theory. As she made her way down the side of the building, something suddenly rushed out from under the hedgerow that grew there and scurried away in the half light.

"Wow! what was that?" She gasped and held onto the cottage wall.

'Oh, it's a badger!' her eyes followed the little creature. 'It's only a young one,' she thought, catching her breath. 'Wow! I must tell my Nan. My first live badger." The little animal ran off down the lane, as fast as it could go.

She proceeded to make her way round the cottage looking for another entrance. She knew that the two windows she had passed on the right side of the cottage were firstly the sitting room and then the study. There were no other windows she could see and then at the back of the building she recognised the high pantry window, and a lower window, the only one in the kitchen. She even saw the flue of the AGA cooker jutting out of the wall, and then after turning left and following the cottage wall she was at the back door, where they had entered the night before last.

Suddenly the moon disappeared behind a large ominous cloud, just now Petra had turned the corner of the cottage and eventually by following the wall would take her back to the front garden.

'This isn't good,' the young girl thought, as she fumbled for her phone, now deep in her jacket pocket. 'I didn't really want to use my torch. Someone might see the light.'

At that moment her foot hit an obstacle protruding from the ground. Petra saved herself from falling flat on her face.

"Ouch, whatever is that?" Petra proclaimed, out loud. She bent down to rub soil off her knees and inspect her injured foot. Then at the same moment some pheasants roosting high in nearby tall treetops, called loudly as they all flew off into the night, making their familiar two note calls, the first note higher than the second.

"I'm sorry," she called after them, "I didn't mean to disturb you." Petra's foot hurt, but it wasn't bad enough to interrupt her mission.

She was inquisitive to know the cause of her injury and shone the light of her phone's torch on the ground. Petra gasped. At that moment she realised that she had found another entrance to the cottage. She stooped and touched a large round grid with a handle.

'So, I am right!' she said to herself.

There on the ground, just a metre from the sidewall of the cottage was a circular, wrought-iron lid. It looked like a cover for something. Maybe an underground room?

'It must be the entrance to the cellar, or even a coalhole.' Petra felt excited with her find and wondered if she dared to go down and explore by herself.

She checked the time on her phone and decided she had plenty of time to investigate. But the lid was heavier than she expected. It was made of cast iron and as much as she pulled on the handle, she couldn't make it budge a centimetre. She was about to give up and go home, when she noticed a stout reinforced wooden pole lying on the grass nearby.

'I imagine this is what the intruders use to enter the cottage surreptitiously. Wow, that's a big word for me!' she thought, as she examined the post carefully. The wood was hard and looked as if it had been chiselled into shape, at one end was a pointed wedge.

"Now, here goes, I'll give it all I've got." Petra picked up the post and proceeded to put the wedge end under the iron lid but alas it wasn't easy. At that moment the moon came out from behind a cloud and shone its light on this side of the house. Now she could see quite clearly and discovered that there was a raised handle in the cast iron lid, just big enough for the wooden post to fit into.

Using all her strength, at last the obstacle gave way and she could push the lid over to one side.

'Grown-ups would have to remove it completely,' she thought. But Petra knew she could angle her body into the space below and easily climb down.

She shone her light downwards and was relieved to see some concrete steps leading down into darkness. The walls were covered in a soft black dust but there was none on the steps. Petra now knew she was right and felt certain this is the way the intruders had entered the cottage.

"I wonder which room it leads to?" she said out loud. Her voice reverberated from the walls of the underground room in a low echo. Petra shivered.

She was now in an underground passage, but it soon came to an end. Before her was another set of steps but this time the steps were leading upwards. She climbed them and found herself in the back of a cupboard in the kitchen.

'So! This must have been where coal was brought into the cottage in the old days. The AGA must be quite new!' Petra was now in the kitchen, and as she examined the wall behind the stove, she could make out signs of where an older fireplace must have stood. A large oak beam was set high in the wall, where an ingle-nook fireplace must have once proudly enhanced the room. The beam was now half buried in the new plaster of the kitchen wall.

At that instant she looked at the time on her phone, 'It's past 1.30am! I must get home.'

But it was when she reached the bottom step in the coalhole that she noticed something of importance. There was a shelf set high in the black dusty wall. She hadn't noticed it at all on her way in, but now with the added height of the steps she could see clearly onto the shelf. Petra gasped.

There was a large chest made of mahogany with a note sellotaped to it and on that note was clearly written 'THE ISLAND.'

6
THE CELLAR

Petra tugged at the chest with all her might, but she couldn't move it.

'What shall I do?' she thought. 'I don't want to leave it here, at the mercy of that couple with the black BMW.' She reached up and gave the box one last pull, but it wouldn't budge an inch.

'I know! I will call Rosie's phone and talk to BB. He can come and help me."

Rosie was asleep with Brown Bear lying heavily on her feet. The bright moon was shining into the window in streams of silver light, when in her dreams Rosie could hear the tune of her mobile phone.

"Are you going to answer that?" Brown Bear had been woken suddenly by the ring of Rosie's phone and was a bit grumpy. "Come on, Rosie, wake up. Your phone is ringing,"

"What's the matter?" Rosie sat up rubbing her sleepy eyes.

"Answer your phone! Hurry before your Mum and Dad hear it. They are only next door in their bedroom."

"You do sound cross, BB!" Rosie fumbled for her phone and slid the answer button across her screen. "Oh! It's Petra. Why isn't she in bed?"

"Just wondering that." Brown Bear moved closer so he could hear the caller.

"Rosie, are you awake?" Petra's voice was urgent.

"Yes, course I am, you are talking to me, aren't you?" Rosie was a bit grumpy too.

"Is that you, Rosie? You sound funny!" Petra was getting annoyed.

"It is me," said Rosie, half asleep.

"Well, listen carefully. I want you to send BB to help me. I'm in Old Mill Cottage."

"Petra, what are you doing there at this time of night?" Rosie was puzzled.

"Please! Rosie, do as I say. Just give your phone to BB, I might get some sense out of him," the sleepy girl passed Brown Bear her phone and snuggled back under her duvet.

"Hi BB, can you find the key the professor gave us and bring it here to me? I have found something very important. Leave Rosie to sleep, we can tell her everything in the morning," Petra spoke with urgency in her voice.

"Right O. I'll be with you in ten minutes," said Brown Bear.

"Thank you, BB, it will be worth your effort." Petra went back to the mahogany chest and stroked it gently waiting in the darkness of the cellar.

'Oh!' she thought. 'I forgot to tell BB about the coalhole. I will have to go and wait by the gate for him."

Petra climbed out of the dusty hole and stood quietly in the warm night air. The nocturnal animals had quietened down now, and as she glanced in the direction of the Welsh hills; she recognised the beginnings of a faint sunrise. A golden glow was streamlining the horizon.

In a while she could hear a bit of a commotion as Brown Bear trundled along the lane towards the professor's cottage.

"Petra dear, what is this all about? How long have you been out of bed? I didn't hear you at all! Whatever is the urgency?"

"Shush, did you bring the key?"

"Yes, of course I did!"

"And where's Rosie?"

"I did as you said. She's fast asleep!"

"Good! Now wait till you see what I have discovered. I was convinced the cleaning woman and her co-conspirator had another way to enter the cottage and I've found it."

"Right O! Lead the way, my dear." said Brown Bear, in a matter-of-fact voice.

Petra led Brown Bear to the side of the cottage where she had left the metal cover of the coalhole half open. She immediately slipped down the gaping gap and put her hand up to guide her pal down the concrete steps. All the gymnastics and dancing she had enjoyed so much were now paying off. At fifteen years old her body was strong and lithe, delving down dark holes in the middle of the night was no trouble to her. But, with Brown Bear it was another story.

"I can't get down there! It's far too small an opening for me," Brown Bear exclaimed in dismay.

"Please just try, BB. It is important," said Petra in frustration. "I can't push the cover anymore. It is so heavy."

"Hold on! I've managed to get my legs and one shoulder just under this cover. Oh my, I'm stuck!" gasped Brown Bear.

Petra was on the bottom step, clutching her phone tightly. She shone the light up to see what was happening and began to giggle.

"It's not a bit funny, I really am stuck!" groaned the big brown bear.

"I told you last time we were on the island you were getting fat," said the young girl still laughing.

"Hey, I am not fat. Just strong and sturdy," he protested.

"Well, BB, I think sturdy is the same as fat," seeing Brown Bear's legs waving in the air she was laughing so much that tears began to roll down her cheeks.

"Now, hey! quit that laughing, Petra," Brown Bear was getting quite cross.

"Sorry, BB, I'll give your legs a tug," and immediately she climbed back up the steps to help her friend, but as much as she tugged it was no use Brown Bear was well and truly stuck.

"I hope what you have found down there is worth all this suffering," he sighed.

"Listen, BB! I have an idea! Get out and go back onto the path."

Brown Bear obeyed and waited for Petra in the side garden.

Petra began to squeeze back through the narrow coalhole cover and once she was alongside Brown Bear, she gave him a quick hug.

"Now!" she said. "We will both push the lid away from the hole and then it will be big enough for you to climb down comfortably."

"About time you had a good idea, Petra. Right! One, two, three, push."

And at last, with the joint effort the lid was moved to completely expose the entire black hole.

"Come quickly, BB, we have no time to waste. It must be getting light by now." Petra showed her friend the mahogany chest high on the shelf. I also found out that if you cross the cellar, there are more steps leading upwards to a cupboard in the kitchen."

"You have been busy. Now let me lift that chest down, so we can examine it together. What makes you think the professor's key will fit this chest as well as the one we have under your bed?"

"Just a hunch."

"A hunch, eh!" Brown Bear placed the trunk on one of the steps and inserted the small shiny key. The key all three friends had protected since the night of the professor's accident on the kitchen floor, which as Petra pointed out was just above their heads, as they stood in the cellar underneath.

"How did you find this coalhole, Petra? It is obvious that is what it was used for, in times gone by, a place to bring fuel into the house," said Brown Bear. "Everywhere is coated in coal dust. The dust is very settled though, I don't think it has been used for many years. We'll both have to have a shower when we get home. Now I'll turn the key."

Petra's hunch paid off and after the sound of a click, the lock gave way and she lifted the lid.

Brown Bear gave a long sigh of relief and lifted out a large package.

"We must have taken the wrong chest in the first place," Petra was puzzled. "I believe the cleaning lady and her companion know about this chest, because the reason I found the coal hole was because I was looking for another entrance to Old Mill Cottage that they could have used."

Brown Bear seemed very puzzled. "Or maybe they don't know about it and that is why the chest was still hidden, high on the shelf."

"Yes, maybe! BB, I'll explain everything tomorrow, but I feel really tired now," Petra yawned. "I think we should just take the package and lock the chest and leave it where we found it"

"Good thinking Pet. Now we must get out of here and replace the cover outside. Come on, hurry, the sun is nearly up."

It was quite a struggle to complete their task, but just at the precise moment the cellar cover slipped into place with a clank, the two pals froze to the spot in the side garden at Old Mill Cottage.

Without warning they both could hear the now familiar sound of the BMW car parking outside on the lane.

"Quick! BB, hurry!" Petra kept her voice low. "We will have to go home over the fields, we can't be seen here at this time of the morning!"

"Yes! Petra, we must get away from here quickly!" Brown Bear exclaimed. "It is very odd that the cleaner comes here so early."

"Yes! I don't think that this time in the morning is a normal time to start cleaning a private cottage," agreed Petra.

Just as BB and Petra were making their way through the tangled hedgerow at the rear of the cottage, a sudden light shone across the pasture beyond, and the sound of a loud engine filled the early morning air. Our two adventurers stood still catching their breath as they watched a large green and white tractor rev into action.

"Whatever shall we do now?" gasped Petra. "We dare not go back to the cottage because of the intruders, and we can't go across the meadows without being seen."

"Leave it to me, young lady. Keep close to the hedge and follow me," retorted Brown Bear, as he disappeared out of Petra's view.

"BB, where are you?" Petra called softly.

"I'm here! Come on jump down into this ditch, it runs all the way round this field," said Brown Bear popping his head up. "Here, take my hand."

And that is how they reached home amidst the mists of dawn on that midsummer morning, quite undetected. By the time they reached their house it was almost broad daylight, and they hurried up the stairs to their bedroom, before Mum and Dad stirred. But Rosie woke and sat up in her bunk.

"What's happening? Why are you both so dirty?"

"Don't worry Rosie go back to sleep. Tell you later," whispered Petra. "BB, I'm going for a shower! You will have to use the hose pipe in the garden."

"Oh! Thanks very much," remarked Brown Bear. "But I'm not dirty," he said indignantly.

"O Yes you are! BB, we are both covered in coal dust. Quick, fast as you can before Mum gets up and sees us like this," Petra was already running the shower when she remembered the folder they had discovered in the coal cellar.

"BB, have you got those papers?"

"Yes, of course I have. I stuffed them under Rosie's bed as soon as we came in."

"What papers?" Suddenly, Rosie sat up wide-awake.

"Shush, Rosie. Not so loud!" Brown Bear could hear their parent's disturbing in the next room.

"Whatever is going on? What are you two up to? Oooo you are

both filthy!" Rosie said, rubbing sleep from her eyes.

"We will tell you everything later. Don't worry we have a breakthrough in our quest," Brown Bear spoke with confidence.

"You mean we are going to the island!" Rosie shouted in excitement.

"Hush, little one," said Brown Bear. "Petra found something last night and this evening we will examine it."

"Yippee!" she yelled again.

"Shush."

Well, that was it! The whole household was awake. Mum at this moment was opening the bedroom curtains, and Dad was trying to open the bathroom door.

"Who's in the shower so early?"

"Hi Dad, it's me Petra I won't be long, sorry!"

"Hurry then, I'm late for work."

Mali decided he wanted a shower too, and all the commotion set the family's pet dog barking in the kitchen.

'Oh! What chaos on a lovely summer's morning!' thought Brown Bear. He wouldn't change a thing, he loved being part of this family.

They had all agreed now there was no more investigating to be done until the evening arrived. He was well house-trained; he wouldn't risk going for a quick nap on Rosie's bed covered in coal dust. He made his way to the garden muttering discontentment under his breath.

"Hosepipe, eh! What I do for these kids."

7
DISCOVERIES

Later that evening, the girls and Brown Bear poured over the contents of the open mahogany chest. The key that opened two chests was now in Brown Bear's keeping.

"At last!" Petra exclaimed in delight. She had sifted through the papers she had found inside the chest in the coal cellar. "Look, BB, this paper is about excavations on the island in the summer of 1998." She took a deep breath. "Now I think we will be able to find out what Professor Mortimer expects of us."

"Then can we go to the island and find its secret?" Rosie begged, pulling at Brown Bear's arm.

"Maybe, little one. But we have a few manuscripts to go through first." Brown Bear sighed, at the large volume of papers that lay spread out on their bedroom floor.

"I know a quick way to wade through them," Petra had an idea. "I'll sort them out into three equal piles, and we can go through them and then decide which are relevant and then decide what to do next."

Brown Bear gave a huge sigh of exasperation. "Has anyone got a pair of glasses I could borrow? My eyesight is not too good these days. I'm all right with distance but those papers have some very small print written on them."

"No!" said Petra. "We haven't any," she looked a little downcast, because she knew Brown Bear would understand all the archaeological jargon.

Rosie leapt up from the floor and went into her parent's room, where the two-family cats were sleeping on the bed. After a bit of a rummage in Mum's bedside drawers, she returned with a pair of spectacles clasped between her fingers.

"Here you are, BB!" Rosie looked very pleased with herself. "Mum's old ones. She never uses these now. I'm sure she won't mind you borrowing them."

In the time it took for Rosie to sort Brown Bear's eye problem, Petra had carefully taken all the papers out of the folder they had found in the chest and made three separate piles on the bedroom floor.

"Now, we are ready to search," she smiled at the others.

"What exactly are we looking for?" Rosie was a little puzzled.

Brown Bear put on Mum's old spectacles and began to sift through his allotted pile.

"To do what Professor Mortimer's requested, we need to find any mention of his excavation on the island." Brown Bear peered over the top of Mum's old glasses and both the girls began to giggle.

"Oh! BB, you do look funny with glasses on, they make your eyes look huge." Rosie tried to stifle her laughter.

"All the better to see you with!" he said in a deep scary voice, as he carried on browsing through the manuscripts.

The two girls fell into fits of laughter.

"That's enough girls! You forget we are on a mission to find the secrets of the island. And I feel it will be a serious business."

After that there was nothing but silence and all three pals got down to the job in hand.

"Hey! You two look at this," said Petra, holding up a piece of sturdy parchment. "This is the way to open the secret compartment in the mahogany chest. Look BB, it shows the points on the lid where we should press on the wood.

"Oh! Yes, it does. Bring me the chest, Rosie," Brown Bear pointed to under the girl's bed. Rosie struggled to pull the chest out.

"Here let me help you, Sis," said Petra, joining Rosie in bringing the mahogany chest into the middle of the room.

Then suddenly they heard footsteps coming up the stairs. They all froze and clung onto the chest, ready to hide it at any second. All ears were expectant, listening closely to the sound. They were all holding their breath.

"It's OK," Petra breathed out with relief. "It's only Mum putting clean washing in the airing cupboard."

"Right! Let's get on with this." Brown Bear kept his voice low. "We have been delayed in our quest for a long time now. We must commit ourselves to the Professor's wishes."

"Yes!" Rosie agreed. "We must!"

The next half hour passed, and our adventurers had answers. By pressing the strategic places marked on the chart, Brown Bear had managed to open a secret hiding place in the lid of the chest.

"Now listen, girls, there are lots of instructions written here and I think it a good idea if you two go down, have some supper and say you are tired and want an early night." Brown Bear stood looking straight into the girl's faces. "What do you think?"

"BB! I can't believe you suggested that idea for one minute," retorted Petra.

"Nor can I," Roses responded, with as much disbelief as her sister.

"Why not?" Brown Bear fidgeted, waiting for a decision from his roommates.

"Because if we go to bed early Mum will be very suspicious, and keep checking to see if we are alright," Petra knew that is what would happen.

Rosie suddenly stood up holding some of the papers, she looked very excited.

"What's up, Rosie?" Petra said, in anticipation.

"Let's photograph all the papers onto our phones and then we can study them when we do eventually go to bed," Rosie was looking very pleased with herself.

"Great idea, Rosie! But there are far too many papers here. We will have to sort out the relevant ones," said Brown Bear.

"Yes! we must," replied Rosie.

"I would say the most important ones are those that mention the island," gushed Petra, equally excited.

"Hang on a minute." said Brown Bear in earnest. "I don't think we need to sort them all because these instructions I just found have done all that for us."

"What do you mean, BB?" Rosie's voice was edged with impatience.

"What does it say?" Petra interrupted. "I am glad we don't have to go through all the papers because some of these documents refer to archaeological finds and burial sites," said Petra, sifting through some of their find.

"Yes, a bit technical I'm afraid," Brown Bear sounded a bit overwhelmed.

"Hey, girls, listen I can hear your Mum calling up the stairs to see if you want any supper, before she cleans up the kitchen," Brown Bear remarked, as he pushed the trunk and papers back under the bunk bed.

"Go on then." he said, ushering them to the door. "Don't worry about a thing. Just leave your phones with me, and I'll have it all sorted by the time you come to bed."

Petra dutifully held out her phone and Brown Bear took it. He had a good plan now.

"And you, Rosie?" Brown Bear's big paw was waiting while Rosie reluctantly held on to her precious piece of technology for a few more seconds.

"I need your phone for backup, Rosie," Brown bear held out his paw.

"Wow! Backup! That does sound exciting BB. OK, here you are then. Why will we need back up?"

"Just in case one of us loses our phone, then we will have all the necessary information on the other," replied Petra, from the landing. She was always quick to interpret Brown Bear's ideas. Rosie was now pushing past her sister to get to the kitchen first.

"Yummy, I can smell sausages"

"So can I!"

"Save me one, please," Brown Bear rubbed his tummy. "Right, off you go then. Now, I will get to work photographing all the relevant documents."

The girls left him to it and followed their noses to the appetising smells in the kitchen.

Brown Bear sat on the floor surrounded with documents, he sighed.

'Now at long last, we have opened the chest,' he thought. He was as excited as the girls were. 'At least, we will have an idea what we are to search for on Swallows Island,' he sighed again, this time in contentment. 'How boring my life was before I met these two adventurous little girls.'

He was very familiar with the girl's mobile phones, he had watched them both use the small slim objects with strange noises, bells ringing, and constant chatter since they were very young. He had been intrigued watching Petra and Rosie playing games, talking to their friends, and in later years they would use them to help with their schoolwork. So, tonight he had accomplished his task. Both the girls' phones were loaded up with the professor's notes, and the cameras now contained a fair amount of visual information.

Later when the girls returned, he was fast asleep at the bottom of Rosie's bed.

"That's a pity, BB won't want his sausage now," announced Petra.

"Oh! Yes, he does," said Brown Bear, sitting up quickly, "Hey girls, I've sorted everything and tomorrow we will find a way to get to the Island. These documents only give hints as to what there is to find on the island. The professor has made notes of many strange phenomena."

"What's phenomena?" asked Roses.

"Wonders, singularities, facts, incidents, happenings, even miracles." Brown Bear listed lots of amazing things.

"Well, I can't wait to go to the island if that's what the professor wants us to search for," said a very sleepy Rosie.

8
HOLIDAY PLANS

Petra woke the next morning feeling a buzz of excitement within her.

"Wake up, Rosie! Wake up, BB! We must get on with planning our trip to the island."

"What island?" Rosie's tousled blond hair covered her pretty face, as she slowly emerged from her duvet, still half asleep. "Where's BB?" she asked in a sleepy deep voice.

"I'm here!" remarked Brown Bear, "I've been up ages preparing for our adventure."

"How do you know it will be an adventure, BB?" Rosie asked, still very sleepy.

"Have you really sorted everything, BB?" Petra was now up and dressed.

"Yes! I have organised everything," he hesitated. "Well, there is one other thing I haven't done."

"The girls felt worried, "Oh, BB! What haven't you done?"

"Well, eh! You two have three more weeks before school starts in September, and I was wondering if you can ask Mum if we can go to the island for a holiday."

"Yippee!" exclaimed Rosie, now beginning to get dressed.

"A holiday?" Petra looked doubtful. "I don't think we will be allowed to go on a holiday."

"Well, you will be perfectly safe with me," Brown Bear looked hopeful. "And I have been down to the quay at 6am this morning and my old mate Lucas has agreed to take us over to the island."

"Oh! Not in that old rowing boat," Rosie was remembering their last trip two years ago. "Petra you were rowing and the sea became very rough and water splashed over us."

"Yes!" Petra remembered too. "And you and I struggled with the tide. Do you remember, BB? We only just managed to find a sea cave where we eventually landed our boat."

"Of course, I do! But it won't be frightening this time," Brown Bear assured the girls.

"How do you know, BB? I was scared," said Rosie.

"It will be fine! Lucas has a new motorboat; he won some money on the lottery. A fair bit I believe. But he wouldn't tell me exactly how much but enough to buy a fine seaworthy vessel," Brown Bear was very fond of his old mate. Lucas had been one of the local fishermen but of late he had started a lucrative business taking visitors out in the bay on fishing trips.

"Why does he want a motorboat?" Rosie always had a question at the ready. She was happy when she knew all the answers to everything.

"Stop asking questions, Rosie, and please hurry and get dressed," Petra was getting a bit worried. "Have I really got to ask Mum if we can actually stay on the island?"

"Yes, I'm afraid so," replied Brown Bear. "According to Professor Mortimer's notes, it will take us quite a while to discover all the hidden secrets."

Suddenly Rosie discarded her sleepy state and dressed quickly. She even brushed her hair, cleaned her teeth and then she was at the top of the stairs ready to go down first.

"What's the rush?" Petra was looking quite amazed at her sister's sudden interest.

"I'm going to ask Mum and Dad if we can all have the last weeks of our school holiday on the island." Rosie really wanted this trip; in fact, she couldn't wait to get to the island.

"Rosie, hold on wait for me." Petra was now ready to go and

ask the question. "I'll come with you. Then she turned to Brown Bear, "BB, I know it is a bit presumptive but, can you start packing for us?" Petra had a determined look on her pretty face. "If that's OK, BB?"

"Sure, I can!" As soon as the girls disappeared downstairs Brown Bear proceeded to find the girls travel bags in the wardrobe the two girls shared. 'I know it is summer, but they'll need warm jumpers and jackets because those caves get quite cold at night,' he thought. On their past visits to the island, they had the choice of the numerous caves, to turn into temporary accommodation.

The girls were a long time and Brown Bear was worried when he heard raised voices. He carried on with the packing, wondering whether he was doing the right thing. But he needn't have worried, the girls returned to their bedroom with big smiles on their faces.

"Hope you weren't worried, BB. That loud voice was mine," said Petra with a gleam of satisfaction.

"I hope you didn't step over the mark, Petra dear." Brown Bear gave a glance of disapproval.

"No, I don't think I did! I just pointed out that Rosie and I are fifteen, in fact nearly sixteen, and we are not stupid girls and that we have a very trusted chaperone in you, BB, and Lucas who is well respected in these parts, and is willing to take us to the island. So eventually they said we can go."

"Well, that is good news!" Brown Bear hesitated. "So, both your parents are in agreement that you two have a brief holiday on the island, Petra."

"Yes, of course they are!" Petra exclaimed. "Don't you know, BB, that I can be very persuasive when I want to be?"

"Well, I have noticed," retorted Brown Bear, deep in thought. "My only problem Petra is not noticing how quickly you are growing up."

"I know it is amazing, isn't it, BB?" Petra gave her pal a gentle thump. Her exuberance was halted for a while, as she saw sadness in his eyes. "Hey, cheer up, BB, don't forget we three have been together every day since Rosie and I were nine years old."

"I know we have!" Brown Bear was subdued.

"Then it is time we grew up," Rosie gave him an affectionate hug. "Don't you think, BB?"

"Ummmm," replied Brown Bear. "I agree to a point, but you do appear to be growing up a little too quickly. Now, come on, we must focus on the task in hand?"

"Do we need to pack our holdalls?" Rosie was feeling excited at the prospect of returning to the island. "And what about a rug or blanket each?"

"Only bring what you can carry yourself," said Brown Bear. "It is summertime and hopefully the weather will be as good as it has been the last couple of months?"

"Can I bring Cyril?" Rosie asked a little apprehensively.

"No! Certainly not," replied Petra. "We are going on a journey to discover the professor's secrets. Not to a….."

Brown Bear interrupted Petra. "Of course, you can, little one."

"But!" said Petra.

"You know how creepy it can be on the island, Petra," continued Brown Bear. "Rosie might need some comfort."

Petra nodded to her trusted friend and went to help her sister finish off the packing.

One hour later, Brown Bear stood tall, almost blocking the doorway of the girl's bedroom. He had one small backpack and a scroll of parchment like paper under his arm. He glanced at the girl's luggage and nodded in approval.

"Now, didn't Mali have one of those portable chargers for his iPhone?" Brown Bear enquired of his companions.

"Yes, he did but he's got a new phone now and never needs to use his charger at all," answered Petra. "I know where it is."

She soon returned looking pleased. "How lucky was that Mali

had left it charging in his room."

"So, we can be off then," said Brown Bear. "I hope you girls have squared all this with your parents.

"Of course, we have," beamed Rosie. "Mum promised to send us a text if there was any news we ought to know about. She told me not to use our phones, to save the life of our batteries, as there is no electricity on the island! And they are only letting us go because Lucas has a new boat."

Petra stood deep in thought. "If Rosie is bringing her menagerie, can I bring my make-up bag?" Petra implored her furry friend.

Brown Bear was about to say, "Certainly not! Who's going to see you on a deserted island?" Then he remembered on both their visits to the island it was not deserted at all. Instead, he smiled at Petra and said, "Why not?"

After some very loud "Goodbyes," the children scurried out of the house as quickly as they could and disappeared round the corner, on their way towards Swallows Village.

"The last time we went to the quay we walked along the sand to reach the harbour, where Lucas moors his boat. But this time we'll follow the road, it is a much shorter route," Brown Bear informed the girls.

"Whatever you say, BB."

The secure home and the friendly village they knew so well was soon left behind, as our little group of friends made their way to the harbour. Brown Bear had decided that once they had reached the edge of the village it would probably be quicker if they followed an old mill workers track across the fields.

As the luscious green grass became trodden beneath their intrepid footsteps, Petra stopped and inhaled a huge deep breath, as the first glimpse of the blue sea caught her eye.

"Look, Rosie! The ocean, it's amazing, isn't it!"

"Yes! Nothing looks as inviting as the deep blue sea," Rosie agreed wholeheartedly with her sister. "But once we are on the island, who knows what we will find?"

"I know, Rosie, it's a daunting thought," Petra clasped her sisters' hand. "Come on, Rosie. I'll race you to be the first to see Lucas' new boat."

9
MISSING

Soon our three pals were making their way along the harbour wall. The midday sun was high in the sky and the waves were splashing against the cast iron jetty. They marvelled at such a picturesque place. The bay's soft yellow sand was bordered by low green hills that stretched for miles along the coastline. In front of them was the secluded harbour with three yachts moored out on the water. They could hear the gentle tinkling of the bells aboard the vessels, as the summer breeze caught the crafts' lines. They all thought it a pleasant jingling sound.

"Look!" called Rosie excitedly. "Lucas is on his boat, and what a nice boat it is too."

"Yes, it looks a splendid vessel," said Brown Bear, as he hailed his old friend.

Lucas waved his sun-tanned hand in a friendly gesture, as his silver hair captured glints of sunshine. "Hey, hold on a minute. I'll be ashore in a jiffy."

"It is a much better boat than the rowing boat we took to the island last time," announced Rosie, who was so excited at the prospect of going to the island for a holiday.

"It won't be a real holiday. You know that, don't you, Rosie?" Petra was about to say more, when Lucas suddenly jumped down from his new motorboat and was beside them all on the jetty.

"Good to see you, Lucas, old mate," Brown Bear greeted his friend.

"And you too, Matey," replied Lucas, looking really pleased to meet his friends once again. "Now come over to the shelter. I have two lots of news for you."

They all followed Lucas who led them along the jetty and onto the harbour wall.

Tucked away beneath the hillside at the end of the path was a rather rustic looking shelter painted dark green. Brown Bear and Lucas were deep in conversation all the way to a small Victorian-style building with the front exposed to all kinds of weather.

"This was made in the days when Queen Victoria was on the throne of England, I presume?" Brown Bear was examining the very ornate shelter.

"Yeh, it was!" Lucas remarked, and then the two pals turned the conversation into a history lesson. Why were beach huts erected in many resorts in Britain towards the close of the 19th Century? The open fronted buildings were popular with bathers and onlookers alike, as they provided a haven from the strong sea breezes. They became very popular and fashionable for the seaside holiday, which the Victorians grew to love.

"And of course, there was the construction of seaside piers about the same time," remarked Brown Bear.

The girls were always amazed that BB and the fisherman were such good friends. And had wondered often how the two knew each other.

"How do you think they met?" Rosie looked puzzled.

"I don't know." Petra answered, just as puzzled. She looked around the harbour. It was a beautiful setting with the aquamarine sea and the array of sailing craft bobbing on the water. Petra and Rosie began to wander away hoping to explore for a while as BB and Lucas continued their deep conversation. But soon Brown Bear called to them.

"Hey, come back, girls. Just listen to what Lucas has told me." Brown Bear had just received some disturbing news.

The sisters quickly returned to the seaside shelter, with

inquisitive looks on their pretty faces.

"Whatever is the matter? You two look very serious!" exclaimed Petra, sitting herself on the long wooden bench under the shelter.

"Now!" Brown Bear began. "Lucas tells me he used to know Professor Mortimer when he lived in our village about twenty-seven years ago."

Rosie sat beside her sister ready to hear the story Lucas was about to tell them. But first he thanked Petra and Rosie for their kind actions.

Lucas leaned towards the girls, "Your BB tells me you saved the old professor from having to spend a night on his cold kitchen slabs." Lucas smiled at the girls.

"Yes, we did!" said Rosie

"I laid them slabs in Old Mill Cottage near on forty years ago now," continued Lucas. "And my old Granddad laid the quarry tiles in the sitting room, that was! Well, it wasn't made into a study 'til Professor Mortimer moved in with all his archaeology books and some interesting finds."

"Exactly how old is the cottage?" Rosie always wanted to know everything.

"I dunno," replied Lucas, deep in thought. "That old mill's been on that site for hundreds of years. It's seen many a miller, but the professor just wanted it as a dwelling place and the old mill wheel hasn't seen action since."

"When did the professor move in then?" Rosie asked, really getting interested in Lucas' story.

"Near on twenty years since the tragedy," Lucas was looking anxious. "It's time to go before the tide changes. If you want to be on the island tonight, we must leave now. I'll tell you more of the tale as we go."

"What tragedy?" Rosie, Petra and Brown Bear looked at Lucas in horror.

"I'll tell you on the way," said Lucas. "Come on, we must get on the boat, or we'll miss this tide."

All three followed Lucas to his motorboat. They picked up their luggage and made their way along the jetty to where the power-boat was moored.

"Lady Penelope the second," remarked Brown Bear looking at the words on the side of the boat.

"No! Rosie exclaimed. "It's Lady Penelope eleven." Rosie started to giggle.

"Rosie, you know exactly what it's called," said Petra, taking her sister's arm as they boarded the shiny new vessel, now bobbing on the swollen tide.

It was a beautiful early August afternoon, and a strong breeze ruffled the waves and spread the white fluffy caps into the wind. Soon they were settled on board.

"Well, I say, old matey, this is luxury compared with the rowing boat you loaned us last time we undertook this journey," Brown Bear was very impressed. "And it has an enclosed cabin and galley. This is very smart."

Lucas carefully guided the craft out to sea leaving the shelter of the harbour behind them. As they looked back towards the shore the girls could see Swallows Village disappearing behind a headland as the vessel motored out to sea.

"The waves are nowhere near as rough as last time when I was rowing," Petra remarked, settling into a comfortable leather seat just inside the cabin.

"Come on, Rosie, sit beside me, it's not windy down here."

"But what about the rest of Lucas' story?" Rosie asked her sister. The little girl was very anxious to know more about the professor and his cottage.

"It will have to wait!" Brown Bear yelled to be heard against the engine noise. "Lucas must concentrate hard now to get us carefully through the dangerous rocks that surround the island."

"Won't be long, girls!" Lucas shouted down towards the cabin.

"It doesn't take long with the help of a motor. We'll be on the island in twenty minutes."

'What time is it now, Petra?" Rosie was getting excited. "This will be our third visit to the island. Oh! Petra, you do have Mali's phone charger safe, don't you?"

Petra fumbled for her phone, she thought she could detect a little anxiety creeping into Rosie's voice.

"It's 3 o'clock and yes, of course I do," said Petra. "Look everyone! I can see the castle in the middle of the island."

"This is great!" exclaimed Rosie. "I can't wait to get there!"

"I'm taking you to a cove on the eastern side of the island," Lucas was shouting over the noise of his engine, "because that is where I always used to land Professor Mortimer and his wife."

"His wife!" exclaimed all three of our adventurers together.

"I didn't know he was married!" said Petra. "There was no sign of a wife at Old Mill Cottage."

"No, there wouldn't be now." Lucas' voice could only just be heard. "She was very beautiful and intelligent, always with the Doc' on his digs," explained Lucas, as he was carefully guiding his boat between the last of the treacherous rocks that rose like huge, jagged teeth that pierced the waters just there.

Both girls were surprised. It hadn't occurred to them that their new neighbour had a wife. Petra thought that Old Mill Cottage showed no sign of femininity at all. She shouted above the engine noise, "So where is his wife now? Especially as he has been injured and has to stay with a friend in the south of England."

There was a rather stunned silence as Lucas skilfully guided his vessel ashore and tied his brand-new boat up alongside a very ramshackle jetty. The tower of the medieval castle overshadowed the harbour just here. The girls were pleased to see it once again. The old ruins of a fine fortress that had once stood surveying the seascape for miles in every direction rose high against the skyline.

"Now come on, I'll show you the beach cottage which the

doctor used as his base while on the island. Then I must be off. I have a trip booked for this evening."

"But please tell us about Professor Mortimer's wife." Rosie pleaded with the fisherman.

"Yes!" Petra joined in. "He wrote us a letter and he didn't mention a wife."

"Come on, Lucas, old mate," said Brown Bear, who felt a bit out of his depth now.

Lucas was deep in thought, as he lifted a large suitcase full of his passenger's belongings onto the jetty. He was silent as he checked the moorings and made his way up the beach. "Come on! This way. I'll show you the cottage. It should make a good shelter for your holiday. Way out of the way of the highest tide."

'Something was wrong here, they all thought,' as they followed Lucas along the shingle to where large sea-worn rocks lay stretched out in the hot sunshine.

'So, Professor Mortimer had a wife! But where was she now?' thought Petra

Lucas remained silent as he carried most of their bags, "We just need to walk round this headland and you'll see a two-storey building at the top of the cove, quite safe from the ocean," stated Lucas.

The island's cliffs were not as high on this eastern shore, as the cliffs our three adventurers knew so well from their last two visits to this island. As they rounded the grassy headland they saw the shape of a stone cottage and as Lucas had stated, it was situated far enough away from the highest spring tide.

"Thanks, old mate," said Brown Bear. "As for our trunk, just leave it here. We'll come and fetch it tomorrow." Lucas was about to say something, but Brown Bear assured his old friend.

"It is perfectly waterproof and it's out of reach of the sea here. Hello, I do believe the tide has started to turn."

Both girls were feeling quite frustrated that BB's friend was not telling them what they were now very curious to know.

"Lucas! Where is the professor's wife?" Rosie couldn't wait any longer and blurted out her question.

Lucas stopped and faced all three companions. Petra noticed he had tears in his eyes.

"She went missing here on this island about twenty years ago."

"What do you mean missing?" Brown Bear asked his friend.

"What I say! She went missing!" said Lucas. "It was a mystery to everyone round here. When Lawrence Mortimer received his doctorate at Oxford, thirty odd years ago, for some reason he chose our village to live in, and there were great celebrations when he introduced his new bride to the villagers. Everyone adored her. She was by all accounts very beautiful and not snobby, very friendly she was! And in the few years they lived at Old Mill Cottage she was amazing with her social skills. Everyone in the village was very fond of her, she would fight the corner of even the poorest villager if need be.

"Then one day in the summer of 1999, I brought them both to the island," Lucas was obviously upset having to relate what he knew. "The Doc said he had work to do on the castle, and Mrs Mortimer was going to study bone fossils in the deep caves. Happy they were that day, a couple in love they were," then he hesitated, "So, I brought their luggage to this cottage here. They were both looking forward to a few days to do what they loved most."

"What happened then?" asked Rosie.

"Mrs Mortimer smiled and thanked me, and that was the last time I saw her," Lucas replied.

"She sounds like an amazing lady." Petra mused over the woman's attributes.

"But what happened to her?" Rosie needed to know.

"Well, I dunno, that's it! Nobody knows." sighed Lucas. "Police searched the island thoroughly, and the professor even hired a private detective, but his wife was never found, and worse still, not even a trace of her was left," the fisherman continued. "Poor man, the Doc, he was devastated! You see they worked together on all the big sites in the world. Quite renowned she was too in the world of archaeology, that is I believe."

"Is that why Sir Mortimer sold Old Mill Cottage all those years ago?" Rosie asked, with deep concern in her voice.

"Yes, I believe it was," nodded Lucas. "Very close they were, and folk around here used to say he blamed himself for the tragedy."

"Oh! That's a shame," said Brown Bear.

Lucas pointed towards the sea. "Hey! I've got to go now, or the tide will be too low, and I'll never get through those jagged rocks." Lucas had been watching the tide and realised he had to leave his friends at once.

Brown Bear gave his old mate a big slap on the back.

"Now, you take care of yourself, and we'll be here waiting for you in three weeks' time."

"Aye now, matey, you all have a good holiday and," Lucas turned to Brown Bear, "You watch these girls like a hawk! Whatever took Mrs Mortimer may still be lurking on the island."

Well, that was it. Lucas had gone, leaving them all filled with questions. Whatever could still be lurking on the island? Petra and Rosie could feel the grip of fear encroach upon their beings. They had stood watching the motorboat until it was a speck on the ocean. Petra was the first to recover.

"BB, you did make copies of all the professor's notes on our phones, didn't you?"

"Yes, I certainly did!" he replied. "But I did better than that. I have brought all his papers with us. So, when we three go through them together, we will each have a copy. You two with everything on your phones, but I thought I will be more familiar with the real thing."

"But it is the real thing, BB!" exclaimed Rosie.

Brown Bear wasn't going to get into an argument with Rosie

about the virtues of the technical age, so he changed the subject and took charge.

"Well, I think now first and foremost, we had better go and see what accommodation that stone cottage has to offer. Collect your bags, girls and hurry, in August it can get dark by eight thirty. We will leave the trunk here. It won't take us long to retrieve it tomorrow."

"I hope the cottage will be warm and dry, I'm looking forward to staying on the island," Rosie picked up her holdall and they all climbed the sea-worn rocks that led to the entrance of the cottage.

The sound of the sea was a welcome and soothing noise, as the waves ebbed away, but suddenly a strong gust of wind caught strands of Petra's hair, twirling it across her lovely face. "Come on. How did we not know about this cottage?"

"Simple," replied Brown Bear. "Because our last adventures didn't give us any reason to set foot on this eastern shore."

"Of course, you are always right, BB!" Rosie remarked, as they made their way up the beach.

When they reached the stone cottage they could see it had a brick-built chimney and Rosie counted a main doorway set in the middle, with one window at the front, on the right side, and two windows upstairs each on opposite sides of the doorway quite high up.

"It's delightful!" said Petra.

Rosie was so excited she couldn't wait and was first through the door that creaked on rusty old hinges.

She disappeared inside and after a few seconds the little girl screamed in horror.

"Oh! No! No! Go away!" Rosie exclaimed, making Petra and Brown Bear freeze on the spot outside.

10
RELICS

Suddenly the sun sank behind some dark grey clouds that were blowing in from the west and a chill wind howled in the lintel of the cottage doorway. Rosie stood there with her face ashen. Petra, still glued to the spot, could see traces of tears welling up in her sister's eyes.

"Whatever is it? What's the matter?" Petra stepped towards the entrance of the cottage mainly to comfort her sister, but of course she was curious to see what had put such fear in Rosie.

Rosie couldn't speak, she was trembling so much that every time she tried to talk her body shook with convulsions and the others could not understand a word she was saying.

"Calm down, Rosie," pleaded Petra. "Here, let me put my arms around you. There now, is that better?"

"Yes, er umm, I think so." Rosie shuddered, not sounding sure that it was better at all.

Petra could feel the little girl trembling from head to foot, as she tried to console her sister.

"Now let me see what has frightened our Rosie?" Brown Bear took charge. He strode towards the door with thunderous steps, patting the girl's shoulders as he passed them to gain access to the old beach dwelling. He pushed open the door as wide as it would go but the sturdy door was hanging on rusty hinges, groaning with reluctance.

"Be careful, BB." Petra called after their friend. She turned her attention to Rosie and could still see her sister trembling.

"Whatever has happened to frighten you like this?" Petra looked all around them in case something strange was lurking nearby.

"Rosie, come and sit down on this rock and try to relax. I'll go inside with BB, I'll keep my eyes on you all the time, so don't worry," Petra patted a nearby rock with her hand, it felt cold and damp.

Rosie did what Petra told her and sat down on the rock; she pulled her hooded jacket tightly around her shivering shoulders.

Within a minute or two the little girl heard Petra scream frantically from within the cottage, Rosie's mouth suddenly became dry, and her body grew more tense, she fidgeted as she waited.

'What shall I do? Go into the horror or stay here and wait.' she thought. The little girl decided she would wait on the rock. She shivered again and pushed her blond hair away from her forehead. A chill wind was gripping at her face and the evening was getting darker by the minute. Then she heard threatening rumbles of thunder in the distance.

Another loud scream from Petra filled the evening air and Rosie didn't have to imagine what Petra and Brown Bear could see inside, because she knew exactly what was in there.

Brown Bear stood tall at the doorway into the cottage. The only light coming into the room inside was through a small window veiled in huge cobwebs. And this is what Petra saw to make her let out another horrendous scream.

"Oh! No! Spiders! Hundreds of them, BB, please get rid of them. I hate spiders," Petra was now shaken up too.

Brown Bear dutifully held up his big furry arm and used his elbow to clean the cobwebs from the glass window.

By now Rosie, feeling alone on the beach, had plucked up courage to go inside. She stood in the doorway glad to be with Brown Bear and her sister once again.

"Look what is in that corner over there," Rosie pointed to a shadowy recess of the room, she was still trembling but doing her best to be brave. "It's those bones! Look, they are moving!"

Petra screamed again and Brown Bear looked on aghast, and to top it all, just at that moment an enormous rumble of thunder crashed in the sky overhead right above the cottage. Immediately it was followed by flashes of lightning, streaking in zig zag blazes across the sky giving light to the room they stood in.

"Oh, my word!" exclaimed Brown Bear. "Whatever have we here?"

"The storm is almost overhead!" Petra exclaimed in horror. "Rosie, come here, get close to me."

"This is not a pretty sight, is it, little one?" Brown Bear was amazed at what they all could see.

"No, it is not pretty, I'm frightened!" Rosie exhaled, with a great shudder.

They were huddled inside the old cottage and there they had to stay for now, as the storm gathered pace and struck with vengeance in the sky above. The rumbling thunder was now crashing louder than the waves on the shore, and huge raindrops were lashing down so heavily onto the rocks outside.

"What a storm!" Petra spoke first, as Rosie and Brown Bear were mesmerised in horror.

Another flash of lightning lit up the room and they could now all see the objects that had frightened Rosie. The room was amassed with old boxes gathering dust and two well-worn trunks with their lids open, exposing an array of skeletons and various bones scattered on the floor. There was a large pile of what looked like a collection of old fossils piled high in one corner.

"Look!" cried Rosie, with new tears welling up in her eyes once again. "Look! Can't you see they are moving?"

Another streak of lightning lit up the room, showing Brown Bear and Petra what Rosie could already see. They looked on in horror because Rosie was right! All the skeletons, fossils and bones were moving.

"Oh! BB, whatever is happening?" Rosie cried out, grasping Petra's hand.

Brown Bear fumbled in his rucksack and found his torch. He switched it on and shone it around the room lighting up the shadowy corners. Something had caught his attention and among all this chaos Brown Bear was pleased to cast the torch beam onto something that might be to their advantage. He quickly beckoned to the girls.

"Don't worry, I have a plan, come with me," Brown Bear's soft voice was very comforting to the girls at that moment. Their steadfast pal led them to a corner of the room, being very careful not to tread near the skeletons.

"I thought as much. Can you see that door over in that far corner? I know its looks like a cupboard, but I think it is the entrance to a stairway. Now watch your footing and follow me." Brown Bear moved stealthily across the room.

The girls obeyed and both could feel their hair standing on end. Fear gripped them again as they were close on Brown Bear's heals, treading carefully on to the first step not knowing what would be beyond.

"BB, what do you think is making all those bones move?" Petra asked, in a half whisper.

"Rats!" announced Brown Bear. "Scores of them!"

And with that remark both girls fled as fast as they could up the stairs and into the unknown. Anything was better than an infestation of rats.

"Ooo! How horrid," Rosie gasped.

"I hate rats!" Petra proclaimed.

"I thought you hated spiders, Petra," Rosie stumbled in her hurry.

"I hate rats and spiders and moving bones. BB, don't you think this is a horrid place?"

There was no answer from Brown Bear, he had stayed on the

ground level and made a terrifying growl. The girls stood still with fear engulfing them both, they could feel beads of perspiration trickling down the backs of their necks.

"BB, BB!" cried Petra. "Why did you make that awful noise? You have really scared us now!"

"Sorry about that, girls, but I had no choice. Look. All the rats have gone," his voice boomed up the stairwell.

Both girls looked down into the first room and thankfully saw hordes of rats scurrying out of the doorway onto the rocks then skittering onto the beach.

"Wow! How did you do that, BB?" Rosie gave a huge sigh of relief.

"Rats don't take much scaring, and personally I don't think they like my smell." said Brown Bear, as he joined the girls at the top of the stairs.

"You don't smell, BB!" Rosie exclaimed. "I wouldn't let you sleep at the bottom of my bed if you did."

By now the three companions came to a full stop. There was no safe room to find comfort in.

"Now what have we here?" Brown Bear was gasping for breath.

"I thought we would be able to enter this room without a problem but look, girls, there is a barrier blocking another doorway."

"What do you mean, BB?" Petra couldn't see a barrier.

"Yes! Look here girls, it is a transparent type of plastic," Brown Bear was now touching a sheet of heavy-duty polythene that had once been hung there to seal the doorway.

"BB, do you think the professor put it there?" Petra asked. "He did live here for a while, I suppose. Maybe when he was excavating the castle."

"More than likely, my dear. Huumm! I'm going to have to break the seal if we want to get in there," replied Brown Bear, taking complete charge of the situation.

"Let's hope we can find somewhere safe to sleep up here. Yes!

Do it, BB, break the seal! Let's get in there because I am not sleeping downstairs with old bones, spiders and rats," Petra was very positive.

"Nor me," joined in Rosie. "The thunder has passed a little, but it is still pouring with rain outside."

"Right then, here we go," Brown Bear was already tugging at the barrier from the top, and slowly it gave way and revealed a door and then a dark room inside. "Wait here."

Both the girls stood in silence outside the doorway and Brown Bear ventured in. He shone his torch all round to discover the only window was sealed too. He soon reached up and tore down the polythene curtain. The rain was lashing loudly against the glass windowpane and a potent flash of lightning lit up the room.

"Wow!" said the sisters together and let out huge sighs of relief.

"There you are girls, no rats, no spiders and no bones," said a very relieved Brown Bear. "Right! I will go down and carry your bags up while you two decide where we shall sleep."

"Well, this is a surprise. I think we can make it cosy here." Rosie's voice was now calmer, as she held up her mobile phone to use the torch to light up the room. "I'm hungry."

Soon Brown Bear was back with the girl's bags, and immediately Rosie was rooting in hers for food. Petra was much more concerned for their surroundings, she held her torch high looking for cobwebs but there were none.

"Hey! look over there, on top of that tall cupboard, I can see an old lamp, and let's hope there is still some oil in it. BB, can you reach it please?" Petra had just managed to get over her fright on seeing so many spiders and was relieved to see Brown Bear bring the lamp down to be examined.

"Good, it feels full of oil. Now all we've got to do is find our box of matches and light it," remarked Brown Bear.

"I have some," said Rosie. "Just in time because the storm had made the sky seem much darker than it should be, for this time of year," she held out the box and Brown Bear took it from her. "Let's hope tomorrow will be hot and we can dry our clothes and then we can explore the island once again."

"I'm afraid Rosie, we have a lot of homework to do first, little one! We must study Professor Mortimer's instructions," Brown Bear looked very serious. "You see, girls, we have to do that or we will never find the secrets of the island."

The storm seemed to be passing and Brown Bear went down to see if he could shut the front door to keep the bad weather out. He had quite a job because the rusty hinges were almost broken through. However, he ventured out onto the rocks and found a piece of driftwood big enough to prop the door shut and keep out the rain.

"I think that will hold till morning. Now girls, let's have our dinner! What have you got for us tonight, Rosie?

"Lucas left our big trunk of goodies on the jetty where we landed, we will have to fetch it in the morning. But I have a load of sandwiches I made before we left home," Rosie was always pleased to play Mum. "We will have to sit on the floor, I'm afraid, this room is void of any comfort. Did you unpack our sleeping bags, BB?"

"I'll do it now," responded Brown Bear. We can sit on them to eat our supper. Come to think of it, I'm starving!"

An hour passed and the storm could still be heard, but it was not overhead now, there were still a few rumbles of thunder moving away across the sea. They lit the oil lamp immediately, as night had fallen and suddenly it became very dark outside.

"That was a good supper, Rosie," said Brown Bear, as he stretched out on the floor of this upstairs room.

"Are we going to study the professor's notes now? The ones you copied to our phones?" Petra gave a big sleepy yawn.

"No, not now! we will do that tomorrow," replied their pal, "I think you girls need to sleep now, it has been quite a traumatic evening."

He didn't even receive an answer, as both girls were fast asleep wrapped up in their cosy sleeping bags.

Soon he was fast asleep too, dreaming about creatures from outer space and the dreaded Hobgoblins.

But they are all long gone. Tomorrow a new adventure would begin.

11
DISCOVERIES AT THE COTTAGE

When the three companions woke the next morning there was no sign of the storm, the sun shone into the upper room of the beach cottage, and all seemed at peace on the island.

Petra was tugging at Rosie's sleeping bag, but the little girl was very tired and didn't want to wake up. Brown Bear was already out on the rocks looking for a larger piece of driftwood to use on the front door.

Petra began to tidy her things away and looked up and noticed another cupboard-like door at the back of the room. She went over to it and wondered why they hadn't noticed it the night before.

"Hey! Rosie, you really must get up now. It's past 8 o'clock and I've discovered something that might be important.

Rosie lifted her tousled head from her sleeping bag; she rubbed her eyes still half asleep and pushed her hair back from her face.

"Where's BB? And what have you found?" Rosie got out of her cosy sleeping bag and joined Petra who had started to pull at the seal that covered a door.

"Strange that we didn't see this last night." Rosie was now beside her sister waiting in anticipation.

"That's what I thought but this part of the room must have been in shadow and we overlooked it." Petra was trying to recall exactly what they could see last night when Brown Bear returned from the beach.

"BB, look what Petra has found! Another sealed-up door." Rosie was very excited, as she relayed their news.

"Come on then, let me help you get that seal off this mysterious door," he had a twinkle in his eye, because he knew how much the girls loved a bit of intrigue.

The door was opened rather cautiously, and it made a loud creaking sound as Petra pushed it ajar. It was another room; in fact it was a beautiful room. Although there was another seal covering on the window, the sun still shone brightly through the panes, enlightening the room.

Petra stepped inside, marvelling at what she saw; there was a beautiful ornate bed, not a four-poster but a bed that had two drapes in fine woven fabric hanging over the bed head. There was a wardrobe with two drawers at the bottom; a very beautiful piece of furniture the wood gleamed in the morning sunlight.

Brown Bear examined all the magnificent pieces in the room.

"Walnut!" he exclaimed, with a certain amount of authority. "Everything is made of walnut."

Then, just as the three were going to explore further, a loud noise reached their ears from somewhere below.

"Hold on girls! I had better go and see what is happening downstairs. Come with me, Rosie, we'll go together," he held out his paw to the little girl and Rosie happily reached out to her friend, and that was it they both disappeared down the stairway to the first floor.

Petra was now alone in the room. She moved over to the window and pulled down the seal that was covering the recess allowing the early morning sunshine to flood in. She turned towards the huge, magnificent bed with an ornate wooden frame.

"Why would such a beautiful piece of furniture be brought to a seaside cottage?" Petra spoke aloud and then she noticed that the bed wasn't the only piece of ornate furniture in the room. She saw a sofa positioned against the far wall. She moved over to this fine piece of workmanship and let her hand gently stroke its soft velvet fabric.

'It's exquisite! What a beautiful shade of turquoise,' she thought. 'Just like the sea on a summer's day.'

Then she heard a noise from below and wondered what BB and Rosie were doing. But as she turned to go back towards the doorway, her eyes caught something else in a recess near the window. There was an object draped in the same material as the door and window seals.

Slowly she stepped nearer and gently lifted the drape. Underneath was another magnificent piece of furniture, a very ornate dressing table probably dating back to the 19th Century. She stood mulling over what she saw. She could hear her own heart beating, pounding away. She stopped and ran her finger very gently over the wooden surface.

"That's odd!" she exclaimed out loud. "No dust! We know this cottage must have been here for at least twenty-seven years."

The young girl was deep in thought again, 'Of course, someone could have built this cottage much earlier, but we do know that Professor Mortimer was last working on the island, excavating the castle, I think that was about twenty-seven years ago, and then he sold Old Mill Cottage and moved away after his wife went missing. Oh! dear, that's very sad. There is a lot more to discover about this room.' Suddenly Petra's thoughts were interrupted.

"Whatever is going on down there?" Petra called down the stairs. "Rosie! BB! Are you alright? I can hear a lot of banging."

She reached the bottom stair and was just about to go and find the others when Rosie called out loudly.

"Petra, do come quickly! Just come and see what we have found!" Rosie called to her sister in an excited voice.

Petra went down the stairs and gingerly stepped into the room with all the skeleton bones, and fossils strewn all over the floor. Suddenly she remembered their fear during the thunderstorm of the previous night. She shivered.

"Whatever is the matter?" She pulled herself together and

called to Rosie. "What have you found?"

Rosie met her at another doorway leading off this main room into a smaller room at the back of the cottage. Petra noticed the floor was actually the rock of the shore beneath her feet. She realised that the entire cottage had been built on the rock-strewn shore, under the cliff.

"Oh! There you are!" Rosie exclaimed. "Look, we have found the kitchen."

Brown Bear appeared behind Rosie with a metal tool of some kind grasped in his paw.

"Well, a bit of a make-do kitchen," said Brown Bear, thoughtfully. "But, there's no doubt it will suffice" He let out a big sigh. "Here, Petra, come and see."

Petra dutifully followed Brown Bear into rather a dark room at the back of the cottage, he looked quite pleased with himself.

He took a deep breath and faced his two companions. "I am going to be honest with you girls because I have been in a bit of a turmoil about us staying here for a few weeks."

"Why? Whatever is the matter, BB?" Petra was curious.

"Because I thought there wouldn't be any fresh water in this cottage. I have been imagining us traipsing every day to that spring we once found, do you remember on our first visit to this island? It was quite near the ravine," he said, stopping to catch his breath.

"Oh! Yes, I remember!" said Rosie.

"We found it by chance, all that lovely pure water gushing out," replied Petra. "That is a long way from the eastern side of the island. So, what have you found here?"

"I was coming to that, my dear. Do come into this scullery, I know it is a bit basic but really it is a godsend."

Petra was intrigued and delighted when she saw a very old stone sink, wedged in between two beechwood draining boards. There was a small window above and she reached up towards the opening set high in the outer wall of the cottage. As she pulled back the threadbare curtains that hung there, the fabric gave way under her touch and immediately disintegrated into fine dust.

"Oh! This place needs some TLC," Petra gasped, as a large spider crawled across her arm. She was about to scream when Brown Bear took her hand.

"Now listen, Petra! I know you can't stand them, but if you always put yourself in the place of any creature that frightens you and try to understand it's fear, then your fear should diminish," said Brown Bear, with a lot of compassion.

"I know!" answered Petra. "But they do just pop out when you don't expect them. Anyway, what was that loud noise I heard coming from down here? Oh! I forgot I have made more discoveries upstairs."

"Well, my dear, that will have to wait. Do come and see what is here. You know, I think the professor must have left in a hurry." Brown Bear put his iron tool down. "Look, the noise you heard was me giving this old pump a bit of a bashing and luckily I found that old spanner under the sink."

"Why did you do that, BB?" asked Rosie. "It made an awful noise."

"To make the pump work, of course, Rosie dear," replied Brown Bear as he took hold of the metal handle situated at the side of the old sink and pushed it up and down until a steady flow of water gushed out from the tap and splashed into the sink. "Look over there, girls, I found some cups." He pointed to a worktop with a cupboard above it.

Petra reached up and passed three drinking vessels down to Rosie.

She carefully examined the cups. "You know these are quite beautiful, I think they are bone- china."

"Yes, you are right!" Brown Bear exclaimed. "Very delicate. Give them a wash, Rosie, then we can taste the water."

"OK, BB," replied Rosie, as she immediately held each cup, in turn in the flow of the sparkling water "Here you are, Sis, you can taste it first."

"Yes, it tastes good," said Petra. "Oh! Can you see what is on the sides of all the crockery?"

"Yes, I can see letters sort of entwined," responded Rosie, holding her cup up to eye level.

"You are right, Rosie. I think they are someone's initials." Petra was now intrigued. "I think the letters are E. J. and M."

"Let me see, girls." said Brown Bear. "The initials can't belong to Professor Mortimer because his are L. B. M. Ummm! Interesting!"

"What does the B stand for? Do you know, BB?" asked Rosie, who expected BB to know everything.

"I'm pretty certain it's Butler!" he answered. "I have read enough of his papers to know that."

"I have an idea. Come with me." Petra said, with a touch of excitement in her voice.

"What is it?" Rosie asked, sensing Petra's enthusiasm.

Petra took Rosie and Brown Bear upstairs once again. They passed through the room they had all crashed in last night and entered the ornate bedroom Petra has discovered earlier.

"Wow!" exclaimed Rosie. "This is an amazing room."

"Yes, it is extremely beautiful. Just go and feel the fabric on that sofa over against the wall." Petra pointed to the exquisite piece of furniture. "BB, why did you think Professor Mortimer left the cottage in a hurry?"

Brown Bear put his head on one side deep in thought. "Well, for one thing all the scattered bones and fossils lying about. The professor would have secured them all in the boxes I would have imagined, and another reason there was no attempt to lock the front door properly."

"I think you are right, BB, but come with me." said Petra, starting to lead them over to the recess with the dressing table under the window. "I have a theory."

"Yes! Walnut," Brown Bear touched the surface. "Well-crafted and far too ornate for an archaeologist's beach cottage," Brown Bear prided himself on his knowledge of wood. He gently pulled open the top drawer and both girls gasped.

"Look at that note paper!" Petra exclaimed. "That was my idea!" She gasped. "I just thought that E J M. would be found somewhere in this room."

"I wonder who E J M is?" Rosie started to open another drawer. "Hey look! A charm bracelet with only one charm on it."

Petra picked up the piece of gold jewellery and touched it gently "Do look both of you. This charm has been carved with initials."

"Do let me see, Petra." Rosie was impatient because a theory was forming in her brain too, and she was anxious to see if she was right. "I bet the initials are E.J.M."

"You are right, Sis, they are! And I wouldn't be surprised if we find more engravings on other things too," remarked Petra, holding the bracelet. "What do you think, BB?"

"Well," he answered, and gave the trinket a quick glance. "I can assure you; I know nothing whatsoever about fine jewellery or anything else fine for that matter. But I do think is it time we all got down to work. We have come here for one reason, and that is to follow the professor's instructions, and unlock the secrets of the island," announced Brown Bear with a very serious tone in his voice. He noticed the girls were rather disappointed. "The only thing I can say of relevance is that the initials belong to a woman!"

"How on earth do you know that, BB?" remarked Rosie, looking closely at her friend.

"Well! I think everything ornate in this cottage is a gift, and anyway time is passing, we must move on, and start the work we have come to this island to pursue."

"So, what's the plan?" Petra inquired.

"Hey! BB, don't forget you have put all the professor's notes onto our phones." Rosie remembered all the hard work Brown Bear had done, so that they hadn't been forced to carry the heavy chests to the island.

"I haven't forgotten," Brown Bear replied. But this morning we'll take a walk back to the jetty where Lucas unloaded our supplies,"

"Yes, good idea, BB!" Petra exclaimed. "I'm getting hungry. Let's go now."

"Right, that is a plan," agreed Brown Bear. "And this afternoon we will have to make notes of the important details I put on your phones, girls. Are we agreed?"

"Indeed, we are, BB," said Petra.

They were just about to shut the door of the cottage when suddenly Rosie had a plan of her own. "Don't close the door, I can do some jobs while you two go and collect the supplies."

"What jobs?" Petra was puzzled.

"For one thing I can wash all that crockery and collect some driftwood for a fire tonight. There must be a fireplace in there somewhere, but if not, we can light a fire on the beach."

"A jolly good idea," said Brown Bear. "Come and help me carry the trunk, Petra, it will only take two of us."

So everything was decided for the day and Rosie re-entered the cottage and filled the sink with water. She thought she would have a rummage underneath and see what else she could find. She let out a cry of joy because all though it was only a quarter full there was a very old plastic bottle of washing up liquid.

"That's lucky," Rosie was delighted. "Now I can wash everything properly."

In the meantime, Brown Bear and Petra were making their way down the beach to the grassy headland to retrieve their waterproof trunk. They rounded the point and were delighted with what they saw. The cove was a lovely inlet with golden sand and a gentle slope into the sea.

"Wow!" exclaimed Petra, "Rosie, will love this. We can come down here and swim every day."

"Hey! hold on, my dear. Don't forget we have come to work for Professor Mortimer and find the secrets of the island."

Brown Bear picked up their luggage and headed back towards the cottage. Petra followed and just as they reached the headland and turned onto the beach they could see their dwelling, nestling under the cliffs.

Then suddenly a blood-curdling howl reached their ears.

"Quick, BB! We must get back to Rosie. As quick as we can!"

12
AN AFTERNOON OF STUDY

Petra was running pell-mell up the beach to the cottage when she saw Rosie rushing over the rocks towards her.

"There's a monster inside!" Rosie was very distressed and started to tremble.

"There can't be anything inside the cottage." Petra hugged her sister. "BB and I heard a terrible noise as we rounded the headland, so nothing can be inside. The noise seemed to come from under the beach, didn't it, BB?"

"It certainly did!" exclaimed Brown Bear.

"I heard it under the sink in the kitchen! I know I did!" Rosie was adamant. "I'm not going back in there!"

"We'll all go in together because I feel certain the noise didn't just come from inside the cottage," said Petra, doing her best to reassure her sister. "I can understand that if you were doing something near the sink, the noise would have been exaggerated to make you think it was right under the cottage,"

"I suppose so. What do you think, BB?"

Brown Bear took the little girl's hand. "Whatever it was has gone now. Come on, let's get this trunk inside and after lunch we will examine the Professor's documents." said Brown Bear. "It is about time we got down to the business in hand."

Rosie rubbed her eyes dry, "I will make lunch, and I can't wait to see what food Mum has packed for us."

"That's the spirit!" exclaimed Brown Bear. "Give me a hand, Petra, this trunk is quite heavy."

Only Rosie felt ill at ease entering the cottage that morning. Petra and Brown Bear had convinced themselves that the noise they had heard must have been the remains of last night's storm, still rumbling around over the bay.

"Rosie, will you make us a nice meal?" asked Petra. "And BB, you can sort out the Professor's papers and I will take our sleeping bags upstairs to the bedroom," Petra, was already sorting out their belongings.

"OK," replied Rosie. "There is a table in the kitchen, I will set out our lunch in there."

"Right ho! I think I'll take all our luggage into the bedroom, there's somewhere to sit comfortably up there," said Brown Bear. "Hey girls! I've just had a thought."

"What is it, BB?" Petra was halfway up the stairs.

"Well, we might as well make the most of things." he said, picking up their luggage. "I don't see why you girls can't sleep on the big ornate bed tonight, and I will sleep on that exquisite sofa."

"Good idea!" called Rosie, from the kitchen. "We should be safe up there."

"Yes! I would like to sleep on that bed," puffed Petra. "At least the rats can't get at us upstairs."

"We should be very cosy, come what may." Brown Bear put the girls' sleeping bags on the big bed.

"BB!" exclaimed Petra. "You do sound cynical."

"I didn't mean to, but we must be prepared for anything." Brown Bear was thoughtful. "I feel this is a much more serious mission than our last two adventures."

"Yes, I feel that too, but I don't know why." Petra rearranged the bedding ready for the night.

"Come on down, you two, lunch is served." called Rosie, from the kitchen.

"Rosie's gone all posh," Petra laughed.

"Ummm, I won't argue with that, my dear," Brown Bear was

glad the girls had got over their fright of earlier, everything seemed normal again, he gave a big sigh of relief. "We're on the way and we are starving," he called to Rosie.

It was just after two o'clock in the afternoon, before our three adventurers had cleared away the remains of their meal, and Rosie had washed the dishes they had used, and left them to dry on the beechwood draining board. The table was now clear and ready for their study.

"Now girls, do come and sit down. You will find all the documentation you will need on your phones. Let me see, what have we got here?" Brown Bear was settled on one of the dining chairs and was having a meticulous root through the contents of the attaché case, the one Rosie had found on the low shelf in the pantry at Professor's Mortimer's cottage.

"Petra, you do have Mali's charger safe, don't you?" Rosie said, looking worried. "It would be awful if our phones stopped working, wouldn't it?"

"Yes! It is safe," replied her sister. "In fact, he charged up his spare one as well, so we should be alright for quite a few days."

"The wonders of technology!" remarked Brown Bear. "But Rosie, go steady on using your phone as a torch, that will soon use up all your battery!"

"Oh! BB, you are right, I will be careful," said Rosie. "Where are our flashlights, Petra?"

"I put them on the bed upstairs, in case we need them in the night," answered Petra, making herself comfortable in another of the dining chairs.

Brown Bear was getting a bit impatient. "Now girls, we will begin."

He did a lot of shuffling of his papers and gave some intensive looks to see if Petra and Rosie were ready to start the search of Professor Mortimer's notes.

"Now girls. I have sorted these documents as simply as I can, for us all to understand," began Brown Bear. "The only parts that will interest us are when this island is mentioned. So, I have arranged them for you both to follow."

"Yes, I can see, look here Rosie." Petra showed her sister the place to begin their work on their iPhones."

"Yes, I've got it too," declared Rosie. "Isn't this exciting! But I wish I knew what we were looking for."

"Just go along with me, little one." said Brown Bear. "Don't forget I have had time to work things out a little, I have a fair idea what we are looking for. Now, quiet everyone, all will be revealed in due course."

For over an hour, their three heads were huddled together pouring over the documents, hoping to obtain answers from Doctor Lawrence Mortimer's files.

"I don't know how you two can read that small print on those phones of yours." Brown Bear interrupted the study session. "I have learnt a lot by just watching you both use different features on your mobiles, but my eyesight is not as good as yours, I could do with bigger print so I could see it more clearly."

"It's easy!" Rosie exclaimed. And began to show Brown Bear how he could stretch the words out on her small screen, making it much easier for him to see the words. "Look, BB. You can even make photographs bigger too!"

"I understand why technology is easy for all you young ones to understand, I became quite proficient with an abacus!"

Outside the cottage the sun shone high in the sky that August afternoon. The sound of seagull's shrill cries came in through the open window, reminding them that at last they were on the island again, with an adventure beginning to unfurl.

"Girls, I would like to draw your attention to Document 31," said Brown Bear, with a very business-like voice.

"Why document 31? Can't we start from document 1?" asked

Rosie.

"No point!" answered Brown Bear. "The island is not mentioned until 31."

"Oh! I see," Rosie sat back on her chair. "Why isn't it mentioned before then?"

"Rosie, darling, I do hope you are not going to interrupt BB all the time?" Petra sounded a bit annoyed.

"It's alright, Petra, I will explain to Rosie," Brown Bear remarked. "As we only have a certain amount of time to find the secrets of the island. And in due course we will present the professor with our findings. I have condensed all the documents we found in the mahogany chests into a program on your phones."

"I know that!" exclaimed a rather indignant Rosie. "Just why are we starting on document 31?"

Petra couldn't help interrupting, "Because only the island is important to us, and all the other notes Professor Mortimer has made up to 31 are about other things. For example, his archaeological dig at Hadrian's wall in Scotland and his dig at the Great Wall of China. There is also an extract about his work in Egypt!"

"Oh! I see." Rosie at last found the document in question on her phone. She studied it intensely. "Yes, I can see his notes on the island and the castle. BB, I am ready to follow your instructions."

"Good girl! Now I will begin," Brown Bear took a deep breath. He began to shuffle some of the papers he had in front of him. Every now and then he would rest his head on his paw with his elbow on the kitchen table.

"What have you found, BB?" Petra asked after a while.

"Just some private letters I haven't read before," replied Brown Bear.

"Oh!" exclaimed Rosie. "Perhaps you shouldn't read them if they are private."

"I know but this one is dated 1987," Brown Bear announced and began to read one of the letters out loud then, as if he thought better of it; he returned the letter to the briefcase.

"Listen, girls, if we are going to find the secret of this island we are going to have to dig deep into the professor's notes."

"Yes, I agree," said Petra deep in thought. "We must find out all we can about his wife. Lucas said she worked with him on many of his digs around the world."

"Yes! We must try and find out what happened to her." Rosie was now very enthusiastic.

"Well!" began Brown Bear. "We do know from Lucas' account, that after the professor's wife went missing, the police were called in and, when the police couldn't find her, he hired a private detective and still she wasn't found."

"This is all very sad," said Rosie, wiping a tear from her eye. "I wonder what happened to her."

There was a long silence then "Hur humm!" Brown Bear gave a little cough. "Now your attention please, girls. We will talk about the professor's wife later. And I will save the private letter till later too, because now we must study the documents concerning his work on the castle on the hill. There are many pages regarding the actual excavation of the castle, most of the work was carried out between 1983 and 1989. Girls, now look at document 31 and you will see we have a copy of the interim report on the excavations that were carried out during the summer of 1993, dated June 28 to July 19.

"Yes, I can see where you are reading," said Rosie. "BB, this seat is very hard to sit on for such a long time."

"I agree," said Petra.

"Well, so do I," agreed Brown Bear. "Just bear with me a while longer, we only need to find all the references to the castle here on this island."

Suddenly both girls collapsed into shrieks of laughter; in fact they laughed so much they had tears rolling down their cheeks.

"What's so funny?" exclaimed Brown Bear.

"You said bear with me," giggled Petra.

"Why is that so funny?"

"Because you are a bear," Rosie couldn't stop laughing.

"I know I am a bear and a bear that is running out of patience."

"Sorry, BB," Petra realised they were being childish.

"OK!" said Brown Bear. "We do need to lighten things up a little. Perhaps I should have taken this venture on my own shoulders and left you girls at home."

"Oh! No BB, we both apologise and now we will be serious, and study all the documents."

All was quiet and for the next few hours the girls' heads were bent over their iPhones and Brown Bear was deep in reading all the important paragraphs that mentioned the castle. Rosie was finding it hard to concentrate and after a while was glad when Brown Bear interrupted the girl's concentration.

"Soon we will have a break, but the professor's work is very interesting, just listen to this." he shuffled his legs a bit under the table and then began to read out loud. "It says here that the tower was completed, by use of a bucket hoist, and a scaffold walk was used as a barrow run. The tower interior was excavated to the earliest medieval floor level and a section was cleared exposing the bare rock. No post-holes or framing for stairways were found," Brown Bear took a deep breath. "Very interesting, don't you think girls?"

"That's strange saying no stairways were found," remarked Petra. "We found a sort of stairway, didn't we? Do you remember, Rosie?"

"Yes, I do, when we were running for our lives on our first visit to the island," recalled Rosie.

"Now girls, listen. It states here that a cistern was discovered near the eastern wall of the round tower," Brown Bear was engrossed with studying the document he had spread out on the table in front of him when suddenly Petra banged on the table and stood up.

"That just can't be right!" she said. "Because the tower we explored was rectangular, not round!"

"Yes!" Rosie exclaimed, fully agreeing with her sister. "On our first visit to the island when the helicopters came to rescue us, we were all on top of the castle tower and it definitely wasn't round."

"Of course, girls! You are both right." Brown Bear agreed. "The tower of the castle here on the island is most certainly rectangular, as were many early castles. It was only in the twelfth and thirteenth centuries that the design began to change."

"Yes, we did it in a history lesson at school, round towers were stronger at withstanding cannon fire," gushed Rosie.

"Yes!" Petra agreed. "Like Conwy Castle in North Wales. Mum used to live half a mile from it when she was little." She was pleased to have remembered a fact about her mother's childhood. "All the towers there were round. We went to see it on holiday once, it was on a river estuary, I can remember it well."

"That would be the River Conway!" Brown Bear looked at the girls. "And the castle building began in 1283 and took until 1287 to complete. It was constructed under the orders of Edward the first, known as Long Shanks, because he was very tall, and a gentleman named James of St George, from a town in France was the king's chief architect." he took a deep breath.

"But girls, you do have a point about the shape of the castle tower on this island, it is definitely of rectangular design, and that fits in with some early castles in Wales, like Dolwyddelan castle in Snowdonia, for example."

Brown Bear turned over his page. "Now girls we really must carry on with our investigation, I am on page thirty-two paragraph two."

Both girls had been listening to every word Brown Bear had read when Petra reached out her hand and touched his furry arm, he immediately stopped reading anymore of the text, and caught Petra's gaze.

"I am so sorry to interrupt, BB, but there is something wrong here."

Rosie looked up. "Whatever is the matter, Petra? I was just getting interested in what BB was saying." Rosie stared at her sister with a puzzled look on her pretty face.

"Look a few lines further on and you will see why I am drawing your attention to the next sentence. I don't think Professor Mortimer is even describing this castle, the one we know that is here on the island." Petra regained her composure and waited for her two companions to catch up.

"Yes! My dear, I do see what has given you doubt, this document describes the excavation of a cistern in a vaulted cellar."

"Well! That proves it! The cellar we explored did not have a vaulted ceiling, and there was no sign of a cistern," Petra remembered quite well their previous adventures on the island. "We know for a fact there was a deep well dug here, up on the hill, so why would they need a cistern?" Petra continued with her theory.

"What is a cistern?" asked Rosie, quite bewildered by now. "Can you tell me, BB?"

"The builders of the castle would dig a large hole to collect rainwater," replied Brown Bear. "Usually in rocky places. Digging a deep well could not be done quickly enough, to water their troops when they first took occupation."

"I see!" exclaimed Rosie.

"These notes just don't agree with what we know about the castle we have already explored," announced Petra.

"Precisely!" exclaimed Brown Bear. "I think! In fact, going by these notes, I am certain there is another castle, somewhere on this island."

"And to discover the secrets of the island," said Petra earnestly, "We must find the other castle."

13
THE GIRL

Petra and Rosie stood dumbfounded, as if glued to the spot. They looked at Brown Bear in disbelief.

"Another castle!" exclaimed Rosie. "But where can it be?"

"BB, You need to check if there are references to the castle on the hill, the castle we have already explored a few years ago." said Petra, deep in thought.

"I have! And there are plenty of reports from Professor Mortimer. Most of them are dated in the late Eighties and early Nineties," Brown Bear paused, he was as mystified as the girls.

"This is quite unbelievable. I thought we had explored everywhere."

Rosie pondered over the idea of there being two castles on the island. "Is it possible, BB? What do you think?"

"Well, I think it is time we had a break," said Brown Bear. "Rosie, is there any quick food in your Mum's parcel? If so, make us a picnic tea and we'll take it on the beach and look back at the landscape, just to see if we have missed anything. Maybe there is another fortress of some kind."

"No problem," replied Rosie. She ran into the kitchen leaving Petra and Brown Bear to go and find a sheltered place, on the rocks outside the cottage.

Soon Rosie was on the beach with their picnic basket brimming over with goodies. Brown Bear looked delighted and announced some pleasant news for the girls.

"We must relax for a while," said Brown Bear. "We have been able to do a lot of work this afternoon, but we must have some fun now." Their trusted companion took each of their hands and began to walk them both towards the ebbing tide.

"The tide is a long way out," remarked Petra.

The sun was shining in a pale azure sky as they walked across the damp sand.

"The air smells lovely after being cooped up all afternoon," announced Rosie, and ran ahead of Brown Bear and her sister. "Look over there, some dry rocks," she pointed to an outcrop under the cliffs.

"Yes," said Brown Bear. "Perfect for our picnic later! I want to walk to the edge of the water just to look back at the island and examine the skyline.

"Do you mean to see if there are two castles?" Petra took the bag of food from Rosie, who she noticed had been struggling a little with the weight of their produce.

"No! It is all right! I will go over to the rocks and set out our meal," Rosie took back their picnic and left Brown Bear and Petra to walk to the edge of the water.

The weather was still warm for a late afternoon in August. Petra and Brown Bear strolled out over the wet sand. The further out they walked they could feel a strong cool wind blowing across the beach, giving the distant waves a ruffle of white foam. High in the sky over the Bay seagulls and gannets were calling to each other with raucous cries.

"Look how deep our footprints sink into the sand, BB. It's getting real, squelchy."

"Yes, Petra," said Brown Bear. "I had noticed. Let's just go a little further. Come on, Petra dear. We must see if there is any other building on the skyline."

They waved to Rosie and she waved back. They walked at the edge of the sea gazing back at the land hoping to see another tower rising above the island. They had no trouble at all in finding the castle they knew so well but, alas there was no sign or even a glimpse of another turret.

"Do you think we may be mistaken and have misread the professor's interim report?" Petra looked at Brown Bear intensely.

"No! I don't think we have." He retorted. "All Professor Mortimer's notes that I have read, and I have studied most of them, are incredibly precise. I don't think he is a man who would allow errors."

"Oh! BB, listen to that roar, the tide has turned!" exclaimed Petra. "We must get back to Rosie. Come on. Look! She is waving at us frantically."

"Yes! I heard it turn," replied Brown Bear.

"So did I!" agreed Petra. "I have often heard it when Mum and Dad took us on holiday to the coast. When the tide is going out you can hear a soft sloshing sound, but when it turns, you hear a mighty roar."

"It is certainly a sound you cannot argue with," said Brown Bear, "Shall we go and have our picnic?"

Petra and Brown Bear walked towards the dry rocks nestling under the cliff on this eastern shore of the island. Rosie was pleased to see them.

"Come on, we have a super dinner," she said, looking pleased with herself. "Mum cooked a ham for us and made a huge salad. And a lemon drizzle cake."

"Ummmm! I love lemon drizzle!" exclaimed Brown Bear. "Girls, you do have the very best Mum!"

"Yes, we know!" The two sisters chorused together.

This evening was the second they would be spending on the island. The golden almost red sun began to set behind the cliffs, casting long shadows along the sand. Our trio of explorers felt very relaxed and happy at last, a bit confused but still happy.

"I am looking forward to spending a night in that luxurious

bedroom" announced Petra. "I think it will be a wonderful experience," she sighed.

"I am too!" agreed Rosie. "It's got to be better than last night in our sleeping bags on a hard floor."

"I don't mind sleeping in that outer room," said Brown Bear. "If you girls want a bit of time to yourselves."

"No, BB, certainly not!" Rosie exclaimed, with a slight panic in her voice.

"BB, it's fine," said a very determined Petra. "You always sleep on the bottom of Rosie's bunk bed at home. We feel safe with you."

"Yes, we do," said Rosie, taking hold of BB's paw.

"You know I will always do my best to protect you two," responded Brown Bear.

"We wouldn't expect anything less," teased Petra, as she handed the big bear another piece of lemon cake.

This proved to be a very pleasant time; eating their picnic on the flattest part of the rocks, digging their toes into the soft dry sand, just sitting munching their food and looking out to sea.

"The breeze is turning very fresh," said Petra. "Are you warm enough, Rosie?"

"Yes, I am, but I'm glad of my hooded jacket," said Rosie. "They are quite cosy when the wind blows. I just remembered it was this time last night when we faced that awful thunderstorm."

"It is much cooler tonight." Brown Bear informed them. "It had been so hot for a few days, and then the hot air met the cold air in a great battle last evening."

"Is that what a storm is?" asked Rosie. "I am really pleased there won't be another storm tonight." She was just helping herself to another piece of cake when suddenly, at that precise moment a different kind of sound boomed over the cove, making all three pals huddle together in fear and anticipation.

"Oh! Whatever is that noise?" squealed Rosie.

"I don't know! Do you, BB?" Petra reached out to her sister and held on to her hand, as reassuringly as she could in that moment.

The three pals had stopped still as they sat on the rocks, the noise they had witnessed had horrified them all, because it was a sudden roaring sound. Even Brown Bear was lost for words

"Oh! Whatever is it? It is so loud it seems to come from beneath the rocks we are sitting on." Rosie reached out and held on to her companions.

"These rocks join on to the cliffs over there," pointed Petra. "I think the noise comes from that direction. I am going to climb a little higher and see if I am right."

"Please be careful, Sis," begged Rosie. "Let BB come with you?"

"No! BB, stay with Rosie," said Petra, in a very determined voice.

By now the darkening evening sky had encroached on the scene and the tide was rushing in with great speed accompanied by a thunderous sound. The dinner party was over! And now fear and trepidation hung above them in the air. The rocks that had provided calm for sustenance a short while ago, suddenly became a hostile place.

"Will you be alright, Petra?" Brown Bear inquired, looking anxious. "I would come with you, but I feel I must take Rosie to the cottage before it gets too dark to see the way back. When I return, I will bring our torches."

"It's OK, I do have my phone as an emergency light." replied Petra. "I will be careful. Once I have climbed the rocks a little and found the source of the noise, I will come back straight away."

"As soon as Rosie is settled, I will return for you." Brown Bear persisted. "I don't like leaving you out here!"

"I'll be alright, don't worry about me, BB. Will you light the oil lamp for Rosie? I will soon be back in the cottage." And with that request, she disappeared from Brown Bear's view.

Petra made her way higher up the jagged rocks. She searched

with one foot above the other in the half-light, proving how sure footed she was, until she reached the top, where the rocks amalgamated with the cliffs.

The young girl reached the topmost ridge of the sandstone cliffs and stood taking in her surroundings. The daylight was fading fast, but she could still make out the headland, behind which was their jetty. In the west, almost invisible now she could see the last embers of the setting sun. She took a deep breath inhaling the pure night air and felt it extremely exhilarating.

"Now this reminds me of our first visit to this island." Petra said out loud, with her words trailing off into the wind. The stiff breeze caught a long tendril of her hair and whipped it across her face.

"Yes! I can recollect clearly the night I climbed the castle tower, and it was rectangular."

Petra was remembering an adventure she alone had, whilst Brown Bear and Rosie were hiding down in the dungeons of the castle. 'And that cellar did not have a vaulted ceiling.' She remembered clearly exactly what the castle was like, and the description of the castle in the professor's excavation notes was nothing like the castle they had all explored on a previous visit.

She suddenly remembered that Rosie and BB would become anxious if she didn't return to the cottage soon, she felt she must accomplish her mission. And at that precise moment she heard the mysterious strange noise once again, this time it was even louder.

She stood up tall on the highest rock and looked closely at the shoreline. A new moon was low in the eastern sky casting a ghostly glow over the rocks before her. The tide was beginning to intrude on the beach and the constant rush of the incoming waves were topped with soft foam reflected white in the moonlight. She clung to the pinnacle for what seemed like ages. The wind blew around her tossing her long blond hair across her face, whipping up the tendrils until they hurt her cheeks.

'That's it! I've had enough of this battering! I'm going down,' she thought to herself. She could not see clearly now as the crescent moon had gone behind a cloud. When her feet were safely on the cliff path, she was relieved to find the wind had abated a little. Petra felt disappointed because she hadn't solved the puzzle of the roaring sound they had now heard twice in two days.

"This island is not going to give up its secret easily, of that I am sure," she sighed. And that was when she heard the noise again, it was right below her. A roar? A growl? Or maybe it was a gurgling sound she could hear. Petra wasn't quite sure, but she was certain the sound came from below, it was a sound just like the one she and BB had heard yesterday.

'Rosie was sure she had heard it coming from below the sink in the kitchen,' she thought as she walked a little further along the cliff and then, immediately in front of her, she saw a fountain of water billowing up from down inside the cliff. It was as if a hole had appeared in the cliff top and a sheer wall of water had been forced up through a gap.

'There is water under these cliffs, and it is not the sea, because it will take hours before the high tide pounds these cliffs.' Petra decided to make her way back to the cottage, as it was getting very dark now. As she reached the bottom of the cliff path and was almost back on the rocks near the cottage, she could see something or someone coming up the beach towards her.

"Hello," said Petra. Who was now alongside the stranger and could see that the shadowy figure was a young girl. Petra, who was on top of the latest trends in fashion, thought the stranger looked rather old fashioned in her style of dress. Petra smiled at the person not quite sure if the image she saw was real, but the stranger did not return the gesture.

A sudden gust of cold air swirled around the rocks, and she couldn't help noticing that the young girl was dressed in a white mid-length, light-weight dress with a flimsy scarf wrapped round very slender shoulders.

"Who are you?" Petra asked, holding her hand out towards the girl.

The girl responded in a soft low toned voice, not with an answer but with another question. "Are you looking for Emily Jane?"

"No!" replied Petra. "I do not know anyone called Emily Jane. I am going to the cottage where I am staying with a friend and my sister," Petra pointed towards the professor's old cottage on the rocks. But when she turned back to look at the stranger, the girl had gone!

14
A MYSTERY

Brown Bear met Petra at the door of the cottage. Inside it felt warm and cosy and Petra could smell mild fumes from the oil lamp and was pleased to hear that Rosie was fast asleep, on the big bed upstairs.

"I've been examining some of these bones," Brown Bear remarked.

Petra interrupted him. "Did a girl come to the cottage? Did you see anyone, BB?"

"No!" replied Brown Bear. "I have been too busy recording these bones."

"Well! I saw a young girl outside on the rocks. I'm wondering if she is real."

"No, I haven't seen anyone except a very tired Rosie, and these bones. You look tired too."

"Yes! I am very tired. I think I'll go up and join Rosie," Petra gave a big yawn and made her way to the stairway. "Sure you'll be alright on the sofa, BB?"

"I will be fine," he assured her. "Don't worry about me. We had better look for the young lady you met tomorrow."

"Yes! I think we should. She only had on thin clothing and it has gone quite cold outside tonight." Petra gave another yawn. "Night night, BB."

"Good night, my dear, I just want to check on the largest bones, they seem familiar, but I don't know why."

"See you in the morning then, Oh! I nearly forgot as I have

been distracted with the girl I met!" Petra was now on the top step. "I have a lot to tell you about what I discovered on the clifftop, but it will have to wait until morning. Night night.

Rosie was fast asleep on the big bed; she must have been hot because she had pushed her sleeping bag down and freed her arms. She looked very peaceful Petra thought as she climbed into her own sleeping bag beside her. It wasn't long before she was asleep too.

It must have been a couple of hours later when something woke Petra. She felt hot too, and reached over to the bedside table, to feel for her phone.

'Three o' clock! I wonder what woke me.'

Rosie was fast asleep, and Brown Bear looked very cosy on the sofa. In the light from her phone she could see his furry chest heaving up and down accompanied by his usual growly snore.

Suddenly she heard a noise on the windowpane, the sound of a stone or pebble being tossed against the glass from outside. Petra switched her phone light off immediately. She had remembered what BB had told her about wasting the charge on her mobile. She fumbled for her torch in her backpack and switched it on.

And then she heard another thud at the window, a bit softer than the last one. Petra got out of bed and moved towards the recess: it was easy to see out because they hadn't bothered to draw the curtains when they went to bed.

The new moon was now very high in the sky and its silvery light illuminated the scene. The tide had turned and was receding, exposing dark, damp sand. Petra was holding her breath as she peered out of the window. She could see where the high tide had deposited reams of seaweed stretched out along the tideline, and she could see the tops of the dark shadowy rocks aglow in the moonlight. She managed to open the window and leaned out.

She had seen the girl again with her flimsy attire being ruffled by a chilly breeze.

"Oh!" Petra gasped. "You can't still be out there in the cold? Stay there. I'll come to you. Where did you go before? Wait, I'm coming." Petra found a thick jersey and placed it round her shoulders, as she rushed down the stairs, and out of the cottage into the night.

She looked up and down the beach but could not see the girl anywhere. But then, as she glanced towards the rocks where they had all eaten their dinner under the cliff, Petra saw her. "Stay there, I will come to you, please stay. I want to talk to you!"

The girl seemed frozen to the spot when Petra approached her. "You are shivering, I thought you would be. It's quite cold tonight," said Petra, "Your dress is of thin material. Do you want to borrow my jumper?"

"I only have one dress and I never feel cold," replied the stranger.

"How long have you been on the island?" asked Petra, intrigued with this young girl.

"I don't know. A long time, I think," was the reply.

"Why did you ask me earlier if I was looking for Emily Jane?" This young woman, who had appeared from nowhere, mystified Petra.

"Because I thought you might be," answered the girl.

"Who is Emily Jane?" asked Petra.

The girl stood there in the semi moonlight. Petra noticed her long thick black hair, as the wind blew it across her face.

"Why did you throw pebbles up at our window?"

"I am not sure. I think I want to apologise to you. I rushed off quickly. Strangers come to this island and scare me. I don't trust anyone!"

"Well, you can trust us!" stated Petra, feeling there was something very curious about this girl.

"I must go now! But if you meet me on the cliff top at midday, I will tell you more," replied the girl.

Petra was just about to say, "Where exactly on the cliff top?" when she felt a cold rush of night air and the girl was gone.

Petra shivered as she looked back at the cottage and saw a light in the bedroom window. 'I must get back,' she thought. 'Rosie has woken up and is worried because I am not in the sleeping bag besides her. Or worse still, I have disturbed BB? Oh, dear! He's going to be very grumpy in the morning.'

Petra trod carefully over the rocks on her way to the cottage that nestled in shadow under the cliff. On entering she made her way through the downstairs room and up the stairs onto the first floor. Luckily it was Rosie who was awake and Brown Bear was still fast asleep on the turquoise blue sofa.

"Where have you been, Petra? I woke and you weren't here. I didn't want to wake BB because you know how grumpy he can be if he doesn't get all his night's sleep."

"Yes! I know Rosie. There is nothing to worry about. Let's both get to sleep and we'll catch up in the morning."

"Oh! I am dreading the morning. BB says we have to go through Professor Mortimer's notes again, as he has found some information about Mrs Mortimer."

"That should be interesting," her sister replied. "We'd better get to sleep now. Night, Rosie."

Rosie was still half asleep and rubbed her eyes. "Where have you been, Sis?"

There was no response as Petra had fallen fast asleep dreaming about a strange girl in a flimsy dress.

Next morning Brown Bear woke first and he wasn't grumpy at all. In fact, he was quite perky and had even put the kettle on to make some tea.

"Come on down, girls. I am making breakfast. We have a lot to do today. It is a beautiful morning and the birds are singing, hur, hum, well actually the seagulls are squawking, anyway it's hot and sunny and it's only 7.30 am."

"Oh! BB, do we have to get up now?" called down Rosie.

"Indeed, you do!" Brown Bear was adamant.

"BB, do I really have to get up this early?" Petra's sleepy voice could be heard from upstairs. "I feel I have only just come to bed. I am very tired."

"You can have twenty minutes more!" he relented. "Bring your phones outside on the rocks. I am packing a picnic breakfast so don't be late."

The morning was filled with glorious sunshine which highlighted the white caps forming into frothy wispy tips on the waves. The incoming tide was accompanied by a stiff morning breeze which was guiding in the inevitable flow of the blue sea. Waves were gently washing over dry sparkling sand, much to Rosie's delight.

"We can all have a swim later," announced Brown Bear, unpacking their breakfast. "When we have studied the professor's papers. You have brought your phones, haven't you, girls?"

"Of course! We never go anywhere without them," exclaimed Petra, with rather a loud yawn. "Sorry, I am rather tired."

Rosie took the breakfast bag from Brown Bear and laid everything out on a red and white check tablecloth. She spread them out on the flattest part of a rock, the one most suitable to be their make-do table.

"Wow! BB, this food looks good. Mum has been very generous, and she knows what we all like. Look! More of that ham she cooks in her slow-cooker, cheese, and a jar of Nan's marmalade and some soft bread rolls that still feel fresh."

"And plenty of fruit, I am pleased to see!" joined in Brown Bear.

Rosie was very alert this morning and began pouring the tea that BB had prepared in a flask. In fact, she was very lively in comparison to Petra. But then she hadn't been up in the middle of the night talking to a strange girl.

"What have you found in the professor's notes, BB?" Petra asked, as she sipped her tea.

"Quite a lot really," answered Brown Bear, as he started to munch on a ham and cheese roll.

"Like what?" Rosie handed out some fruit.

"What have you found that we don't know already?" said Petra.

"Well, for one thing Mrs Mortimer was not into studying old buildings!" Brown Bear informed the girls.

"Oh! I understood that his wife accompanied the professor on all his digs around the world!" exclaimed Petra.

"So did I," said Rosie.

"Well!" explained Brown Bear. "She was an archaeologist in her own right, but her main interest was excavating animal bones."

"Well, that is a very interesting fact," Petra took in a deep breath. "I suppose that explains all the fossils and bones in the downstairs room in the cottage."

"Yes, that is what I thought too, hence my interest in them last evening, when you came in from the beach," replied Brown Bear.

"I remember, BB," said Petra. "You said you wanted a good look at the larger bones, because they reminded you of something, but you didn't know what."

"Yes, my dear, my precise words, those large bones do remind me of something in my past." Brown Bear looked deep in thought. "No doubt it will come back to me when I am not expecting it."

Rosie seemed quite disinterested with all this talk of bones. She had carefully packed all the used breakfast things away; she was looking longingly at the sea. The summer wind was getting stronger and blowing white fluffy clouds across the sky. Then came a sudden rush of the incoming tide rolling in and was now halfway up the golden sand. The wind upped its speed and was now driving in the waves with much more force. Sudden gusts had stirred up high breakers, to roll them in torrents of frothy foam and deposit them with great force crashing on the shore. The endless white caps were encroaching the beach and covering the sand, washing over thousands of glistening pebbles and then drawing back to make way for the next impatient wave.

"Come on, let us swim now while it is so perfect," cried Rosie in glee. The little girl discarded her shorts and T-shirt and was running down the beach to splash in the inviting water wearing her new swimsuit.

Within seconds Petra joined her and Brown Bear watched on, enjoying seeing the girls so happily frolicking at the water's edge.

"Come on, BB. Please come." called the girls together. "It is so warm you will love it."

Very soon Brown Bear joined his two best pals and for a while they were all enjoying swimming around one another and squealing when Brown Bear disappeared under the water, then suddenly, to their surprise emerged again a short distance away making the girls shriek with laughter.

What a wonderful time they were having all three together on their beloved island.

"This is a great holiday!" exclaimed Rosie, "The sun is hot and the sea is warm and nothing to spoil it. Yippee!"

"Yes, it is lovely," agreed Petra. But she held a secret. And she began to wonder when she ought to tell the others about the girl.

Brown Bear stood up and began to walk in the shallows, as he did so he shook his thick dense fur, so that all the sparkling droplets landed on the girls making them squeal.

"Race you to the rocks!" yelled Petra.

All three, ran splashing through the waves to the dry sand.

"I'll win," announced Petra and she did. "What time is it? Rosie, have a look at your phone for me."

"It's eleven thirty," answered Rosie.

"Right," said Petra. "I'll help you get all this stuff back to the cottage. Then I have to be somewhere at mid-day."

"Where do you have to be, Petra?" Rosie looked most puzzled.

Brown Bear was still shaking himself dry, much to the girl's dismay.

"Hey BB, that's enough!" cried Rosie. "As fast as I'm drying myself, you are wetting me again."

There was so much fun and laughter going on that Petra avoided giving her sister an answer. She wasn't ready for questions yet. She must keep her midday meeting and find out a lot more about the girl.

15
SECRETS OF THE CLIFFS

Once back at the cottage all three went their separate ways. Rosie was in her element washing the breakfast cups and plates and generally tidying the small kitchen. Brown Bear brought a pile of the professor's documents and spread them out on the dining table. And, as for Petra, well we know by now, she has plans of her own.

"Hey, you two!" she called to the others, as she crossed the threshold of the cottage and stood out on the rocks. "I'm going for a walk on the cliffs. I won't be long."

"Hey!" called Brown Bear, "I have just remembered the letter the professor wrote to you, Petra, telling us he was staying with his friend Eustace."

"Yes! I remember. Didn't he mention he had employed a cleaner or something like that." Petra called back, as she was anxious to keep her cliff top appointment with the girl.

"You are right!" Brown Bear replied, "I'll just go over his papers again before lunch."

"I won't be long! I'll help you when I get back." Petra was off over the rocks and up the cliff path as fast as she could.

The tide was in now as far as the rocks, so there was no beach visible for Petra to walk on. But that didn't bother the young girl who was as agile at climbing up the rocky cliff path now, as she was in her early gymnastic lessons. She had been a proficient pupil while attending her primary school.

She eventually stood on the cliff top that beautiful summer's day looking down at the surf-capped waves, as they crashed on the rocks below and at the cottage. She could feel her long blond hair, still wet from her swim, falling lankly on her shoulders. Suddenly there was a loud shriek from a gull directly above her, she gave a gasp of surprise, and then she saw her!

There was the girl sitting on the grassy cliff path just a few metres away, still dressed in the same flimsy dress. She hadn't seen Petra and sat there with the wind blowing her hair in strands across her face. Petra had a few moments to study a very beautiful face and a young woman with the longest black hair she had ever seen.

"Oh! There you are!" the girl exclaimed. "I thought you wouldn't come to meet me."

"Why did you think that?" replied Petra. "I always keep my word. Anyway, I find you intriguing."

"I see!" the girl replied, getting to her feet and facing Petra. "I keep my word too! Come with me. There is a place just along here out of the elements."

Petra followed the stranger to where there was an overhang in the rocks, a perfect shelter from the buffeting wind that had helped drive the sea inward that morning.

The girl spoke first. "I watched you all arrive two days ago. You landed at the old jetty and the man who brought three of you to the island returned to the boat and steered away to the mainland."

"And were you pleased?" Petra looked straight into the girl's face and realised she looked older than she had originally thought.

"I don't know what to feel pleased is like."

"Oh! I am sorry to hear that," Petra felt there was something very odd about the stranger. "Where do you live?"

"I have made a dwelling place deep underground," the girl replied in a quiet voice.

"I would like to see your home," said Petra.

"I can show you one day. Tell me about your friends and why

you have come to this island?" The girl looked as if she was really interested in our little company.

"Let's sit down on the grass and I will tell you all about my sister and Brown Bear, who we call BB," Petra began to tell the story of how Brown Bear was very wise, and about Rosie her sister and their new neighbour's cottage in their village, and how they have come to the island to find the secrets of the island for the professor.

"The professor?" exclaimed the girl, whose beautiful face was suddenly overshadowed with concern. "This professor has a secret?"

"No!" Petra exclaimed. "No, he hasn't got a secret! It is the island that holds a secret!"

"How interesting because I know some secrets of this island," the girl astounded Petra with her answer. "Over there a fountain of water escapes and gushes high into the sky."

"Yes! I have seen it," Petra was about to ask the girl some more questions when suddenly the resounding noise they had all heard yesterday boomed up in the sounds of growls and groans. And it was the same sounds Rosie had heard coming from under the sink at the cottage. They had heard the same blood curdling disturbance as they entered the cove yesterday after they had both returned from the jetty with supplies they had brought from home.

"Whatever is that noise?" Petra asked the girl, but when she turned to face her, she had gone. "Hey, where are you? Please come back."

Petra searched the cliff top, but there was no sign of the girl. She walked higher up the cliff path and peered over the edge to see if she had gone down to the shore, but there was no sign of her anywhere.

The wind ceased a little and the noon sun soared high in the sky. Petra could hear gorse pods popping all around her. The seagulls were shrieking in the endless blue sky. She believed the noise had disturbed the birds too. She made her way higher up the cliffs to where the grass had stopped growing and more rocks appeared. They were tall and jagged like broken teeth jutting crookedly out of the landscape. Petra started looking amongst them hoping the girl would be hiding there, but there was no sign of the strange girl.

"Where did she go?" Petra was starting to feel annoyed with the girl and her sudden disappearances. "Where does she go? It is not a very well-mannered person who does that! And just as she was opening and talking to me." Petra felt frustrated.

Just as she came to a place on the path where the rocks appeared in front of her like stalagmites in a cave, she stopped to examine her find and suddenly without warning a mass of water appeared in front of her, spurting into the air.

'It's like a fast jetted fountain,' she thought. 'Maybe it is, the high tide escaping it's bounds from under the cliff? But no, it can't be because when I saw it yesterday the tide was far out.'

"Hello, where are you? I don't even know your name." yelled Petra, desperately. She felt sure the stranger was nearby, even though she couldn't see her.

Petra searched and searched but there was no sign of the girl.

'Perhaps I imagined her,' she questioned herself. 'But no, I am not that kind of person. I know she was real. She seems so lost and alone, I feel I must find her and discover how I can help her.'

She was about to climb further up the cliff top when she heard Rosie's desperate cries resounding on the breeze.

"Petra, Petra where are you?" The wind caught Rosie's words and spun them round and round, making them resound off the cliffs and echo in the air.

"Oh! I forgot Brown Bear and Rosie, because all I have been thinking about is the girl," Petra said out loud, as she made her way back down the cliff path and landed with a crunch on the shingle.

"There you are! Come quickly! Brown Bear is cross because you have made us all late starting lunch." Rosie took hold of her sister's hand and pulled her along. Petra said nothing and followed her sister.

As they reached the rocks on which the cottage stood, it started to rain and heavy moisture-laden clouds began to obscure the sun.

"Where have you been, Petra?" Brown Bear did sound grumpy.

"I am sorry I am late, but let's have lunch and I'll tell you everything afterwards!"

Well! That was it! Brown Bear never stayed grumpy for long. The three sat round the small dining table and tucked into a meal, which Rosie had prepared.

"I made a casserole by mixing a tin of corned beef and a tin of baked beans together," said Rosie apprehensively.

"It's very good," said Petra, tucking in.

"Excellent!" Brown Bear exclaimed. "Very tasty."

Rosie sighed with relief as she hadn't been sure if her companions would like her cookery invention. She felt very pleased with herself. There was a chocolate cake to follow, and everyone was happy and content.

As soon as the meal was over Brown Bear made an announcement.

"Petra, Rosie, I need your full attention if we are going to solve the mystery of this island." He sat upright on his chair and ruffled through the professor's documents.

"Well! You have it," said Petra, in earnest.

"And you have mine," agreed Rosie. "I thought we had to find a special secret."

"Well, yes! I thought so too, but I haven't come across one in all the professor's notes. But I have found something about the second castle with the round tower."

"Oh! BB, why didn't you say that before?" Rosie questioned her furry friend.

"Because I only read about it just before our meal, and I didn't want you to get too excited about it. Not before lunch anyway!"

"BB, how could you keep it from us," said Petra, a little annoyed.

"Come on, BB, please tell us now." Rosie was beside herself with excitement.

"Right, girls, please settle down, my news is quite exciting."

"Do tell us, BB. What have you found out?" Petra settled herself at the table, looking straight into Brown Bear's big brown eyes.

"Well, looking at the professor's notes more closely I think the round tower he mentions is quite near to the rectangular tower we have already explored."

"How do you know that for a fact, BB?"

"O…kay," he said slowly. "I have found a place on a small map of the island amongst the papers." Then, he sat very upright, and pointed to the document laid out in front of them. "I think the round tower is just here!"

"But that isn't very far from the castle we all know." Petra looked very puzzled.

"I know!" came the reply.

"Let me see." Rosie begged to have a look.

"There are some depth measurements on the professor's interim report," said Brown Bear. "I am about to check the depth of the round tower."

"This is getting a bit complicated for me," Rosie screwed up her nose.

"No! it's not complicated!" exclaimed Petra. "I think this makes our search easier."

"All we have to do now is to go and search the castle dungeons more thoroughly," Brown Bear gave a big sigh.

"We didn't explore all of them on our first visit," Petra was deep in thought. "Don't you both remember we were far too busy helping those pilots we befriended, well rescued, escape from the enemy."

"Yes! I remember it all," intervened Rosie. "We all had to leave the island in a hurry."

"Right then!" announced Brown Bear. "At first light tomorrow morning we will go to the parts of the dungeons we didn't have time to explore a few years ago."

"Why can't we go this afternoon?" begged Rosie.

"No, we need to plan our exploration most carefully. Petra you can find our climbing equipment, and Rosie you can fill a holdall with food, enough for a day or two."

Rosie and Brown Bear began to move and soon were bustling about in urgent preparation for the journey tomorrow.

Petra sat upright with her shoulders against the back of her chair stretching her arms into the air and yawning.

"I must go for a walk," she said. "It's a bit stuffy in here."

She was thinking of a way to make an excuse to go back up the cliff path and search diligently for the girl.

"All our climbing gear is still packed, BB, I'll sort it later, I won't be long!"

"Petra, it is pouring with rain now, you'll get soaked. Please don't go out in this weather," pleaded Rosie.

"But I must, I really must!" Petra took hold of her waterproof jacket and disappeared out of the cottage door. The only thought she had in her head was to find the girl.

16
ANOTHER CASTLE

As Petra reached the top of the cliff path, she began to wish she had heeded Rosie's warning. It had been a lovely summer's morning, but as the day wore on the weather had turned to deliver its worst. Petra pulled the hood of her jacket tightly round her head, as the wind buffeted her face making her cheeks sting with the incessant force of the rain. The downpour was so heavy it was making her way underfoot fraught with difficulty.

Soon she arrived at the spot where she last saw the girl. The path had collected small pools of water making the rocky way slippery, and incredibly treacherous. Petra was wearing trainers on her feet and soon they became soaked by unavoidably stepping into the puddles. Feeling her feet getting more and more sodden she decided to give up her search and go back to the others.

With the rain stinging her face she turned to go back down the cliff but standing in the middle of the path was the girl.

"Oh!" Petra exclaimed, in surprise. "Please don't disappear again, I want to talk to you." Surprisingly the girl wasn't very wet, and she was still wearing the same flimsy dress.

"Come with me." She beckoned for Petra to follow her.

A few minutes later the two girls stood on the level rocks, near to where Petra had witnessed the sudden gush of water. The high fountain that had stood before her like a wall of water now towered into the air above her.

"This is a special place," the girl said in such a very quiet voice, that Petra could barely hear what she was saying.

"Do you mean it is a secret place?" Petra asked.

"It can't be secret because I know of it!" exclaimed the girl.

"I thought," said Petra. "That it might be one of the secrets of the island."

"If you want to know all the secrets of the island," the girl remarked. "When you earn my trust, I will show you what you want to know."

"That sounds really promising! But my sister and Brown Bear must be in on this secret too."

"I am not sure about meeting anyone else. I have been alone here on this island for a very long time," replied the girl, looking beseechingly into Petra's eyes.

"Listen, you can come and meet Rosie and BB, later this afternoon and have some tea with us," Petra was enthusiastic. "But I haven't told them anything about you yet."

"I am not ready, but if you are on the beach early tomorrow, I will come and see them briefly." The girl seemed to relent, but Petra wasn't at all certain that she would be there to meet them all the next day.

"Alright, that will be good, I know they will be friends with you because you are my friend now," Petra made to link arms with the girl, but she shrugged away. "That's OK," Petra smiled. "Can I tell them about you, at least?"

"Yes!" said the girl. "Come and see this."

The two girls stood overlooking a deep cleft in the cliff top, a hole in the rocks that didn't seem to have a visible bottom that Petra could see.

"Does this join up with the ravine? We explored it on our first visit to the island. My sister and I were only ten years old then," explained Petra.

The girl looked into Petra's blue eyes, "No, the ravine is in the centre of the island, nowhere near here. How old are you now?"

"My sister and I are twins, we are both 15 years old," replied

Petra. "May I ask how old you are?"

"I don't know my age, but I have counted lots of hot seasons and many freezing cold ones," the girl moved away from the opening in the rocks. "I must go now. I will meet you all on the beach in the morning. Look, the sky is brightening. It will be a fine day tomorrow!"

And with that remark the girl disappeared once again. Petra could do nothing but go back to the cottage, to change out of her soaking wet clothes.

"Rosie! BB! Where are you? I need to tell you both something very important," called Petra, as soon as she was dressed in dry clothes. "Rosie, where shall I leave my wet shorts and T-shirt?"

"In that small sink in the kitchen, of course," Rosie shouted down from upstairs, where she and Brown Bear had been engrossed studying the old map of the island that Brown Bear had found amongst the professor's papers.

"That's fine, I'll give them a rinse," Petra was soon in the ornate bedroom with her two companions, reaching for her dressing gown which she had left on the back of the bedroom door.

"What is the matter, Petra my dear? You look somewhat distressed," asked Brown Bear.

Petra noticed that Brown Bear and Rosie had quite a few of the professor's documents spread out on the big bed. They looked in some sort of order and had not been placed in a haphazard way.

"Where have you been, Petra?" Rosie was curious. "BB, and I think you are being a bit mysterious."

"No! BB, I am not in any distress! Maybe I am being a bit mysterious. I climbed to the top of the cliff path, and then I was caught in a downpour. I have never seen such heavy rain before, and that's why I have left my wet clothes in the kitchen," explained Petra, as she scrambled up on the bed beside Rosie.

"Now! Look here, Petra. I was just about to read part of the professor's report to Rosie," said Brown Bear.

Petra bent over the papers Brown Bear was pointing at, "So what have you found, BB?"

"Well! I have studied Professor Mortimer's interim report with great intensity. In fact, he has given precise references and detailed descriptions of what his excavations have uncovered," Brown Bear took a deep breath. "But I have come to the conclusion that his findings do not relate to the rectangular medieval castle that stands majestically in the middle of this island."

"I know, BB! But we have thought that before." Petra was drying her hair with a towel, a very exquisite one that she had found in the drawer in the dressing table.

"That is hard to believe!" exclaimed Petra. She lay back against the ornate satin pillows."

"I can't believe it either." Rosie joined in too. "What does it mean exactly? What are you telling us, BB?"

"If what you say is true, BB," sighed Petra, now raising herself up on her elbows to face her furry friend. "Where is the castle he has excavated? And where exactly on this island are we likely to find it?"

"To be honest, my dear, from what I understand of his notes I really believe the second castle with the round tower is somewhere on the eastern cliffs. I do not know but I have studied his references concerning the second castle thoroughly, I believe they are far deeper underground, than even the lowest recorded depth of the rectangular castle we explored."

"You mean lower than the dungeons we went in years ago?" Rosie explained with a certain amount of disbelief.

"Yes, I do!" Brown Bear was convinced he was right. "Let me read this to you and as I do, take yourselves back to the time we first found the steps to the dungeons and went down to explore." He made himself comfortable on the sofa ready to read to his companions.

"I remember everything!" Rosie cried out in excitement. "I

even remember the damp walls and the musty wet smell that was down there."

"That's the way," Brown Bear seemed pleased. "Remember every detail, Rosie, and as I read this new document, interrupt me if anything is different from what you both recall of our first adventure."

"We will, BB, we are ready," Petra answered for both girls.

Outside the sun was shining brightly, drying up all the rain. Petra looked up and wondered whenever was she going to get the chance to tell the others about the girl.

"Presumably it is the professor's actual excavation notes which I am reiterating to you girls. Now concentrate!" said Brown Bear, giving a little cough before he began reading.

"The south facing entrance between the buttresses or flanking walls stood four metres high above the rock: hewn floor. We discovered the entrance had been blocked early in its existence but fortunately we discovered the cellar entrance over a metre down and the wall below had been poorly built and a drain had been placed for the collection of rainwater," Brown Bear stopped to see if the girls were concentrating and was pleased to see both their eager faces intent on his every word. "I'll carry on then."

"Yes please, BB," said Rosie.

Petra just gave him a nod of approval.

"Right then," Brown Bear found his place and resumed his reading.

"The second area where work was concentrated in the excavation of this summer Nineteen-Ninety something?" Brown Bear gave a sigh, "I can't see what year it refers to exactly. Look, girls. It has been smudged just here! Anyway, I'll carry on." He commenced reading aloud. "Now, let me see. Ah! Yes, work was carried out on the external stairs of the round tower."

"Well! That's not our castle, is it?" interrupted Petra. "The rectangular tower we climbed up in our first adventure definitely didn't have external stairs."

"You are right, Sis!" exclaimed Rosie. "Even the turret at the top of the tower only had some internal well; worn steps, leading to the very top."

"Yes, I remember it all exactly," said Brown Bear, in a positive voice. "I am convinced the professor was definitely writing about another castle somewhere on this island. But where exactly, I have no idea?"

"Are there any grid references?" asked Petra.

"Grid references! Why would they need grids?" Rosie asked, with a puzzled look on her pretty face. "Unless, of course, it would have been for the ancient rainwater that collected in that drain."

Petra couldn't help laughing at her sister's remark. But Brown Bear didn't see Rosie's joke at all funny so, he explained very seriously to the little girl what a grid reference was used for.

"Rosie, dear! Numbers and letters can find a grid reference on maps and other documents, where a reference indicating a location using a series of vertical and horizontal grid lines identifies the spot."

"Oh! BB, this is all very complicated for me. When can we go and play on the beach again?" Rosie wasn't much wiser, but she did remember her geography teacher mentioning something similar last term.

"Very well, Rosie!" Brown Bear said in a gentle voice. "I know all this is complicated, but you and Petra did promise Professor Mortimer that you would come here instead of him, and find its secrets."

"Yes, we did!" intervened Petra. "We did promise him in the ambulance when he was being taken away to the hospital, with a broken ankle."

"I know," said Rosie reluctantly. "But it is the last three weeks of our summer holiday. Can't we move things on a bit, BB?"

"Well, I don't know how we can." said Brown Bear, deep in

thought.

"Actually, I do," Petra remarked quite casually.

"How?" exclaimed Rosie, in a flush of excitement.

"What time is it now?" Petra searched for her phone. "It's nearly five."

"Yummy! Tea time!" said Rosie. "I will pack a picnic and we can eat it on the beach."

Brown Bear and Petra agreed. BB returned the important documents back into the briefcase, making sure the documents were returned in order. He sighed with relief when they were all returned safely to the fine leather case in which the professor had placed them for safekeeping.

Rosie soon had a full picnic basket in her hand and Brown Bear had found a two-metre square of tarpaulin behind the kitchen sink.

"Right! Let's go," he said, holding the big front door open for the girls.

They were all surprised to find how warm it was outside, as they stepped through the cottage door onto the rocks.

"Let's walk over to that headland," Brown Bear pointed in the opposite direction to the beach with the landing jetty. "We have never explored any of this eastern side of the island before, have we?"

"You are right, BB," replied Petra. "Our last two visits were mainly focused on the North and West shores."

Rosie nodded agreeing with her sister.

"Now! Petra," bellowed Brown Bear. "What did you mean by telling us you know a way to move things on a bit?"

"Yes, Sis' I want to know too, because all these history lessons aren't getting us anywhere, are they?" Rosie blurted out her true feelings.

"Hur, Hum!" Brown Bear interrupted. "I beg to differ! We have learnt a great deal, Rosie. Now, we know that somewhere on this island there is another castle, already excavated by our professor. And if nothing else we are going to discover exactly where that fortress is standing."

"Petra, are you going to tell us how we can move things on a bit?" asked Rosie.

"Yes!" exclaimed Brown Bear. "And what is with this business of you going out into the night? And these walks up to the clifftop you are taking alone?"

"What walks in the night?" exclaimed an indignant Rosie. "Petra, is there something that you are not telling us?"

Petra swallowed hard, in that moment she didn't think her sister or BB would believe her about seeing the girl.

17
EMILY JANE

Brown Bear and Rosie decided on the place for their picnic tea. So, they both placed the tarpaulin on the sand near the dunes, which were soft and golden and glinted in the late afternoon sun.

"This cove isn't as wide as I thought it was," said Rosie, unpacking her basket of tea things. "It's a cosy cove! Don't you think, Petra?"

"It's fine!" replied her sister, not really concentrating on what Rosie was saying.

"Are you OK, Petra? You seem miles away." Brown Bear glanced over towards the sisters. "Is anything the matter?"

"Well, actually there is," said Petra. "I need to tell you something."

"Oh!" exclaimed Rosie, as she stopped what she was doing.

"Uuumm," said Brown Bear, as he sat down on the tarpaulin. "I thought there was something going on. You have been a bit distant for a while now."

"Whatever is the matter?' Rosie was puzzled. "Please tell us, Petra. I haven't noticed you being distant."

"Well, alright I'll tell you everything, but Rosie, do put all the food out now, I'm hungry." Petra helped herself to a corned beef sandwich.

Brown Bear and Rosie sat upright in expectation of Petra's explanation.

"Now, I did say I know a way to move our investigation on a bit further, in regard to finding the other castle, but you must listen carefully." Petra settled herself down on the tarpaulin.

"The second day we were here on this island," she began. "Do either of you remember we all heard that unexplainable noise, coming from deep in the rocks."

"Yes, of course I do!" exclaimed Rosie. "It was the same noise I heard under the sink in the cottage. I was very frightened."

"I definitely remember," said Brown Bear. "It was coming from under the cliff, and we left you to climb higher up because you thought you knew exactly where the noise was coming from."

"Yes!" Petra was looking closely at her family. "When I was high up, as high as I could go, a wall of water gushed out of the rocks, just like a huge fountain."

"Wow!" exclaimed Rosie. "Why haven't you told us before?"

"Because there's more! Much more! I have seen a girl here on the island!"

"What do you mean?" asked Rosie. "Why haven't we all seen her?"

"I think because she has chosen me," sighed Petra. "At first I thought she was real. But now I'm not so sure?"

"Oh, Petra." Brown Bear was looking very worried. "You think you are seeing a ghost?"

"Yes! I think she must be!" exclaimed Petra. "I didn't at first because she talks to me, but then after a short time she disappears, always making excuses and saying she must go. And then she just disappears!"

"What does she look like?" Rosie was feeling excited and frightened at the same time."

"Don't worry, Rosie darling." Petra continued. "She is very gentle and wears a flimsy white dress and when I asked her if she was cold in the night air, she replied that she never felt cold, and only had the one dress."

"A white dress!" Rosie exclaimed in horror. "That proves it! If her dress is white then she's a ghost!"

"What else has she told you, Petra dear?" Brown Bear looked concerned.

"Now, let me think." Petra closed her eyes deep in thought.

"When she first came up to me looming out of the darkness, she asked me if I was looking for Emily Jane? I told her I didn't know an Emily Jane and I was staying with you two in the cottage. I remember pointing to the cottage and when I turned back to talk to her, she was gone, completely disappeared."

"Oooo!" said Rosie.

"She does sound like a strange girl." Brown Bear looked thoughtful.

"Umm, I know! She is very strange, she told me she has lived on the island for a long time, and she didn't know for sure how old she is." Petra gave a big sigh. "And then when we talk, I feel I am getting some way with understanding her, and then she just disappears again."

"Oh! Petra, I think she is a ghost!" Rosie sounded as if she had made up her mind. "Tell me again what she said. Who did she think you were looking for?"

"She just asked if I was looking for Emily Jane?"

"Umm, Emily Jane?" Rosie was deep in thought. "The initials are E. J."

"Yes, they are! What of it?" Petra was puzzled.

"Petra, surely you remember all the crockery in the kitchen?" said Rosie excitedly. "And all the note paper in the bedroom drawer? Everything has the initials E.J. embellished on them."

"Yes," replied Brown Bear. He joined the conversation somewhat confused with all the mysterious initials "But the initials on all the crockery and the stationery were E.J.M."

"Yes, I know everything must belong to Emily Jane, but Emily Jane who? I wonder if there is a connection somewhere." Rosie said thoughtfully. "What could the M stand for on all those belongings?"

"Could be anything." Brown Bear joined in the conversation, sceptically. "Now listen girls, it is getting late. We ought to get back to the cottage because I feel another summer storm is on the way."

"Really! No! we don't want another storm, especially like the one we had on our first night!" Rosie exclaimed, with fear in her voice.

"Don't worry, Rosie," comforted Petra. "It won't be like the first night we spent here on the island, this time we will be cosy in our amazing bedroom."

"Yes, of course," came the reply. "I think it was the lightning lighting up those bones and the rats. It was the rats that frightened me most."

"You are right, Rosie, I had forgotten the rats, but we haven't seen any since, have we?"

"No," agreed Rosie, with an unsure voice.

"And you won't see them again! Not while I am on this island," stated Brown Bear with authority.

"We are pleased about that, BB," said Rosie. "But what about the terrible roaring noise? And the ghost?"

"And the mysterious second castle?" Petra added, raising her eyebrows.

"Yes! And who is Emily Jane?" said Rosie. "We have so many mysteries to solve."

"Well, I suggest we have an early night," Brown Bear was in charge again.

"Oh! I forgot to tell you both something very important," remembered Petra.

"About what?" Brown Bear and Rosie asked together.

"We have a meeting on the beach early tomorrow morning,"

"Who with?"

Petra took in a deep breath of the salty evening air. "With the girl of course!"

It was mid-August, and it was starting to get dark earlier than usual. The sun had set, and all was quiet over the island, there were a few last shrieks of seagulls, who had spent half the afternoon hovering over an inshore trawler which was now returning to the mainland to land its catch.

Back in the cottage, Brown Bear told the girls he needed to examine the larger bones that were scattered about in the downstairs room.

"Those bones puzzle me," he told the girls. "I won't be long. You two make yourselves comfortable upstairs."

"Do you really think there will be a storm tonight, BB?" Rosie asked their friend, before he got too engrossed with his examination of the skeletons.

"I do, young Rosie!" he said. "I will just step out onto the rocks to see what the tide is doing."

Brown Bear stepped out of the cottage door and gazed up at the sky. "There are storm clouds gathering but the tide is going out. Rosie, don't worry it won't be anything like the storm the other night!"

"OK, BB," the little girl looked relieved, as Brown Bear re-entered the cosy dwelling.

"I have left you some supper in the kitchen and I am taking mine and Petra's supper up to the wonderful room upstairs."

"Thank you, Rosie, I'll enjoy it when I have examined these bones more closely." Brown Bear closed the cottage door as best he could with the piece of driftwood he had found. "You girls take the oil lamp and I will use my torch. It isn't really that dark yet."

"See you later," called Rosie, as she carried a tray of supper, up the stairs for her and her sister to eat later.

"Hey! Rosie, come and look at all this." Petra's voice was urgent.

"Whatever is the matter?" Rosie placed her tray on the bedside table.

"You or BB, haven't been back up here, sometime today, have

you?"

"No, of course not!" Rosie assured her sister. "Why?"

Petra beckoned her sister to join her at the dressing table, set in the window recess. She had opened the top drawer and pointed inside. "Look, all the stationary is missing!"

"No! It can't be," Rosie examined the open drawer. "Perhaps it is in the lower drawer, or in the two side drawers?" Rosie was perturbed, as she searched all the dressing table drawers to no avail.

"No there is nothing there, I have already thought of that," replied Petra. "I've looked everywhere, even in the wardrobe."

"Maybe BB has been studying them," said Rosie. "He's downstairs studying those bones, shall I go and ask him?"

"No, he wouldn't be interested in note paper, he's just fascinated with old fossils, and bones, and historical things, not a female's writing materials."

"Why do you think they belonged to a female?" asked Rosie, looking behind the large piece of ornate furniture. "Just a thought," she saw her sister's frustrated look.

"Only that the crockery and stationery are so exquisite, umm, I suppose I mean girly," said Petra, wistfully. "Let's eat our supper now. I'm hungry. What delight have you made tonight?"

"Not very much, we are running out of supplies."

"But Rosie! Mum packed loads of food!"

"Yes, she did, but we three have really big appetites," Rosie's voice was half full of apologies. "I was thinking of asking BB to go fishing for us."

"What a brilliant idea! You are so clever Rosie, to think of it!"

"Well, it wasn't hard to think of, as we are surrounded by the sea."

Petra became very enthusiastic, "Hey, we could scout the rock pools for shrimps and crabs. I think BB might enjoy that."

"Good idea, now do you want any super, Petra?"

"I do but I also want to know where all the stationery has

gone?"

"Let's ask BB, he just might know what's happened?"

The girls were about to call Brown Bear upstairs, when he suddenly appeared at the bedroom door.

"Hey girls, I have brought my supper with me, so we can all eat together."

"Yes, that will be nice," said Rosie. "Sorry it's not much tonight, but I am having to eek out our supplies."

"Oh! don't you worry Rosie, it looks a fine meal to me!" remarked Brown Bear. "Cheese, crackers, grapes and an apple each. It is quite enough. Oh! You both look sad whatever is the matter?"

Petra volunteered first. "It is a bit worrying BB, but all the stationery from this drawer is missing."

"Missing!" Brown Bear exclaimed. "Have you searched for it?"

"Yes, of course! everywhere in this room, it was so beautiful with initials on every piece." Rosie looked extremely worried. "You remember E.J.M?"

"Indeed!" boomed Brown Bear's deep voice, filling the room. "E.J.M. is on all that exquisite tea service downstairs in the kitchen cupboard. So, everything beautiful in this cottage belongs to Emily Jane."

Rosie started to nibble at her cheese. "Are we all in agreement that we think the professor brought all these luxury goods here to the island to please his wife?"

"He must have," added Petra. "And that theory solves the mystery of who the girl was talking about when she asked me if I was looking for Emily Jane?"

"That's it!" Brown Bear was assertive. "Yes! I am sure the initials belong to the professor's wife, Emily Jane Mortimer! What do you girls think?"

"Of course! Why didn't I think of that?" Petra tossed her long fair hair away from her face. "You know so much is happening here. But I don't know if I told you, BB?"

"Told me what?" Brown Bear took his tray over to his bed on the beautiful sofa on the far side of the room.

"That the girl wants to meet you and Rosie on the beach early in the morning. I will introduce you both!" Petra gave them a lovely warm smile.

"Depends on whether ghosts keep appointments," giggled Rosie.

"So, first thing in the morning we are meeting the girl," confirmed Brown Bear. "We must find out what she knows about the Professor's missing wife."

Rosie replied sleepily, "Yes, and she might know all the other secrets of the island too."

18
ROCK POOLS

Brown Bear had woken the girls at 6.30 this morning. Usually, they would moan and protest but not today. Petra and Rosie were elated at the prospect of this important meeting with the girl. Rosie was excited at the thought of meeting a real ghost, but Petra was filled with a certain amount of doubt, as the stranger had disappointed her by suddenly vanishing into thin air.

"Come on, girls" called Brown Bear. "The tide is going out and the rock pools are uncovered, a good time to go fishing."

"OK! We are coming," Rosie appeared on the rocks outside the cottage with a large kitchen sieve and a bucket.

"Wow! Rosie, you mean business," said Petra, stifling a yawn.

'Yes, I do!" replied Rosie.

"That's the spirit!" Brown Bear sounded very jovial this morning. "It is going to be a hot day. Did either of you girls hear the thunder in the night?"

"No!" replied the girls in unison.

"I told you it wouldn't be much of a storm," said Brown Bear. "I heard a few rumbles of thunder in the early hours but no lightning."

They arrived at the rockpools at the foot of the cliffs. Rosie put the bucket down with a thump and immediately took off her flip-flops and laid them on a dry rock beside a picnic basket she had prepared earlier.

"Shall we eat first?" asked Petra.

"No!" boomed Brown Bear, with a positive response. "We must

see what fish we can find. Then if we are successful, we can enjoy our breakfast later."

With that remark both girls walked over to the nearest pool, they had to clamber carefully over the rocks that were still slippery with algae. The tide hadn't gone out very far and dark green squishy seaweed remained washed up on the sand, still wet and glistening in the morning sunshine.

"There seems to be a massive amount of seaweed washed up on the shore today," announced Rosie. "Why is there so much, BB?"

"Well!" Brown Bear stood deep in thought. "I can only imagine that the storm the other night has caused it."

"But how?" Rosie looked up at her friend. She knew Brown Bear would have a plausible explanation.

"Many varieties of seaweed grow deep under the oceans and storms sometimes are so strong with the way they toss the waves about on the surface, and all that movement uproots the vegetation growing on the seabed," said Brown Bear stopping to catch his breath. "Girls, can you remember the journey we endured getting here to this island last time?"

"Yes, of course," said Petra. "I remember rowing our boat in and out of the rocks. That was a ferocious storm we had to overcome that night!"

"Indeed, it was! Well, plants growing on the seabed are ripped up and eventually float to the surface and in due course are tossed onto the nearest beach and lay strewn on the sand." Brown Bear stopped for breath.

Rosie had tired of the geography lesson and wandered off to see what was in the nearest rock pool. "Look, BB, come and see what's in here," yelled Rosie. "Lots of shrimps swimming around. We can fry them for our lunch with some potato chips."

"That's good, carry on, my dear!" Brown Bear had decided on a pool further along the beach. He stooped over it and seemed very pleased with what he had found.

"Hey! Girls, bring that sieve over here, there are some small fish trapped in this pool. This is good news, as we won't go hungry. Best thing for our health is to eat fresh fish."

"I know!" responded Rosie. "One of our teachers told us, first class protein."

"Quite right!" Brown Bear was about to give a lecture on the benefits of fish, when a flock of terns squawked overhead with their 'chit chur tut rrrr chip' chirping and drowned out his words.

"Seeing as there is an abundance of fish, can we eat our breakfast now and collect some fish later?" asked Petra.

"Yes! Why not?" replied Brown Bear "While it is cool because later it will be so hot that we'll need to take cover indoors and study the professor's work and plan for our journey tomorrow."

"What journey?" Rosie looked a bit puzzled.

"To search for the other castle, of course!" Brown Bear exclaimed.

"But we don't know where to start looking, do we?" said Petra.

'I have an idea," Brown Bear assured the girls, as he moved to another pool.

"Don't forget, Petra, we are supposed to be meeting the girl. I mean the ghost," said Rosie.

"I know," replied Petra. "I have been looking out for her."

"Hey, girls!" Brown Bear sounded very excited. "Come over here and see what I have just found."

Brown Bear had wandered off to a pool of his own. Within seconds the girls were by his side, staring into a lovely deep reservoir of emerald green water. They forgot about breakfast and wondered what he had found.

"What is it, BB?" Rosie inquired looking into the water.

"What a lovely pool!" exclaimed Petra, bending down to study it closer. She noticed the rocks were a dark bluish grey and the water looked quite deep.

"Bring your bucket over here please, Rosie." Brown Bear

couldn't hide his excitement.

"What is it, BB?" Rosie handed him the bucket. He took it from the little girl with one paw and he plunged his other furry arm into the pool. And out of the water he produced the largest crab the girls had even seen.

"There you are, girls!" He exclaimed. "Tonight's dinner!"

"I've never seen a crab before," said Rosie.

"Of course you have," said Petra. "We always used to go 'crabbing' with Dad and Mali when we were on holiday in North Wales."

"But they were tiny! Not big enough to eat," answered Rosie.

"Uummm, it is a good big one. There is plenty of tasty meat on this fine specimen," Brown Bear was very pleased with his catch. "Let's see if we can see another one?"

By now the sun was shining down brightly on the pool of green sea water and its surface was being teased by a gentle morning breeze. All three gazed closer into its depth, looking for another prize. They realised the colour of the pool was determined by swaying fronds of sea grass and long sword like spears of seaweed closeted together.

Suddenly, the seagulls and the terns were silent, not a squawk nor a shriek. All that could be heard was the dull slosh, slosh of the receding tide. And then a dark grey cloud blotted out the sun and a sudden gust of an icy cold breeze engulfed them all.

Then Rosie screamed!

"Oh, look!" Petra gasped in horror. "Can you see what I can see?"

"Indeed, I can!" Brown Bear was disbelieving, but because the girls were aware of what was in the pool, he felt in that strange moment, he needed to look closer at what had disturbed the girls.

Then a weird silence and an icy cloak of dark mist was blotting out the warm morning sunshine and all three of our protagonists were slowly coming to terms with what the rock pool had revealed.

Petra spoke first. "Did you both see her?"

"Yes, I did!" exclaimed Rosie. "But I don't understand. Is that the girl you have been meeting, Petra? The ghost?"

"No, it isn't, but tell me what you can see." Petra urged her sister to reveal what she could see in the greenish waters of the rock pool.

"A face in the water!" gasped Rosie. "I can see a woman's face, just below the surface."

"Yes!" Petra agreed. "It is just as if someone is here on the beach looking over our shoulders, and her reflection is captured in the pool."

Rosie shivered and looked behind her but there was no one there.

At that moment the ripples increased and the dark mist disappeared, evaporating into the morning air. The sun once again shone on the green water of the pool, and all was as it had been before. The face had gone.

"That was so weird!" Petra looked all around, but there was no one there at all. "BB, tell me exactly what you saw."

"Umm, very interesting," said Brown Bear, who was as calm as he always was in challenging moments. "As I gazed into the waters, all went very quiet and a gentle breeze moved the surface of the pool and I saw the face of a woman, not a young girl but a woman."

"Yes!" Petra replied. "It wasn't the girl! The girl has long black hair and this woman had long dark hair too. although she did look similar. But you are right, BB, this woman looked in her late thirties, and although the girl isn't as young as I first thought she was, I don't think she can be much older than her late teens." Petra sighed.

"Perhaps we all imagined her," said Rosie, looking hopeful.

"No, we certainly did not imagine what we have just seen,"

Brown Bear was sounding positive. "Who do you think we saw in that pool, Petra?"

"I don't know," she replied.

"Hey! Come on then, girls, a few more shrimps, and we had better carry our catch back to the cottage, out of the sun."

"Yes, you are right, BB," agreed Petra. "It is getting really hot. Is there time for a quick swim?"

"Alright then," replied Brown Bear. "I will just sit here a while and you two catch the tide."

"Oh! Yippee!" cried Rosie ecstatically and tore off her shorts and T-shirt revealing her new swimsuit.

"I think I will just paddle," said Petra, beginning to walk in the water. "You will have to hurry Rosie, the tide is going out quite fast now."

Rosie wasn't listening because she had thrown herself into the cool water and was having fun splashing about in the shallows. After a while she looked to the shore to catch Petra's eye, but her sister wasn't looking her way at all.

Then Petra saw the girl, and the girl wasn't alone. Albeit she was some distance away but sure enough it definitely was the girl. Petra saw her companion and realised she was a woman, a tall slender figure that moved gracefully along besides the girl.

"Hey! Wait! I want to talk to you," Petra yelled at the top of her voice.

But the girl hadn't heard her cries and appeared to be oblivious to Petra. The girl just carried on walking with her companion alongside the edge of the sea going further and further away.

"What is the matter, Petra dear? Why are you yelling into the air?" Brown Bear, who had been snoozing, was suddenly aroused by all the noise. "Whatever is the matter?"

"Look along the shoreline, BB. Can you see those two people walking in the wet sand?"

"No! I'm sorry I cannot see anyone!" Brown Bear exclaimed.

"Are you feeling alright, Petra? The sun is getting far too hot for us to be outside!"

"I'm fine, I thought I saw the girl I was telling you about. I saw her with a companion walking at the water's edge. Petra held her hands up to her eyes, using them as a sunshade to scour the now deserted beach. "I'm sorry I must have been mistaken, as there is nobody there now?" Petra had lost sight of the two figures.

She was about to run along the sand to try and catch up with the two strangers, but the noonday sun was now beating down from the clear blue sky with a ferocious power. She stopped suddenly quite out of breath. She quickly thought of her sister. Where was Rosie?

"Hey Rosie, where are you?" Petra was struck with fear as she couldn't see Rosie anywhere.

She looked back at the sea where she had last seen her sister frolicking in the shallows, of the outgoing tide. Fear gripped her heart in long tenuous chains pulling tight and taking her breath away.

"What have I done?" she tortured herself with all kinds of dreaded thoughts. Petra looked all along the shallow waters of the ebbing tide. There was no sign of Rosie.

Petra was really worried now she looked all the way along the edge of the sea with its annoying sloshing sound, but there was no sign of her sister. She looked in the opposite direction hoping to see the girl and her companion still walking together along the wet seaweed strewn sand, but they had gone.

The beach was deserted.

Petra started to yell at the top of her voice, "Rosie! Rosie! Where are you?"

Brown Bear was most concerned, "I was watching you both and I nodded off and I shouldn't have done, Oh Petra, I am so sorry."

"It's not your fault, it is mine. I am obsessed with the girl. I was watching her when I should have been watching Rosie."

"The girl you keep seeing?" Brown Bear asked, with real concern in his voice.

"Yes! It was, but there was someone else walking alongside her at the water's edge," Petra was glancing up and down the beach. But there was no one to be seen, now

"Do you think it might have been Rosie with the girl?" Brown Bear looked towards the sea. "I think we should follow the footprints. The indentations should still be there, as the tide is going further out by the minute."

"Good idea, BB!"

The midday sun was searing down on them as they followed the ebbing tide line.

"Look, BB!" cried Petra. "There are footprints here! Can you see the prints in the wet sand?"

"Yes, I can!" exclaimed Brown Bear. "But I can only see one set of prints and they are far bigger than Rosie's dainty little feet."

"Yes, you are right! But I saw two people walking together and I am positive Rosie was not one of them," said Petra. "We must go back to the rocks where we left our bucket of fish. With this heat I'm sure they will all be cooked by now."

Soon they were back at the rock pool where they had witnessed a woman's reflection in the water. There was no reflection now and there was no sign of the bucket or sieve. Petra looked all around for Rosie's flip-flops, but there was no sign of them either.

"She must be back at the cottage. Quick, we must find her." Brown Bear sounded really worried now.

The door to the cottage was wide open and the bucket of fish had been placed just inside the door in the cool stone room. Petra rushed in and shouted at the top of her voice for her sister. She ran upstairs and searched the bedroom, with the exquisite array of furniture but there was no sign of her sister.

"Where can she be?" Petra gave an enormous, exasperated

sigh.

"I have no idea!" Brown Bear replied. "We will have to search the rocks and the cove. It is not like Rosie to go off on her own, is it?"

"No, it isn't! We will go back to where she was splashing about in the sea. Maybe she brought the bucket back to the cottage to keep the fish cool. And then went back to the sea." Petra was already running back to where she had last seen Rosie. Still blaming herself for thinking about the strange girl, rather than her own precious sister.

"Rosie, Rosie, where are you?"

19
WHO ELSE IS ON THE ISLAND?

Petra and Brown Bear had searched frantically for Rosie. The heat from the sun was now unbearable. So they found shade on the shale beach under the cliff.

And then it happened.

"Whatever is making that noise?" Petra jumped to her feet. "BB, it is so loud! Can you make out where it is coming from?"

"I think it is coming from under these cliffs but it's not a steady sound, it's moving."

"Where is Rosie?" Petra was in despair; she had never been separated from her twin sister for very long.

"We'll find her!" Brown Bear was very reassuring. "Listen. The sound is now moving away from us."

"What can it be?" Petra wiped a tear from her eye. "We have only been on the island a couple of days, and we have heard that roaring noise every day. BB, I am so worried about Rosie!"

Petra was far more upset than she let on to Brown Bear. She couldn't remember a day when Rosie hadn't been in her life. She was about to walk back to the sea when suddenly down the cliff path came her sister, running pell-mell towards her.

After a few moments Rosie threw herself at Brown Bear, who scooped the little girl up off the beach and into his strong, furry arms.

Rosie seemed very upset and confused and it was a while before she calmed down.

"I have seen something very strange; I was frightened!" Rosie exclaimed between sobs.

Brown Bear took charge of the situation, as was his custom.

"Right!" he said. "Come. Firstly, let's go back to the cottage and have some lunch. Would you like that, Rosie dear?"

"Yes, I would," she gave one big sob and rubbed her eyes.

Petra reached up and gave her sister a tissue. "We have been so worried about you, and we heard that noise again."

"I heard it too and it seemed very near when I was underground," Rosie wiped her eyes.

"What do you mean, Rosie? Underground?" Petra exclaimed in horror. "Why did you go off without us?"

Brown Bear stepped in, "Petra, dear! Not now! Let us have lunch first then, Rosie can tell us all about it later," he put his charge down on the sand. "Phew! You are getting to be a heavy young lady!"

"I don't know why you two are making such a fuss," volunteered Rosie. "I was enjoying being in the water and I saw Petra rush off along the shore, and BB, you looked as if you were dozing in the sunshine, and a girl approached me, and she told me she would show me the secrets of the island."

"And did you believe her?" Petra was so glad to have her sister back with her.

"And who is this girl?" questioned Brown Bear.

"Ursula!" exclaimed Rosie, enjoying the attention.

"Ursula? Ursula who?" expressed Petra in astonishment.

"Very interesting!" said Brown Bear, deep in thought. "I have heard that name before, but I cannot remember where I heard it."

"I asked her what her name was," said Rosie with a sigh. "And she said her name was Ursula! Oh! Do you think she is the same girl, Petra, the one you have been seeing, the ghost?"

"Could be. Well! Yes, she probably is the same girl, but I have never asked her name."

"OK girls! Now I will make lunch, so you two can go clean up."

Brown Bear was out of his depth now with so many girls on this island. "I'll cook the fish!"

It was about one o'clock when they had finished their meal of fried shrimps. Brown Bear had said he had prepared the crabmeat ready for their dinner that evening.

"We could survive here for ages," said Rosie. "We could live on seafood and berries."

"We could!" announced Petra. "But we don't have to, as the school term starts in September."

"Oh! No," cried Rosie in despair. "September always comes round too quickly. We haven't found the secret of the island yet."

"Now! Rosie, please tell us all about what happened when you went underground with Ursula?" Brown Bear sat on the rocks outside the cottage. "I had planned to search for the other castle today, but we were distracted by the fishing and you went missing."

"Yes! I must tell you two everything I found out. Remember I was splashing about in the sea. Well, that was when I first saw the girl, she was on the cliff path beckoning me to go to her," Rosie stopped for breath.

"But you couldn't have seen her at that precise moment in time because I saw her, walking along the beach with a stranger," said Petra, puzzled.

"No! Petra you couldn't have seen her. I'm telling the truth, I saw her, and I went to meet her. I carried the bucket of fish back to the cottage and she met me outside."

"Something really strange is happening here." Petra replied. "I know what I saw!"

"And I know what happened," replied an indignant Rosie. "Ursula took me up the cliff path and showed me an entrance into another world."

"Whatever do you mean, Rosie? Another world? Young Rosie, you are not making any sense," Brown Bear adopted an avuncular stance and looked at his charge more closely. Usually, Brown Bear was phlegmatic but today he was far from his usual calm self.

"I will show you! Petra, BB, please, will you just come and follow me?" Rosie took them outside and took the lead to take her two companions up the steep, cliff path. The afternoon sun shone less brightly, as a hazy mist rolled in from the now distant sea.

Soon they all reached the cleft in the rocks where Petra had witnessed the sudden spurt of water, the geyser that soared up many feet into the air.

"Oh look! There it blows again!" exclaimed Petra. "Why is there water under the cliffs, BB?"

"I really don't know." Brown Bear was deep in thought.

Suddenly a gust of wind caught the fountain, and the spray was driven in a shower towards them all.

"That was unexpected," squealed Rosie. "But look who is here." The little girl ran about two metres higher up the path to welcome her new friend.

"This is Ursula." Rosie introduced the girl to Brown Bear.

"I am pleased to meet you, young lady," he gave a courteous nod to the girl.

"We've met!" said Petra curtly.

"Yes, we have," replied the girl. "I have a lot to show you. Will you all come with me?"

No one spoke. The girl's request seemed like an order, so everyone formed a line on the narrow path and followed the girl.

"Where are you taking us, Ursula?" Petra was puzzled.

"She's taking us to the underground caves!" exclaimed Rosie, in a very positive voice. "It is where she took me earlier."

"Yes," said Ursula, taking hold of Rosie's hand. Then she faced Petra. "When I first approached you Petra, I really thought you had come to the island in search of Emily Jane, but now I realise you are just here on holiday." The girl smiled at the others.

"No! It isn't a holiday," Rosie blurted out, and received a

disapproving look from Brown Bear.

"Oh! I don't understand," said Ursula. "What other reason could bring you here?"

At this point Brown Bear realised he needed to take charge of the situation. He turned towards the girl and looked her straight in her eyes.

"Your name means Little She Bear in Latin."

"I know that!" stated Ursula.

"BB! How do you know that?" exclaimed Petra.

"I picked up a lot from my old Gran, back in the forest," said Brown Bear. "Now young lady, where are you taking us?"

"This way," Ursula led the way past the borehole that was now dormant once again.

When they reached the highest point on the cliff top Ursula stopped and turned to the little party of followers, she pointed to a hole in the ground almost hidden amongst the rocks

"This is the way to find the secrets of this island. I was born on this island, and I have grown up here. It has been lonely, but you seem to have come with a mission, and I know I can help you all with that." The girl stepped aside.

A cool wind blew across the cliff top as Brown Bear took the initiative to be the first to venture into the gaping hole. He disappeared inside and Petra and Rosie held their breath. Rosie held out her hand to the girl and she returned the gesture. Petra was about to follow Brown Bear when suddenly he returned a bit dishevelled.

"Girls, we can't go down there without some equipment. I insist! I can see danger, we must regroup in the morning, when we have tools and provisions for a long journey."

"OK then!" exclaimed Petra. "But can Ursula stay with us in the cottage tonight?"

"By all means," replied Brown Bear. "That is if she wants to?"

"Yes! I would like that," said Ursula, with a smile on her face.

"You know you are very pretty when you smile," Petra smiled back to the girl's delight.

It was a happy scene in the cottage that evening. The girls had taken Ursula upstairs to the big ornate bedroom to show her some of their clothes she might like to wear, the following day.

"I only have this one dress," said Ursula, quite mesmerised by the array of shorts, jeans, and tops Petra had laid out on the bed.

"Oh!" exclaimed Rosie. "How do you keep warm in the winter?"

"I rarely come outside if it is wintertime. It is so cold on these cliffs," said the girl. "It is warm where I live. I have everything I need down below! I will show you everything tomorrow."

At that moment Brown Bear called the girls down for supper. I have made a soup out of all the fish we caught this morning and flavoured it with herbs that grow near here.

"It smells very nice," said Ursula, as Brown Bear politely held out one of the kitchen chairs for their guest to sit on.

"Welcome to the cottage," said Petra. "It is so nice to have a friend on the island."

"I am glad to be here in your company," she smiled at them all. "I have been here many times. I used to examine all those bones and fossils. Some of the bigger ones are from foxes and wild pigs but the large ones, well, I am hoping Mr Bear, that you can tell me."

"I have examined some, but I need to be sure before I divulge my findings," exclaimed Brown Bear. "By the way, you can call me BB, like Petra and Rosie do."

"Thank you, BB," she said softly, as she took a piece of bread from the plate Rosie was offering her.

"I knew I had seen bones like the ones collected here, but I couldn't quite remember where," Brown Bear remarked. "I have vague memories of my young days in the forest caves of Northern

Europe."

"What plans have you made for our journey tomorrow, BB?" Rosie asked excitedly.

"I am hoping Ursula will take us underground," replied Brown Bear. "And show us where she lives, maybe we may even find the second castle."

"I'll show you the castle," replied Ursula. "You may be disappointed," said Ursula, casting her eyes downward.

"That may be true! But now I think we need an early night, so we can be up very early in the morning." Brown Bear went off to the room upstairs where all their equipment was stored.

"Right!" Petra exclaimed. "Rosie, can you find us some food to take with us tomorrow?"

"Okey Dokey!" Rosie sounded very cheerful. "Petra, can you show Ursula the big sofa in our bedroom. I'm sure she will be comfortable there tonight."

"Will do! Come on, Ursula. It is a very beautiful room, not like the rest of the cottage."

"I know," Ursula replied. "I find that fact strange."

As they made their way up the stairs Petra realised that the girl must have been in and out of this cottage many times over the years, while she had been alone on the island. She was about to say something when Brown Bear knocked on their bedroom door.

"I have set up a camp bed out here in this room for me to sleep on tonight," he informed the girls. "I have decided to give you all a chance to chat about girly things. I won't be far away,"

"BB!" said a delighted Petra. "That is very kind of you."

It wasn't long before Rosie came up the stairs to join the girls. It had suddenly become dark outside, and Petra lit the oil lamp. The room became a hub of activity, as Petra and Ursula were deciding what to wear for the journey the next day.

"What is it like underground, Ursula?" asked Petra. "It must be very warm, as you only wear a flimsy dress."

"Yes, it is sometimes, I think you will like where I live." The girl seemed quite at ease with her new companions.

"Right now, girls! Time to sleep, I am getting you up at sunrise," Brown Bear called from the outer room. "Rosie, I hope you have managed to find enough food for us to take on our expedition."

"We are completely out of bread and milk!" uttered a very sleepy little girl.

"Don't worry," said Ursula. "You won't go hungry. I have a larder full of supplies," She climbed up onto the turquoise blue sofa. "Good night, Petra and Rosie, I am very comfortable here."

There was no reply, as Petra and Rosie were so tired after their extraordinary day, they had fallen asleep as soon as their sleepy heads touched the silky softness of their pillows.

It was after midnight when something disturbed Brown Bear. He woke up wondering where he was. But then he realised he was on a camp bed in the spare room. He sat up listening intently to a low droning sound far out in the bay. He decided to go out onto the rocks to see if he could see a vessel on the water. He felt instinctively that it was a boat of some kind.

The evening air was still, and the incoming tide was in no hurry to wash upon the sand that night. He could still hear the noise of an engine coming from the sea, far out beyond the cove. It was a humming sound and was coming nearer.

Brown Bear made his way to the low headland to the right of the beach. Once there, he could see the shadowy shape of the jetty against the backdrop of the ocean. Gentle waves were washing around the iron posts that had once been cemented in the rocks, to form a small but convenient, landing stage. A gentle breeze was scurrying light fluffy clouds along in the midnight-blue expanse of sky. And then the moon came out from behind the clouds giving enough light for Brown Bear to capture the scene. He took a step nearer and stood on the planking of the old jetty, making it creak with his weight.

"Very convenient of you 'Old Moon' my friend, to come out just then. Now I can see exactly what is going on," said Brown Bear out loud.

There out in the bay he could see a fishing vessel. There was only one white light to be seen on board. He believed the boat should have sidelights, a red light to indicate its port side and a green light on the starboard side. So, at that moment he knew the trawler wasn't active in the process of fishing offshore. Brown Bear let his thoughts drift off into his past.

Sometimes a white and a green light would appear on the stern of some vessels, as green light was sometimes used to attract the fish at night. Brown Bear knew a lot of interesting facts and fishing interested him as his old friend Lucas was a fisherman.

After a few moments of gazing out across the water, Brown Bear could see a lot of activity on board the vessel. A rowing boat was being lowered down on ropes into the relatively calm waters of the bay.

'My eyesight isn't what it was, but I am sure I can see two people rowing to shore,' he thought. 'That's a risky business with those sharp rocks around the island. Lucky for them it is a very high tide tonight or they might end up as mincemeat.'

As he watched the small boat, he noted that it was not travelling towards him but appeared to veer away from the direction of the jetty and seemed to head towards the northern shore of the island.

He watched for a while longer and then he heard the trawler restart its engine and head off towards the mainland. He was certain the rowing boat had not returned to the trawler.

At that moment Brown Bear was worried. He felt certain that the small boat was going to land on the island. He glanced back towards the cottage but there was no light on there. Thankfully the girls were all fast asleep, unaware of what he had just witnessed.

Slowly he walked back along the sand, and then he smelt smoke from a newly lit fire. He stopped in his tracks but then decided to make his way back to the shoreline, and sure enough he saw a tall spire of smoke, billowing up from the cove that lay around the headland, on the left side of their cove. He gave a huge sigh of relief as he felt assured that their abode on the eastern shore would go on undetected.

In that moment he was pleased to know that the professor's beach cottage was secluded amongst the rocks under the cliff. Nevertheless, he was extremely worried for the girl's safety if some strangers were landing on the island under the cover of night.

'We certainly don't want trippers on this island, especially not now. We are all here on an important mission at Professor Mortimer's request, and we don't want anyone coming here to find the secrets of the island before we do.'

The tide was coming in fast now and he had to race the inky waves up the beach. He satisfied himself that the cottage was well hidden, even from the sea.

'We must all be careful and make sure the intruders don't find us!' he thought, as he made his way up the beach. The moon had disappeared behind some clouds now, and darkness had suddenly descended all around him. Brown Bear could hear the roar of the incoming tide behind him. It sounded like a warning, and he felt the presence of danger, on that late summer's night.

He decided to tell the girls about the trippers in the morning. But then without any warning the roaring noise they had all heard before came again even louder than the sea itself, encircling his whole presence. He turned back to the shore, and he heard a woman scream, a hysterical shriek captured on the night air.

'Ah! The intruders have heard the noise too. Well, let's hope they are gone by morning. Then just as he had smelt the newly lit fire, he now caught a whiff of extinguished flames being carried his way on the breeze.

'Obviously that noise has scared the trippers!' he thought. 'Be gone by morning,' Brown Bear hoped that would be so. With all his knowledge and a wily feeling within him, he knew that wasn't going to happen! The last thing they wanted right now was somebody else on the island.

20
INTRUDERS

Brown Bear woke early the next morning just as the rising sun cast its misty beams directly into the cottage. He had decided not to worry the girls with his findings of the night before. He felt he had to be sure someone else was on the island before he mentioned it to them. He was certain the discovery of intruders would upset Rosie and make Petra angry. He wasn't at all sure how Ursula would react to anything.

'That girl is a real mystery,' he thought as he made his way to the kitchen to see if Rosie had prepared a rucksack full of food for their day underground.

Rosie was up and dressed and was stuffing as much food as she could into the very large picnic basket she had found on a high shelf in the kitchen.

"Good morning, Rosie! Have we enough food for our journey?" Brown Bear asked her with a rather worried look on his face.

"Yes, I think so. Mum packed loads of snacks for us and Ursula told me when we reach the place where she lives underground, we won't go hungry."

"Well!" Brown Bear replied. "I hope she is right because we all have enormous appetites."

Very soon Petra and Ursula appeared in the kitchen dressed and ready to go.

"Good morning girls," said Brown Bear. "Oh! Ursula, you do look different."

"I know!" she replied. "I love these clothes that Petra has given me. They feel so comfortable. I am so grateful to meet you all and be friends and anyway my old dress almost disintegrated as I took it off last night."

"Did you really only have that one dress?" asked Rosie, quite curious.

"Yes! I found it in the wardrobe in the bedroom upstairs some years ago now," replied Ursula.

"What did you wear before?" asked Petra. 'Could it have been one of Emily Jane's dresses, left in the ornate room before she had mysteriously disappeared?' she thought to herself.

"I don't remember," the young girl sighed.

"Well, never mind," said Brown Bear. "We must get on. Now please lead the way to your abode, Ursula."

By the time everyone had sorted out what they wanted to take with him or her, it was almost seven o'clock. The dawn sky was not promising a particularly pleasant day.

The early morning's golden light was now streaked with ominous long black clouds, stretching out in elongated ribbons, vying with the soft yellow haze of dawn. A penetrating early autumn mist was wetting the cliff path beneath their feet making the climb more arduous than usual.

"Careful Rosie, the ground is very slippery this morning," remarked Brown Bear.

"I know," said Rosie. "I am being careful, BB!"

In a while they reached the highest point on the cliffs where they towered above the cottage nestling on the rocks far below. The three girls waited for Brown Bear to catch up.

"Can you all see those heavy grey clouds coming in from the west?" he puffed a little, catching his breath after the climb. "They mean torrential rain for later!"

"Good thing we are going underground," stated Rosie, struggling with her basket. "It is quite scary down there, you know. That noise we have been hearing is much louder and it echoes around caves and…" Rosie's voice trailed off as Petra's phone rang to say she had received a text message.

"It's from Mum," Petra looked at her screen. "It's not good news, I'll read it to you." Rosie, Brown Bear and Ursula all got closer, as Petra took in a deep breath and began to convey her mother's urgent message.

> Hi, I hope all is well, but I must tell you that there has been a burglary at Old Mill Cottage. Cleaning lady reported it to the police. I've contacted Professor Mortimer and he can return home in two weeks' time if he is well enough. The good news is that his ankle is mending well. Someone broke in through a kitchen window the night before last. The study at the cottage had been ransacked and forensic officers were called in today to dust every room for fingerprints. According to Mrs Evans from the village, who the professor has recently employed temporarily to look after his property, she told the police that something must have been stolen. Something valuable and personal to him must have been hidden under the floorboards. It must have been very important because the burglars ripped half of the boards up in the study to find it. Apparently the police have two suspects - a man and a woman. But they can't arrest either of them because they have disappeared.
> Come home Petra. I do not want you or Rosie in danger. I'll send Lucas to bring you back at high tide this evening. Let me know you are all ok. Love Mum.

"That's the longest text message I've ever read." Petra was trying to catch her breath. "Whatever do we do now, BB?"

Rosie was dismayed, "Oh, we can't go home yet!" she exclaimed.

"We must find the secrets of this island."

"Shall I talk to your Mum?" Brown Bear was looking worried.

"No, definitely not BB!" Petra was worried too. "Mum only indulges us when we tell her things you say, she doesn't really believe you can talk."

"Of course, she does," cried Rosie with indignation. "When I told her how intelligent BB is and how he looks after us, Mum said, "I'll humour you this time."

"There you are, Rosie! See she doesn't really believe us," remarked Petra. "Don't you remember when Mum was collecting recycling stuff for the tip? And she left a box in the hall for Dad to take to the skip, and unbeknown to him our darling BB was in it. It was Mum who put him there, remember Rosie?"

"Oh! I had forgotten that!" Rosie looked very downcast at that moment.

"Well! I haven't forgotten that morning!" exclaimed Brown Bear. "I was about to be thrown in a skip with a load of rubbish, when your dad rescued me and sat me in his van. Phew! That was a near thing!"

"Oh, yes," sighed Rosie. "And we were so pleased to see you safe and sound, BB! Mali had driven us to town to rescue you!"

"That must have been an awful experience for you all. You never mentioned you have a brother. How wonderful! I would have liked a brother," joined in Ursula.

"Now listen, Petra," said Brown Bear. "Text your Mum and tell her we are all fine, and we will come home in a few days." He decided that was the best thing to do under these circumstances.

"Good idea!" agreed Petra. "I'll text her now."

It wasn't too long before their mother replied by ringing Petra's phone.

"Hi Mum," said Petra, in her coolest voice. "No need to worry, we are all fine. Yes, I promise if we feel in any danger, I will ring you straight away. But Mum, Rosie and I are nearly sixteen, and we are very sensible. Yes! I will! Yes! I promise! Send our love to Dad and Mali. Bye Mum." Petra switched off her phone and put it in her short's pocket.

"So, what did she say?" begged Rosie.

"Well," said Petra. "After a few 'ifs and buts,' Mum agreed we can stay a few days longer."

"Great!" exclaimed Rosie in delight.

"That settles it!" Brown Bear said in an urgent voice. "We must get a move on and explore down this hole, and hope we find some secrets. But girls there is something very important I must tell you. First, we must walk a little way along the path here which will take us to the cliff top that overlooks a cove on the north shore."

"Whatever for, BB?" Rosie exclaimed.

"Come! You will soon see something worrying, but we must all be quiet and don't look over the edge until I tell you." Brown Bear kept his voice low.

The three girls followed quietly and in a few minutes were waiting in anticipation behind their big furry friend.

"What's down there?" Rosie asked, doing her best not to step nearer the edge, to see for herself what was on the beach below.

The early morning sky had been a warning of what the day had in store. It was overcast with dark grey clouds rolling in from the west, carried on a stiff sea breeze.

"Listen carefully, girls. I was waiting for the right moment to tell you. We are no longer alone on this island!"

"What do you mean, BB? Who else is here?" Petra stepped closer to the edge of the cliff.

"I am not sure. But now you can look over into the cove down there," Brown Bear took in a deep breath of relief, because he hadn't wanted to frighten the girls unnecessarily.

Petra was the first to respond. "I can see a boat pulled up high on the beach."

"Yes, I witnessed a boat being rowed ashore late last evening,"

Brown Bear began to relay the happenings of the night before.

"I was awoken by a noise, and it turned out to be the engine of a fishing vessel out in the bay. I watched as a small boat was let down on ropes into the water. Then I heard the trawler restart its engine and head back to the mainland. The rowing boat landed here on the island, and as you can see is still here."

"Oh! BB, that doesn't sound good." said Petra.

"Are we going down on the beach to see who it is?" Rosie pulled at BB's arm.

"Indeed, we are not!" exclaimed Brown Bear. "Whoever it is must not know we are on the island."

"Keep down everyone!" Petra ordered urgently. "I can see them!"

They all obeyed. Petra was now flat on her tummy on the wet grass, getting dangerously close to the edge. She could see a man and a woman leaving the beach to walk up a path on the far headland that led to the old castle, and immediately recognised the woman.

"I know who it is!"

"Who?" chorused the others.

"It is the couple we saw at the professor's cottage," stated Petra positively. "The woman we thought was a cleaner and the man who drove the black BMW."

"By Jove, I trust you to be right, my dear!" replied Brown Bear. "Now, why are they on the island?"

"Do you think they are the burglars Mum told us about in her text?" Rosie asked, as she too was on her tummy pushing towards the edge to get a better view.

"Yes, I do! And we know they made a mess of the professor's packing boxes in his study," said Brown Bear, giving a long sigh. "They must have found something that has led them here."

"Like the mahogany chest?" Petra exclaimed.

"No!" said Brown Bear, who was deep in thought wondering

what was the best thing to do next. "As I told you, I saw them coming here last night and when they first arrived, they lit a fire down there on the beach. I caught a whiff of smoke, but then that awful roaring noise sounded out from the bowels of the earth, and it scared them."

"How do you know that, BB?" asked Rosie, as she moved closer to her friend, she was feeling a little scared now.

"I know it because they immediately extinguished their fire, and as for them being scared, I have a very strong sense of perception."

"I do wonder what that roaring sound is? We have heard it every day since we arrived on this island!" said Rosie.

"I can help you with that!" Ursula volunteered, much to the surprise of the others.

"How?" Rosie looked puzzled.

There was no time to answer; the sound of shouting from the far side of the cove stole their attention. Heated voices rose up to invade the morning air. A soft persistence drizzle stung the girl's faces, as they strained their ears to hear the conversation coming from the beach below. The couple began to walk up the path towards the castle. A plan started to form in Petra's mind.

"When they have gone further up the path to the castle, I'm going to climb down!" exclaimed a very determined Petra.

She knew she had been a competent gymnast, best in her class a few years ago. 'Well, eight years ago,' she thought. 'But never mind, I'm still good.'

"Be careful, my dear," Brown Bear was a little concerned. "What will it achieve?"

"Look towards the old castle, I can see the intruders walking up the path. I'll be alright! I just want a nose round. They might have made camp in a cave. I won't be long. I just want to find a clue that will prove there is a link to the professor." Petra took a deep breath. "If I do find something with links to him, we will have proof that they are the burglars!"

"Alright! but we must start our journey now, Petra," Brown Bear took charge. "You can follow us later but be careful." Then he coaxed Rosie and Ursula to move towards the hole in the rock that would be the way to find the secrets.

"Oh! We can't go without Petra!" Rosie exclaimed, near to tears.

"Yes, you can, Rosie darling," Petra squeezes her sister's hand. "I just have an idea and I want to see if I am right."

"Come on, girls, let's get out of this rain," Brown Bear took charge. "Ursula, will you lead the way, please?"

Soon the cliff top was empty; Petra was on her way down to the beach and the others disappeared underground.

Large rain clouds had descended all over the island and the cool air brought goose bumps to Petra's bare arms, as she reached the slippery rocks of the cove on the north shore. Soon the young girl found a red rowing boat dragged high up on the shingle in a corner of the cove, but as she peered inside there was no sign of anything to reveal the identity of the intruders, who were now making their way to the ruined castle that stood high on the grassy hill.

'I haven't much time, so I'll just check the caves along this stretch of the coast. There must be quite a few,' Petra thought, as she made her search. Luckily the second cave she entered showed signs of occupancy.

Rolled up at the back of the cave high and dry, onto white silvery sand were two sleeping bags and a hamper full of food. And to her delight, there, spread open on a dry rocky shelf was a briefcase with the initials L. B. M. artistically worked into the soft brown leather. Inside it she found a letter addressed to Professor Lawrence B Mortimer, Old Mill Cottage, Mill Lane, Swallows Village.

"This is a real find!" she exclaimed out loud. And then she

thought about what they already knew from their visits to the professor's cottage. 'This proves we were right, to think that the woman we thought was the cleaning lady and the man who had driven the black BMW car were baddies, and up to no good!' Petra sighed. 'And especially after Mum texting us about the burglary at the professor's cottage.'

Petra went back to the cave entrance to check that the couple were still on the hill. The beach was empty, all was quiet, and Petra sighed with relief.

'I think this proves someone else wants to find the secrets of the island.'

21
CLOSE ENCOUNTER

Petra stood at the entrance to the cave. In front of her there was a very angry sea whipped up into grey walls of surging water with foam-capped waves. She could hear the roar of the incoming tide and the drizzle that had so cruelly stung her face earlier was now a sheet of persistent heavy rain. Her T-shirt and shorts were soaked through. Petra decided she would have one more look in the cave and then she must follow the others underground.

The cave was warm inside and she was reminded of their first adventure on the island when she and Rosie were only 10 years of age. What an adventure they had with BB on this island.

Petra began to search the open briefcase.

'These people are travelling light,' she thought. 'I must be careful to leave it exactly as I find it. I wonder what interest these two people have in the professor.' Her hand felt the smooth soft leather as she searched deeper inside and then the texture changed and she could feel stiff paper. She took a deep breath as she withdrew her find out into the musty atmosphere of the cave.

In her hand she held an envelope containing a letter written on exquisite note paper, it had already been opened. Petra immediately pulled out the folded notepaper and with it came a small piece of firm material. She looked at it closely but couldn't make out if it was a piece of parchment or an old fragment of linen, stiffened with the passing of time. She could see some faint markings on the remnant but in the limited light couldn't see what they were. Immediately she reached for her phone and took a photo of the letter. She noticed it was handwritten and was on the same kind of note paper with entwined initials as they had found in the ornate bedroom, back at the beach cottage.

She delved deeper into the briefcase. The remainder of the papers looked like bills and receipts. 'This must be one of the items stolen from the Old Mill Cottage. I feel sure this briefcase must have held important documents belonging to Professor Mortimer.'

'Wait until I tell the others what I have found,' she thought, replacing the letter back into the envelope, but she decided to keep the piece of material.

'I shouldn't have done that really, but how else can we find the secrets this island keeps.'

Suddenly Petra stiffened in fright. She had heard two disturbing sounds. The first was the angry roar of the sea bringing in the furious tide. The wind had gained strength and the sea was flooding in fast, covering the sand and pounding the rocks. Petra moved to the shingle outside the cave and to her dismay could hear raised voices buffeting against the wind.

"Oh no!" exclaimed Petra out loud. "The intruders are coming back to this cave! I must hide before they find me." She carefully put the piece of old material and her phone into her pocket. She gave a last glance around the cave to see everything was as she had found it. She stepped outside into the blustering wind and rain and keeping close to the rocks she made her way along the shingle beneath the cliffs. 'I daren't climb the path back up to the top now or I will be seen!'

The young girl looked for somewhere to hide, but the rocks were well worn and certainly not large enough to hide behind. Petra felt desperate, her heart was pounding deep in her chest. She could feel raw panic set in as the voices grew nearer. And then she stumbled across the red rowing boat pulled up high on the shale below the cliff.

'This will have to do as a hiding place,' she thought. 'I have no choice. I just hope the couple don't come this way.' Luckily there was a sheet of tarpaulin folded on the deck of the boat, Petra lay flat and pulled the cold wet cover over herself. She lay still for what seemed to be a long time. She could hear the voices getting closer, in fact so near that she could hear what they were saying to one another. The woman spoke first.

"Well, what a waste of time that was, absolutely nothing of Mortimer's at all! I told you there must be another castle on this island." Her tone was hard and agitated.

Then Petra could hear the man's voice coming nearer to her hiding place, closer than she would have preferred. She held her breath and her body froze in apprehension of being caught. The man was now almost beside the boat, Petra could hear him walking on the shale nearby. She could hear it crunching under his feet.

"I'll just get my jacket, Jo! I am sure I left it in the boat." It was the man speaking, and suddenly she felt the boat move. She lay there waiting to be discovered at any moment.

"No, it's not in there!" she heard the woman's voice. "You left your coat in the cave, I saw it this morning," the woman retorted, much to Petra's relief.

'Fear can be so sour and alleviation so sweet,' Petra felt in the moment that she was reprieved.

"I'll need it tonight," the man replied. "It was freezing in that cave! How much longer are we staying on this barbarous island?"

"Until I say we can go! And that won't be until I find what Mortimer has been hiding from me." replied the woman.

"What you got against the professor then?"

"Plenty!" snarled the woman. "He owes me big time! I am going to light a fire to get warm."

"After hearing that terrible noise last night do you think that's a wise move?" he replied. Petra was certain she could hear a tremor in his voice.

"I am! Come to think of it, you can do it for me," exclaimed the woman. "I am soaked through. Light a fire here at the entrance to this cave, and then we must look through the briefcase again, we must have missed something."

"Well, you are not going to find much in there. You said the mahogany chests are where the professor kept all his secrets." Petra thought that the man was the underdog in this situation, she detected fear in him.

"Yes, the chests were the places where he used to keep all his important stuff, when I used to work for him, but he obviously didn't bring the chests to the island."

"But we know neither of his chests were anywhere in his cottage," said the man. "We gave the place a good going over! So, where do you think they are?"

"I have no idea.' The woman replied. "Come on, let's get out of this atrocious weather." The pair disappeared into the cave and Petra gave a huge sigh of relief.

She waited a few minutes to be sure the couple were occupied in the cave before she cautiously lifted the tarpaulin and peered out. There was no one in sight, so immediately she climbed out of the boat and made her way over the rocks jumping from one to another, so relieved the intruders hadn't caught her. It didn't take her long to locate the cliff path and quickly climb to the top. Soon she was at the place where she had left Brown Bear and the girls, she could now see the entrance to the underground.

There was no sign of anyone on the beach below, but she could smell smoke. Petra slipped her hand into her shorts pocket to feel for her phone. Yes, it was safe and so was the piece of material.

'I can't wait to tell the others all I have discovered. That woman is obviously a disgruntled secretary of the professor's, someone in his past that can't let him go,' she thought to herself.

Petra slipped through the hole in the ground. She had been expecting a steep drop but there was none, just a steady decline leading to a very smooth floor. She was about to relax and follow the passageway in search of her companions when she heard a deafening gush of water. The path she was on remained dry, but about a metre below her was a watercourse filling with the rushing torrent, speeding below her on its way out of this underground cavern. The noise of this water was so loud Petra reached for her phone and lit the torch facility to view the deluge.

"I must get away from here quickly," she said out loud, her voice being drowned out by the furious surge of water. Petra began to run along the pathway and was delighted to hear Rosie's voice.

"Come on, Petra. Come this way. We are safe up here," Rosie had remembered her torch in her backpack, and was shining its light on the ground, so that her sister could see the way to safety.

"How do I climb up there?" Petra could see the faces of Rosie, Ursula and Brown Bear staring down at her. She could only see a smooth rock face with no footholds.

"Follow the beam of light from my torch," said Rosie, shining her light for a metre or so further up the passageway and then Petra sighed with relief, because now she could see some steps leading up to her companions who were high and dry above the watercourse.

"Am I glad to see you all. I have had a sort of adventure. And just wait till I tell you what I have found out about the intruders."

"Look, if you all follow me," said Ursula. "I will take you to where I live, and we can have a rest and some food and then Petra, you can tell us what you have discovered."

"Ummm! That's a great idea," Brown Bear took Petra and Rosie's hands and gleefully followed their new friend along the passageway. "I feel a new adventure coming on."

"Yes, I do, too," joined in Rosie, who felt happy that they were all together again.

The euphoria Brown Bear and Rosie felt in that moment would not last. For in the days ahead there will be danger, fear and sorrow that will change all their lives forever.

22
UNDERGROUND RUINS

Ursula took the lead along the underground passage. The furious torrent of water was now far below them and did not interfere with their journey, only the noise of the rushing water could be heard. Brown Bear, Petra and Rosie were excited about getting their quest underway at last. It had been a long time since the day a new neighbour had moved into their quiet country village and made his request to Petra and Rosie. But now they felt it wouldn't be long before they all found the hidden secrets the professor had mentioned.

After about twenty minutes of continuous decline Brown Bear realised the path had levelled out. Ursula stopped suddenly facing our three adventurers with her right arm held high with the palm of her hand facing her newfound friends.

"We must stop here. Before we go any further, I want to show you something that I know you have shown interest in," said Ursula in a very serious tone of voice. "I know it is very dark in this passage with only torches to light the way."

"Yes, it is! How much further must we go until we can have a rest?" asked Brown Bear.

"How much longer until we see your home?" Petra was tiring too.

"It's not that far but I want you to see something first. I just want you to shine your torch up high, Petra," and then Ursula instructed Brown Bear to shine his light to the left of where they stood. She wasn't surprised to hear gasps of dismay from all three of her companions.

"It is a pile of rubble! In fact, a massive amount of rubble," sighed Petra. She shone her torch higher, and its beams were lighting up stones and boulders that had collapsed in what must have been a cataclysmic event. It was a sorry sight witnessing the remains splayed out all around in this underground passage. The stones were of all sizes scattered forlornly on the floor of the tunnel.

"What is it?" asked Rosie.

"Well!" exclaimed Brown Bear. "I do believe it is the remains of the second castle that was mentioned in the Professor's notes."

"Do you really think so?" Petra questioned her mentor.

"I do! It is approximately where it should have been located, above here," he pointed upward, "Up there is the eastern shore of the island according to the professor."

"What professor?' Ursula almost demanded. "I have never heard of a professor."

Brown Bear was about to tell Ursula some details about Professor Mortimer when Petra gave him a disapproving glance. Then at that precise moment an horrendous roar boomed out encircling them in the underground passage, making Rosie almost jump out of her skin. She clung to Brown Bear, frightened by the all-consuming sound.

"It's that roaring noise again," cried Rosie. "I told you it was louder in the underground caves."

"Listen! Rosie." Ursula was reaching out to hold Rosie's hand. "Please don't be afraid. It is only a noise! I'll explain later."

By now Brown Bear was already examining the pile of fallen masonry. Petra had followed him to get a closer look. He gave his head a quick scratch and then announced his findings to the others.

"Alas!" he said, "Girls, I'm pretty sure that these stones are the ruins of the second castle, mentioned in the Professor's interim report. Look here, girls." Brown Bear was now getting quite excited witnessing what lay around him. "I can make out many stones with rounded sides and fallen buttresses that were utilised in this fortress's erection."

"BB! What is a buttress?" asked Rosie. "I have heard of them in a history lesson, but I have no idea what they were used for." The little girl looked at Brown Bear in anticipation. She knew he wouldn't fail her with an explanation.

Brown Bear stood tall in the torchlight. Petra felt sure a lecture was imminent. Rosie stood looking at him adoringly as she was about to hang onto his every word.

"Well! I will tell you what I know," Brown Bear's words boomed around the underground cavern. "In medieval architecture, buttresses were used to support walls of many a castle especially when it had a roof. It was a structure used to support a wall, to hold back outward pressure from an internal wall, to stop them collapsing."

"Oh!" Rosie gasped. "Weren't the builders clever even in those days. So, how did it work?"

"It made the outer wall stronger and stopped them from bowing out under pressure of a heavy roof, so I believe."

Ursula interrupted the history lesson but Rosie didn't mind. "My mother told me the castles on this island were built in the 12th century, and that's all I know about this castle, except it was a victim of the earthquake," replied their new friend. "But I did say you would be disappointed not to find it in better condition,"

"Well! Yes, I am perplexed," Brown Bear felt a little deflated. He had put a lot of hope into finding this castle with the view of having some questions answered."

"Mr Bear," Ursula took his paw in her hands and gave him a squeeze. "In due course I will tell you everything I know, but I am getting tired too. So, please follow me. I will lead you to a much more comfortable place where we can sit and relax."

"That sounds nice," said Rosie. "I need a rest! I'm worried that you are taking us nearer to that growling noise. Are you?"

Ursula was about to answer when another horrendous torrent of water came gushing down the passage below them, making them all hesitate before following their new friend any further.

"What is it with this water? Petra gasped, as she held tightly onto her sister.

"I hope the water won't come this high." Rosie held back a tear.

"No, it won't," said Ursula, in a very calm voice, which amazed the girls. "All the flood water stays in the course it has made for itself and when the pressure is too much, it gushes out of the bore hole on the cliff top. Remember you have seen it in action."

"Yes, of course we have all seen it," replied Petra, quite relieved. "So that is one worry out of the way then. Now we only have those blood curling growls to contend with."

'There is a lot down here that is quite terrifying, no wonder my girls are apprehensive,' thought Brown Bear, beginning to doubt whether he was doing the right thing allowing this exploration. 'But then,' he thought again. 'It was not my intention to bring them on this mission. I must not forget that fact, this is Professor's Mortimer's mission and not mine.'

"I will explain in a little while, just come with me." Ursula seemed to read Brown Bear's thoughts. She was now making her way further up the passage and was followed closely by Petra and Brown Bear, who had now picked Rosie up off the rocky floor into his big strong arms to carry her.

After a while Ursula stopped and held up one arm to halt the others. She saw apprehensive looks on all three faces.

"I knew you would be shocked at seeing the castle ruins," Ursula said, a little out of breath. "I must explain! There was an earthquake here about twenty years ago, not a very big one, but enough to do a lot of damage. Within three years, there had been one earthquake and a landslide. I don't remember them because they happened before I was born."

"Oh! Goodness me!" gasped Brown Bear. "Are we safe down here, my dear?"

"Yes, I know when there is danger, but my only worry now is getting you all back to my home before it gets too dark," Ursula hastened her steps and they all followed.

"But it is already dark in this passage!" exclaimed Rosie, still in Brown Bear's arms.

"Yes, I know, you are puzzled. As soon as we enter my home territory you will all know what I mean. Come on."

There was a bend in the passage and then it widened out into a larger cavern. Everyone followed Ursula on a path that led deeper underground. After a while they knew they were in a tunnel because they could see light ahead.

"Not far now, we will soon be able to rest and eat a meal," Ursula seemed delighted with the prospect of showing everyone her underground home where she had lived alone for many years.

"I hope you will tell us everything about yourself and why you live so deep underground." Petra wanted to know every detail about this strange girl.

"I will, I promise, but we are not far away now. Now look here. This used to be a blockage caused by the landslide so we need to climb now."

Ursula pulled herself up and passed through a rocky opening, a metre or so high in the wall of rubble. "This was caused by the landslide," she said.

Beyond the wall they could see another cave and she urged the others to follow her. Petra and Rosie slipped through easily but Brown Bear being much larger had a bit of a squeeze to join the three girls on the other side.

"Wow!" exclaimed Rosie. "This is a fantastic place!"

"Amazing," announced Petra.

"I know that smell!" pondered Brown Bear.

"What smell?" retorted Petra. "The only smell I can detect is ozone. Do you know what I mean? Like the sea but more delicate!"

"What can you smell, BB?" Rosie asked her companion. "Because I can smell blossom and trees and the perfume of sweet scented flowers."

"I can't put my finger on it," Brown Bear looked puzzled. "It could be a smell from my past. Umm, I'm not sure!"

Petra used the light on her iPhone to briefly take in her surroundings. All three were amazed to be in such a beautiful place. It looked like a tropical paradise but how could it be? They knew perfectly well they were on the island they all loved.

"Excuse me, Mr Bear," interrupted Ursula. "Let me show you where we can all sleep tonight and then tomorrow you can search for the secrets you want to find."

"Yes!" he replied. "My girls are very tired now. Is there somewhere near and comfortable where we could make beds for the night?"

Within the first hour of entering this unusual place they were all settled on soft green grass with their jackets wrapped around each individual backpack for a pillow. They had finished off all the snacks their Mum had given them and drunk fresh clean water from a fountain that Ursula showed them set in the rocks.

"It got dark very quickly," said Petra. "Is this where you live, Ursula?"

"No, it isn't! But in the morning I will show you my abode," she answered in a sleepy voice. "We have to lie low now because it is not safe to wander here after nightfall. If you hear strange noises in the night, just ignore them because nothing can get to us here."

"Oh! Ursula! I'm never going to get to sleep now!" exclaimed Petra. But she did!

They all woke early the next morning and Ursula showed them a way beyond the shadow of the rocks and the grassy dell. The girls followed their new friend into warm, early morning sunshine while a gentle breeze ruffled their hair. Soft green grass lay beneath their feet. Then Ursula came to a halt.

"Where are we?" asked Petra. "This place seems unreal. There is an abundance of colourful flowers and a lake! It is an amazing place."

"This is near to where I have lived all my life," replied Ursula. "It is not a lake! It is a lagoon! You can make out the sea beyond those dunes!" The young girl pointed towards the horizon in the direction of the sea.

The scene in front of them was the most idyllic coastal haven. Brown Bear, Petra and Rosie stood in amazement absorbing the scene. It appeared to be a large cove but nothing like the other coves they had all become familiar with. This cove was dominated by the lagoon; its water was of the deepest blue. There was a beach of fine white sand that invitingly lay to one side of them. And then the sand gave way to large rocks of a bluish grey colour, and behind them were higher rocks and boulders. Beyond they could see glimpses of a dark green forest beckoning to them in the distance.

"How enchanting!" exclaimed Brown Bear. "I find it hard to believe this is still the island we know."

"I assure you it is, Mr Bear!" Ursula told him in a very positive voice.

"What else do you know about the castle?" he asked

"Not much really, but I have always known it was here. But I know it collapsed when the earthquake happened. It destroyed the castle and caused damage to some of the caves too. The castle had stood for hundreds of years until that fateful day, that is when everything on this island changed!"

Petra could see Ursula had tears in her eyes. "Oh! You don't have to tell us anymore if you don't want to."

"But I do!" she exclaimed. "Even though it is very painful to remember!" she said, rubbing tears from her eyes.

"Now listen!" Brown Bear was always ready to take control of an awkward situation. "We must have breakfast and then we can all talk and catch up. Petra, I think you were going to tell us about an adventure you had before you followed us all underground, yesterday."

"Yes of course!" Petra replied. "There is a lot to tell you and a bit I have worked out."

"Right then," answered Brown Bear, "Now do we have any food left?"

"Not much!" said Rosie. "Ursula said we didn't need to bring a lot of food."

"Yes, that is right as I have a good store near my home cave, but for now I will show you where we can gather some fruit," said Ursula. "Then later I will show you my emergency supplies."

"That sounds good!" Petra and Rosie responded in unison.

They spent a pleasant hour collecting ripe fruit from trees nearby.

"This is wonderful," said Brown Bear, tasting the orange-coloured specimens. "Tastes like very sweet apricots."

"Yes!" Ursula agreed. "I'll show you the lagoon now. Please come with me."

"It's great here!" announced Rosie.

And then they all heard the noise again. This time the blood curdling howls were even louder than ever. Rosie screamed, Brown Bear growled, and Petra pulled Ursula to the ground.

23
THE LETTER

Since their first day on the island they had been aware of a noisy disturbance, but today's incident had been extremely frightening. The fast response from Brown Bear was very reassuring to Petra and Rosie, they felt his threatening action to nearby danger was most comforting.

"BB, I have never heard you growl before!" exclaimed a rather upset Rosie.

"Nor have I!" agreed Petra.

"A basic response to an unexplained noise!" said Brown Bear calmly. "But I feel the noise is not unfriendly."

"Well, it sounds very unfriendly," Rosie was hovering behind Brown Bear.

After a while they all recovered, and Ursula spoke first. She smiled warmly and Petra thought in that moment how beautiful the girl looked, with piercing forget-me-not blue eyes and black, silky hair that grew down to her waist.

"Come. We will go and sit by the lagoon." The young girl led them to the shore of the most peaceful stretch of clear blue water. They all made themselves comfortable on the silvery white sand and gazed expectantly at their new friend.

"I need to leave you for a while but don't worry I won't be long!" With that remark Ursula disappeared.

"Where did she go?" Petra sat upright on the sand.

"It is hot and beautiful here," said Rosie, wiggling her bare toes in the soft sand. "Why do you think Ursula has left us?"

"Never mind that!" Petra interrupted. "But listen! I really have something important to tell you both. I don't want Ursula to know what I found and what those intruders were doing on the island."

"Oh! Why can't Ursula know?" Rosie looked puzzled.

"Firstly, we don't know who she is." Petra spoke quietly.

"Yes! Pet, you are right!" Brown Bear looked all around them. "So, what did you find out?"

"I found the cave where the couple are staying and luckily, they had left an open briefcase inside and I found a letter addressed to the professor, from his wife inside it. Look here. I photographed it and now have it on my phone," Petra handed her phone to Brown Bear.

"Let me see," begged Rosie.

"Well done, Pet! You have a brave streak in you, which I admire!" Brown Bear remarked and took hold of Petra's phone.

"What does it say, BB?" Rosie was getting a little impatient.

"The letter is written on the same notepaper we found in the bedroom," observed Rosie, when at last she could see the letter for herself. Petra's camera had captured every detail.

"The paper that went missing," said Petra. "We never found it, did we?"

"No, but it doesn't explain the missing stationery, because the date on this letter is 30 July 1999, she was writing on her own notepaper all those years ago," said Brown Bear.

"Was there anything else in the briefcase?" Brown Bear looked intensely at Petra.

"Oh yes! I nearly forgot," Petra handed Brown Bear the folded piece of cloth she had found in the same envelope as the letter.

The three pals studied the remnant as best they could. Petra spoke first.

"I don't think this is a very old specimen," she said in a hushed voice.

"There is a cross with some letters," said Rosie. "Look! S.E.N.W.,

I wonder what they stand for?" she pondered. "Oh! I know! It is the letters of a compass!"

"Clever girl!" remarked Brown Bear. "Now let me see, I would think it is about a hundred years old at least. It is a well-worn piece of linen; the edges are very frayed."

"Yes, I can see," said Petra. "I must be quick in case Ursula comes back. It's okay, BB, I will read the letter out loud," She held up her iphone and began to read.

"Yes, please do, my dear. I can hardly see the writing on your phones. How you young ones manage, I don't know?"

"Yes, please do Petra!" Rosie sat on a nearby rock.

"My Dearest Larry," Petra began

"Who's Larry?" Interrupted Rose.

"Short for Lawrence," tutted Petra. "Now listen."

Petra continued to read the letter aloud.

My Dearest Larry,

I am missing you so much, but you will be glad to know my work here is nearly done.

So, sorry you were called away, but I know your work is as important to you as mine is to me. I forgot to say how much I adore the new bedroom furniture. You were very secretive finding all those antiques for me and bringing them all to the island for my comfort. I bet you arranged for Lucas to transport everything over here. I hope you rewarded him well.

I am enclosing a small piece of old cloth I found in the cellars of the castle that took a tumble when the earthquake hit the island. You were so determined to find another fortress and I am so glad you did! But who would have thought it would have been constructed on the rocky shore, on the eastern side of the island? I suppose it made sense a thousand years ago to have two means of defence on the island. Now regarding the piece of cloth, well, I think it could be old linen. First, I thought it was parchment as it was so stiff. The markings on it indicate where the vital cave is, the cave I could not find in all the weeks I spent searching for it, that last time we came to the island. I believed that it was where I would find remains of prehistoric animal bones. But I decided to use the map myself to go in search of my precious treasure and I have now located that special cave. I did tell you about it before you left in such a hurry. I plan to go there tomorrow. I have made a copy for myself so I am enclosing this original one for you.

I hope you reminded Lucas to come one evening to pick up your stuff; I will give him this letter so he can leave it at Old Mill Cottage for your return from Oxford. How I miss you right now but I will soon complete my investigation and hopefully store any finds in my 'charnel' room at our lovely hideaway here on the island.

Last night before I went to sleep I thought of something that made me laugh. I decided neither of us has changed since the day we first met amongst the Egyptian Pyramids back in 1988. There we were beneath the Sphinx, you with your quest for stones and me with my continual search for bones. What good times we have had together through all these years.

I am looking forward to your return very much, and maybe we can have some time to relax here on the island. I have some wonderful news for you. I know you will be as thrilled as I am.

Your ever-loving wife

EJ x

Petra and Brown Bear looked at each other both deep in

thought.

"Oh! BB," Petra broke the silence. "Isn't that romantic? They do seem to have been very much in love, don't you think?"

"Hur hum! I don't know much about being in love." Brown Bear mused. "Back in my day in the wild forests of Europe, my family just got on with things!"

Petra feared in that moment he might go into intimate details about happenings deep in the forests, but Rosie broke the silence.

"I wonder what E.J.'s wonderful news was." Rosie looked downcast. "It is so sad she went missing before she could tell the professor. What do you think it could be?"

Suddenly there was a disturbance at the mouth of a cave nearby. Ursula appeared covered in blood.

"Whatever has happened?" Petra was astounded to see her new friend in such a state.

"It's all right I am not hurt! But the clothes you gave me are ruined," replied Ursula.

"But whose blood is it?" Rosie was most concerned.

"I'll have a quick swim and get changed and then I'll show you one of the secrets of the island."

"Wow," exclaimed Rosie. "You can have some of my clothes."

"Thank you so much! You are all so kind to me," and with that Ursula threw herself into the lagoon, rippling the perfect turquoise water into ever decreasing circles.

While they all waited for Ursula to wash, they sat on the sand dipping their toes into the deep blue lagoon.

"She seems very calm under the circumstances," said Brown Bear.

"I wonder where the blood came from," Rosie pondered looking at the stained clothes.

"Well, I'm convinced there is something very strange on this island. A secret Ursula has known about for a long time," remarked Petra.

"Ummm, I think you are right!" said Brown Bear. "I think the professor's wife knew what it was too. But I'm pretty sure Professor Mortimer knew nothing about it at all."

"Before Ursula comes back, let us quickly sum up all the facts we know." Petra guided them to the nearest rocks, and they all sat down watching Ursula splashing in the deep blue lagoon.

"We just haven't had time to discuss very much," said Rosie. "Okay then, what do we actually know?"

"We know the professor's wife went missing, and this might be the last letter she ever wrote." Petra started to make mental notes. "And we know there are intruders on the island looking for some secret treasure."

"There is a lot we don't know as well," joined in Brown Bear.

"Like whatever is causing that loud noise we have heard ever since we came to the island!" exclaimed Rosie.

"I think Ursula knows more than she is letting on," Petra announced. "Look, here she comes, and I think she is older than you or me, Rosie."

Ursula was running across the silver sand towards them. Petra threw her a towel and she caught it deftly.

"Hey, do I look clean now? Have you some dry clothes for me, Rosie?"

"Yes, of course." She fumbled in her backpack for a moment. "Here you are, clean shorts and a T-shirt,"

"Thank you, Rosie. It is so good to have friends."

"Where did that blood come from? It was far more than a cut on your skin," asked Rosie. "Are you hurt?"

"No! It wasn't my blood!" Ursula replied.

"Whose blood was it then?" Rosie was now very curious.

"I will tell you later, when we have had some lunch." Ursula dried herself quickly and put on the clean clothes.

"Can you make a fire on the beach, BB? Look over there. Petra,

I can see some edible seaweed growing amongst the rocks at the edge of the lagoon. We can barbecue some prawns and anything else we can catch. Rosie, come with me. I will fetch my fishing net!" Ursula gave her orders in a nonchalant way. No one mentioned the blood again.

"That sounds wonderful!" exclaimed Rosie, thinking how beautiful her new friend looked with her dark, long hair forming damp ringlets around her shoulders.

"And BB, see if there is any driftwood among the rocks. Maybe a high tide has deposited some there. Perhaps you will oversee making a fire."

"Right, I'm on it!" Brown Bear was mesmerised with all this femininity.

For the moment there was a very pleasant scene to behold, on that exotic stretch of the island. Everyone was busy with the task of making lunch. The sun shone high in the sky and the turquoise waters of the lagoon lapped softly on the silvery white sand.

After a while they were all full and content, having enjoyed a meal of prawns and fresh fish, cooked over charred driftwood, with blackberries for dessert. It wasn't long before they all fell fast asleep on the warm soft sand.

Petra was the first to wake disturbed by Brown Bear's snoring. She sat up and shook some sand from her hair.

"Where's Rosie?" she yelled and began to frantically search for her sister.

"What's the matter?" Ursula was now wide-awake.

"Rosie is missing," retorted Petra. "She was right beside me when we lay down after our lunch"

"Now, calm down Petra, she can't be far away," consoled Brown Bear.

They began to yell at the tops of their voices for the little girl.

"Rosie!"

"Rosie, where are you?"

"Please, Rosie, where have you gone?"

But there was no answer, only the shrill call of the gulls overhead. The lagoon still deposited soft sounding waves on the shore and the sun wandered high in the afternoon sky.

"She never leaves our side! Does she, BB?" Petra's voice was burdened with anxiety.

"No, she doesn't!" Brown Bear was now anxious about his missing charge.

"We must look for clues in the sand." Ursula joined in.

"Good idea!" They started to search in the area where they had all been snoozing.

"Look! Look!" cried Petra. "There are strange marks in the sand and then they disappear."

"Yes, and here are Rosie's footprints close by, she's wearing her flipflops," Ursula looked towards the cliffs and the large cavern with its gaping hole, now looking black and mysterious and not at all inviting. "I hope Rosie hasn't gone in there." The young girl had a strange look on her face.

"What's the matter?" Brown Bear's voice was deep and urgent.

"Nothing!" quickly retorted Ursula, with her head turned down, towards the sandy beach.

"There is something wrong." Petra seemed to read what their new strange friend was thinking. "Ursula, why do you look so worried?"

A cool breeze stirred, and way out across the lagoon the sea gave the roar of the turning tide. A golden glow of the late afternoon's sunshine gave the scene an eerie, quiescent feel. Ursula still did not speak.

"Ursula, you are holding something back from us." Petra stared towards the cavern entrance. "What is it? Tell us?"

"Does Rosie like rabbits?" at last Ursula spoke.

"Of course! That's it!" Brown Bear exclaimed. "The markings in the sand are rabbit prints. Look girls, now I can see clearly, Rosie has followed a rabbit into the caves. Come on, we'll go and find her."

Petra was relieved and followed Brown Bear towards the cave.

"No! No, you can't go in there," yelled Ursula at the top of her voice.

"Why ever not?" Brown Bear gave a frustrated grunt.

"Because inside," Ursula calmed down and wiped tears from her eyes, she now spoke quietly, "There is a special place, my place."

"I see!" exclaimed Petra, in surprise.

There was a long silence in which no one spoke. Petra was worried sick about her sister. Brown Bear stood still. He was not used to dealing with so many girls. He eventually spoke in a soft voice selecting his words carefully.

"Well, we won't intrude on your space, young lady, but Ursula, please will you go in the cave and find Rosie, she may be lost in there."

"I will!" said the girl. "And tomorrow, as soon as it is light, I will take you to see something amazing on this island."

"You keep saying that but you never do," Petra was getting annoyed with the strange girl.

"I will, I promise, but the time is not right yet. Give me time and everything will be revealed"

"But will we ever find the secrets of this island?" asked Petra.

"I think so!" replied Ursula. "And with my help you surely will."

24
THE SHRINE

Rosie woke suddenly from her afternoon nap. She sat up on the warm white sand being aware that something had touched her cheek.

"Hey, little thing, what do you want?" Rosie reached out to a little rabbit, but it was too fast for her. "Hi, bunny, come back here. I think you've hurt your paw."

Rosie looked at her companions lying on the sand. All three were fast asleep. She could hear the roar of the tide out beyond the lagoon. Ursula had told her it was safe on this beach. Only on rare winter days, in really bad weather would the sea flood over into the shallow waters of the lagoon.

"Come here, bunny, I can help you."

Rosie noticed a small amount of blood on the little creature's back foot, as it scurried off into the cavern. She looked back at the others and picked up her flip-flops. No one stirred so, she decided to follow the tiny rabbit into the system of caves.

She entered a cave very quietly and could see the rabbit sitting washing its ears at a point where the passageway veered off to the left.

'That is strange,' Rosie thought. 'I didn't notice this junction before when Ursula first brought us this way to the beach.' Nevertheless, Rosie followed the little creature along the tunnel as far as she could see. Then suddenly the passage started to narrow and she found herself in a weird half-light.

'I wish I had my phone!' she thought. 'I could have used the torch.' She decided to find the injured animal and went on a little further along the passage, but there was no sign of the rabbit.

After a while of feeling her way along the rocky wall Rosie could no longer see where she was going. She had almost decided to go back to the others, when a short way ahead of her she could see a light. She was sure it wasn't daylight, as the glow ahead was a shimmering pale pink haze.

The little girl felt afraid of what lay ahead but carried onwards resisting the desire to go back to the safety of her companions. But something strange possessed Rosie, urging her to go forward and on towards the light. Deep within her chest Rosie could feel her heart pounding, pumping away until she could feel it was hard to breathe. She stopped and took three deep breaths and found that helped.

'Should I go back now?' she asked herself. 'No, I must see what is making that light. Maybe it is the work of Sea Sprites.' Rosie sighed remembering that in a previous adventure together with Petra and Brown Bear she had encountered the little sea creatures a few times.

'No, it can't be the little sprites, because where I am now is a dry cave situated a good way from the sea. We three found out that the little sprites cannot survive far from seawater. She quickly dismissed that idea and took a few steps forward reaching a perfectly rounded sandstone arch.

'Whatever am I going to find now?' Rosie thought, as she cautiously stood by the arch and looked through into a small room, which again had been moulded out of the rock, carved by ancient seas through the passage of time. This secret place was bone dry with blades of marron grass, strewn on the rock floor. Rosie gasped as she beheld what lay in front of her.

'This is a sanctuary! A shrine!' Rosie realised, hardly daring to breathe. The cave was so quiet, with two large pink candles burning brightly on what appeared to be a stone altar in the centre of the cave.

A note to my readers: you would expect Rosie to be terrified and run back to the others, but she wasn't afraid at all. She just stood and marvelled at what she saw. She felt calm and at peace with herself. Rosie's heart was quiet and serenely beating steadily deep within her.

'I wonder who built this,' she thought. 'I'm sure Ursula knows about it. Who else would light the candles? I think we have a lot to find out about the strange girl.'

Rosie stood back and tried to memorise the scene, so that she could recall everything and be able to describe to Petra and Brown Bear exact details.

'It looks as if the stones have been carried in here to make the altar,' she thought. Then she noticed down on the floor stood a chest. Rosie stooped down and carefully opened the lid, it creaked as she did so. The rhythm of her heart stirred again as she looked inside. The little girl found it half full of large candles., the same as those already burning on the altar. The lid was too heavy, and Rosie let go, it made a loud thud that echoed round the cave, disturbing the sanctity of this place. Rosie stood still and listened to the silence and then the peace was shattered.

Then suddenly something startled her; she could hear voices in the passageway outside. Whosoever was there were too close for Rosie's comfort.

She could hear a man and a woman arguing. 'What shall I do?' Rosie thought. 'I want to get back to the others.' But she froze with fear on the spot, her heart pounding once again. And then something strange happened, the candles on the shrine started flickering and at the same time she felt something take hold of her hand and lead her calmly into the shadows.

"Who are you?" she whispered. Rosie felt she ought to be afraid and run back along the passage and out into the sunshine, but she wasn't afraid at all. Whoever was holding her hand was gentle and very reassuring. She just let herself be guided away from the warring couple into a dark corner of the cave.

Time stood still; it seemed like an eternity. She could hear the voices, getting closer now. She stiffened as she could hear a male voice getting nearer and nearer, unbearably loud as the man came even closer. Rosie knew that if she reached out her hand she could touch him. She shivered at the thought. Then he spoke to whoever he was with.

"You are not going to find any trace of the professor's secrets down here!" said the man. "We should scour that old castle and find out if there are treasures in the rubble. Why was that castle built underground, anyway? I want to take what we can and get back to the mainland. I've had enough of this godforsaken island."

"Of course, it wasn't built underground!" Rosie could hear a woman's voice now, "Fred, you have no sense at all," retorted the woman. "Couldn't you see that there has been a subsidence, don't you remember? There was an earthquake in the nineties that hit this island. And then a few years later in the summer of 1999 there was a landslide," the woman paused for breath. "Pity it didn't wipe out the whole island, then we wouldn't have to be here now, tying up loose ends."

"What loose ends?" retorted the man.

"You know exactly what loose ends I mean, Fred," answered the woman. "And no! No! I am not ready to leave yet, I want revenge!"

Rosie was now certain that it was the voice of the woman; they had all heard the night they hid in the garden at Old Mill Cottage.

Again, something touched Rosie's hand and gently pulled her towards the way that led out of the caves, in the direction of the beach and the blue lagoon.

Rosie was about to ask. "Who are you?" When the squabble between the man and the woman grew louder and more aggressive. In that moment Rosie was glad of the hand that held hers. She didn't need to strain her ears to hear, as the voices were extremely loud, she could hear their conversation clearly.

"What have you got against the professor?" The man asked his companion. "And why do you want revenge?"

There was no reply from the woman.

"Jo! Will you have the decency to answer me?" Rosie trembled as she could detect a deep frustration within the man.

"You know why? Fred, I have told you often enough,"

"Because he jilted you all those years ago! Is that it?" retorted the man. Rosie was certain it was the same couple that had intruded into the Professor's Cottage.

"Yes!" the woman replied. "But there was a lot more to it than that!" Rosie could detect a great deal of bitterness in the woman's voice.

"Well? tell me then," the man was still angry.

"You know I worked for him, don't you? And he took me on all his digs," reflected the woman.

"Yes! You told me, you were eighteen when you first met him," the man seemed calmer.

"We were both young. We were studying archaeology in Dorset university! But I decided it wasn't for me, so I left and took a secretarial course in a local college, just so I could stay near him."

"So, what went wrong?" the man asked,

"What went wrong? What went wrong? Everything went wrong!" The woman yelled at the top of her voice.

Rosie shivered as she stood in the shadows.

"He met her, that student," shouted the woman. "I hated her so much I can't even say her name. That's what went wrong! And that was it! He dumped me like a hot potato! She and Larry were studying on the same course that first year. They became inseparable and that was the end of me in his eyes."

Rosie felt the hand let go of her and then a howling gust of wind blew through the cavern. The candles flickered once again this time with a fury from within. The woman screamed and Rosie could hear the man take a sharp intake of breath.

"What the hell?" he said, with a trembling voice. "Who's this woman, dressed in a long flowing garment?"

"What woman?" replied his companion, as she looked where the man was pointing into the shadows.

"No! No. It can't be her! It can't be! We must get out of here now," yelled the woman. "Now! I mean now! Fred, run for it! This place is haunted! I've seen enough! Mortimer can keep his secrets. I'm getting out of here now! It's her, she's haunting this island!!"

"Who?"

"You know very well who."

"Right, let's get back to the boat. Quickly! Come on!" responded the man. Rosie wondered who the man could be, as he was subservient, quite used to the woman's orders.

She could hear their screams and fading voices, going back along the passageway. She wondered how the couple had found the underground tunnel. Could they have come from the sea? Or did they follow us down the hole on the clifftop? She had heard them mention a boat, so more likely by sea. Then, they knew about the second castle lying in ruins and how the intruders had found the shrine was a mystery to Rosie.

Then she realised and everything became clear to Rosie. Of course, Ursula has built this altar and keeps the candles alight in the memory of her mother. Rosie stood glued to the spot she couldn't move. She took in a deep breath and could once again feel her heart pounding deep inside her. Rosie blinked in the darkness and could smell extinguished wax. 'Something or someone must have put out the candles.'

'I must find my way out of here, right now!' she thought, as she felt her way along the dark passage wall. Then at last she could see daylight at the opening of the cave and made her way towards it. As she stepped out into the golden glow of the evening sun, she felt something brush against her foot.

"Oh! There you are, bunny. Why did you go in there?" Rosie bent down to pick up the injured rabbit, but suddenly it hopped away onto the beach. "Well, your foot looks better, I expect you will be alright now." She watched as the little creature disappeared into the grassy dunes. "I must find the others!" That was Rosie's main task now.

As Rosie made her way back to the beach, she felt a sharp gust of wind swirl round her. She shivered in the cool evening air. She thought back over her encounter with the ghost! 'Yes, I'm sure it was a spirit that held my hand,' she questioned herself. 'And that couple certainly saw something that frightened the wits out of them.'

At last Rosie stood on the sand, her eyes blinking with the bright glow of the setting sun.

"Oh! There you are Rosie!" Brown Bear exclaimed with relief in his voice.

"Yes! I'm here, but I have had a strange experience! Wait till I tell you everything that just happened."

"We woke from our nap and you had gone," stated Petra. "Where have you been?"

Then suddenly without saying a word Ursula rushed past Rosie and ran into the caves.

"Oh! my word!" exclaimed Brown Bear. "Our new friend doesn't look happy."

"No, she won't be," said Rosie. "You two come with me to sit on the rocks and I will tell you what I have found."

In a little while all three reached the shelter of the rocks, the sun was now very low in the western sky, casting its final beams in a strange shimmering haze over the lagoon.

"Now tell us, Rosie. What has happened?" Brown Bear looked closely at the little girl. He was thinking how much she had grown lately. "Are you alright, my dear?"

"Yes, thank you, BB, I am fine now but I just had a very

disturbing encounter. I'll be quick. First, there is a strange presence deep in the caves. I found a shrine, a stone altar with lit candles on it. And more candles in a box on the rocky floor just underneath. I think Ursula knows all about it."

"Knows about what?" Suddenly Ursula appeared among the rocks, startling the others.

"Oh! Nothing!" exclaimed Petra.

"Look! I know I owe you all an explanation. In fact, I will take you now, as I have a sort of emergency," Ursula beckoned to them all to follow her.

"What kind of emergency?" Rosie asked the girl.

"Come I will show you and maybe you will all discover one of the secrets of the island."

25
SECRETS

Ursula led our three adventurers along the beach. She headed for the shallow waters of the lagoon. The sun was low on the western horizon. Here on the eastern side of the island it was impossible to see where the sun set, as the castle on the hill rose high above the island, casting its shadows and impeding the views of the west. As Petra, Rosie and Brown Bear followed their friend they could see the golden clouds that tapered into pink and crimson ribbons commanding the sky, forerunners of the ominous dark clouds that herald the night.Ursula turned to face them at last.

"We have to wade in the water a little way to get to my special cave. We had better take off our sandals, the water is shallow just here. Then I will show you where I have lived for all my life. It is a bit of a trek though."

Brown Bear, Petra and Rosie followed the girl in silence. Rosie had got over her fright and was pleased to be with the others.

"What's that light shining out at sea?" Brown Bear was getting familiar with his surroundings, as he was the tallest in the group he could see the waves on the ocean, far out beyond the island.

"It is a trawler," replied Ursula. "It is not fishing. There are no lights to indicate the trawler is working. It will be waiting for those strangers to row back over the water to rejoin it."

"Oh!" Petra exclaimed. "How do you know about them?"

"Of course, I know! I know everything that happens on this island," stated Ursula. "Those two people are thieves; I have seen them here on the island a few times before you three arrived." Ursula looked at them all intensely. "Petra, did you realise the note paper went missing from the bedroom drawer in the room at the cottage where you girls are sleeping."

"Yes, we did!" exclaimed Petra. Brown Bear nodded in agreement.

"Have those two stolen all that lovely writing set? It was beautiful, with initials on every piece!" exclaimed Rosie.

"No! I did!" replied Ursula. "I took it away for safety."

"But why?" Brown Bear joined in.

"Because, as long as I can remember there have been beautiful things in that upstairs room," said Ursula incensed. "I didn't want them to steal the notepaper. They even stole a briefcase with historical manuscripts inside, and they were about to steal some of the bones and fossils in that first room at the entrance to the cottage, until they saw me. They dropped armfuls of relics they were carrying, just threw them down and ran away. That room has always been full of bones ever since I first saw it. I must have been seven years old when I managed to climb out of the underground cave. I felt I must explore the island. I was lonely and missing my mother."

"You have a heart-breaking story, my dear," Brown Bear was sympathetic towards the girl.

"Yes, I know," she replied. "And it gets worse!"

As they walked along it became clear to Petra that Ursula must mean the briefcase she herself had found in the cave, where the intruders were camping. 'It obviously belonged to the professor. Now, that proves the intruders are the same couple we saw at the professor's cottage in our village. So, they brought it here to the island! What a good job we took both his mahogany chests and hid them in our house for safekeeping.' She was just about to mention those facts to Ursula when a strange howling sound was heard, The girl led them away from the waters of the lagoon to some high rocks.

"We must go quietly the rest of the way," said Ursula. "Because, I think we have been heard already."

Rosie shivered in fright, her imagination running wild. "Who has heard us? The intruders?"

"No! Not them!" replied the girl, as she led them deeper between the rocks. "Don't worry, I have dealt with them."

"How?" Brown Bear was intrigued.

"I've scuttled their boat," the girl said with a grin.

"You've what!?" exclaimed Petra.

"I made lots of holes in the planking of their dinghy, they won't be able to row back to the trawler now," Ursula sounded very pleased with herself. "In fact, whatever they have stolen from the cottage will have to stay on the island now, where it belongs."

"But what if they use their mobile phones to call for help?" Rosie asked feeling rather apprehensive.

"Because, I have their phones! As I said, those two won't be going anywhere. Now, quiet everyone, we are getting near to my secret cave where I have survived ever since I can remember."

Just as they all were about to step inside Ursula's home territory, there came an horrendous roar, followed by a series of low deep throated growls.

Brown Bear scooped Rosie off her feet and into his big furry arms. Rosie gasped but was pleased to be safe.

Petra took a firm hold of Ursula's hand. "Of course!" she said. "This is the noise we have been hearing ever since we arrived on the island and now that we are up close it is so much louder. What is this mystery? It is something you are keeping very secret. Come on, please tell us."

"Yes, I will. I hope you are ready for some surprises. You must keep very quiet and follow me, and in a while, I will show you," she said in a low voice. "Mr Bear, you stay a little way behind, as I will have to introduce you carefully, or you may be killed."

"What!" Rosie exclaimed in horror.

"Ursula! Where on earth are you taking us?" Petra stopped in her tracks. "We are not going anywhere until you have told us everything you are keeping from us. Are we in real danger?"

"No, not really! So long as I go first. Just trust me." Ursula replied. "I know everything is strange to you all, but this is the life I have had to get used to."

Brown Bear put Rosie down and faced the girl.

"I have always felt responsible for Petra and Rosie, ever since I introduced them to this island a few years ago," said Brown Bear.

"Yes! BB has always looked out for us," announced Petra.

"Yes! He has always known what was best for us in a tricky situation." agreed Rosie.

"And there have been a few of those!" exclaimed Brown Bear. "I think young lady, you owe us an explanation."

"Yes! I know I do!" Ursula faced them all in the fading light and beckoned them to sit beside her on a large tree trunk that had fallen some years ago. Petra and Rosie sat close together and Brown Bear sat beside them.

"You do owe us an explanation, young lady," he said, making himself comfortable. "You must tell us everything you know. We are good listeners."

Rosie felt it was so good to be amongst her little family again. She thought they were now in a very unusual place. The fallen tree was lying on the ground beside some very tall rocks. In the background, only metres away, she could see a forest.

There was no loud noise to disturb the peace, and our three adventurers could only hear the gentle lapping of water somewhere inland accompanied by a gentle whispering breeze ruffling the leaves high in the canopy. The moon, large and silver, appeared low on the eastern horizon.

"Look, girls, the moonrise!" said Brown Bear. "It will be a full moon tonight."

Ursula looked fragile in the moonlight as she began to tell her story.

"It is quite true that I have lived here all my life. Have you ever wondered how I speak English so well? It is because my mother taught me."

"Your mother!" Petra and Rosie exclaimed in surprise.

Brown Bear leaned forward. "Well! Yes, my dear, you do use English grammar correctly, I did wonder."

"Where is your mother now?" said Petra.

"I will come to that in a while, but I feel I must explain what the loud roaring noise is first," replied Ursula. "But listen, why don't I show you my home so we can eat and be more comfortable. What do you say, Mr Bear?"

"Indeed! What a good idea," replied Brown Bear. "I am getting a bit peckish."

Ursula stood up and beckoned them all to follow her. After a while they reached their destination because hidden among the tall rocks was a cave, Ursula entered first and immediately she reached for a torch that she kept inside on a stone ledge.

"It will only be dark for a short distance and then we will have to climb over some rubble. I will show you a part of the island I call home."

They entered the cave and were surprised to find a short tunnel and all followed Ursula in silence. After a while they came up against a wall of fallen rocks and stones. Ursula climbed up and over the rocks and was soon lending a hand from the other side to help everyone into her abode.

Brown Bear, Petra and Rosie climbed through a gap about a metre high in the wall of fallen rocks.

"Ouch!" exclaimed Rosie, as she caught her arm on the rocky wall.

Brown Bear was concerned.

"I'm fine, don't fuss, BB. It's only a scratch."

Minutes later they all stood in an illuminated cavern.

"Well! I never!" Brown Bear remarked, looking round the cave in amazement.

"Wow!" exclaimed Rosie and Petra in unison.

"Welcome," said Ursula, with a warm smile on her pretty face. "We won't need a torch now. Come, I will show you everything."

"And explain everything I hope." Brown Bear stood tall.

"Of course, Mr Bear, I assure you I will!"

And then it happened again. The noise they could hear was an unbearable roar that seemed to be so close to them that they all looked around the cavern not knowing what to expect. Petra and Rosie stiffened in fright, but Brown Bear seemed delighted.

"Lead the way, young lady. I don't think there will be anything to frighten us here."

Brown Bear stood still, smelling the air. He seemed to recognise a certain odour.

"What do you mean, BB? It sounds like a monster." Rosie reached for his arm.

"Your BB is right! There is nothing to frighten you. Come with me and soon you will see for yourselves," Ursula reassured the girls.

The cave that Ursula called home was a magical place. Once our adventurers had followed their host away from the fallen rubble, they found themselves in another wonderland. It almost appeared to be a replica of the cave and beach of the lagoon. But now they observed another beach of silvery white sand and a lake of vibrant turquoise blue water surrounded by forest and the tall pinnacles of rock. The sky was high above them, visible through a large hole in the roof. The light of the full moon illuminated this huge cavern.

"It's like daytime in here! But what is making that noise?" Rosie looked puzzled. "And where did that blood you were covered in come from?"

At the far end of the cave there was access to the outdoors. Ursula went to sit on a rock at the edge of the lake and made a very strange sound.

"Come and meet my close companions who have helped me cope with my life since I was young." She made a sound and the girls thought it very strange. It was like a low growl made deep in her throat. "Look, watch the trees at the far side of the lake."

Then in answer to the girl's call, three dark objects propelled themselves across the lake to where our group were waiting. Everyone was mesmerised with disbelief at what they saw.

"I'll go to them and bring them to meet you. Be careful not to make any sudden movement," said Ursula and immediately jumped into the lake. She swam strongly towards the shapes in the water.

Petra and Rosie looked on in amazement.

"Oh! Look, BB! Whatever they are, they are swimming to meet Ursula," said Rosie.

"They are really pleased to see her," agreed Petra. "Oh! They are all playing chase. BB, can you make out what they are?"

"Indeed, I can!" exclaimed Brown Bear. "Three brown bears."

"What!" the girls exclaimed together.

Brown Bear appeared to be delighted to see members of his ursine family.

"Come on, let us go to meet them. Move slowly, girls." He led the way to the very edge of the lake and took a drink. "It is fresh water, how amazing! This is how Ursula has been able to survive down here."

There was a sudden loud splash in the lake.

"Stand back, girls. Here they come. All three are bound to shake the water from their fur and it will probably soak us."

An incredible scene followed. Brown Bear couldn't resist being first to shake paws with the three robust creatures and then one by one the bears nuzzled up to the girls. They were quite familiar with little girls. Ursula examined the smallest bear's front paw.

"There you are, Star. All mended. I told you not to pick up sea urchins. They can give a nasty scratch." She gave the little bear a pat on his head.

"Ursula, do you have names for all your friends?" Petra asked while gently stroking the smallest bear and realising that this is where all the blood that had spoiled Ursula's clothes must have come from.

"Well! Yes, I have, but it was my mother who named the adult bears Kent and Moonlight, but that was before I was born. The little bear was born a few years ago," Ursula gave a big sigh. "I named him Starlight, because the night he was born here in this cave, there were myriads of stars shining in through the hole in the roof. It was quite wonderful."

Petra was intrigued. "So, these friends of yours are the cause of all those horrendous noises that we have heard on the island, and this is where the blood came from?"

"Yes! I'm afraid so, but I think they consider me as a mother figure, and when I must leave here and go about my errands, they don't like it, so they howl till I return."

"Oh! That is lovely for you to have creatures who love and miss you," remarked Petra smiling. "So, tell us all about your mother and where is she now?"

"She's dead," Ursula said sombrely.

"Oh no!" Rosie exclaimed in horror. "It must be awful not to have a mother."

Petra and Brown Bear looked on and for once, they were lost for words. Ursula looked extremely sad, and the girls gave her a long warm hug.

"It is awful to remember what happened!" Ursula remarked with tears welling up in her lovely blue eyes. "But I have had to cope alone for so long now. I was so pleased when you girls arrived on the island and especially, that your friend is a bear too."

Everyone wanted to ask what had happened to Ursula's mother, but Ursula looked so mournful that all three were lost for words.

It was the bears who broke the silence. Starlight, the smallest bear, was a cute little animal and was quite happy nuzzling up to Rosie, when suddenly one of his parents made a strange low growl deep in its throat, and all three returned to the water and swam back across the lake in the moonlight.

"Don't worry about them, they like to roam the forest at night. They are descended from the wild cave bears of Northern Europe. Studying ancient animal bones was a passion of my mothers, she taught me all about them. There is a cave on the other side of the lake where my mother found ancient ursine bones." Ursula pointed across the water.

"Ursus spelaeus!" announced Brown Bear. "Stone age relatives of my family! So, your friends are descended from cave bears." Brown Bear became very interested in Ursula's secrets. "Are there larger, deeper caves on the island? I ask because I would expect there to be very large caves somewhere nearby. The species would winter in them for safety, and hibernate of course."

"Yes, there are! Some go out under the sea. I haven't been there yet, but I am sure my mother did. I think some of those bones in the cottage are extremely old. Maybe she found them down there."

"It is incredible how their species have survived here." remarked Brown Bear. "I thought they became extinct about twenty-five thousand years ago but if the island bears have adapted from herbivores to carnivores, then that could explain it. One day I would love to see the deep caves. Will you show me, Ursula?"

"Of course I will, BB! Yes, these three eat everything, and this lake is very deep. It holds many species of freshwater fish. And of course the forest flora and fauna are plentiful."

"Very good, indeed," remarked Brown Bear. "And your ursine

friends have access to the sea, I presume? A perfect larder for your friends, Ursula."

"Yes, there is access to the coast, but it is a long trek through the forest."

"You are so clever BB, you know everything!" said a delighted Rosie.

"Is Ursus Spelaeus their scientific name?" asked Petra.

"Yes, it is!" Brown Bear was certain, and Ursula nodded in agreement.

They all looked at Ursula in anticipation of more information. "Don't worry. I will tell you everything I know later. But now I will show you my stores and then we can have supper and after that I will show you where we can sleep tonight. You will be quite safe with me."

All the rocks were smooth and flat where Ursula had laid a bed of moss and bracken, collected from the woods, to form a large sleeping area. The roof of the cave was overhanging here, a sheltered place where Ursula had prepared a cosy bedroom for herself. Tonight, she was happy and very pleased to offer her friends such unusual accommodation.

"Now you have met one of the secrets of the island and in the morning I will tell you about another," she gave them all a tired smile.

"Another secret!" Rosie exclaimed.

"Yes! Come on now, we must get some sleep." Ursula was very pleased to have guests for the night. "Here everyone, do take a pillow."

"Where do you find pillows on this island?" asked Brown Bear.

"From the cottage of course," Petra and Rosie said in unison and then began to laugh, and Ursula joined in too.

"That's what I like to see, all my girls happy," Brown Bear took a pillow and settled down for the night.

As Rosie lay on the comfortable bed trying to sleep, her mind was very active. She remembered she had found a secret too. She had been about to tell the others about the altar with the lighted candles she had found, but then she thought it better not to tell them until the time was right. And for some reason she didn't think the time was right.

Rosie realised in that moment that her thoughts about the ghost had been correct. When she had been in the cave that afternoon, when the quarrelling intruders had run away scared, she thought the place was haunted. Now she was sure that it was because there was no other explanation for what had happened.

Rosie shivered. 'Of course,' she thought. 'What I have found is a shrine for Ursula's mother. The ghost held my hand and showed me the way out of danger. It was kind to me but,' Rosie took a long deep breath and realised that the ghost must have turned on the intruders in anger, and that was why they ran away in terror.' Rosie shuddered remembering her encounter.

'I think Ursula knows that her mother is not at peace. Could that be what she means when she said she would tell us more tomorrow? Or does she know of many more secrets on this island?'

At last Rosie fell asleep dreaming of big growling bears and ghosts in flimsy attire haunting the forests of the island.

26
URSULA'S STORY

The next morning Ursula provided a delicious brunch for her newly found friends and later she began to tell her life story. The lake beside them dazzled in the glare of the mid-afternoon sunshine and the waters rippled gently in a light breeze. Playful growls could be heard coming from the woods.

"The bears seem happy when you are near them, Ursula," said Rosie, realising that it was Ursula's ursine friends that had been causing all those horrendous sounds they had been so frightened of ever since their first full day on the island. "Their noises really frightened us, you know."

"Yes, Rosie, I do know and I'm sorry, but I couldn't tell you anything about them until I got to know you all. And of course, you two girls arrived with a bear. And that was scary for me because I thought how awful it would be if all four creatures got into a fight, and we could not separate them."

"Of course!" exclaimed Petra. "I can see now how worried you must have been. We understand but now you know how much of a big softy BB can be, everything will be fine."

Brown Bear sat looking pleasantly surprised, "I am only gentle with my girls. I can fight like any other animal. To the death if I have to."

"Hey, steady on, BB," Petra put her hand on his arm.

"I'm just saying," Brown Bear relaxed. "Lovely place you have here, young lady."

"Yes, thank you, BB," replied Ursula. "Would you like to see the entrance to the bear caves? It is a lovely walk and we could pick some blackberries for our supper."

"That sounds like a great idea," said Brown Bear. "Have you a basket, Ursula dear?"

"Yes, I have!" she replied.

A very pleasant afternoon was had by all. They found the bear cave entrance, but it looked to be very dark inside and Brown Bear was a bit annoyed because he had forgotten to bring his torch.

"Never mind, BB," said Rosie. "Maybe we can come another day?"

"Yes we can," replied Ursula. "But now we must get back to my cave before it gets dark."

About an hour later they were all back in Ursula's home cave relaxing on her stone sofa with all its comfortable cushions. The moon looked full again tonight.

Brown Bear and the girls could hardly wait for more of Ursula's story, but all were very polite and waited patiently for their hostess to carry on with her intriguing tale.

"Those blackberries were delicious," said Brown Bear, "What time is it on your phone, Petra?"

"It is just after nine o'clock," she replied.

The moon was now passing over the opening in the cave roof, and when it was almost dark, Ursula lit an antique oil lamp and two candles.

"Hurhum," interrupted Brown Bear. "May I ask, my dear, that if you have been alone for years on this island, where did you manage to find oil and candles?"

"From the cottage!"

"Ermmmm, makes sense," he said, sitting back to get comfortable, and admonishing himself for asking something that was so obvious.

Ursula began her story as her new friends sat around her in the cave she called home. In the distance they could hear the bears in the woods with sounds of trampling of undergrowth, and the odd grunts from the parents and then a sudden higher pitched growl from the youngster as the trio explored deeper into the forest.

Petra and Rosie were no longer afraid of the noises the bears made, to be inside Ursula's home territory was quite an experience for them both. Ursula had arranged plenty of soft cushions on a low rocky couch, and even had some flowers in a vase on a rock shelf. There was even a large wooden chest that contained an arrangement of supplies, mainly food that she had gathered from all over the island.

"This is all very cosy, young lady," remarked Brown Bear. "Top of the class for initiative!"

Ursula looked pleased with his remarks.

"Now, I will tell you all I know. The landslide brought so much earth and rubble into some of these caves that my mother was trapped underground."

"Your mother must have been very scared," Brown Bear was deeply concerned.

"I am sure she was, but she was a very practical person, she didn't waste time being sad. She just carried on and was marvellous the way she taught me so much even when I was just toddling around."

"So, Ursula," said Petra. "You can remember as far back as that!"

"Yes, I can, as there wasn't much else to distract me. I only knew my mother and the bears, Kent and Moonlight. I remember lots of instances but as I was so young, it was hard remembering a timeline."

"You are doing just fine, carry on."

"Thank you, Mr Bear, you are so kind. No wonder the girls love you! Well, I had better start from the beginning."

"Yes, that is a good idea," Brown Bear was now relaxed amongst the cushions.

Ursula began to explain how she had survived alone on the island.

"It was in the middle of the 1990's, when an earthquake struck the island. It was only a small quake, quite low on the Richter scale. My mother told me that one day when we discussed planetary disturbances. I was older then of course!"

"Your mum must have been very clever," remarked Rosie.

"Yes, she was," replied Ursula. "She worked for many years as an archaeologist. And then after the dust settled, they couldn't resist coming over to the island to do some work of their own. But they both had many commitments, and it wasn't until the late summer of 1999, that they had some spare time to come and work here on the island."

"Who were they?" asked Petra.

"I don't know," replied Ursula.

"So, what happened?" asked Rosie.

"Whoever was with my mother received an urgent message. All she told me was that it was urgent, something about a robbery and he had to go to the mainland but promised to return to the island the minute everything had been sorted with the police."

"So, he was a he!" queried Rosie.

"Ah yes, I did say he, well it must have been then." Ursula sat with her eyes closed trying to remember.

"I can't recall what my mother told me when I was younger," said Ursula, deep in thought. "I became aware of everything when I was six. I know I was six because my mother told me that it was my birthday, and she said we would go for a walk in the afternoon to the far side of the lake, and we could pick late raspberries and blackberries and make a dessert for tea, to celebrate my birthday."

"That was nice," Rosie smiled.

"So, what happened next?" Petra asked, intrigued with Ursula's story.

"My mother told me of her being left alone on the island, and that was when she discovered the bear caves. She had always felt the ancient European wild bears had a cave somewhere on the island. There is a big one in Kent, the county in the south of England. That is why she called the big male bear Kent."

"Oh! I see," Brown Bear gave a nod.

She told me that she had discovered a map written on very old cloth that marked a certain cave and immediately she followed the details and eventually found the caves deep underground and some going down under the sea."

'That must have been the piece of cloth we found in that personal letter,' thought Rosie, not quite sure where all this was going.

"Was there another earthquake?" Petra asked. She also was thinking about the piece of cloth.

"No, only the one a few years previous, but that had all settled, or my mother would not have come to the island to work. Shall I carry on?"

"Yes, please don't stop Ursula." Rosie was captivated by this strange girl's account. "Do you know what your mother did next?"

Ursula shut her eyes and screwed up her face trying to remember every detail. "My mother said she stayed in the cottage that first night she was alone, and the next day packed up some food, found her torch and set off in search of the bear caves marked on her map."

Eventually Ursula opened her eyes, "And then it happened, I think my mother was so brave!"

"What happened?" asked Rosie, holding her breath.

"A landslide! She told me she felt the intense tremors and ran back to the cave where she had entered this system of caverns, but she was too late, the landslide had caused rocks and rubble to fall into the caves and the entrance, or rather her way out was blocked."

"Oh! no!" All three of her new friends gasped in horror.

"So, Ursula, your mother was trapped and there was no other

way out?"

"That's right. She knew of no way to escape," the girl sighed. "And my mother, to her dismay, realised she was pregnant, expecting a baby with no help, and the knowledge that no one would miss her, immediately or ever at all."

"Now, that would be a terrible predicament to be in, wouldn't it?" Petra looked straight into Ursula's eyes. "And that baby was you!"

"Yes, Petra it was me!" replied the girl.

Brown Bear gave a grunt. Rosie thought she knew why. 'He was not used to talk of babies, or more teenage girls for that matter.'

"Do you know how your mother coped with her pregnancy, and of course the loneliness?" Rosie asked, most concerned.

"Yes! She told me everything as soon as I was old enough to understand. The night I was born the female bear Moonlight, helped my mother, and brought her fruit and nuts to eat and apparently cared for me, while my mother slept."

"This is an amazing story, my dear!" announced Brown Bear. "Did your mother try to escape?"

"No! She was completely trapped down here; she could only go out to the lake. She taught me to swim before I could walk. She was so brave and never once complained."

"My mother would tell me lots of stories as I grew, my favourite was how she met and fell in love with my father," Ursula's eyes twinkled in the moonlight.

"Oh! Who was your father?" Brown Bear asked the young girl. "Did you find out who he was?"

"No! I didn't," replied Ursula. "My mother often talked about him, but by the time I was six she had begun to lose all hope of him ever coming to find her." She gave a deep sigh.

"Oh!" Rosie took Ursula's hand. "Why do you think she gave up?"

"Because in the first few weeks she told me she could hear

dogs barking, and helicopters circling high above searching the island, but one day all fell quiet, they had given up. My mother had almost been buried under the rubble. But thankfully she was saved from the impact of the landslide itself."

"But could never leave the island again." Brown Bear's voice was deep and troubled.

"No! She never did!"

"So, what happened then?" asked Petra.

Ursula was pleased to have an audience. She felt it wonderful to have human company and it was comforting to reminisce about her mother.

"It is so good to be able to talk to you all," she said as she wiped a tear from her eye. "I do, miss my mother."

"Of course, you do, my dear," Brown Bear was very sympathetic. "Carry on, my dear, we are all very interested in what you are telling us."

Ursula nodded and continued.

"The landslide happened on the day she explored the bear caves, she had gone deep into them and when she returned to this place, she found loads of debris had been distributed and was blocking her way. She cleared most of the rubble that had fallen in the first cave, where the hole is now, but she could never pass through it. The gap was too small for her and in the end, as she grew bigger with me growing inside her, she gave in to her predicament and told herself she didn't mind being trapped. She submitted to her new life and devoted herself to me. She would swim in the lake and the two bears became her friends. There was plenty to eat and drink and the forest was accessible in parts. Anyway, the bears looked after her!"

"Absolutely amazing," Brown Bear stretched his legs. "Do carry on, my dear."

"You see, there was no way to get back to the main part of the island. Eventually with the aid of some pointed rocks used as a chisel, she worked away at the fallen stones that blocked her way, then eventually one day she broke through and she was so happy."

"You had an amazing mother," said Rosie, engrossed in Ursula's account of events.

"Let me tell you everything and then you can ask questions afterwards if you are not clear about anything in particular."

"Okay!"

The three companions sat still and quiet waiting for Ursula to explain the strange existence she had been forced to endure.

"Your mother was so brave!" Petra exclaimed, thinking how she would feel if something like that happened to herself and Rosie.

"Yes, she was incredible. I only have vague memories of my first few years, so I will tell you what happened through my mother's experiences," Ursula's voice was soft and clear. A breeze gently swept through the cave and the flames on the candles flickered. Rosie and Petra shivered in the half-light.

"My mother was very loving towards me and we were happy. We could only go as far as that first cave, it was the cave we came through," continued Ursula. "Do you remember we had to climb through a gap in the rubble?"

"Yes, indeed we do!" answered Brown Bear for all of them. "Do continue, my dear."

"I have very vague memories of crawling around on the rocks, swimming in the lake with my mother and the two bears, swimming with us, but that is all really." Ursula's voice trailed off as if she was trying to remember more. "But one day my mother called me to her side and announced that I was now five years old, and it was time she told me exactly what had happened to us."

"Oh!" Rosie gasped, holding onto Brown Bear's big paw for comfort.

"That was the day my mother told me about her own life, growing up on a farm in the remotest part of Wales. As a young girl she was fascinated with all the animals and when some of them died she would help her father bury the poor creatures in an unused area of their hillside farm. Later she told me she would dig them up after a few years to see how they had decayed."

"Uck!" exclaimed Petra.

"Oooo!" Rosie gasped.

"Burying dead animals on the farm wouldn't be allowed nowadays," Brown Bear sat up straight and informed them. "Must be registered and collected,"

"Yes, yes, BB, we know you never break any rules!" Petra gave him a frustrated look. "Let Ursula finish her story."

Ursula looked at them all. "I'm sorry but you did want all the details?"

"Yes, of course we do." Petra and Rosie answered in unison.

"Then my mother told me that one day her own father suddenly surprised her by saying, 'Come on, girl, go and apply to a university, you've always been the clever one in the family. You passed all your A levels last year and I realise now how selfish I have been expecting you to work on the farm with your three brothers. You are good enough for Bangor or Aberystwyth universities, I'm sure of it! Then you can study prehistoric bones till they come out of your ears.'"

"Ouch, that sounds painful!" exclaimed Rosie.

"Just a figure of speech!" Brown Bear pointed out. "So, what did she do?"

"She had already passed many exams in school," replied Ursula. "So, with her father's blessing she applied to the university in Poole, Dorset so she could obtain a degree in archaeology, first."

"First?" Petra questioned.

"Yes," replied Ursula. "She needed a degree in archaeology before she could go on to study for her Masters."

"What would she have needed a Master's for?" Rosie asked, all three were mesmerised with their new friend's account of her early life.

"I think it was to obtain more qualifications in certain prehistoric studies. Remember I was very young when she told me about her own life. It was hearing my mother's story that I was beginning to realise that we were both confined to the island forever."

"So what happened?" Brown Bear leaned forward.

"Well, she completed her course at the college on the south coast. She passed everything. She was so clever. In fact, she taught me to read some of her old books when I was three."

"Incredible!" exclaimed Brown bear.

"So, we were completely trapped in the caves and could not get back onto the island, but when I was a bit bigger, she would lift me up and I could see out of the hole she kept chiselling away at, and I was beginning to understand what she was doing."

"So, how long have you lived here alone?" interrupted Brown Bear.

"I don't really know. One day my mother managed to get out through the opening, but she told me to stay and wait for her," said Ursula. "I hope you don't mind but I'll tell you more about that later."

Petra could see Ursula's eyes were filled with tears.

"That's fine, you are extremely brave to tell us your story. So, how did she find the bears in the first instant?"

Ursula wiped away her tears with another tissue Brown Bear had gallantly handed their hostess.

"Thank you, BB. Well, she told me it was the map that brought her to these caves. She had found animal bones on the island, but her passion was to find ancient bones from the Palaeolithic era."

"Do you know what happened to the map?" Petra asked, deeply interested in all Ursula had to tell them.

"No, I don't. I did look for it in the cottage, but it wasn't there. I was seven when I first found the cottage, I had been alone for over a year by then, I did miss my mother very much. She was like a walking encyclopaedia, especially with her knowledge of zoology and archaeology. She was happiest when she was teaching me."

"You were so lucky to have her, but was she able to give birth alone?" Petra asked gingerly. "She must have been terrified."

"Yes, she was, to start with, remember I've already told you a little of that night. She told me all of it, she said when she knew her time had come, suddenly the big female bear Moonlight arrived in the cave, and helped her," said Ursula. "The bears have been entwined in our lives ever since I was a new-born baby."

"Yes, I know you already told us, but it's still amazing!" exclaimed Petra.

"Yes, incredible!" sighed Rosie. "I didn't know where babies came from until I was eleven. You have known since you were six!"

"Yes, quite astounding!" exclaimed Brown Bear. "Wild bears have lived alongside man for thousands of years, and usually very compatibly." He loved to impart historical facts to the girls. "I hate to ask this, Ursula, but when did your beloved mother die?"

"I don't know how or why. I just know she was murdered. Eventually she had chiselled away at the wall of rubble and suddenly one day a whole lot of rocks fell away and the hole it left was big enough for her to pass through." Ursula stopped for breath. "And she said one day there would be a boat she could wave to and possibly get us help." Ursula paused again. "She would go out for a little while most days. I do remember her saying if she had a buggy, she would take me. Of course, I didn't know what she meant. I still don't, actually. Then one day she did not return. And I knew she was gone."

"That's so tragic," said Petra. "How long have you been alone?"

"Well, I have never really been alone, the bears have stayed with me and then a few years ago, they had their own baby bear and we have been like a family living down here ever since."

"But what happened to your mother?" Petra asked.

"She was murdered!"

"How do you know that?" Rosie was following Ursula's account closely.

"Because she told me," said Ursula.

"How could she tell you that if she is dead?" remarked Petra.

"Because her spirit is here with me always," said Ursula.

"It is!" Rosie stated profoundly.

"How do you know, Rosie?" Petra asked, disbelievingly.

"Remember when you thought I had got lost in the cave, when I had gone to help the baby rabbit?" Rosie was the most serious she ever had been. "Well, I found a shrine! I think it is a shrine." She looked at Ursula and raised her eyebrows.

"Yes, you are right, Rosie!" the young girl proclaimed. "I built it in memory of my mother, so she will always be near me."

Brown Bear was getting worried, finding himself out of his depth.

"Well, she definitely is here!" exclaimed Rosie. "When I was lost, she kept me safe while the intruders were searching the caves and arguing. She held my hand and guided me to safety."

"Yes, her presence has always been here since the day she died," Ursula had tears in her eyes, welling up about to brim over.

Brown Bear reached into his jacket pocket, "Here you are." He passed her a tissue. "I always carry them with me in case the girls might need one."

"Thank you, Mr Bear," Ursula wiped her eyes gently. "It feels strange crying, I thought I had taught myself not to cry. It all seemed futile."

"Well, it is not futile now!" said Brown Bear. "You have us three to care about you now. Isn't that right, girls?"

Petra and Rosie nodded and both girls gave their new friend a hug. Ursula hugged them back in one of the longest hugs they had ever had.

"Let us sit by the lake and I will tell you everything that has happened since that fateful day I lost my mother."

"Is she really dead?" Petra found all that Ursula was telling them hard to believe.

"I have never found her body but yes, she is dead! And she haunts this island. You know that to be true, don't you, Rosie?"

"Yes," replied Rosie. "That is true. She held my hand. She is very gentle, but she frightened the intruders. She put a dreaded fear in them, and they ran away as fast as they could."

"Good! I am glad because they caused her death," Ursula stopped at the edge of the lake. "Look, it is like daylight, the moon is still high above." The young girl sat on a ledge of rock and the others gathered round her.

"Now, I will tell you exactly what happened!"

Brown Bear interrupted. "Ursula, my dear, you do realise it has passed four o' clock in the morning?"

"Ooo, that's late," said Rosie. "Sorry, I can't stop yawning."

"No, it's very early," Petra yawned too.

"Never mind," said Ursula. "I will continue later."

Something very frightening happened the next day and it was quite a while before Ursula could continue her story.

27
THE RIVAL

The cool grey walls of her new flat did nothing to subdue the intense anger that Joanna Newsome felt on a sunny afternoon in June 1990. She had just read an article in the 'Just Married' column of the national newspaper she had picked up on her way in from the local newsagent a few doors down. She was in the process of moving to the market town of Petersfield, where she had recently chosen to live out her spinsterhood. She threw the paper onto the pile of removal crates, her face red with anger.

"How could he! How could he!" she exploded. "After all I gave up for him! Even spending some of my grant on accompanying him to China. I hate him and the woman he dumped me for! I'll never forgive him or her! I hate them! I really hate them!" Her face was flushed, and tears stung her eyes, as they overflowed and trickled down her cheeks. This was the day Joanna swore to take revenge on Lawrence Mortimer, and the rest of her life had been spent planning that revenge in detail. Joanna's only problem was that life over the years had got in the way.

As she stood in that newly painted room, she reflected on her life so far. She did however feel pleased that she had broken away from the county that had given her most grief. She reflected that her only reason for staying in Dorset back in the spring of 1988, after he had made excuses for them to part, was to stay near the man she loved. The previous year she had even managed to get on the same archaeology course as Lawrence Mortimer. She had stuck it out until the Christmas term ended. During those months she had been constantly reprimanded by her tutors, one in fact, Jeff Lacy had accused her of being 'star struck'.

"I have no idea what you mean, Sir." She had replied, but of course she had.

Joanna had scraped through her school examinations to gain her place at the same university as the young man she had met whilst exploring an ancient medieval castle, on the Welsh borders.

It had been on a beautiful day in July 1986. She clearly remembered the green lawns of the site had been newly mown that day, leaving the smell of the sweet cut grass lingering in the air.

Standing at the window of her new living room she smiled, as she remembered the first day, she had set eyes on him. She closed her eyes now, and there he was tall handsome with dark brown hair and piercing blue eyes. She had wanted him from the moment she saw him. The two of them seemed to be the only visitors to the magnificent castle on that glorious summer's day.

In front of her in her mind's eye was a stone archway and her intention was to pass through it. She took a step forward, but this young man was trying to pass through from the courtyard on the other side.

"After you," he had said politely.

"No, after you," she had replied, noticing his blue eyes twinkling like jewels on that far off day.

Joanna smiled to herself remembering, they had both taken a step forward and ended up in each other's arms. After many apologies he had invited her for coffee in a nearby tea shop and later that week he had taken her out to dinner.

And that is how Joanna Newsome first met Lawrence Mortimer, and it hadn't taken very long for her to fall in love with him. But it was not a healthy kind of love, more an obsession. She was jealous of everyone he spoke to and by the end of the year Lawrence began, not surprisingly, to tire of her.

Now four years later, her new flat was supposed to be a fresh start, but as she looked around the open plan layout and saw many boxes waiting to be unpacked, her seething jealousy and hate still simmered dangerously within her.

"That Lewis woman can't possibly love him as much as I do! How dare he dump me for her!" She had questioned herself day after day throughout the years. "And for him to marry her is more than I can bear!"

Then she heard a car engine stop outside, bringing the present day back to her troubled mind. Part of her wanted to stay in the past, but a loud knock came at her front door and brought her back to reality.

"Come in, Fred, it's open. I'm glad to see you received my message! Why don't you ever answer your telephone?"

Frederick Newsome was her long-suffering brother. He had witnessed many a tantrum when his younger sister had lost the plot. Their parents had been on holiday in Switzerland and had unfortunately been killed in a freak cable car accident when both siblings were only fifteen and sixteen respectively. Life changed for them both suddenly, and Frederick always felt that Jo had blamed everyone she met for the tragedy. So often had he been the mediator in many an argument.

"What's the hurry, Jo?" asked her brother. "Why couldn't your news have waited until tomorrow? I said I would come and help you unpack."

"No! It couldn't wait! Just look at this." Joanna handed him the Times newspaper.

Frederick took hold of the paper and began to read the article Joanna was pointing to.

"Oh! Dear Jo, I am so sorry," his voice was troubled, as he read the announcement. Her brother reached out for his sister's hand and gave it a light fleeting touch. "Why was the wedding in Oxford?"

"Larry apparently moved there to take his Masters. I feel sick!

He's mine! Not hers." Joanna was furious. Tears began to smart her eyes, "What am I going to do, Fred?"

"You will just have to be strong and pretend you don't care," Frederick passed his sister a folded handkerchief.

"I know. I will. But I do care," Joanna wiped her tears. "I will get my revenge! You see if I don't."

"That's a big burden to carry around with you, Jo." Frederick knew how vindictive his sister could be. "Well, who is this girl Larry has married? How did he get to know her?"

Joanna gave her brother an ominous glare, "I was so stupid relinquishing my place at university. I got bored of archaeology and went to work in an estate agent's office, as you know!"

"Yes, but you told me you stayed in the same town to be near him!" Her brother was finding his sister inconsolable.

"Yes, I did! but I couldn't be with him all the time. Anyway, it is all my fault. I should have stayed at university and not given Larry a chance to meet Emily Jane Lewis," Joanna paced the room up and down.

"What does it say about them in the newspaper? Let me see now," Frederick started to read out loud.

"The marriage of Lawrence Butler Mortimer of Ripley, Surrey and Emily Jane Lewis of Aberystwyth Wales, was conducted in a ceremony at St Mary's Church, Oxford, on Saturday June 6th, 1990, where they were pronounced husband and wife, by the Reverend Hubert St -Clair, of the parish." He looked up at his sister.

"It all sounds rather grand, don't you think?" remarked Frederick Newsome.

"It doesn't matter what I think, does it? I was his first love. It should be me there in that paper and not that Welsh girl." Joanna had vengeance in her eyes. "I'm never going to get over this. Cheating on me behind my back! And....?"

"Well, Jo, if you remember correctly, it was you who cheated on him first, with Giles Cranford, your boss at the estate agents."

"You clearly think I am at fault!" Joanna yelled at her brother.

"No! I don't! You are my younger sister and I will do anything for you. You know that. I promise."

"I will hold you to that! Anything did you say, Fred?"

"Yes, now, or in the future. I will be there for you."

So, it was on that day that the siblings made their fateful pact. And severe consequences would be felt in the years to come.

Over the years Joanna tried to forget Larry. But time passed by slowly for her, she could not forget Lawrence Mortimer. As years progressed, his position in Oxford became quite prominent and through the years Joanna would find snippets of his life and career at the university in the newspapers,

Apparently, he had met his future wife whilst on a visit to Egypt and the two had been inseparable ever since. And the latest news was the couple had bought a home in a sleepy Welsh village near the coast.

Joanna sat upright in her chair and moved the paper nearer to the light coming from the window, she gave a great sigh, she didn't want to miss a detail. She carried on reading, most intrigued, as to what was happening in the life of her only love.

Another day she read in an article dated September 10th 1996, a minor earthquake had rocked an island in Swallow's Bay. This was not very far from the mainland village where Professor Lawrence B Mortimer and his wife had secured a base in Wales, by purchasing 'Old Mill Cottage' in Swallows Village.

Then years later in the summer of 1999 she found another article as she was browsing through her evening newspaper.

> Doctor Lawrence Mortimer and his wife, the eminent bio-archaeologist, Doctor Emily Jane Mortimer were both spending a summer break on Swallows Island,

studying and excavating the ruined castle that rose from the island's centre. His interest in ancient buildings and Mrs Mortimer's great interest in ancient zoology allowed them to combine both their careers.'

Reading that article in the evening paper, dated the 2nd August 1999, made Joanna feel totally sick with jealousy, and tears drenched her face.

For a while, she gave up searching for anything to do with Professor Mortimer but one evening a headline caught her eye and she could not resist reading the frontpage story.

THE WIFE OF PROFESSOR LAWRENCE MORTIMER IS MISSING.

The account was accompanied by a photograph of Emily Jane Mortimer which Joanna ignored. The snapshot showed Emily Jane at her most beautiful, with shoulder-length, black hair and deep blue eyes. There was no way Joanna could compare with her and she knew it. She dismissed the photo and began reading the account of the tragedy.

> Renowned Oxford Professor, Lawrence. B. Mortimer's wife went missing yesterday on Swallows Island, a small island, rich in history, off the Welsh coast. Doctor Emily Jane Mortimer disappeared on the island and Lawrence Mortimer was distraught at the loss of his beloved wife.
> Apparently, seismologists agree a sudden landslide occurred, probably caused by the instability of the island since the minor earthquake on the island three years ago. Professor Mortimer is devastated. Even after a thorough canine search of the castle and dungeons and even coastal

caves, there was no sign of his wife. Then came a systematic search of the island by police helicopters, including the beaches and coves. But unfortunately, there was no sign of Emily Jane.

The saddest thing for Joanna was she read the same article year after year. She received a certain amount of pleasure from knowing that Larry was alone and that Emily Jane her rival was lost to him, and he could no longer be wrapped up in his wife's company. Every year in August Joanna would reach up to find a box she kept on top of her wardrobe. She would bring it down, sit on her bed and mull over its contents.

She had kept everything that reminded her of the relationship she has enjoyed with Larry, the man she still loved. She had kept everything that reminded her of Lawrence Butler from the Castle ticket on the day she had first met him, to souvenirs of their visit to China and unbeknown to the professor she even had locks of his hair, stolen while he slept. So, every year since the day of their breakup she would stew over her lost youth that was forever entrapped in her troubled and sick mind.

Twenty years later, in August 2021, when she had finished her annual reading of the article, she reached for her phone to call her brother.

"Fred, I need to see you. How about tomorrow?"

"What's the matter, Jo? I haven't heard from you for weeks. What have you been up to?"

"I want you to make arrangements to take me to Wales," Joanna almost spat out her words.

"Wales! What on earth for?" Frederick had not heard from his sister for a while. He had been meaning to ring her. But she was always in a black mood since her breakup from Larry. And sometimes he felt leaving her alone was a good thing to do from time to time, for his own sanity at least. How he wished he could turn the clock back to happier times.

"Look, I can't talk now but I'll ring you this evening."

"OK! Make sure you do!" Joanna tossed her phone onto her bed and looked through her window onto the street below.

'Why did I leave that course?' she asked herself, and the answer inside her head was loud and clear. 'Because you weren't good enough!'

Later her brother did call and that was the night when a plan was concocted between the siblings, a very dangerous plan with many significant consequences that would eventually involve the children and the island.

28
KIDNAP

The light from the moon was fading fast as it began to descend on its illusionary journey into the sea below the western horizon. The eastern horizon was now aglow with iridescent marshmallow clouds floating in pink and gold ribbons, heralding the sun.

"Look!" exclaimed Rosie. "The dawn is breaking and we haven't been to bed yet."

Petra yawned and stretched her arms above her head.

"I am really tired," Ursula yawned too. "I hadn't realised how late it was. I will show you where we can sleep. I will tell you more tomorrow."

"This yawning is catching," agreed Brown Bear.

"Look everyone, we can rest here," Ursula led them to some soft green grass. "It is quite springy and cosy and dry."

"Yes, this is nice," said Petra. "So near to your home cave too."

Within minutes they were all fast asleep. The island was still and quiet as the sun rose in the sky. It was well past midday when they awoke.

"What's that noise?" mumbled Rosie, waking suddenly and rubbing sleep from her eyes.

Brown Bear woke up too, "It sounds like the engine of a motorboat." He stood up, "I'll just climb up these rocks and see what is going on."

"No! BB, please don't, you are far too big to go up there. Anyway, you will be seen by the intruders if they are around."

"Yes, you are right Petra. You go!" exclaimed Brown Bear,

stepping aside for Petra to climb the pinnacle of rock.

When she reached the top, she had a good view over the sea. The lagoon lay to her left sparkling in the afternoon sun. She could also see the far headland and the beach where the intruders had left their rowing boat. To Petra's dismay she could see a large motorboat docking at the jetty they had all used on the first day they had arrived on the island.

To her horror she could see at least two men trying to land a large metal cage. They struggled to hoist it on to the jetty, but the tide was high, and waves were rocking their boat making such a task impossible,

Petra watched intently, as the strong breeze and the unrelenting tide were deterring the men from landing the cage. She sighed with relief.

"What can you see, Petra?" Rosie cried out over the roar of the wind. Brown Bear put his arm around Rosie.

"Shush, little one, wait until Petra comes down. No doubt she will give us an accurate report."

All three stood in silence waiting for Petra to return.

The motorboat engine had stopped, and Ursula gasped and uttered something that Rosie and Brown Bear could not hear.

"What's the matter?" Brown Bear thought Ursula looked very agitated,

"I can hear the bears, I must go," she yelled and was gone.

Brown Bear and Rosie just stared at each other, not at all sure what was happening.

At that moment Petra descended the high rock and stood beside them.

"Where's Ursula? I need to know something important," Petra was in quite a distressed state. "Where is she?"

"She rushed off," said Rosie.

"Where to?" Petra questioned.

"She just said she could hear the bears and rushed away,"

Brown Bear answered but now he felt uneasy.

"I saw men in a motorboat trying to land on the jetty," announced Petra.

"Whatever for?" Rosie held on to Brown Bear.

"I have no idea," replied Petra. "I wanted to ask Ursula if there is a beach we could get to, if we walk right through the forest?" Petra sighed seeing that Ursula was nowhere to be seen.

"Why do you need to know about another beach?" asked Rosie.

"Because the motorboat the men are in has now headed further down the coast," Petra looked extremely worried. "We must find Ursula! Come on we must go after her and warn her, those men are up to no good, I'm sure! BB, will you lead the way? You are so good at tracking."

They entered the forest and found a way between the trees. After a while it grew darker, as the sunlight could not penetrate beneath the thick canopy of foliage. Occasional waves of light danced at their feet, as the treetops moved with the wind disturbing leaves in the tallest branches. Brown Bear switched on his torch.

"Look here is a path the bears have made; we must follow it!" Brown Bear was quite confident in that moment that they would soon come across Ursula and her beloved ursine family. Petra and Rosie were close behind him, as he went deeper into the woodland. In the semi darkness of the forest was an uneasy silence that unnerved the girls.

Brown Bear intrepidly led the way deeper into the forest. The girls followed with their hearts beating fast. There was no sign of Ursula or the bears.

A breeze high in the treetops rustled the leaves and occasionally allowed the sun to filter down, casting a flimsy light on the woodland path.

"This is a long way to get to a beach, my legs are getting tired," moaned Rosie.

"Won't be long now," replied Brown bear.

The three pals carried on trying to avoid the much-tangled undergrowth, but it wasn't an easy task. Brambles and ivy had closely entwined together creating a hazardous walkway beneath their feet, though obviously no trouble to big heavy bears.

"We are on the right track. I can smell the sea!" Petra hastened her step.

"Listen!" exclaimed Rosie. "I can hear screams."

"Quick, it is Ursula, she's in trouble!" Petra reached for Rosie's hand.

"Not so fast, girls! I will go ahead and see the lay of the land," Brown Bear took charge, he sensed imminent danger. "I can smell the sea too; we are near to the shore."

"BB, I didn't get time to tell you exactly what I saw, when I climbed the high rock," Petra gasped for breath. "Everything happened so suddenly, Ursula disappeared and here we are pursuing her, I just didn't have time to tell you!" gasped Petra. "I saw men trying to land a cage on the jetty."

"What kind of cage?" Rosie asked, looking puzzled.

"You know, the kind of large cage they have on animal documentaries." Petra commented, as she did her best to keep up with Brown Bear. Suddenly he stopped in his tracks.

"A cage can be used to catch large animals. Ummm, I don't like the sound of that. I truly hope no one is after the bears. Look!" he exclaimed. "There's a bit of a raised area ahead. Let's make for it. We might be able to see the sea from there."

In a while they reached the patch of higher ground. Although trees were still dense, they could catch glimpses of a grey sea with white foam-topped waves being whipped up by the wind out in the bay.

"Wait!" said Brown Bear. "Stay under cover of the trees. I have a bad feeling about this. Stand back while I will go nearer to see exactly what is happening."

Then at that moment they heard blood curdling howls that made the hairs on the back of their necks rise.

"That's Starlight!" exclaimed Brown Bear. "I know it is! He has a ferocious growl for a youngster!" Brown Bear pulled the girls close to him. And then Ursula screamed again, a loud distressed scream, and then there was silence.

"Oh no," thought Petra.

After a while they were all on the beach with the forest behind them. They stood in the shelter of some gorse bushes, witnessing an horrendous scene. The sun was beginning to set and an eerie glow captured the scene.

"What's happening, BB? I can't see," Rosie clung on to his furry arm.

"Stay down behind these bushes," he exclaimed. "Whatever happens we must not be seen, at least until I have a plan."

"Oh! BB!" cried Petra. "Ursula is screaming desperately and look, there are strange men trying to capture Starlight! That is the cage I saw them trying to land on the jetty and because they failed, I feel sure they have sailed around the headland to get here."

"This is terrible, BB, please help her." Rosie was clinging on to Brown Bear, not really believing what she was seeing.

"Quick! BB," cried Petra. "We must do something. This is a crime!" Petra's voice was shaking. They watched quite helplessly from the edge of the forest until Petra stood up, "I am going to do something even if I only cause a distraction!"

"No! Indeed, you are not!" Brown Bear stood in her way. "I am not taking responsibility for any of us getting shot!"

"No! don't go, Sis. BB's right, they have got guns! I could see a weapon in one of the men's hands. Petra relented and went back with her companions to wait quietly.

All three stooped down behind some low bushes at the edge of the forest witnessing the scene. The high tide was pounding the boat, but nothing seemed to be deterring the villains from this outrageous act.

Brown Bear could see that as well as weapons the men were carrying coils of rope. One was holding Ursula's arms behind her back, as the other man was holding open the cage door ready to capture the little bear who was growling ferociously, trying to break free.

"We have got to stop them!" Rosie exclaimed, fighting back tears. "BB! Will you do something to save the baby? He is terrified! Oh! Look! Ursula is trying to kick the person who is holding her. BB, this is a nightmare! Please help them. Please, please do something." The little girl broke down in tears.

Brown Bear was about to jump into action when Petra pulled him back.

"No! don't!" she exclaimed, "Look that motorboat is just offshore now. They must have steered around the headland from our cove near the cottage. So, it is possible to find a way to the forest along the coast instead of the underground way, Ursula showed us."

"Don't worry!" Brown Bear pointed. "It is too shallow to land a vessel that size on this beach. I can see the boat clearly. And guess who is on board?"

"I can't guess!" replied Rosie, still with tears in her eyes.

"Is it the intruders?" Petra asked. "Remember the man and the woman, who's boat I hid in, and Ursula, scuppered. How have they acquired a motorboat? Unless they had another phone and called someone, a device Ursula missed when she hid, or took their phones. I'm not exactly sure what she did. I think what she thought was to remove their only means of communication."

"Yes! That could be it! But I don't know what we can do to help without getting hurt ourselves. Those men look vicious." Brown Bear scratched his head in thought. He really had a problem now.

"Look!" yelled Petra. "The boat is attempting to land. Surely they realise it will run aground if they come ashore here."

"BB! Can we intervene and somehow rescue Ursula?" yelled Rosie. She was not frightened of being heard, as the noise from the commotion on the beach was even louder than the sea.

"No! those men will overpower us all with their guns." Brown Bear's words terrified the girls.

"But!" Rosie stood up. "We can't let them take the little bear, and if they do, they will have to take Ursula as well. By the look of things, she is really putting up a fight."

"Listen girls! I have a plan, but you must promise me you will stay on this beach and remain well hidden."

"Alright we will, but whatever you are going to do, be very careful." Petra squeezed his paw and Rosie gave him a hug.

"What are you going to do?" she asked her dear friend.

"Better you girls don't know." And with that remark Brown Bear disappeared back into the forest.

29
THE CAGE

Ursula's screams filled the evening air as attempts were made to capture the young bear. Petra and Rosie gasped in horror as they watched from the cover of the trees. The perpetrators had steered the motorboat around the headland and abandoned their previous plan to land on the jetty and use the facilities of the cottage.

Joanna Newsome had visited the island from time to time, over the years, unbeknown to her brother. Then years later she started to make plans to return to the island as her conscience was getting the better of her, annoyingly reminding her of loose ends she had not tidied up on her fateful visit in 2006.

She returned two years later with Rick and Marcus who had become excited about the fact she knew of a deserted island and wanted to see if the terrain was suitable for drug smuggling and whatever lucrative business they could muster up there. They were in league with a local boat owner who was making a fortune with his undercover businesses.

Joanna had agreed to show them the island and it was in the summer of 2008 that the three of them landed on Swallows Island. It was Marcus who saw the girl first. It was almost dusk when he grabbed hold of Joanna's arm.

"Look!" he pointed to a shadowy figure down on the beach. Joanna and Rick could see a very young girl in a white flimsy dress. "Quick! Let's hide in this cave. It's a ghost.'"

The following evening when she was back in her cool grey walled sitting room Joanna sat deep in thought.

She decided to let Marcus and Rick think what they liked and encouraged them to believe the island was haunted by a young girl. It suited her plan to have control over this gang she was forming. Joanna realised that the girl in the flimsy white dress who looked about eight years old was the daughter of Emily Jane. There was no doubt the ghostly figure was endowed with beautiful long black hair just like her mother's.

Joanna shuddered as she remembered her love rival's pleas, "No don't kill me, please. I have a young daughter."

There was a chill wind blowing in the bay and, to the girls' horror, they could see the motorboat following the action a few metres offshore.

"Where's Ursula?" yelled Rosie, "I can't see her now, I hope the men haven't captured her!"

"She's alright but look she won't let go of Starlight. One man is trying to put a rope around the cub, and Ursula is lashing out at them," Petra's voice was shaking as she stood with her sister watching all the happenings. "Oh! Where is BB? We need him here!"

"He's been hours, I'm sure," said Rosie. holding back tears.

"We'd better go and find him." Petra was about to go back into the woods to find BB, when Rosie grabbed her arm so tightly it really hurt her,

"Ouch, Rosie, don't…" Petra's words trailed off as there was a lot of commotion down on the shore.

"Three more people are in the motorboat; I can just about see them as it is getting dark!" exclaimed Rosie, "Look, the two intruders are with those men!"

"This is real trouble now Rosie. It looks like they are trying to beach the vessel here on the sand. They are stupid because the tide is turning," replied Petra. "I wish BB would hurry up. Where do you think he has gone?"

"I wish I knew. I am really worried about him."

"Me too!"

Petra and Rosie stood helpless, as they watched the melee from their hiding place. One of the men on the beach was struggling to overcome the angry, frightened bear, but it was strong and was fighting back. The man in the boat called to the man on the shore, something that petrified the girls.

"Hey! Marcus, use your gun!"

The girls clung to each other trembling with fear.

"No way, Rick!" replied Marcus. "We were told to look after our prize! No money for damaged goods, that's what the boss said. Remember, Rick, this is no ordinary bear. Jo said it's prehistoric!"

"What do you mean prehistoric?" yelled Rick, the man who was steering the boat. He watched as Marcus struggled with the weight of the young animal.

"Come on Marcus," yelled Rick loudly. "Quick! push that bear into the cage, just pull the rope you tied round it. Come on, what are you made of, man? It can't be that heavy."

"You just come and try it yourself, Rick." Marcus replied as he was struggling with the captive.

"Hey! watch the girl." Rick shouted from the boat.

"What do you mean? I can't watch her and deal with this archaic monster at the same time?" shouted Marcus.

"I said prehistoric, not archaic you idiot!" Rick was having difficulties with the boat at this stage.

"Oh! Where's the boss?" shouted Marcus. "I thought she'd want to see all this."

"Oh! No! Damn it! the girl has got inside the cage now!" exclaimed Rick, as the boat almost grinded to a halt.

Joanna Newsome appeared on the deck.

"Well, that's a bonus, Jo here looks very pleased," said Rick. "Ma'am I can't go any nearer the shore, the tides going out!"

Marcus was struggling with the cage, as waves were washing round it on the sand.

"Throw us a rope, Rick? You'll have to use the boat to pull the cage," yelled Marcus

"What do you want the girl for anyway?"

"Revenge!" came the reply but Petra nor Rosie could hear who spoke that word.

Moments later the two passengers, Joanna Newsome and her brother Frederick, scrambled out of the boat and waded through the shallow waves, looking very dissatisfied with the ruffians they were employing to carry out this wicked deed.

"Come on, here's another rope! Tie it to the cage and we'll all pull at once. When it's afloat we can all get it on board." Frederick spoke with little enthusiasm in his voice.

Alas Marcus and Fred were making a bit of a mess with the rope. Nothing was working to plan. as the tide was taking the boat further offshore.

"Why can't you two do anything right?" shouted Joanna. "Time is running out! It will be too late to catch the high tide on the mainland. Bumbling lunatics! Both of you!"

Rosie recognized their voices. "It's the people I heard arguing in the caves when I found the shrine! the woman we thought was a cleaner and the man who drove the black BMW."

"Yes, I think you are right, stay hidden!" said Petra. "Where is BB? Why is he taking so long?"

"I just can't imagine," Rosie replied, trying hard to see what was happening. "He's been gone for hours. I want to go and kick and scream and help Ursula, but we must stay here, mustn't we, Sis?"

"Yes! We must, I want to go too," replied Petra. "But those people will overpower us and probably take us with them wherever they are going. And then BB will return and he won't know where we are."

"Yes! We must stay. BB will know what to do." Rosie agreed with her sister in a positive voice. Deep down she was worried. She thought to herself that as children they had been in some tight spots on this island, but nothing as serious as this. Marcus just stood there, and Rick remained on the motorboat, who was no help at all.

It seemed ages to the girls just waiting there for BB to return. The sun had long gone from the sky and night had taken hold of the scene. A cold wind blew from the east and the tide had turned, leaving the villains floundering in the shallows. There was a strange mist rolling in from the sea and the girls shivered. Someone on the boat lit a lamp with a wide beam as the girls watched the upsetting scene.

"I do wish BB would come back," sighed Rosie. "What time is it? Let's look at the time on our phone. I have an idea! Have you got yours safe?"

"Yes! Of course, I have, and a lot of charge left in it too, because we only made one call to Mum, and she used her own phone to call us back. Why do you want it?" Petra fumbled in her rucksack and brought out her phone. "We must be careful with the torch; the light is so bright! What are you thinking, Rosie?"

"Well," replied her sister. "We could see if there is anything in the old mahogany chest about the Professor's past, something that might give us a clue as to who these people are. BB made all the contents of the chests into files on your phone."

"Yes, he did! Good idea, Rosie!" Petra handed her phone to Rosie. "Remember the intruders have the letter to Professor Mortimer from his wife." She said while keeping her eye on the happenings on the shore.

"Yes! I didn't think of that before, but these people must have broken into his chest at some time, otherwise how did they get the personal letter?" Rosie sighed, as she searched for the files BB had copied on that calm sunny afternoon back at the cottage, as part of their study session.

"Yes! You said you took a photograph of it in the cave, I wonder what she was going to tell her husband? Ahh, but we do know now, don't we? She was never able to tell her husband that she was expecting their baby," Rosie cupped her hands to shield the light. "Oh, good! BB copied many of the professor's documents for us. Do you remember?"

"Yes, I do," replied Petra. "But look what is happening. Quick, Rosie, our detection will have to wait!"

Down on the beach the two girls could see what was happening where the waves met the dry sand. Petra recognised the two people who had intruded on their island, days ago. She felt sure it was the man and the woman who were camping in a cave. She was certain that it was the same couple who had arrived and alighted a trawler out in the bay and rowed to the island late at night.

Petra breathed in deeply remembering what BB had told them about the smell of the extinguished bonfire they had lit that night. The two must have found driftwood and lit a fire on the beach and hurriedly extinguished the flames when they were bombarded with the sound of horrendous eerie growls that frightened them. The same people who were in possession of a briefcase in which she found the original letter, to the Professor from his wife. Petra had no doubt that these visitors were the same two people who they all knew had found a way into 'Old Mill Cottage,' in Swallows Village, and were the same people who had ransacked the professor's belongings, days after he had moved into his new home, in the quiet village. And just days after the girls had found him injured, lying on his kitchen floor.' Petra remembered it all.

"Oh! Look!" cried Rosie. "They have locked the cage and have Ursula and the little bear captured inside and now they are dragging it into the water," Rosie was sounding hysterical. "All four are trying to get the cage on board the boat."

"I don't think they can, the tide is going out, the water will get too low for the motorboat to come any further in shore," Petra took her sister's hand. "Come on, we must try and delay them.

Oh! Listen to Ursula's screams! She sounds terrified!"

"Petra, Petra, look something is happening?" Rosie's voice was now touching the edge of hysteria. "They have dropped the cage in the water and Ursula is getting wet, we have to help her somehow?"

"Don't worry the little bear has lifted her up, out of the waves!" replied her sister.

At that moment Petra felt everything was getting out of control.

"I'm worried about BB, why is he taking so long? We don't even know what his plan was."

Then suddenly ear-piercing howls could be heard on the early morning air. And to the girls delight out of the forest burst Brown Bear, with the two adult bears that Ursula loved so much, following him close behind.

When the large bears appeared on the beach the mist that surrounded them made them look bigger than they were. Their dark brown fur was on end with rage, as they headed down the beach to rescue their cub and their beloved mistress.

"Oh BB! Thank goodness you are back here now; it has been awful not knowing where you were," There was such relief in Petra's voice.

Brown Bear comforted the girls and Rosie burst out crying with relief as she cuddled up to him.

Petra pulled at his arm, "Look! BB, we must help."

"No, we must stay here. Leave it to Ursula's ursine friends. They will have her back with us soon, but don't forget you are witnessing parental fear and rage combined in the anger of this prehistoric species."

The two ferocious bears raced down to the water's edge. As soon as the villains saw them towering above the tree line, they abandoned the attempt to lift the cage on board their motorboat.

The woman and the three men were petrified now, at the sight of angry animals tearing towards them. Suddenly they stopped knee deep in the water and were immediately stunned to hear the engine of the motorboat start up without their orders.

"Hey! Wait," Joanna called out to the boatman. "Hey! Stop, I demand you turn off that engine."

"Yeah, what you playing at, wait for us," called out Marcus, his menacing character had now turned into a babbling wreck. "Come back. Please don't leave us here with all this wildlife! You, you traitor, p- p-please! Come back!"

Their boatman took no notice but swerved the vessel around and headed out to sea.

Joanna and her brother Frederick began to wade back to the cage, and the two ruffians tried to swim after the boat. There was mayhem on the shore, and it was starting to get light as the dawn was seeping through the dark clouds of night and sending a welcome glow across the dawn sky.

"Right! Now girls, come with me while I think what is best to do," came Brown Bear's reassuring voice.

Then suddenly without any warning, from far away over the eastern horizon they could hear the droning of many engines in the sky, coming nearer and nearer to the island.

"Whatever is that noise, what's going on?" exclaimed Brown Bear.

Then just as suddenly they all heard the roar of many motorboat engines, crashing through the waves.

"What is happening?" yelled Rosie, trying to be heard above the noise.

"Oh BB! We need to get Ursula and the baby bear out of that cage."

"Petra, come to me and you too Rosie. If this is what I think it is, we will all soon be safe." The girls followed Brown Bear to the safety of the trees. They huddled together trying to make out what was happening at the water's edge.

Suddenly the island was flooded with light. Light from above and light from the sea.

The girls huddled down behind Brown Bear, not yet sure of what was happening.

"Oooh! It's the police!" announced Rosie.

"Thank goodness," sighed Petra. "Now surely Ursula will get some justice."

Soon the beach was as light as day. The motorboats had landed using their own portable jetties to reach the sand, and many armed police officers were scouring the beach and the woodland that edged the shore.

"Come on girls, this nightmare should be over now. Let's go and introduce ourselves." Brown Bear was looking forward to meeting the establishment.

"Can you both see what is happening in the shallows?" cried Rosie, in a state of excitement. "Look, the cage is unlocked, and there is no sign of the bears."

But Ursula was still inside, sitting calmly talking to a policewoman. Another of the police officers passed in a blanket and a cup of something hot.

"Shall we go and talk to them," asked Rosie.

"No!" replied Petra. "They will come and talk to us when they are ready! But where have the bears gone?"

"All the bears have gone back to where they live! The parents have rescued their cub and retreated to the forest and caves beyond. The police aren't interested in them," Brown Bear leaned his big furry head towards the girls. "It's these criminals they are after. And it looks as if they have been betrayed by the boatman."

"Well! I am glad he betrayed them; those thugs have been cruel. And what about Ursula? She had the worry of her safety and the cub drowning," said Rosie, whilst looking bewildered with all the goings on.

"Look, here they come now," Petra felt relieved. She stood up to greet the police officers.

"Hello, girls, are you alright?" asked a big burly officer. "I am Detective Sergeant Cooper."

"Hello," said the girls in unison. "We want to go to Ursula, she is our friend, and we care about her living alone on this island." Rosie looked beseechingly into the policeman's eyes.

"Well! That is why we are here. I understand that Mr Bear here is an old friend of Lucas Oliver. Is that right, Sir?"

"Yes, it is!" said Brown Bear very positively. He stood up tall, very pleased to be addressed as 'Sir'.

"We have been watching this island for a few days now," the officer's voice was loud and to the point. "Ever since Mr Oliver had suspicions about strangers in the area asking questions about boat trips out to the island," the police officer informed them.

"Oh! We never knew that!" exclaimed Rosie.

"No, you wouldn't, young lady, it was top secret." The policeman gave her a smile.

"Our unit searched this island twenty-two years ago, but drew a blank," he said.

"Was that when the professor's wife went missing?" asked Petra.

"Yes it was, but we found no trace of her. Years before that there had been a minor earthquake, and then three years later a landslide, but we searched everywhere and found no sign of Mrs Mortimer," the policeman was quite forthcoming, thought Brown Bear.

"Are you here to search for her again?" asked Rosie.

"No, but we are here to arrest the two leaders of a gang and their accomplices."

Suddenly another officer came over to them, he seemed in a hurry.

"Sir, the Supa' wants us to get a move on, and the young lady wants all of her friends to meet her at the cottage on the beach."

"Oh! Yes!" said Rosie. "We all want to see Ursula as soon as possible. Have you seen the bears? Are they all safe?"

"What bears? We know nothing of any bears!" exclaimed DS Cooper. "We have come to arrest a murderer."

Brown Bear indicated to Rosie not to say another word." Right then officer we will make our way underground and meet you all at the Cottage."

"Underground?" The Detective Sergeant looked puzzled. "I have orders to take you round the headland by helicopter and land on the beach by Professor Mortimer's Cottage.

"O! How exciting," exclaimed Rosie. Petra felt a buzz of excitement too.

"Is that ok, Sir?" The Policeman looked at Brown Bear for approval.

"Fine by me, officer," Brown Bear looked round at the girls. "It won't be the first time we three have travelled in a helicopter! Will it, girls?"

"Oh! when was that?" DS Cooper was intrigued.

"It was in our first adventure on this island," Rosie gushed out her words. Petra and I were only ten and we escaped from the Hobgoblins.

"Oh! I see," replied the officer, but he clearly didn't. 'All grown ups know there is no such thing as hobgoblins.'

"We rescued some helicopter pilots from the castle dungeons," joined in Petra, remembering the exciting time they had spent on this island, when they were young children.

"Right, girl's enough of that! I'm sure the officer doesn't want to hear all that now." Brown Bear was getting a little embarrassed.

"It's okay Sir," the policeman nodded to Brown Bear. "Sounds good fun, I've got a couple of kids back home. They love Hobgoblins!"

Suddenly, there was a loud thrust from one of the helicopter engines. The pilot was under orders to carry three witnesses to be questioned by Superintendent Harding in a makeshift incident room at Professor Mortimer's beach cottage on the east shore.

"Transport ready to go any minute!" another officer beckoned them all to the helicopter. "Superintendent Harding is already at the cottage, with WPC Denton and the girl."

"Right! We are on it! Come on, after you," DS Cooper stood aside until they were all strapped into their seats, aboard the police vehicle. "We will be landing in four minutes. It is only a short distance."

"Wow!" exclaimed Rosie, as the helicopter soared into the early morning sky.

"Look, there is the cottage," said Petra. She gazed down at the beach. They had soon come around the headland. She could see quite a commotion in front of the cottage. A large white tent had quickly been erected, as the police officers had found the size of the cottage far too small, to hold their inquiries.

"A small bump and then we are down," said Detective Sergeant Cooper. "This shouldn't take long. We need to establish exactly what you all know about Joanna and Frederick Newsome, and their gang, of course!"

The helicopter landed and the senior officer helped them all down safely onto the shale under the cliff. Rosie gave him a big smile and caught hold of Brown Bear's paw. But before she could say anything else, there was Ursula being followed by a female police officer rushing towards them, looking none the worse for her ordeal.

"Come this way, if you don't mind," gestured the policewoman. "We have set up a makeshift incident room, as we couldn't all get inside the cottage."

"That's fine," said Ursula. "I have a lot to tell you!"

"Now! That is what we want to hear, young lady." WPC Denton smiled and showed them inside the tent.

"May Ursula go upstairs to our bedroom to change into dry clothes," asked Petra.

"Of course! I can see you girls all need appropriate attire."

"Yes of course!" said Rosie. "We are still wearing our shorts and T-shirts."

"Be as quick as you can! The Superintendent has limited time." WPC Denton nodded to the girls. "He is only here because Professor Lawrence Mortimer is an eminent archaeologist, and his missing wife has been an unsolved case for many years now. I think he is hoping for a connection,"

"Well! my mother has been missing since I was six years old," Ursula informed the officer.

It suddenly dawned on Brown Bear that the Professor's wife and Ursula's mother were the same person.

'Oh dear!' he thought. 'Whatever have we got ourselves into this time?'

30
INVESTIGATION

Superintendent Harding had everything under control when the girls were seated in front of him in the makeshift incident room outside the cottage. All three girls had assured the police company present that they were not at all tired and wanted to get on with the investigation.

It was now six a.m., and the early autumn sunrise was spectacular. WPC Denton had used her issued travel stove to make everyone a cup of tea. The girls were watching the Superintendent closely waiting for his questions.

"Now, young ladies this won't take long, but tell me all you know about our two suspects, Joanna and Frederick Newsome."

Petra spoke first "We became aware of them a few days after Professor Mortimer moved into a cottage near to where we live in Swallows Village. We didn't know their names or anything. I thought the woman might be a cleaner as they appeared to have access to his cottage!"

"Did you see what they did in the house?" The Policeman was quite pleasant.

"No! Not really, but we heard them arguing in the study."

"Where were you then? Inside the Old Mill Cottage?"

"No, we were in the garden at the back. BB had gone back to look in the study window."

"And you are sure you heard their voices, and could you recognise them again?"

Petra and Rosie nodded.

The Superintendent leaned back on his chair looking at Petra closely. "I will cut to the chase. We know all about the Professor breaking his ankle and asking both of you," he looked at Rosie and gave her a smile. "Yes, I believe he asked you two for help to find some secrets here on the island, because he was incapacitated himself. Is that correct?"

"Yes! Secrets of the island!" volunteered Rosie, smiling back at this important policeman. "And we have found two of them already."

"And what have you found?" He looked very serious now. He furrowed his brow as he waited for Rosie to speak.

"We found Ursula! We thought her very strange at first. She told us she had survived alone on the island for a very long time. Then the other day she took us underground and showed us where she had lived with her mother down by a lake with the bears."

"What!" exclaimed the Officer. He stood up immediately and called to one of his fellow officers to bring DS Cooper to join them.

Rosie went pale and looked at Brown Bear for his disapproval, but he showed none. The little girl thought she had let the secret of the bears out of the bag.

There was a bit of a commotion as DS Cooper was located. At last the officer appeared inside the makeshift incident room in front of his commanding officer.

"Now, DS Cooper, how old are you?"

"Forty-one, Sir." The D S replied.

"Old enough to have been involved in Operation Pyramid?"

"Yes, Sir, I remember it well! My first investigation, Sir."

"I wasn't part of it. Still in London back then," Superintendent Harding looked directly at his Detective Sergeant, "Do you remember searching a lake here on the island?"

"No Sir! definitely no lake found on the island. Just a ravine that splits the island in two. Bit of a creepy place that was."

"Right then DS Cooper, as soon as the girl has recovered from her ordeal, you and WPC Denton must accompany her underground and find that lake, er, umm, what is her name?"

"My name is Ursula, Sir," she interrupted. "And I will be very happy to show you where I was born, and the lake where my mother taught me to swim."

"It is a pleasure to meet you, young lady," replied Superintendent Harding, who was assigned to Swallows Valley Police. "Now, tell us all you know about your mother." The officer was looking straight into Ursula's eyes.

"Yes! I will, but I don't know very much as I was only six when she left me alone in the cave!" Ursula was fearless.

"So, she actually left you alone?" The Superintendent seemed surprised.

"Yes Sir! She went out one morning to see if she could hail a boat or draw attention to our existence."

"I see!" said the Superintendent.

"No! I don't think you do, sir," replied Ursula. "It wasn't like her just popping out one day, as I suppose would be a normal expectation."

The police officer gave a sharp irritated cough. "So, carry on, what would it have been like?"

Brown Bear had been listening close by. Not only has he, his two girls to protect but nowadays Ursula as well. "Excuse me Sir, this young lady has surely had enough for one day."

"It's Okay BB, I'm fine"

Ursula turned to Superintendent Harding. "Well Sir, I will tell you what it was like! The first day my mother was trapped in the cave, she was aware she was pregnant with me. She told me when I was little that she had been determined on that day to find her freedom again. Soon she found some sharp rocks to use as a Chisel, to work away at the rubble that had blocked the exit to the cave; the landslide had made her a prisoner."

"Quite extraordinary, what courage!" said the Superintendent.

"Then one day ages later, she told me whenever she got the chance she would work at the rubble endlessly, then one day she broke through, lots of debris fell away and made enough room for her to squeeze through the opening. It was that day she felt free to go out onto the island. She said it was too dangerous for me to go with her. So, off she went knowing the bears would look after me until she returned."

"Did she mention why she thought it was unsafe to take you with her?"

"No Sir," Ursula replied.

"Did she go out often?" WPC Denton asked the girl.

"She would go and climb up to the top of the castle tower. She would only be away for a short time, just long enough to see if there was a vessel close to the island. It was exciting when she came back the first time, she brought some nice things from the cottage."

"May I ask, like what?"

"Just luxuries to make life more comfortable like soap and cushions!"

"I understand," said Superintendent Harding. "Now I have a teenage daughter at home and if she had endured anything like you have today, she would be cosy in bed by now."

"Well Sir, I wasn't going to interrupt your investigation" Ursula responded. "But I am very tired now. I was fine and then it came on suddenly."

At that moment Petra and Rosie started to yawn.

"Right! That is settled then, we will all get some rest now, and regroup at two o'clock." He gave them all a smile and then turned to his officer.

"DS Cooper, get some of the others to go back to the mainland in the Choppers and send a message to Lucas Oliver to return to the island. What a good man he is! He must guard this coast like an eagle."

"A hawk! Sir, I think you mean a hawk," Brown Bear couldn't resist correcting the Superintendent.

"If it wasn't for Oliver, we would not have caught the gang," stated Jack Harding, looking very pleased with life. At that moment a call came over his radio, the senior officer took a few steps away from the girls to answer it, "Yes! Yes! Very good, Sergeant, thank you for letting me know."

"Great news! Both the Newsome's, Marcus Morgan and Rick Ragsworth, are in custody, and for starters have been charged with theft and attempted kidnap." The senior police officer looked extremely pleased. He turned to his D S.

"Would you say, Cooper, that's about half of Jo Newsome's gang?"

"No, nowhere near! She's always picking up layabouts to do her bidding, there could be a lot more." replied the Detective Sergeant and asked to take his leave of his commander so he could organise the departure of the helicopters.

Superintendent Harding turned to the girls with a huge beaming grin on his face.

"This afternoon we will hear more of Ursula's life story. Now, Mr Bear, see you take great care of these girls."

"He always does!" exclaimed Petra and Rosie together.

WPC Denton climbed the stairs inside the cottage to check that the girl's accommodation was secure. The officer turned the bedcovers down and looked in the wardrobe. She even checked the catch on the window.

"Right! We must be careful in case there is another member of the Newsome gang still lurking around here. Anyway, it looks very cosy in this bedroom, and I admire the taste in choosing such exquisite furniture."

"Yes! I do too," said Ursula. "I have no idea why it is here! I came in this cottage once or twice. It was never locked. I think there is a connection with my mother, I vaguely remember her talking about it once. She told me she had worked as a bio-archaeologist and even when I was young, I remember she taught me about ancient bones and fossils."

"Is that why the room downstairs is full of them?" remarked the policewoman.

"Yes, I think so, she had worked on lots of historic sites and loved her work, she was interested in all kinds of bones especially bones from the Pliecerine era." At that moment Ursula felt very proud of her mother. "I do find something extremely odd though."

"And what might that be?" asked the policewoman.

"I find it strange that all the relics are placed so higgledy-piggledy. My mother was meticulous about anything she found. Always in date order and labelled. I have read some of her books she'd published. She encouraged me to learn about everything."

"Where did the books come from?" asked the WPC Denton.

"I'm not sure, but once mother could get out on the island, I was not much more than six and I just accepted everything as normal. I knew nothing else. She would bring things from the cottage. I didn't ask her whose they were or anything." Ursula gave a long-tired sigh. But it is odd how the relics look as if they have just been thrown in that room and not arranged neatly as I know my mother would have placed them."

"So, what do you think is the reason?" asked the WPC.

"That it wasn't my mother who put all this stuff in this cottage. Someone else did!"

"I see, I'll take it up with my sergeant," WPC Denton replied.

"Did your mother ever mention these relics?" Brown Bear was curious and had been catching Ursula's every word.

"No, Mr Bear I don't think she did, I can't remember. I only know I was six when I last saw her." Ursula gave a big yawn. "I remember my sixth birthday really well, because of the raspberries and I have never had anyone to celebrate a birthday with me ever since."

"That is something we can rectify," said Petra in the middle of a yawn.

"Right! Now everyone, you must get some sleep," said the policewoman. "It has been a very long morning for us all."

"It has, Petra and I have been looking for Ursula since yesterday and we have been awake all this time," mumbled a very sleepy Rosie.

"Yes, you are right, Rosie!" responded Petra. "Do try and sleep Sis' we just might be able to get two or three hours before we meet with the officers at two o'clock."

Both girls jumped into the great big bed, but Ursula hesitated.

"Are you alright, young Ursula?" asked Brown Bear. "You are a very brave young lady, I am proud of you, standing up against those crooks."

"Yes, I'm really fine, I was just thinking it's wonderful to be back with my friends."

"I'm very pleased to hear that. Well, I'll bid you girls farewell."

Brown Bear was very concerned, knowing the ordeal their new friend had just been through, at the hand of villains! It must have been distressing for her and Starlight. He turned to the policewoman.

"I'll come with you now so the girls can get some sleep."

The two stood on the rocks outside the cottage below the canopy, the makeshift incident room. They could hear the sea and the flapping noise of the canvas roof relentlessly blowing in the stiff breeze.

"Goodbye then, Mr Bear, I must report to D. S. Cooper. What a morning it has been," said WPC Denton as she made her way down over the rocks.

"Yes, indeed it has, and I feel this afternoon will prove just as interesting," replied Brown Bear. "I'm going for a walk before I have a rest, I have a lot to think about."

But the policewoman was out of earshot now, as she was about to join her fellow officers staked out along the beach. Brown Bear shrugged his shoulders and made his way along the shale. He could smell smoke wafting in the air reminiscent of the night the intruder's landed on the island. He realised the police officers had lit a fire to cook their breakfast, a little distance away, under the shelter of the cliffs.

Most of the unit had returned to the mainland in the helicopters with orders for his old friend Lucas, the fisherman, now a proud motorboat owner, to meet with the police officers at 2pm sharp.

Brown Bear shivered, the early autumn air was cold, and the wind ruffled his fur. The sea was on its way in again. Hopefully the tide will be high enough for Lucas to land at the jetty.

Something was worrying him, and he wasn't quite sure what it could be? He found a place to sit on some dry sand high on the beach, well away from the police officers. He sat under the cliff that rose behind him like a shadowy monster.

'If there was ever a monster,' he thought. 'It is that hideous woman, the one we thought was the Professor's cleaner, and her accomplice who the police told me was her brother.' Brown Bear sat there deep in thought. After a while he was startled by one of the officers.

"Hot cuppa for you, sir!" DS Cooper passed a steaming cup of tea to Brown Bear who took it graciously. "Fancy a chat?"

"I do! sit yourself down," Brown Bear patted the sand beside him.

"Sorry, mate! I'll just stand, I'm still on duty."

"I suppose you want to ask me questions." Brown Bear took a sip of his welcome beverage.

"Well, yes just one," replied the policeman. "How well, do you know this island, sir?"

"If you had asked me that a few weeks ago I would have said like the back of my paw er hand but now I'm not so sure?"

"Why is that?" The policeman looked puzzled.

"Young Ursula, who we only encountered here on the island a few days ago, has now shown me areas of lake and forest and underground gullies and caves that I had no idea existed."

"Who is she?"

"All we know is what she has told us; she was born here in an ancient cave where descendants of cave bears helped her mother in her confinement. She is very intelligent, and my girls are getting very fond of her. That is all I know," Brown Bear took a deep breath.

"So, what happened to her mother? Did she die in childbirth?" asked the policeman.

"No! I told you the bears helped her, and Ursula told us that she was only six years old when she last saw her mother. The girl is well-educated. Apparently her mother taught her to read at a very young age. She has perfect vocabulary!"

"So, what did happen to her mother?" the officer asked, in an urgent voice.

"Ursula only has vague memories of her mother, as she was very young. The day she lost her mother on this island must have been devastating for the little girl."

Brown Bear stood up suddenly. "Are you here to find her mother? I think you should because something bad must have happened to her all those years ago. The girls and I believe she haunts the island!" Brown Bear caught his breath. "There is a mystery to be solved here. Anyway, your Chief said Ursula will have the chance to tell her story later today."

"Yes! That is right he has requested that Lucas Oliver is to attend. Now I must report back!" He reached out his hand to Brown Bear, "You finished with that cup?"

"Indeed! I have and very nice too, here you are, officer. Thank you."

Brown Bear was alone again on the sand, he could hear the incoming tide still far out in the bay. He and the girls were experts when it came down to what the tide was doing! The sudden roar that Rosie had taught him to listen out for was a sure indication the tide had turned. He walked back to the cottage, stewing over everything in his mind.

'Two women missing on this island, not possible surely?' he thought, as he neared the cottage. 'Oh dear! They have locked me out! Never mind! I'll just have a rest here, under the white tent now abandoned until the investigation resumes.'

As he felt himself drifting off to sleep, he could see in his mind the image of a beautiful woman, whose face they had seen reflected in the pool on the beach. That was the day I had taken Petra and Rosie fishing. I believe I can solve the mystery and find all the secrets of the island. I am looking forward to a reunion with Lucas and hearing all he knows about the ruffians that almost kidnapped Ursula. Brown Bear's mind was running riot and he couldn't settle, he tossed and turned on the sand trying to make a comfy hollow. Then he remembered the sight of the young bear and Ursula in the cage, and the Newsome's and their gang wading knee deep in the water trying to carry out their dastardly scheme. And then suddenly he remembered the hours he had spent copying all the professor's notes onto the girl's phones.

"That's it! I need to look at Petra's phone. There must be a link in this drama somewhere. Maybe tomorrow I will find another secret of the island.'

31
WORRYING THOUGHTS

All was quiet in the upstairs room as the girls slept. But something woke Ursula, she sat up in the enormous bed she was sharing with her two new friends. She listened intently trying to hear what had awakened her. There was the roar of the incoming tide being driven in by the wind. Then she became aware of the bedroom window frame creaking with each gust pushing against it. Ursula shivered as she remembered her horrendous ordeal in the cage with the little bear the day before.

'As if I wouldn't put up a fight to rescue him!' she thought. 'I do hope the bears are safe. With all the goings on they will have hidden themselves deep in the forest. Oh! this island used to be so tranquil when my mother was with me. I really must go to find Starlight as soon as I can. Ursula started to think deeply about her mother. She had been heartbroken when she realised she would never see her mother again. It was the bears that had kept her strong. Now she felt even stronger than ever having BB, and the girls for company. I must do something for my mother before it is too late.' She had an idea and tugged at Petra's arm.

"Are you awake? If not, please wake up! Petra, I need a witness."

"What is it?" Petra woke up, "What's the matter, Ursula? Can't you sleep?"

"No, I can't! I want to ask you something important. Will you come with me? I want to find my mother!"

"You have an idea where she is?" Petra sat up in bed beside her enthusiastic friend. "I thought you said your mother had been murdered. You know that is a very serious claim to make?"

"I know it is, but it is true. I have an idea where her body might be!" Ursula spoke the words softly.

"Do you know for certain she's dead?" Petra whispered, trying not to wake Rosie.

"I'm certain! Her spirit has never left me. It's not knowing what happened to her that plagues my mind. Look I'm going to have to go over all this with the police, I don't want to do it twice. It is very painful!"

"Yes, I am sure it is. Rosie and I really feel for you. Can't this wait?" Petra replied, rubbing sleep from her eyes.

"I just thought I would go now!"

"If only you can wait until this afternoon and tell the police what you are thinking. And then they will search for your mother," Petra was starting to feel exhausted. "I am too tired to come with you now, but lie down and I will listen to your theory."

"Hey, it is not a theory!" The girl was now becoming very perturbed. "The police won't help, because my mother told me years later that they had abandoned the search for her. There had been a landslide as you know. Someone must have reported her missing, I remember her telling me that at first, she heard dogs and helicopters searching the island. Then one day all was quiet."

"That fact alone must have been heart breaking for her. You know for your mother to realise no one would be looking for her," exclaimed Petra a little too loud and woke Rosie.

"What's happening?" Rosie sat up pushing her tousled blond hair from her face.

"Shush, keep quiet, we are just making plans for later," replied Petra, trying to keep her voice low in case someone could hear them.

"Plans for what?" Rosie was very sleepy.

"Listen! Ursula," said Petra urgently. "There is nothing we can do now with Swallows Police force here on the island. But we will talk it over with BB, and if he agrees we can all look for your mother."

Ursula reluctantly agreed and snuggled down under the duvet on this luxurious bed. The girls lay there quietly, and minutes later it was only Petra who remained awake. Her mind was running on overdrive. Petra thought about everything that had happened on the island from the day of their arrival to the horrific kidnap attempt yesterday. The beautiful woman's reflection they had caught a glimpse of in a pool on the beach, and the strange footprints in the wet sand that same day. It is obvious now and perhaps Ursula is right, that it is her mothers' ghost trying to tell her something.

Petra was remembering everything, even Rosie going missing, putting great fear in herself and Brown Bear. Also, later Rosie telling them all that she had found a shrine with lit candles burning on it in a cave, and the angry voices of the two criminals, Joanna Newsome and her brother who had now been caught by the police officers. She worried about how Brown Bear's old friend Lucas, had come to guide the police to the island. I feel positive Lucas must have shown them the way through the rocks. Then some officers arrived by air and once that sudden swoop on the island had begun, Ursula was rescued and now the criminals were held in a cell somewhere on the mainland.

Petra was arranging all the happenings of the last few days in her mind, putting the incidents in some sort of chronological order, trying to make sense of it all.

She wondered if it was Lucas who had tipped off the police. 'He was well aware we three were here on the island,' Petra became deeper in thought. 'Of course, now he has a new motorboat he must have been asked many times to bring tourists here safely through the treacherous rocks that surround the island. Some of the locals know about the jagged pinnacles when they are exposed at low water, but I can't wait to hear what Lucas has to say! And now Ursula's mother's name is Emily Jane, the same name as Professor Mortimer's missing wife. Was Petra beginning to paint a true picture of the events.

'Who owned the trawler that enabled the strangers to land on the island?' Petra's mind was truly troubled. She couldn't rest. 'All the beautiful furniture and delicate tableware and even the exquisite notepaper that Ursula had said she, herself had taken for safe-keeping, were gifts from a man who was hopelessly in love with E.J.M. or Emily Jane Mortimer!'

Petra's thoughts had turned into a dream or rather a nightmare as it became obvious that the Professor's wife and Ursula's mother were the same person. 'But how on earth can we tell Ursula the truth? And worse still, how can we tell the Professor he has a daughter?'

'Oh no!' said Petra out loud, amidst her turmoil. Thank goodness she hadn't woken the two girls sleeping besides her. She was now positive that even the bed was a gift Professor Lawrence Mortimer had brought to the island with Lucas' help.

'All these beautiful pieces were brought here for the comfort of his beloved wife. So, what had happened to Mrs Mortimer?' Petra's mind carried on delving into all the facts they had collected. How could she have been missing for all these years? If she had been in an accident surely her body would have been found long ago? I do feel she must be dead; Rosie would never have lied about someone or thing taking her hand and leading her to safety, away from the cave where she heard the two people, I presume were the kidnappers, the intruders, the couple Rosie had heard in the cave near the shrine, squabbling, quarrelling. And obviously they were the two who arrived at Old Mill Cottage in the dead of night in that black BMW and must have had a free hand rummaging through all the Professor's papers. And yes! That is where they found Emily Jane's letter, of course.'

Petra also remembered Ursula being very upset when she

hadn't wanted anyone to go into the cave where Rosie had just appeared from after following a rabbit. Ursula had declared it was her space!

'Oh! That reminds me I must tell the police about the cave on the shore, where I found the briefcase. I photographed a letter from E.J. Yes, Emily Jane. Of course, there is the connection! That's the proof we need to connect the Newsome's with the Professor.'

Just then she saw Rosie turn in her sleep.

'Oh, I must stop my mind from rambling, I'm going to wake everyone if I don't stop.'

It was amazing with her mind in a state of such turbulence that Petra would ever get to sleep, but she did, and of course she was the last to wake later that morning.

After a quick lunch of fruit, cheese and biscuits and a hot cup of tea handed round by WPC Denton, the investigation commenced under the canopy once again. Brown Bear arrived looking a little dishevelled.

"Oh! BB, your fur is full of sand," said Rosie. "Hey! Don't shake it off near me!"

"Not surprising after the morning I've just had, trying to get a nap under this tent, with my head full of worries," he remarked.

Petra was sipping her tea quite calmly, but she too hadn't slept well.

"Me too, BB, I was trying to piece everything together, but it didn't all fit."

"Now don't you worry about all that!" DS Cooper arrived, looking smart and fresh with a big smile for everyone. "That is why we are here but, alas, Superintendent Harding had to leave a while ago. Something urgent cropped up at headquarters this morning. He has left me to finish things up here. His officers have had a good search of the old castle and its dungeons and even the ravine but no trace of Mrs Mortimer."

"Who is Mrs Mortimer?" asked Ursula, with a puzzled look on her face.

Brown Bear purposely interrupted, "Excuse me, Detective, we don't have to worry about that now do we?"

At that moment they all heard a motorboat engine and, to the girls' delight, it was Lucas keeping his appointment with the constabulary of Swallows Bay. Petra and Rosie asked leave of the police officers and tore down the beach to the jetty excited to see an old friend of their beloved bear.

Brown Bear caught hold of Ursula's hand, "Come meet a very good old mate of mine, we became great friends many years ago."

Once again, the faithful tide was coming in and making it easy for Lucas to land and secure his vessel. The sea water was lapping at the jetty, but Lucas jumped off the bobbing boat to greet Brown Bear and the girls.

"Don't worry I haven't come to take you home yet, girls. You still have a few days of holiday left!" He sensed something was up when he glanced at Petra and Rosie.

"We've had a spot of bother here," said Brown Bear, shaking Lucas' sunburnt hand.

"Aye, I know," replied the fisherman.

"Come on everyone. DS Cooper is ready to conduct his enquiries," the policewoman called loudly. "This shouldn't take long, then Mr Oliver will take DS Cooper and myself back to the mainland."

The Detective Sergeant carried a wad of papers under his arm and beckoned to the others to be seated under the white canopy.

"Now all I need is a statement from this young lady," he nodded to Ursula.

"Right now, are you happy to answer a few questions?"

Ursula looked at her new friends and could see they all gave their approval.

"Yes! I am," she stated clearly.

"Okay then, what is your address and your name?" continued the Detective Sergeant.

"This island is my address of course!" she gave an exasperated reply.

"Right! You see I must fill in this form with your details, name, age, address, *et cetera*, and I must be specific, but if you can't be more helpful, just tell us your story and I will make notes for the Superintendent."

"Excuse me, Sir! It isn't that I am not being helpful. It is because I genuinely don't know who I am." Ursula's voice was tinged with indignation.

"I am sorry, but I will be in trouble if this form isn't filled in correctly," said DS Cooper. He looked over to WPC Denton.

"Do you fancy dealing with this, PC Denton? I am out of my depth here!"

There was a bit of debate between the two officers but in the end, it was the policewoman who befriended Ursula and encouraged her to tell her story.

WPC Denton was calm and, at this moment in time, Ursula needed a woman's touch. The officer sat back in her chair, one that had been brought out from the cottage kitchen. She picked up a large notebook and turned a page. "I don't suppose there is any chance of the internet anywhere on this island?"

"Yes, but it's infrequent," replied Petra.

"Now in your own words, tell us what you remember of your early life," said WPC Denton.

"Shall I tell you everything I know?" Ursula didn't seem to mind being the centre of attention,

"Yes, Ursula please do," replied WPC Denton.

There was a long pause, then Ursula spoke out in a clear soft voice. The officers were soon intrigued.

"You are certain the woman and those three men who tried to

kidnap me and my pet bear are securely locked up, and can never get near me again?"

"They are all being detained in cells at headquarters and our fellow officers on the mainland are making a case against them all. In twenty-four hours we will know exactly what happens next," said the WPC with a satisfied smile on her face.

Brown Bear sat upright listening to every word the young lady uttered. Nothing was different. It was the same story Ursula had told him and the girls.

"There had been a landslide her mother had told her when she was old enough to understand. That was the day Emily Jane had discovered the ancient bear caves, she had been exploring the caves and had become aware of strange noises. And when she tried to return to the cottage where she had been staying on the island, she realised her way out was blocked. That was why her mother had escaped with her life. The falling debris of rocks and sandstones being flung around that terrible day. Half the cliffs were destroyed and a castle that had stood guarding the eastern shore had crumbled and fallen with all the mediaeval masonry collapsing below ground level and it remained there to this day. My mother was trapped in an underground grave, well it could have been if days later when the island was still again, she found the strength to search for a suitable rock and through the first years she just prodded and poked until some of the stones gave way."

By now Ursula had tears welling in her eyes and Rosie passed her friend a tissue. Ursula diligently used it to wipe her tears of sorrow from her lovely face. As she composed herself, she looked at the girls and gave them a watery smile.

"That was the hole we all climbed through to get to my home. Do you three remember?" Brown Bear, Petra and Rosie nodded.

DS Cooper sat up straight and looked into Ursula eyes.

"I am sorry I have to ask you this, but after your mother went missing, were you happy living alone on this Island?"

"Yes, I was, but it took a long time to realise I would never see my mother again! At first, I waited and waited for her to return. But she did not return! So, I decided I would climb out of the hole she had made in the fallen rubble and go and find her myself. Perhaps she had fallen or something. I knew even at a young age it must have been something serious to stop her coming home. She adored me and would never have left me to fend for myself."

The two officers talked together for a few moments then DS Cooper turned to Ursula.

"Why not come with us and have a couple of nights in a hotel on the mainland until you recover from your ordeal?"

"What is a hotel?" Ursula asked, with a puzzled look on her face.

"Don't you know?" The WPC looked amazed.

"No! I don't. My mother taught me to read by the time I was four. She used to go back to the cottage and bring whatever she could carry, mainly books on archaeology and pass everything through the hole to me. I read lots of her books but there was never one about a hotel. What is a hotel anyway?"

"It is a big place, a building with lots of rooms and sometimes a swimming pool. And a bar," gushed Rosie.

Detective Sergeant Cooper stood up and pushed his chair back from the table, "I think we are finished here for now." he said. "Right, to give you a breather, young lady, I just want a short statement from Mr Oliver."

Lucas had been sitting quietly listening to every word that Ursula had just said.

"Oh! Right-oh," said Lucas. "Ask away!"

Lucas' statement surprised them all and revealed yet more secrets.

32
LUCAS

By six o'clock that evening everyone was very tired, and DS Cooper decided it would be better to continue the next day. So it was agreed they would meet again at nine o'clock in the morning. Lucas said he would sleep in the cabin on his boat.

Petra and Rosie decided they would have an early night; both were exhausted after the excitement of the last few days. Brown Bear and Ursula sat on the rocks outside the cottage talking about the species Ursus Spelaeus for a long time. As it grew dark the police officers advised them to get some sleep.

The next morning started hot with low white clouds capturing the summer heat. The tide was coming in with less vigour today and the seagulls flying overhead were enjoying communicating with each other by giving out raucous cries.

Lucas chose to sit out on the rocks close to the two police officers who were patiently waiting for the boatman to commence with his statement.

"Mr Oliver, will you please tell us what you know about the Newsome's?" DS Cooper asked the first question.

Lucas wrinkled his furrowed sun-tanned brow while he thought. "Never heard of them 'til around the turn of the century, probably late 1990's. They found me on the quay mending fishing nets for the trawlermen."

"And what did they say to you?"

"Well, to start with they were both agitated, especially her, not a nice soul," Lucas was thoughtful.

"Why do you say that?" asked WPC Denton.

"She did most of the talking and was demanding. I didn't like her at all!"

"And her brother Frederick?"

"Aah! I didn't know they were siblings!" Lucas took a deep breath. "Her brother was alright, not angry like the woman, he was a polite bit of a gentleman so to speak."

"And what did they ask of you?" DS Cooper looked tired.

"Aah, they wanted to know if anyone hired out boats in these parts,"

"And!" exclaimed DS Cooper who was getting a little impatient, he needed sleep. He had been on duty since the first tirade of Police officers landed in the early hours, yesterday.

"Well, I asked what they wanted a boat for? And they said they wanted to go to the island. And I told them the waters round the island were treacherous. Many a wreck in the olden days!"

"What happened then?" asked WPC Denton.

"Asked if I would take them, but I refused! I didn't like them, you see!"

"So did anyone take them?"

"Not sure but Rick, one of the men you just caught, had a boat, even in them days. He was young then and a bit shifty, do anything for anyone at a price," Lucas made moves to get up, "I must stretch my legs, aah, ouch, give us a pull up matey?" he held his hand out to Brown Bear, who helped his old friend to his feet.

"Well, can you remember anything else, Mr Oliver?" DS Cooper shuffled his papers together.

"Yes, I know a lot more!" said Lucas.

"Like what," the police officer stood up too.

"Like the time I brought all that furniture to the island. It took four trips, but I was happy to do it with the help of my nephews."

"That would have been hard work," said the policewoman.

"Aye it was, but folks around here would do anything to help the Professor!"

"You knew Professor Mortimer?" DS Cooper looked surprised.

"Of course, he was very well liked in these parts. I brought his wife to the island in the summer of ninety-nine. She was a good-looking wench and the Doc idolised her."

"Did you help in the search for her when she went missing?" asked the detective.

"No! I was on a trip to South Africa with my cousin, not a holiday, just working!" said Lucas. "And it wasn't 'til I got back did I hear about the lady going missing on the island." He pulled out an old spotted handkerchief and wiped his forehead.

"Phew, it's going to be a hot one, late August can be like that! Now I remember going fishing when I was a young lad......"

DS Cooper interrupted, "I have to finish your statement, headquarters want it straight away." The Detective Sergeant felt under pressure. "I must get on, the Supa' wants a detailed account, Sir."

"Will it be used as evidence?" Lucas looked intently at the officer.

"I expect so, if the case gets to court," DS Cooper stifled a yawn. "Now after the landslide in the late summer of 1999, a top unit from the city were dispatched here and they searched every inch of this island but found no trace of the missing lady. Now, I am led to believe that you are familiar with this area and the seas around here, Mr Lucas, do you have anything to add?"

"Aye! Problem with this island is that there is more beneath than above. There are many underground caves and the ravine for starters?" Lucas seemed pleased to be the centre of attention, all eyes were on him. "If as you say the police searched everywhere for the lovely lady, I cannot add anything to that! I am sorry I do not have the answer, nobody does?"

"Well, it looks like it will remain a mystery?" said the officer. "Well, we will have to leave it there now, as we have to be ready for our ride home." He reached up to the canvas roof and began to bring down the white tent and canopy.

"Here, we'll help with that," Brown Bear was on the job of putting the cottage back to the way it was before the unexpected and much appreciated visit from the constabulary.

"Hey, girls, a cup of coffee would be nice!"

"Come on, Ursula, and you, Rosie. Let us make ourselves useful," Petra called to the girls.

Soon the makeshift incident room was packed neatly away in a large holdall WPC Denton had produced. The two officers were busy tidying everything up around the cottage.

"There, all done, umm thank you, miss," DS Cooper took a coffee cup from Rosie and took a sip.

"Sir," WPC Denton interrupted her superior. "We need to inform the young lady what will happen next."

"Why yes, of course, Miss Ursula," DS Cooper met Ursula's gaze. "There is nothing to worry about, but you might have to come to the station to make a formal complaint against the gang that tried to kidnap you?"

"Surely that is not necessary, Detective!" Brown Bear stepped in. "You all saw what happened! In fact, the Newsome's and the two ruffians were caught in the act."

"Yes of course! I did say might, but the one thing I forgot to ask you young lady, is how old are you? What is your Birth date?"

"I don't know, I have tried to work it out over the years, but I'm not sure. I've counted full moons and I have counted seasons. All I really know is that I was born the year after the landslide. That is what trapped my mother underground, and it was her interest in prehistoric and ancient bears that saved us. I suppose I might be twenty years old?"

Petra thought that was probably right! Even on that first night when the girl appeared out of the darkness, on the rocks outside the cottage, she always felt she was older than the fifteen years she and Rosie were.

Suddenly from the eastern sky they heard the noise of a helicopter engine and as it roared nearer the noise drowned out anything else that was said. The craft came to land high on the beach, causing a storm of sand particles to rise in the air. At last, the two police officers said their farewells and boarded the aircraft.

"Thank you for everything," yelled Brown Bear. Within minutes the vehicle was out of sight on its journey to the mainland.

"Now, Lucas," said Petra. "Come and have tea with us."

"Aye, I would like that, but I must watch the tide. Got a few hours before I must head back." Lucas looked pleased especially when Rosie said she would prepare the food and the others could find out what Lucas knows about the Professor and his wife. Deep down she hadn't forgotten that Ursula had said her mother had been murdered. But none of that was mentioned by the police. Rosie went off to busy herself in the kitchen and Petra and Brown Bear began to plan their own investigation.

"Who is this Professor?" Ursula demanded. "The police mentioned him, why is he so important?"

Brown Bear took charge, as was his custom when things got a bit difficult. Petra swallowed hard, her sleepless morning had answered a few questions in her mind, but now was her chance to tell BB, something she thought she might have discovered during her mental turmoil.

"Ursula! Why did you say your mother had been killed?" questioned Petra.

"No! Not killed, murdered!" Ursula exclaimed, with certainty in her voice. "The day she left me in our cave was a summer's day. I remember her telling me it was going to be hot outside. For many weeks she had been working away every day pulling out rubble from the hole, you know the one I took you through to get to our home in the cave."

"Yes! we remember!" said Petra

"That must have been hard for her knowing she had a child who depended on her," Brown Bear remarked.

"I know it was very hard for her," replied Ursula. "But she never complained or ever got angry however hard life got and it was hard, especially in the winter. It was so cold in that cave but one year, when I was a baby, my mother told me later how the bears had been very curious one day and ventured out of the woods to come and sit and just stare at my mother feeding me. She was amazing. She seemed to be able to communicate with them."

"Incredible!" exclaimed Petra. "Do you know if she had studied them in the past?"

"Yes! I told you ancient bears were her main passion; she studied their prehistoric bones and went around the world searching for information. Sometimes mother would pretend I was in school, and she would be my teacher. As I grew bigger, she would tell me about other countries where she went in search of ursine bones. She told me that during the summer of the year she had graduated from university she travelled to Romania and visited a large cave in the Apuseni mountains. The cave had been discovered in 1975 and 140 skeletons of prehistoric bears that had walked the earth twenty-seven thousand years ago were discovered." Ursula sounded as passionate as her mother must have been. "And because of her love for her work, she named me Ursula."

"Ursula! Why, what does it mean?" Petra was deeply interested now.

"It means Little She Bear!" Brown Bear couldn't help coming in with a snippet of knowledge.

"Aye it does!" agreed Lucas. "In the night sky you can look to the North and you can see Ursa Major high in the Heavens."

"Oh!" said Petra. "That comes from Latin. I think it is another name for the Great Bear."

"Yes, it is! Ursa Major means Great Bear!" Brown Bear

continued with his words of wisdom. "Some refer to it as the Plough."

Suddenly there was a burst of activity outside the cottage door. Rosie appeared with her arms full. "Hey come and help. We still have some food, I found a packet of wraps and 3 tins of Tuna, and dried Apricots and Raisins and custard creams for pudding."

Petra and Ursula went to help carry out the trays laden with food and carried them down to where the rocks were at their flattest. The sun had disappeared behind a large white fluffy cloud, and it wasn't quite as hot as earlier, the tide was still high with persistent foam edged waves washing the sand.

"Here you are Lucas," said Brown Bear, passing his old friend a rolled-up tortilla busting with tinned Tuna. "Now all we want to know is what it was like on this island when you came here alone after you arrived back from Africa? What damage had the earthquake done? To be honest the island doesn't seem very different to the last time we came. In fact, I am surprised the old castle on the hill didn't get a battering." Brown Bear took a big, long breath to recover from his intense question and then tucked into his afternoon tea.

"Aye! You be right there my friend, but it was the subterranean levels that took the brunt," said Lucas. "I went down those old stone steps into the ravine that now totally splits this island in two and the old Eastern fortress that stood precariously on sandstone bedrock has disappeared except for a pile of rubble."

"But we saw it on our way underground," said Petra.

"For over twenty years it lay as it fell on the eastern shore," said Brown Bear. "And then the landslide took it underground."

"Yes, Lucas you are right, but we saw it, as we made our way underground to where Ursula lives," stated Rosie.

"It has been at least twenty years since I came here alone to look for Mrs Mortimer," Lucas finished his wrap and Rosie thought he looked very serious. "You see I felt responsible for her disappearance in a way."

"Why ever did you feel responsible, Lucas? I'm sure no one blames you," Brown Bear gave his old mate a pat on his shoulder.

"Well, I brought the Mortimer's to the island."

"Wasn't it dangerous, so soon after the quake," inquired Petra.

"The Doc said he had someone from the University over to check if it was safe for them to come." Lucas looked very serious as he related his account. "He would never have taken any risks! Anyway, it was declared safe. Apparently, it had not been an earthquake on a large scale, just a few tremors that had loosened some bedrock."

"So, that is why the old castle still stands and the castle the Professor had theoretically discovered on the eastern shore was devastated," remarked Brown Bear, who was listening intently to Lucas' tale.

"The Doc was interested in the castle remains and planned a vacation with his wife searching for whatever they could find. He had bought Old Mill Cottage in 1994 and he and his beautiful young bride became part of the village," Lucas continued.

"So what year did you bring them here?" asked Rosie.

"It was 15 July 1999. I remember it clearly! We had had a few days bad weather and had to cancel their first choice. Then the morning on the fifteenth dawned bright and sunny and as planned we met on Swallows Quay. It was the first time I met Mrs Mortimer, but I had seen her in the village. I remember she asked me how I was and how long had I been a fisherman? And then as Jamey and me loaded their luggage aboard my boat, she commented on how tall I was! And I said, all of us Oliver's are tall, and she gave me a lovely smile that would melt an iceberg." Lucas sat back and finished his meal.

"So, I presume you and your nephews have installed all that beautiful furniture before that day." Petra was intrigued. "So was that the last time you saw her?"

"No, I was summoned by the Doc. He'd remembered something crucial and wanted me to sort it. He had asked me to call in and take him to the mainland."

"See, it was all arranged that I call in at the jetty every week to bring his post. A very busy man he was," Lucas took a breath. "Anyway, he had to get to his office urgently. So, they said their farewells and Mrs Mortimer waved him off, looking beautiful standing on the jetty, lovely long black hair she had. The Doc was a bit worried about leaving her alone, especially after the earthquake a few years ago. But she kept reassuring him she would be fine. She told him she had plenty of work to do exploring the underground caves for prehistoric bones and fossils, all that kind of thing." Lucas was deep in thought.

"Now if I find any bones, I make a stew with 'em!"

Everyone laughed.

Lucas continued, "Come to think of it, it was about that time when I first set eyes on that couple. Ummm, when those Newsome's took an interest in hiring a boat."

"Oh! no!" Rosie yelled out. "They must have been watching the Mortimers even then. That must have been over twenty years ago, Lucas."

"Oh! They looked like young kids then, fresh out of college. Well, the man did! But she didn't look the studious type, far too much make up on her. Now, Mrs Mortimer, as she was called by the village folk, didn't need a scrap of makeup, she was a real beauty!"

"Did you ever see her again?" asked Petra.

"Yes, a week later I called in at the Jetty and Mrs Mortimer gave me a letter to take to her husband at 'Old Mill cottage.'

"Just post it through the letterbox," she said. "He was called away to Oxford, but he needs to pick up some documents from the cottage. I know he'll be back there soon."

"And that was the last time you saw Doctor Emily Jane Mortimer?"

"Alas it was!"

Suddenly Lucas jumped to his feet, "Hey I must go! Look, the tide has well turned. Don't you kids worry now! I will keep my eye out for strangers lurking round the Quay." He made his way along the jetty and jumped on board his new motorboat. "Hey! Look what I forgot to give you."

Brown Bear was tall enough to reach out to the departing fisherman, "What is it my old mate?"

"Package of food from your lovely Mum," replied Lucas, as he let go of the ropes.

"Oh, and she said to remind you that school starts on September fourth. And with that he was gone.

"Urrrrh," said Petra and Rosie together.

Ursula had been very quiet, in fact she hardly spoke at all.

"Now listen up girls, you know what that means, don't you?" announced Brown Bear. Petra replied. "Yes, BB! It means we only have a few days left to complete what the Professor asked of us. You know, don't you, Rosie?"

"Yes! It means time is running out and we need to get a move on if we are going to complete our mission and find all the secrets of the island."

"Right!" exclaimed Brown Bear. "We will have an early night, be up early, do some necessary chores and then be ready to follow Ursula and find the caves."

33
THE CAVE BEARS

It was early afternoon and the midday sun had been fierce, the tide was high splashing waves against the jetty. The island was quiet again as everyone concerned in the kidnap attempt had been gone a while, and for once even the seagulls were silent. Brown Bear and the three girls looking out to sea far across the bay could see clearly the reason for the bird's absence. A fishing trawler was at work almost on the horizon and there in the sky following along behind the vessel they could see a huge flock of seabirds.

"What birds follow fishing boats? BB, can you see any from here?" Rosie was straining her eyes to see the activity over the water.

"My eyesight's not as good as it used to be," answered Brown Bear. "But I can see the bigger ones! They are mainly Black backed gulls, but I can make out some Puffins and a few Cormorants. They are all after the bits of fish entrails the fishermen are shucking overboard."

"Yuk!" exclaimed Petra.

"Well," said Brown Bear. "The birds are not daft; they can smell a fishing boat from twelve miles away. It saves them diving into the briny and having to find a dinner for themselves!"

"BB, you are so knowledgeable," said Ursula. "Petra told me you were educated in the Northern forests of Europe by the elder members of your family. Have you ever come across bears like mine?"

"No!" he replied, feeling very pleased that Ursula was talking to them all again. He had put her silence down to the shock she had endured at the hands of Joanna Newsome.

"No! not exactly," his eyes met the young girl's. "Your ursine friends are descended from Ursus Spelaeus, a species the archaeology world thought was made extinct about 24,000 years ago, in other words your friends are descendants of the Cave bear."

"I am sure you are correct!" exclaimed Ursula. "I remember my mother being excited one day, yelling, 'I've found them! I've found them!' And then as if she realised her outburst had startled me, she put me on her knee and explained that she was an archaeologist and she had discovered creatures from deepest history living close by, not very far from our cave."

"I would agree with your mother, but didn't you say your friendly bears live in the forest! And not in caves," Brown Bear seemed to choose his words carefully.

"They go to their caves in the wintertime!" exclaimed Ursula. "If you want, I will show you! I want to go there soon, because I want to check if Starlight is alright after his ordeal!"

"Will you really take us to see their caves?" Rosie was excited, she felt a deep love for bears especially BB! "You chose an amazing name for the little bear," she said. "He is a star after trying to defend you in that awful cage."

"We defended each other, but I was really scared for him! Those wicked people might have sold him to a Zoo or even worse." Tears were welling up in Ursula's eyes.

At that moment Brown Bear took charge.

"Right! We must find them! Let's go right away, young lady! We need to take food with us! Remember we haven't yet looked inside the hamper Lucas brought from your Mum, girls."

"I'll fetch it!" exclaimed Petra. "I can't wait to see what Mum has sent us!"

"Me too!" Rosie ran with her sister to help carry the supplies. "Amazing! We were nearly out of food. Good old Mum!"

Soon the two girls joined Ursula and Brown Bear, who took hold of the well packed hamper.

"Now, are you all ready?" Ursula put her finger to her mouth. "Try and keep quiet because the bears will be easily spooked after their ordeal. I think they will be in hiding."

"Okay lead the way, Ursula," Brown Bear kept Petra and Rosie on either side of him, as they followed Ursula towards the cliff and up the path behind the cottage.

"We will have to go down the hole at the top of the cliff, as we cannot venture around the headland because of the high tide," explained Ursula. "We'll soon be in my home cave, and then if the bears are not around, we'll have to take a trip around the lake to the forest."

They all managed to climb down the bore hole at the top of the cliff. Brown Bear struggled a bit while holding on to the precious hamper, but in the end reluctantly passed it down to Petra who caught it deftly. It really was heavy, so she decided to leave it on the rocky floor. Brown Bear retrieved it and carried the hamper to their destination.

The journey didn't take them as long as it had done the first time when Ursula initially showed them the way to her underground home. This time no one remarked on the tumbled down castle or the gushing water in the gully below them. Eventually they were about to pass the cave with the shrine which Rosie had discovered. There was no steady glow from pink candles this time: there was only darkness. Brown Bear held his torch up high.

"I have been too busy lately to light the candles on my mother's shrine."

"Ursula, what do you mean?" asked Petra.

"What shrine?" Brown Bear puffed under the weight of the hamper that was slowing him down.

Only Rosie remained silent. But she realised that she hadn't had a spare minute to tell her sister or BB, about the shrine, or to tell them about her encounter with the ghost. At that moment she had to ask Ursula one thing that had puzzled her.

"Where did you find pink candles on the island, Ursula?"

"From the cottage," Ursula replied. Then she realised what was obvious. "Of course! Rosie, you have been here before haven't you!"

"Yes, I have! But I didn't have time to tell any of you, I was going to tell you, but all that has happened got in the way!" replied Rosie. "How did you know I have been here before?"

Ursula's voice came out of the torchlight, "My mother told me!"

There was a sharp gasp from Petra, she looked at her sister. "That must have been that day Rosie, when you got lost following a rabbit." Petra remembered clearly.

"Yes!" Rosie nodded. "It was!"

"So, if your mother told you, Ursula, then she can't be dead, as you have said she is," Petra insisted. "I just want to know the truth!"

"Will you please listen to me? My mother is dead! And has been dead ever since I was six. That day she went out to see if she could hail a passing boat, as she had done a few times before, but that day she didn't return. I knew something was wrong, she would never have left me alone. She would always see that one or other of the bears would look after me, when she went out for something. But that day she said she wouldn't be long! So, no need for a chaperone bear." Ursula glanced around at them all and they could see she was near to tears.

Brown Bear felt her pain. He thought she carried a heavy burden around with her and had the appearance of a little girl lost.

At that moment Brown Bear and the girls believed what their new friend said to be true, as she was so adamant that her mother really had lost her life somewhere on this island.

"Your mother must have had great trust in those fellows." Brown Bear put down the hamper of food. "Can we stop for a bite to eat?" he sat on the cave floor. "For one thing I'm starving and for another if you girls eat a lot the hamper will be lighter for me to carry."

"It's not far to the Lagoon," remarked Ursula. "We could have something to eat there and then I am hoping the bears will come to us. Otherwise, it is a long trek around the lake to the forest beyond, to search for them."

"Can I get something straight?" Petra caught hold of Ursula's arm.

"Yes of course! What is it?"

"If your mother could get out of your home cave, as you call it. Why wasn't she able to go to the rescuers?" Petra was puzzled.

"Because it was years later when the wall gave way under all her chiselling." There was a little exasperation in Ursula's voice. "In the early years of captivity there was no way out!"

Rosie leaned forward and touched Ursula's arm.

"When we came to the island in search of its secrets Lucas brought us as you know, and it was he, who mentioned that Professor's Mortimer's wife had gone missing on the island some years ago," announced Rosie, regretting immediately what she had just said, seeing Petra and Brown Bear's glaring looks of disapproval."

"What's that to do with me?" Ursula stepped over the hamper of food and walked to the entrance of the cave. "Come on, they are all here!"

Soon they were all in the fresh evening air on the shores of the lagoon. Brown Bear took the hamper and carried it to some nearby rocks. He felt the tension in the young lady who he had grown very fond of, but he knew that soon she would have to learn the truth about her parents.

"Where are the bears?" Petra asked. "I thought you said they were all here. I can't see them."

"They are here!" replied Ursula. "Look, they are playing in the water just behind those blue grey rocks on the far side."

Yes, the family were having fun. Kent was floating on his back and Starlight was busy climbing playfully up on top of his father, while Moonlight was relaxing in the shallows looking calm and serene as usual. The water was turquoise blue and rippled with ever decreasing circles. Sunlight was reflecting down through the opening in the cave roof and the late August day was mellowing into one of those golden enigmas of summer bliss.

In a while Rosie and Brown Bear unpacked some of the food and handed out wonderfully aromatic pork pies and sausage rolls, and a jar of homemade pickled onions. They all tucked in and were delighted when Rosie opened a big round tin and inside was a delicious Chocolate cake already cut into slices.

"Girls you have a wonderful Mum," Brown Bear said without thinking and immediately Ursula burst into tears.

"Oh! My dear, I am so sorry," Brown Bear apologised profusely. "You miss your mother of course! We understand, don't we, girls! I am sure she was wonderful in every way!"

"Yes, she was!" replied Ursula. Petra and Rosie felt so sorry for their new friend at that moment.

"Are you alright to carry on with your story about what has happened to you?" said Brown Bear, softly.

"Yes, I am alright, and I feel better, in fact, I feel better for a cry! Do, you remember when we first met, I told you I thought crying was futile. Here I was all alone, with no one to see my tears or hear my sobs. So, when I felt tears well up in my eyes, I would just blink them away and scold myself for being weak."

Ursula now looked different, more confident with a radiant smile of her lovely face.

"Right Petra I will answer your question and I will carry on with my account of events. The reason my mother could not go to the rescuers," Ursula bravely carried on with her narrative. "Or even the police when they came at the time. She told me when I was about three or four years old that the earthquake had caused the Eastern castle to fall, as you have all seen." The young girl nodded to her audience.

"You see it is a bit complicated because it was a few years before the earthquake had struck the island. Mother told me that in the summer of 1999 she arrived on the island ready to work, but the ground must have been made unstable causing a landslide that filled some of the subterrain caves. Mother had been trapped in the cave you now know, as the cave we called home."

"Why was she in these caves? When all her things were in the cottage!" asked Rosie.

"Doing what she loved most!" replied Ursula. "Hunting for ancient bones, of course."

"And she was trapped because of the rubble?" Petra remarked.

"Yes, with no food and only the clothes she had on. She used to tell me everything! She had worn blue jeans, a cotton floral blouse and a Gilet."

"What's a Gilet?" Rosie had not heard that word before.

"It's a type of waist coat, a body warmer," replied Petra. "Pronounced jillay!"

"My mother was incredibly brave. It took years to shift the stones in the cave wall. You know you all climbed in that way," continued Ursula. "But by the time I was six she could get outside through the hole in the wall, if need be. I did tell you about the bears caring for her in her confinement and from that time the two bears were her close friends."

"Amazing!" said Petra. "So, was she able to get out and go to the cottage then?"

'Yes! She told me everything about living down here. Remember she had no way of exploring the landscape, she knew nothing of the headland around which she could have reached the beach with the jetty. The first few months were hard and very lonely for her but once I was born, she said she was very happy and just accepted her new life.

"And the bears were part of it?" remarked Brown Bear.

"Yes!" agreed Ursula. "Her days were now busy caring for me. The bears cleared out all the fallen stones from the caves. And even taught my mother where to find the best places in the lake to catch fish, and they even showed her every nut and fruit bush in the vicinity."

"How incredible," stated Rosie. "Did she ever want to go to other parts of the island, maybe just to see if someone was still looking for her?"

"Well! No, not in the beginning! Because she couldn't!" exclaimed Ursula. "She was totally trapped down here and if it wasn't for the continued assistance of these wonderful creatures neither of us would have survived for very long."

"You and your mum were so brave," said Rosie.

"I am not really brave. I just didn't know anything else." Ursula gave a lovely warm smile to them all. "You have changed my life for the better. I am so glad you all came here."

"We are pleased too," said Petra, and Rosie agreed.

"Remember my mother did not know about the way into these caves from the cliff top. I found that myself years later. So, no, she never left the cave for years, and I only found the bore hole and the passage I brought you down here, when I was a lot older just by being curious. I loved exploring the island. Well, I had nothing else to do. And then you arrived at the cottage that night of the storm, and I kept watching you, I was fascinated with your freedom."

"Well! That's expected!" said Brown Bear knowingly. "Now there is something we have to tell you. Something very important!"

"Oh, what ever is it?" Ursula looked aghast.

"We have worked something out, haven't we, girls?" Brown Bear nodded to the girls.

"Yes, we have!" joined in Petra.

Brown Bear continued, with his steady gaze on the young lady.

"Did your mother ever mention Professor Lawrence Mortimer to you at all?"

"No, I have never heard of him. She used to talk about someone called Larry, but I never heard her mention a professor or a Lawrence Mortimer. I would have remembered if she had. No! it was Larry she talked about all the time, well, every day in fact. She would tell me how incredible he was, how intelligent he was, and how thoughtful he was, and how very, very, loving he was too," Ursula looked puzzled. "But he was someone she met at university when she was eighteen years old! Not a professor."

Brown Bear gave a short cough. "Well, since we arrived on the island and meeting you, a lot of facts have put themselves together," Brown Bear could hear himself talking but the more that came out of his mouth the more he could feel himself floundering. How he wished his ursine family had taught him more about delicate matters like this one, but that had never happened and until he met Petra and Rosie, he had never realised how complicated young females could be. He gave a nervous cough but managed to muster up enough verbal stamina to tell Ursula the truth.

"We believe that Professor Lawrence B. Mortimer is your father!" exclaimed Brown Bear.

"What do you mean? My father!" Ursula exclaimed in shock and surprise. "Mother would have told me if I had a father."

"Well!" said Brown Bear. "She probably thought you were too young to take all that on board. Six! Did you say you were just six when you last saw your mother?"

"Yes, I was," Ursula was deep in thought. "You are probably right. she only ever talked about positive things to me. It was quite difficult living down here anyway without added stress. I know she loved Larry whoever he was. She was confident that one day he would come and find us."

"Well actually that is where we come in!" stated Rosie. "Isn't it, Petra?"

"Yes! Rosie is right! It is a bit of a long story," said Petra. "We will tell you everything later, but one day in July this year Professor Mortimer moved into a cottage in the village where we live. Apparently, he had lived there many years before with his wife Emily Jane Mortimer!"

"Yes, our teacher Mrs Roberts announced the news in our history lesson," continued Rosie. "And we were having a famous Archaeologist as our new neighbour. A famous professor who was moving back to live in our village. We both went round on his first evening to say Hello. 'Old Mill Cottage' is the name of his home, so we went to introduce ourselves. You know we were just being good neighbours."

"No! I don't!" interjected Ursula. "The bears are the only neighbours I've ever known. I remember seeing initials on objects in the cottage on the beach."

"Yes, we saw them all, as you already know, Ursula," said Petra. "When we arrived on the island, we only knew that the Professor asked us to find the secrets of the island. He had planned to come and find them himself but on that first night back in our village after twenty-seven years away, unfortunately, when we arrived to welcome him to our village he had already fallen and broken his ankle."

"Oh! Goodness! How awful! Poor man!" exclaimed Ursula.

"It was so fortunate that we were a bit nosey and wanted to meet him," joined in Rosie. "We called the paramedics and as he lay in the ambulance he beckoned Petra and me to go inside, and he asked us to come to this island and find the secrets."

"When was this?" she asked.

"A few weeks ago in July, just before we broke up from school for the summer holiday," answered Petra. "Brown Bear didn't know anything about this until I needed his help the night I found the Professor's Mahogany chest in the cellar of the cottage."

"Yes, my dear all that is true," announced Brown Bear. "And it wasn't until Lucas was steering his motorboat towards this island, on a very hot afternoon in early August that we knew anything about the Professor's missing wife."

"I see," said Ursula in a subdued voice. "E.J.M. Emily Jane Mortimer."

"Precisely!" exclaimed Brown Bear. "As extraordinary as this all seems, I don't think there is any doubt that the Professor's missing wife and your mother are the same person?"

"Were the same person!" exclaimed Ursula in her sorrow, stating the past tense.

"Yes!" Brown Bear took the girl's hand in reassurance that she wasn't alone in her tragedy. "We will help you find out what happened to your mother."

"Thank you, Mr Bear and you two wonderful girls. I am just so happy we have met. I have been very lonely, and it has been amazing for me to have such great company. Now all we must do is find my mother's remains.

"Hey! listen Petra your phone is ringing," remarked Rosie. "It is amazing it still has some battery left."

Petra searched in her rucksack and pulled out her active mobile. "It is only because of Mali's super charger, normally it would be dead by now."

"Quick, answer it. Is it Mum?" asked Rosie.

They could all hear Petra talking but it wasn't her Mum, "It's the police," she told them aside. "Oh no, when did that happen? We thought they had been taken to the cells in Swallowfield Police station."

Brown Bear held his paw out for the phone, "Yes, Officer," he said. "That is not good news. Oh dear, how has that been made possible?" Brown Bear listened a while longer. "Right then, that alters things! Yes, we will remain vigilant. Goodbye, Sir."

All three girls looked on in a state of great anxiety. "What is it, BB?"

"The Magistrate's court has only let the Newsome's out on Bail! Now we really are in danger! Petra ring Lucas if you can? We need him here at once."

"No, I can't, he hasn't got a mobile," said Petra. "And the battery on my phone isn't going to last much longer. Those villains are bound to come back to the island."

"What are we going to do?" cried Rosie.

"We must find my mother's body." replied Ursula. "I have been in contact with her many times over the years and I always feel she is still on the island, but I have searched everywhere, and I can't find any sign of where her remains might be."

"Ooooo!" exclaimed Rosie. "What about in the forest? Do the bears live in caves deep underground?"

"They do! but she is not there!" replied Ursula. "They both searched with me as soon as she went missing, but of course we only had access to the cave we were trapped in, and the lagoon. The bears were lost without my mother, the female went off her food for a while and lost weight, animals grieve the same way humans do."

"We have a dog and two cats at home and Yes, we know they feel everything just like us humans," said Petra.

"Kent helped her and soon she was eating again," Ursula smiled. "I was very relieved."

"You are very in tune with your ursine friends," remarked Brown Bear. "You must have an inkling of an idea where we might find your mother."

"I know she isn't at rest! I feel her presence, as if she is trying to tell me something."

"Like when do you feel that, Ursula?" asked Rosie. "I'm sorry to ask but perhaps we can find a clue."

Ursula was deep in thought, her long black hair being disturbed by a soft evening breeze, she reached up with her suntanned fingers and wiped an annoying strand away from her cheek.

"Well, Rosie, you may be right!" she said looking at Rosie's expectant face.

"To be honest, since the day my mother failed to return though the hole that she had worked so hard to achieve, pounding away at the stones and rubble day after day, breaking down the wall of landslide debris. I have never felt she has deserted me. You see we were prisoners in there because of that wall." Ursula stopped to take a breath. "Oh, I just remembered it was the bears who made her a crib for me when I was tiny and pulled out their own hair to line my bed, so it was snug and cosy for me."

"Oh, what wonderful companions for her in those hours of need," said Brown Bear. "I think I will go and have a chat with them! They might well give me a clue as to what had happened to Emily Jane, your dear mother."

"Yes, please do that, BB." Ursula called after him.

Brown Bear did not have time to answer because at that moment a police helicopter flew over the island.

34
TRAGEDY

It took them a while to make their way around the headland the next morning. The tide was out, but the sand was still wet. They were anxious to know why the police helicopter had landed on the island again.

"BB, do you think it is safe here now?" asked Petra.

"Safe for what?" asked Rosie, trying not to get her trainers wet in the squelchy terrain.

"Well!" exclaimed Brown Bear, "We just need to be cautious because I am sure someone is on the island. I know that was a police helicopter that landed and took off almost immediately and to me that only means one thing."

"And what might that be, Mr Bear?" asked Ursula.

"That the police are aware that the Newsome's might return for some devious reason to the island, to accomplish their plan," he said as he held onto Rosie who was finding the soft wet sand a problem. "Are you alright, my dear?"

"Yes, I am if I can hold on to you while we climb over these rocks," Rosie held on to Brown Bear, as he guided her through a tricky bit of the rocky coastline. Then after a struggle they rounded the headland and back onto the beach with the jetty.

"Oh! Look everyone, the cottage!" Rosie was overjoyed.

"Nice to be back!" Petra ran up the beach ahead of the others. "Oh, the door is locked! We didn't lock it, did we, BB?"

"No, we couldn't," he said. "It seems to be locked from the inside. I will have to give it a shove. Stand back everyone!"

At that moment, they all nearly jumped out of their skins, as the old familiar sounds of howling and growling of the bears could be heard coming from the bowels of the earth.

"They are not happy!" exclaimed Ursula. "I must go to them!"

"Hey steady on! Someone is definitely on the island!" Brown Bear looked very worried. "That helicopter didn't land for fun. I would prefer us all to stay together. Let's sort this door out and get inside the cottage and then if your ursine friends are still disturbed then I will come with you to check on them!"

Ursula didn't look happy but nodded all the same. "All right but I love them dearly,"

"Now I'll have to get a tool to help budge this door," Brown Bear looked around for a heavy object.

"No! BB, you don't have to!" exclaimed Rosie. "I left the kitchen window off the latch, I'm the smallest I can squeeze in that way and open the door from the inside and let you all in."

"They have installed a Yale lock." Brown Bear noticed a shiny round lock high up on the door.

"BB, who do you think did it?" asked Rosie.

"The police, I presume," he replied.

"Oh," said Rosie. "But I want to help."

"I can squeeze in too," said Petra.

"Yes!" Brown Bear was deep in thought, he knew he was always responsible for Petra and Rosie. He was aware they were growing up fast and becoming young ladies with strong minds of their own. And then suddenly everything seemed to be taken out of his hands and the great oak door groaned on its hinges and opened unaided.

"Wow!" exclaimed Rosie. "Who did that?"

"That's really creepy!" Petra looked on in amazement.

Ursula stepped forward towards the black void that lay before them. Brown Bear pulled her back. "Better be careful, young lady, I don't understand the vibes I am feeling about all this."

"It's my mother!" exclaimed Ursula.

"So, she is not dead?" Petra was puzzled.

"Of course, I keep telling you she died when I was six!"

Petra caught hold of Rosie's hand. But Rosie pulled away and entered the cottage.

"It's alright, I feel her presence," Ursula stepped inside quite unafraid.

"I do too!" Rosie had experienced something in the cave where Ursula had built her mother's shrine, and she felt the same now. She was aware of something strange inside.

"Well," said Brown Bear. "I am an animal, and I am not sure I am privileged to the supernatural. Stop, girls, let me go in and check everywhere first."

The girls waited while he entered. He went into all the rooms but he neither saw nor felt anything untoward. "Okay! I just thought it might be the Newsome's hiding away in here."

Even though Rosie and Ursula detected a presence, nothing had been disturbed since they both were last here. Rosie went into the kitchen and filled the kettle.

"Who would like a cup of tea?" Rosie enjoyed looking after the others. "And there is some of Mum's cake left!"

After they had refreshed themselves, Petra went upstairs to sort out some clean clothes.

"We have worn the same things for ages," she said out loud, as she laid some jeans and tops on the big ornate bed, but as she did so she felt something touch her hair.

"Who's there?" Petra exclaimed. For the first time she experienced a presence in the bedroom. She turned around but there was no one there.

Petra felt a chill surround her and then out of nowhere a piece of material scrunched up in a ball dropped to the floor in front of her. She bent and picked it up and for no reason she could think of, she opened one of the dressing table drawers and popped it inside. Then she ran down the stairs and out into the sunshine to join the others.

She found them sitting on the rocks watching a motorboat heading in the direction of the North shore. Brown Bear was looking very agitated.

"What's wrong, BB? Petra sat down beside him.

"I would like to know who is in that boat?" But before he could see the occupants clearly the vessel disappeared behind the headland.

"Oh! I am getting old!" he sighed. "I can see birds flocking around a trawler, but I can't see the faces of people."

"Don't worry Mr Bear!" Ursula was concerned. "You probably don't recognise them because that boat was moving very fast!"

"Yes! you are right, young lady," he exclaimed. "Now what would interest someone on the North shore?"

"It is just a sheltered haven with high cliffs," Ursula explained.

"How can we find out who they are?" Brown Bear was getting more agitated.

"There is a cave hidden away in the rocks," remarked Petra, remembering her adventure down in the cove. "That was where I found the letter from…."

Brown Bear interrupted her. He knew what she was going to say, but he thought, 'we cannot tell Ursula at this point, that they had all read a private letter to the Professor from his missing wife.'

"You know girls I am convinced the occupants of that boat are the Newsom's, breaking their bail conditions."

"Yes, BB you are probably right!" Petra sighed with relief. She knows that she sometimes says things, before she gives her words without enough thought.

After a while they all walked down the beach to the jetty. This time they could see that many of its black iron girders were exposed and quite visible in the water. The morning sun shone down into the deep, revealing fronds of various seaweeds that grew there, swaying in the incoming flow.

Rosie was the first to look up. "Look! Another motorboat way out at sea!" She noticed a brightly coloured vessel.

"It's Lucas!" yelled Petra. "And someone else is with him."

"He's waving frantically. I wonder what is going on?" Brown Bear was waving back to his old friend. "I think he will have a long wait before he can land, the tide has a fair way to come in yet."

"And so will that boat be heading for the North shore? It looks like Lucas has followed the first boat. Come on let us go and wait for him at the cottage, girls we ought to wash out some of our dirty clothes."

"I'll come and help," said Ursula.

"Yes," said Rosie. "Everything should dry quickly in this heat."

"We could do with a clothesline and pegs," replied Petra, jokingly.

"I know where there is one and a basket of pegs," Ursula informed them, "Come with me. I will show you."

She led them around the back of the cottage where there were gorse bushes growing under the cliffs. There was a wire line tied to two of the highest scrubs. Petra and Rosie were delighted.

"Ah, the pegs," asked Petra.

"I know!" exclaimed Rosie. "I have seen them in that cupboard under the kitchen sink." She went inside the cottage to fetch them, "This is a stroke of luck. I have found an old box of washing powder too."

The three girls busied themselves for the rest of the morning with the laundry and soon jeans, shorts and T-shirts were billowing in the summer breeze.

The noonday sun was climbing high in the sky. The tide had turned, and its familiar roar blotted out everything our little group of adventurers were saying.

It was well over two hours before Lucas was tying his vessel up alongside the jetty.

"Come on, old Matey, good to see you again," Brown Bear helped steady the boat. "Now what is going on? Why have the Police let those two scoundrels out on bail?"

"I dunno." Lucas jumped down off his bright red motorboat. "This is Jake, my nephew, he's come to be of assistance, if needs be."

"Are you expecting trouble then, old pal?" Brown Bear looked closely at Lucas.

"Come on! I can tell you know something."

"Aye! I do that, but let's get nearer the cliffs. There be a fair wind and it can carry voices to the next cove if you aren't careful."

Soon they were all sitting on the rocks outside the cottage. Jake introduced himself to the girls and Rosie went inside to bring out refreshing drinks of lemonade. Lucas began to tell them what he knew, they were all silent for a while listening to Brown Bear's old friend.

"Well, it's like this you see," Lucas said, in a low voice. "I've been hearing things about those Newsome's, and what I've been told is not good." He took a sip of his lemonade. "Swallows village is full of gossip and old Mrs Jones at the post office knew the Professor and his wife over twenty years ago, when they lived at Old Mill Cottage."

At that moment there was a loud howling from the bears and Ursula got up to go to see what was troubling them.

"I have to go! I won't be long," she said with determination in her voice. Then she disappeared up the cliff path and disappeared down the blow hole.

"Where has the young lady gone?" Jake asked.

"Big long story I'll tell you later," replied Petra.

"Aye! Then I will carry on," said Lucas. "It was six o'clock this morning when I was down on Swallows Quay checking out my craft and I was approached by those siblings. I was wary, as Mrs Jones had said they had been seen in a black motor one evening outside Old Mill Cottage."

"Do you know exactly when they were seen?" Petra was watching the fisherman closely.

"Aye! I do, around the time when everyone in the village were excited about Professor Mortimer's return to the village, late June or July I think it was."

"Oh yes!" said Rosie knowingly. "It was in early July that Petra and I found the professor lying injured on his kitchen floor."

"Oh dear, that must have been you that called the ambulance." Lucas gave a smile.

"Yes, it was, and it was when he was placed on a stretcher inside the vehicle that he called Petra and I to go inside, as he had a request for us to fulfil!"

"Can I ask what that was?" Lucas was intrigued.

"It was for me and Petra to find the secrets of the island," said Rosie. "Apparently, that was why he had moved back to the village."

"Yes! The village heard that he'd come back to look for his Missus," said Lucas, deep in thought. "Just such a pity she went missing all of them years ago. In the late 1990's they had both come here to the island to do some research after that earthquake. They had waited over three years for the dust to settle, so to speak. Should have been safe by then."

"But apparently not!" exclaimed Brown Bear. "So, what happened this morning, Lucas?"

"O, Aye. Sorry," Lucas composed himself. "Them Newsome's arrived in a taxi on the quay, rare sight in those parts nowadays. I haven't seen a taxi down there for years."

"And?" Brown Bear was getting a little impatient, as the sun was soaring overhead, and he felt so hot in his thick furry coat.

"They wanted me to bring them to the island, but I refused. Not very happy they were and even offered me twice the going rate, but I still refused."

"Good for you!" said Petra. "So, what did they do?"

"They went off, I dunna know where. But next thing that old rouge Les Lescott arrived in his boat, tied it up at the quay and next thing those no-good Newsome's returned, and got on board his boat!"

'Who is this Lescott? Is he a crook?" asked Rosie, fascinated with Lucas' story.

"No! Not really just a troublemaker and a nosey parker!"

"Oh! we don't like nosey parkers, do we Petra, remember? Troy Gardiner in year seven?'

"Yes! Rosie, I thought we agreed not to mention him again!" Petra turned to Lucas intrigued with his story. "Please, tell us more about Professor Mortimer and his wife. Did they get married in the village church?"

"Alas no!" Lucas was in a distant state, as if he was remembering every detail of the Mortimer's life in the village. "No! The grapevine says they married in Oxford amongst their undergraduate friends."

"Wow!" stated Petra. "I want to go and study at Oxford University one day!" she looked around at the others. "If I really work hard that is where I would like to be, because I have a future and when I settle down, I hope I will have achieved a degree first. I feel very impressed with what Mrs Mortimer achieved; I believe from Ursula that her mother was an archaeologist in her own right." Petra took a deep breath. "Lucas! Do you think I could ever achieve anything like that?"

"Well! I am not the one to tell you anything along those lines," Lucas sighed. "I missed out there. But what I can say is, do what you are comfortable with and don't let anyone stand in your way!"

"Thank you for that, Lucas, I think you are very wise!" Petra turned to Brown Bear.

"Do you think we should go after Ursula?"

"Not yet!" he remarked. "Those bears have been her whole life. We'll give her a little more time."

"Yes, BB, you are right." Petra then turned to the fisherman again.

"Lucas, please tell us everything you know about the Mortimer's, where they very much in love?'

"Well, my dear, I am a humble bachelor and I have very little knowledge of such matters, but Mrs Jones in the village has been married three times and I am sure she must be an expert in affairs of the heart."

"Oooo!" exclaimed Rosie. "Did she know anything about the Professor and his wife?"

"I am sure she did, but a very discrete lady she be," Lucas was deep in thought. "The only bit of gossip I did hear was in the first weeks of their occupation of Old Mill Cottage back in 1994."

"Can you tell us, Lucas, or is it very personal?" Petra asked.

"It is personal but seeing that the whole village knew at the time I will tell you, because you all seem to be very involved with the professor."

"We are, Lucas! Yes! We are involved and as Professor Mortimer asked us personally to find the secrets of the island for him because he found himself incapacitated, we are involved, and have found some of the secrets already!" proclaimed Petra.

"You have? Well, that is good. And yes! I will tell you what I have heard, and I would not repeat it if it weren't true."

"What is it, Lucas? Please tell us." begged Rosie.

Brown Bear looked perplexed as he was worrying about his girls. Up to now he had censured everything he heard that was not suitable for their young ears. Brown Bear gave his old friend a pat on his sunburnt arm.

"You had better tell us what you know."

"Aye I will," Lucas made himself as comfortable as he could on the rocks and carried on with his saga.

"They came as newlyweds, lovestruck so to speak. The villagers were very fond of them as they didn't act like strangers looking down on everyone. They were the nicest couple you could meet. The Professor was highly respected by everyone and as for her, Mrs Mortimer she was loved by the community, you know the kind of lady who was interested in everyone who she met." Lucas looked round at everyone. "She was devoted to her husband and helped him with his work, as well as her own."

"Oh!" said Petra. "That is so nice to hear, Lucas. What did she look like?"

"There wasn't anyone who made her acquaintance that didn't love her. Very beautiful she was with long wavy black hair and piercing blue eyes she had, and not a bit snobby, even though she was a professor herself and married to the eminent archaeologist. All in all, she was a lovely friendly woman."

"She sounds amazing!" Rosie was impressed too.

"She was," Lucas smiled. "She helped with the mobile library that came around once a month and even helped in the church sometimes, arranging the flowers for the Sunday service. Mrs Jones used to say how accomplished she was at everything." Lucas took a long deep breath.

"So!" said Brown Bear. "So, what happened?"

"Well, within the first few weeks of coming to live in these parts, one day there was great excitement because news got round the village that the very popular couple were expecting a baby."

"Oh, how lovely for them," said Rosie.

"Very nice," said Brown Bear.

"Well, it wasn't all nice!" exclaimed Lucas.

"What do you mean?" asked Petra.

"Well because there had been such happiness in the village it came as a great shock when one morning an ambulance arrived at 'Old Mill Cottage' and the Professor had been called back home, and he accompanied his wife to the hospital."

Both Petra and Rosie looked alarmed, "Oh dear!" said Petra. "Why? What had happened?"

"No one knew anything all that morning, but by early afternoon the Professor arrived back at the cottage without his wife!"

"So, what had happened?" Brown Bear was extremely interested in his old friend's account of the happenings back in 1994.

"Well, it remained a secret for a while, I think the Doc' was allowing time for his wife to recover."

"Lucas, please tell us what happened?"

"Later there was a rumour going round that Mrs Mortimer had lost their child, and it was no fault of her own," Lucas wiped tears from his eyes.

"Oh! Lucas, why are you so upset?" Petra asked the fisherman in a soft gentle voice. "Did something happen to make her lose her baby?"

"Yes, it was cruel. She and the Doc' were so happy. Very popular with everyone in the village, not snobby like a few of the villagers were expecting, you know, having a distinguished college background and all that!"

"Did anyone in the village at that time have any idea what actually happened?" Rosie's voice was low, and she couldn't hide being upset too.

"There was a rumour at the time, but it wasn't until months later that it became actual knowledge. Mrs Jones at the post office found out first, then it circulated round those parts like a forest fire, and it was exactly twenty-seven years ago, when the couple moved away!" Lucas stood up. "Ouch these rocks get harder I must stretch my legs or I'll get cramp."

"Me too!" Brown Bear stood up too. "So, what had actually

happened then?"

"Well, it breaks my heart to tell you, but the Doc' had been away back to Oxford we think, and Mrs Mortimer was alone in 'Old Mill Cottage' for a couple of nights!"

"From what I have heard she was awakened in the middle of the night by an intruder. She must have screamed but no one lived near enough to the Old Mill to hear her. Someone had tied her by her wrists to the bedpost, and the intruder ransacked the downstairs rooms, and a few valuable items were later reported missing. Even a sentimental necklace that had been a special gift to Emily Jane from the Doc."

"How awful!" exclaimed Petra.

"She was left tied up all night, a prisoner in her own home, and it wasn't until the post lady came in the morning and found her in great distress that the police were called."

"That's really terrible!" Rosie was near to tears. "So, what happened?"

"Well, the Professor was called home and when he arrived later that morning he called an ambulance, and he went with his wife to the hospital. The whole village was in shock at the robbery and the police were called but nothing came of it! It wasn't 'til a few days later we heard Mrs Doc' had lost the child. Whole village was in mourning for them. Very, very, sad it was and for them a real tragedy."

"Lucas!" Petra looked straight into the fisherman's eyes. "Did they ever find out who the intruder was?"

"No!" Lucas continued. "They didn't arrest anyone, if that is what you mean? But you know what village folk are like! There was gossip about an old flame of the Professor's, someone who had been dumped and held a massive grudge, someone who through the years had wanted revenge on the Professor's lovely young bride."

Now it was dawning on Petra, as to whom this woman might

have been! Through no fault of Emily Jane's, this evil person was so jealous that she would do anything to once again seek the affections of Lawrence B. Mortimer, even murder! But she obviously did not know him well enough, for he had been devoted to his wife.

There was a stunned silence among this little company, no one had expected to hear such a horrifying account. Petra decided that all they can do now is find all the secrets of the island. As each day passed their task was becoming more and more complicated.

35
CONFESSION

There was an awful lot of information to take in on that evening as Petra and Rosie prepared a picnic meal for their supper. There had been no sign of Ursula and after their meal Brown Bear had decided to walk with Lucas to the jetty.

"Listen I'll leave Jake my nephew, he's starting his new job as a police cadet; I think you call it. He seems to have a lot in common with your girls. If the Newsome's are on the island, then an extra pair of hands might be useful, if you get my meaning?"

"Yes, Lucas I do," replied Brown Bear, as they made their way down the beach. "Do you know why the police released that pair on bail?" He remarked. "Weren't you and old Sergeant Bannering drinking mates at one time?"

"Yes! We were when I was younger but these days there aren't much of the old crowd left," said Lucas. "But I heard a whisper when I was in the Post Office!"

"From old Mrs Jones?" Brown Bear was glued to every word his old friend uttered.

"No!" said Lucas. "She passed on, must be over three years ago, Delyth, her daughter runs it now and she is married to Constable Douglas Henshaw, and he likes a chat down at the Cross keys on a Saturday night. Not that he'd repeat anything top secret you know!"

"Of course not! So, what was the whisper you heard?" Brown Bear asked, as they approached the jetty. The tide was high, and Lucas' boat bobbed on its moorings, the sun had begun to sink low in the west.

"Tell me! I must get back to the girls and if Ursula hasn't returned then I will have to go and look for her." There was a great deal of anxiety in Brown Bear's voice.

"Who is that girl Ursula?" asked Lucas. "And doesn't her name have something to do with bears?"

"We don't know who she is. Petra met her first one night in the dark outside the cottage. Look I have to go, and so must you or you will miss the tide," Brown Bear patted his old mate on the shoulder. "Come on, tell me what the whisper was?"

"Well, as you would expect there was much disgust with the decision to let them go even though it is on bail, but someone suggested it was that the cops hadn't got enough evidence to charge them with murder. And as Mrs Mortimer is still missing, everyone became aware during the nineties that Joanna Newsome had a grudge against the Doc'. Apparently, she was at the same college as him and his misses, not that they were married then! Just kids starting out."

"Right!" said Brown Bear, "That is enough for me. So, that wicked couple will be here to look for the lady's remains. And if they find any that will prove their guilt to Superintendent Harding."

"Yes! That's about it!" replied Lucas. "But a long time has passed so, probably not much hope of that! Aye that be it then, I'll be back in the morning. I'll see if Lescott's boat is back at the dock. If not, I'll do a bit of enquiring as to his whereabouts."

"Yes, thanks I would appreciate that old pal, well goodnight,' Brown Bear hesitated.

"Oh! One more thing, you know this island like the back of your hand?"

"Aye, I do that!" answered Lucas.

"Have you ever seen bears on this island, you know, wild brown bears?"

Lucas looked totally amazed. "No! I ain't seen bears running wild, nor did I ever see that girl before and if the professor's wife is found on this island, I will be very surprised, because back in the day there was a massive land and sea search for her. At the end of it the police gave up ever finding her. And as for the Doc' he was a broken man, heartbroken to the core he was."

"The gentleman has my sympathy, tragic tale," replied Brown Bear. "Right Ho! See you in the morning." And with that he waved as Lucas started the engine of his motorboat and steered away in the direction of Swallows quay, approximately five miles across the water.

Brown Bear rushed back to the cottage, but when he arrived the girls weren't there. The sun was beginning to set, and a strange golden shimmer spread along the horizon, the sea took on a burnished glow and an east wind stirred the marron grass on the top of the cliffs. The high tide whipped up pink tipped waves that were now being buffeted by the wind.

Brown Bear didn't want to shout out to the girls, as he was aware there might be other people on the island. He pushed the door of the cottage and fortunately the lock had been left off the catch. He could smell perfume coming from the first room, he thought that was very strange. It was the room he and the girls didn't use, as the floor was covered in fossils and ancient artifacts, they all believed had once belonged to the Professor's wife.

He decided to look upstairs for the girls, after all, they must be very tired by now and probably sleeping. He climbed the first two steps and heard something move ahead of him. The light in the cottage was very dim. He had forgotten his torch and he had no idea where to look for the oil lamp they had found on their first evening.

Again, he heard a soft sound, and the aroma of the perfume filled the air overpowering the static musty smell that enveloped this old beach dwelling.

Brown Bear could feel the heckles on his neck stand on end. He had to admit he was a little scared of the unknown. He was now in the bedroom over by the ornate dressing table that he now knew the Professor had installed in this exquisite room for his much-loved wife.

Then suddenly he heard a rustling noise, as though of crinoline brushing against a ballroom floor. What little light remained at the window was fading fast and, as he looked out into the night, he could see the moon very low on the eastern horizon. He could feel his bristling heckles on the back of his neck rising and a buzz of fear urged him to move towards the door that led to the room, at the top of the stairs. Then he heard the rustling sound again and there at his feet was a screwed-up ball of paper.

"No, it is not paper!" he said out loud, "I am not quite sure what material this is." Then the swirling sound of taffeta brushed past him once again and in the next second it was gone. Brown Bear shivered. He told himself he was not afraid but just puzzled.

Brown Bear was finding himself in a strange place! He was feeling and hearing things he had never felt or heard before. In that moment he felt paralysed, still, unable to move.

'Whatever was happening to him,' he wondered. 'Was this experience what Rosie meant, by feeling a supernatural presence?' He suddenly felt claustrophobic, he felt hot and there was no air! As a faint light moved across the window of the upstairs room, he knew he had to get out. The gentle moonshine gave him energy to get away as fast as he could. He flew down the stairs clutching the rolled-up piece of material that he found on the floor. Had he imagined the voice he could hear, a calm controlled voice saying, "Don't go I am here, I am here."

He reached the front door and banged it open, crashing it on its jamb. Brown Bear gulped in fresh air and collapsed to the rocky ground outside. Then he heard a scream that brought him to his senses. It was Rosie's scream.

"Rosie, what is the matter?" He called out into the still evening air. "Come over here, come to me." And then he saw the three girls running pell-mell towards him along the sand, as if they were being chased. "I am here. Whatever is the matter?"

All three girls were almost collapsing after their run, gasping for breath. Brown Bear took charge and guided them all inside the cottage. He didn't like seeing them all so upset.

"I will go and make some hot chocolate, now wait here and calm down, then after a nice, sweet drink you can tell me all about what has upset you all so much."

"Tha tha thank you BB," stuttered Rosie between her sobs.

"Thank you, BB," Petra gave him a feeble smile.

Ursula seemed the calmest of the three. "You are very kind, Mr Bear. Can we all go and sit on the big bed upstairs? My legs ache from running."

"And mine do too," sobbed Rosie, still with tremors in her voice.

"Well, that's a bit tricky!" exclaimed Brown Bear.

"Why ever not? We want to rest up there. We are very tired. We have run all the way from the North cove!"

"Okay. I'm just being a bit silly!" Brown Bear's voice was hushed. "I just thought there was someone up there!" He led the way upstairs to see if it was safe. "Now! what made you run so fast, as if you were being chased?"

"We were being chased by those wicked Newsome people and an ugly man with a gun!" said Rosie.

"A gun!" exclaimed Brown Bear. "I will go and lock the door," he said, and made his way to the front door. He glanced out over the shoreline and the tide was starting to wash into the cove. He could see a vessel moored out at sea.

'That is strange, no lights! So, it cannot be trawling,' he thought, as he shut the door and pushed up the metal catch on the new lock.

He made the hot chocolate and found a tray to carry the drinks up to the exhausted girls. The white object was no ordinary kitchen tray! He stooped to reach for it, as it had been pushed in a crevice between an old kitchen unit and the stove. Brown Bear pulled it out and there in an intricate design were the entwined letters of E and J!

"Emily....Jane," he said out loud.

And at that exact moment a gust of wind blew open the small kitchen window and made it slam shut with a bang.

He picked up the tray and carried it upstairs to the girls who had made themselves comfortable on the big bed. He could hear a lot of excited chattering, obviously they had recovered from their fright and the gruelling run home.

"Quick!" exclaimed Rosie. "BB, is coming, do you think we ought to tell him?"

"Tell me what?" Brown Bear opened the door calmly and placed the tray of hot chocolate on the dressing table. He kept his cool even though he felt very alarmed inside.

Petra saw the look on Brown Bear's face, she knew he was very perceptive so there was no reason to delay the truth.

"Come and sit down, BB, we have something important to tell you!"

He held the tray of drinks out for the girls.

"This is the last of the chocolate powder, in fact our supplies are getting very sparse now. We will have to think about going home soon." He found a comfy place on the sofa and waited for someone to speak.

"Oh no!" exclaimed Rosie. "We can't go home until we find the secrets Professor Mortimer wants us to find."

"Don't forget, girls, school is looming on the horizon. Now what have you got to tell me and why were you all on the nsorth shore?"

Petra took charge and began telling the story of the late

afternoon. Rosie kept fidgeting and Ursula put her arm round the young girl to comfort her.

"Well, BB! You were quite a long-time seeing Lucas off on his boat and Rosie and I got a bit bored and decided to go and find Ursula. We were going to go the underground way but then she came running to us on the beach and she told us to follow her to the North cove, as she had something important to show us." Petra met Ursula's eyes and the girl nodded in agreement.

"Yes, that is right!" Ursula's face suddenly lit up, as if the sun shone brightly into the room, even though the sky outside the window was getting dark.

"I was on the way back from checking to see if the bears were all right because that loud howl, we heard told me there was something wrong, but when I found them by the lagoon my fears were in vain and to the contrary, they were totally happy and something wonderful had happened!"

"Now, don't side-track my dear, do concentrate and tell us what drew you to the North cove." Brown Bear was getting tired after the long day.

"Sorry, BB, but I do have something nice to tell you later. Now back to this afternoon, I found a boat moored to an old post among some rocks and I heard three voices in the distance," said Ursula, in an excited voice. "I knew there was a cave nearby, but I had never been in it before,"

"So, you felt you had to go inside to hide," said Brown Bear.

"Of course!" exclaimed Ursula. "At the back of the cave I found three rolled up sleeping bags and I realised who they belonged to. At that point I decided to come back here when I bumped into Rosie and Petra on the beach so, I took them back to show them what I had found, but luck was against us, and three voices came nearer and nearer, and we were trapped hiding at the back of the cave. I am positive it was those dreadful Newsome's and their boat man they called Les."

"Yes, Lucas was telling me about Les Lescott who he told me was one of the biggest rogues on the mainland," Brown Bear stretched his leg and rubbed his knee.

"What's the matter, BB, are you okay?" said a rather concerned Rosie.

"I am just getting a bit older, and my knee bothers me sometimes. It will be alright in the morning. So, what happened next?"

"Well!" exclaimed Petra. "The three of us went right to the back of the cave, and just as Ursula said, there were rolled up sleeping bags and a hamper of food. But at that point the Newsome's and the boat man returned, and it was real luck they did not see us."

"So, what happened then?" Brown Bear took a sip of his drink.

"Well, we lay flat on the cave floor behind their bags."

"Yes!" said Rosie. "They started to talk about Emily Jane."

"And what did they say?" Brown Bear was very interested in the girl's account of the events.

"Well, if ever I thought that my mother might still be alive!" Ursula looked straight at Brown Bear. "There is no doubt now! I know that the Newsome woman killed her, she took her revenge here on this island. She was boasting to the two men that it had given her great pleasure to be rid of the person who stole her lover, some man she had adored back in her college days."

Brown Bear stood up and went over to the window in the ornate bedroom. He opened the window that creaked on its hinges and drew in an enormous gulp of the fresh sea air.

"And what did this woman say then?" he felt sick and worried in that moment

"She was delighted in the fact that she had gained the two men's whole attention," Petra took up their account. "And she described how on one hot day she had come to the island alone, even dared facing the voyage through the perilous rocks that surround these waters, and she even said it was lucky that she had seen her rival sitting by a rock pool with her back to herself, looking out to sea.

So, she crept up on her victim and took her off the scene forever. She gloated as she told her brother and Lescott that now, Emily Jane could never distract her old lover again. He would not belong to Emily Jane ever again!"

"What a wicked woman!" exclaimed Brown Bear.

"Well, yes," said Petra. "She is wicked and what she said next was very shocking, especially as it was Ursula's mother she was talking about, but BB, our new friend was amazing and kept her cool."

"Oh Ursula!" said Brown Bear. "I am so sorry you witnessed all that."

Ursula nodded and gave him a knowing smile.

"Yes BB, it was terrible what she did to my mother!"

Rosie's eyes welled up with tears once again.

"Don't cry Rosie darling. You three have been so brave! Come on, let us finish our chocolate before it goes cold."

Brown Bear looked at these three young women and could only imagine them lying flat on the sandy cave floor, hidden and very scared and not even daring to breathe, whilst listening to what had happened to the girl's mother. He shivered and shook his head in disbelief, as one by one the girls unravelled the horrors of the afternoon.

"BB, we were very frightened being so close to those Newsome people!" exclaimed Rosie. "I am certain the man who I think was her brother was neatly dressed but the boatman was rough and ready! You know what I mean, don't you, BB?"

"Yes! Indeed I do!" replied Brown Bear. "What did the woman say next?"

Ursula left the comfort of the cosy ornate bed where the girls had been resting and moved to the sofa and took hold of Brown Bear's big furry paw.

"Joanna Newsome, I believe that is her name, carried on

boasting to the two men! She told them she picked up a rock and crept up behind my mother, the most beautiful and the most loving woman in the world," cried Ursula.

"Oh! Ursula my dear girl, this is so terrible," Brown Bear held her in his arms, this is awful for you to hear, I am so sorry," he said. "Only tell me more if it doesn't distress you too much."

"Ursula was crying now, and Petra stepped in to tell Brown Bear the gory details and Rosie comforted their friend as best she could.

"BB! From the depth of that cave, we heard a confession, that Joanna Newsome had crept up behind her victim and raised her hand which was holding a rock ready to strike. Emily Jane saw her reflection in the water of the pool, and she turned to face her assailant and was cruelly attacked."

"Oh no!" exclaimed Brown Bear shocked to his core. He sat with his head in his hands.

Petra continued. "That wicked creature had hit the side of her head and Emily Jane ran for her life in the direction of the cottage. And that Newsome woman was proud to tell her captivated audience, her brother and that Lescott man what she had done. BB, you wouldn't believe how much she boasted, she was relishing in it all again, as she went on to say how much blood was everywhere and she told them she was about to chase after her victim to finish the job when she had to stop in her tracks, as an enormous wild animal placed itself between her and her badly wounded victim. I think it was Kent!"

"Yes, it would have been Kent. He adored my mother."

Petra was out of breath and let Rosie carry on. Rosie was very upset but was not frightened of repeating all they had heard whilst hidden in the cave.

"It is all very gruesome, and I don't want to upset Ursula, any more than she is but apparently, Joanna Newsome ran away from the animal and Emily Jane made it to the cottage. You see BB, it was so uncomfortable hiding down on the cave floor, we were getting tired of lying still, the sand was thin, and the rocky floor was getting harder, when her brother started to talk to the other man."

"This Les Lescott?" asked Brown Bear.

"Yes, that was the name they called him," replied Rosie, in a very quiet subdued voice. Rosie could see that Ursula's face was wet with tears.

"I was only little when these people took my mother away from me at a time when I needed her most!" At last Ursula sobbed her heart out in the safety of Brown Bear's strong arms.

After a while he spoke. "That was wicked! What happened next?" Brown Bear could hardly hold in his rising anger.

"Remember BB, we were getting cramps with having to stay still and quiet," said Rosie. "But the man I'm sure was her brother, because he seemed scared of his sister. I had noticed that fact when they intruded into the cave with Emily Jane's Shrine. Well, he said he and Joanna had gone back early the next morning to hide Emily Jane's body. He said the tide had been in at roughly midnight that day and by the next morning there wasn't a drop of blood to be seen anywhere, they were convinced the sea got rid of any incriminating evidence, and he and Joanna thought Emily Jane couldn't have made it inside the cottage and at best, as his sister had said at the time, 'hopefully she had been washed away by the outgoing tide."

"So, they knew her name. They knew exactly what they were doing! Did they say anything else?"

"Oh! they said a lot more," Petra had recovered and was ready to continue. "It was very interesting to hear criminals talking amongst themselves like this, and especially knowing they have been let out on bail."

"When we get back to the mainland," said Brown Bear. "We will go straight to the police and tell them everything you three heard the criminals say! but listen girls I have an idea! Will you all come with me now to the room downstairs?"

"The creepy room? The one where the thunderstorm frightened us on our first night. on the island," Rosie shivered remembering.

"Yes!" replied Brown Bear. "The room with the fossils and arrays of bones."

"Why?" Petra asked, very curious now. "There's no sign of dried blood or anything like that in that room. We would have noticed. Anyway, this all happened at least fourteen years ago."

"Yes, you are right, but I have just thought of something else," Brown Bear made his way to the stairs and all three girls followed close behind.

Soon they stood in the room. It was the first room in the cottage, it could have been a hallway, but Petra had decided it was too big for that. Brown Bear had thought it probably had been a dining room, as the kitchen they had found at the back of the cottage was adjoined to this room. So, yes, maybe that was what it had been used for but now in the light of Petra's torch, it looked dark and mysterious with only a sliver of silver moonlight penetrating the gloom.

"I didn't have time to tell you," Brown Bear informed his companions. "But I had a strange experience when I was here alone. Like Rosie had in the cave, I too felt a presence here in this cottage."

"I have experienced it many times over the years," Ursula was pleased BB, was now thinking like she had done and hopefully together they would all find a clue to where her mother's remains could be!

Brown Bear moved to the back of the room carefully treading his path between the piles of calcified bones. "I am amazed the police did not search here all those years ago when Mrs Mortimer first went missing."

"Back then!" Petra, remarked. "They would not have known that she was still alive trapped in the underground caves!

Remember they had no clue what happened to her. They might even have surmised that she had been washed out to sea, like Jo Newsome had hoped."

"In all those papers and documents, we found in the old mahogany chest, there was no death certificate for Emily Jane." Brown Bear looked at the girls. "But I do remember a letter from a Solicitor addressed to the Professor stating that as no certificate had been submitted their hands were tied, and without further legal documentation Mrs Mortimer's assets had been frozen".

Suddenly a sharp gust of wind blew through the cottage, they all trembled. Rosie saw something moving in the corner of the room by the back wall.

"BB, shine your torch over here." gasped Rosie. "Look everyone! A screwed-up piece of paper moving in a draught."

Petra ran to retrieve it quickly and took it to the light of Brown Bear's torch so she could see it clearly. "It's not paper, it is the same material as the note I kept from inside the envelope I found in the briefcase in the villains cave. You know that was probably the Professor's case, the one that was stolen. But look! I'm sure this is a riddle of some sort."

"Let me see?" said Brown Bear, holding out his big furry paw. "It is a riddle! I will read it to you girls!" He held the torch high so he could see the very neat handwriting. "We did lock that front door, didn't we girls?"

"Yes! Of course we did, BB!" exclaimed Rosie. "And the back window! No one can get in unless they happen to be a ghost?" She felt the heckles on the back of her neck stand up as she said those words.

"Listen now," said Brown Bear, as he began to read. "This is a riddle! Of which I am certain. It is in an old form of text."

"Once I was strong but made so weak
I am the treasure which you seek

Not high above but hidden below
To find the secret venture so
Where ursine relics may be found
You will find me underground."

There was a stunned silence in the room. Rosie spoke first, "Do you think it refers to the castle on the east shore? Once it stood strong and now it is weak lying in a mass of its own rubble."

"Well thought out young Rosie," uttered Brown Bear, deep in his own ideas. In the next moment his thoughts were suddenly interrupted by Ursula's positive voice.

"It is my mother! I know it is! The riddle refers to my mother."

'Yes! I agree with you," said Petra. "I too believe your mother is far from the rest she deserves." Petra gave a weary sigh. "Emily Jane certainly is trying to tell us something."

As they stood staring at the message they felt out of their depth. Rosie held out her hand to Brown Bear, he duly passed her the riddle.

"I know what this means!" exclaims Rosie.

"What does it mean?" Petra asked her sister, while Ursula and Brown Bear waited in anticipation.

"It really could refer to the eastern castle: Once it stood tall and strong!" Rosie's voice was confident. "Then the earthquake made it weak and defenceless, as it crumbled to the ground. We all have seen it lying in rubble in the underground passage."

"Oh, yes!" said Petra. "Rosie, I think you are right! And we did think that Professor Mortimer knew of some treasure within that castle."

"Well, some secret," joined Brown Bear. "Maybe."

A few minutes of silence passed while they gathered their thoughts.

"I see what you all mean," remarked Ursula. "But I think the way the riddle is worded means far more than the ruined castle.

Think about it. What are ursine relics to do with the castle?"

"That's a good point," retorted Brown Bear.

"I think the riddle is to help us find my mother and not treasure! I really feel she could be buried here in this room. This is the only place it could mean," Ursula's voice sounded adamant.

"You are so right, young lady," Brown Bear felt a huge surge of excitement. "We must find a shovel and I will dig!"

At that precise moment they heard a loud rapping on the front door of the cottage and a torchlight beamed through the downstairs windows. Rosie clung to Brown Bear.

"Whatever is happening now?"

36
IN PLAIN SIGHT

"Whatever is the matter, Officer?" Brown Bear slipped the lock and opened the door. "Oh! And I see you have young Jake with you."

"Yes, sir! He has joined the police force, aiming to work in CID eventually, his family are very proud of him," replied Detective Sergeant Cooper, who they all recognised as one of the police officers who had responded to the attempted kidnap of Ursula.

"Very good, Jake! Very commendable, young sir." Brown Bear took a step outside. For one reason there wasn't much room inside for more people and for another he felt he and the girls were so close to discovering the mystery surrounding Emily Jane's disappearance that he didn't want anyone else trampling over the cemetery of bones and fossils that had meant so much to the Professor's wife. Brown Bear stood tall and exuded as much authority as the senior officer.

"How can we help you?"

"I think you will all be aware that one of our choppers landed on the island," responded DS Cooper. "We were sent ahead of the release of the Newsome family, I will explain. Superintendent Harding, who is SIO on this case, gave the orders. Their release was agreed by the magistrate, who was in on a plan, so that the Newsomes can be free to condemn themselves and lead us to the scene of their crime!"

"In other words," retorted Brown Bear, "you have no evidence to actually charge them with murder."

"Murder!" exclaimed the Detective Sergeant. "No, it's not murder we want to convict them of, that boat sailed ages ago! The Supa' believes that Mrs Mortimer's body was washed out to sea many years ago. There was an enormous search at the time, of the whole island and the rocky coastline. No trace of her anywhere. Saying that, we do not expect anyone to be charged with murder."

"So, what's the big deal with these Newcome folk then?" Brown Bear asked, he wanted to blurt out what he and the girls knew but he thought better of it. 'We have no proof either,' Brown Bear thought to himself.

"So, what news do you have to offer us then?" Brown Bear stretched out his arm to protect Petra and Rosie from going outside.

"Jake here was ordered to stay close to the Newsomes, watch their every move and he followed them to the remains of an underground castle, where they have begun digging for treasure," DS Cooper stopped for breath.

Brown Bear turned to face Jake, "Treasure. Is that what they are looking for?"

"Yes. That's what the woman said," answered Jake, who was a tall good looking young man. "She is the boss. The men she hires are frightened of her."

"I see! So what, DS Cooper, do you require of us?" Brown Bear stood tall facing the two men.

"We know it is late. 9pm to be exact. But we were hoping that Ursula would come with us to the fallen castle and identify her kidnappers."

"She has already identified them!" Brown Bear snapped out his answer. "The day you arrested the gang and took them into custody! We all witnessed who the perpetrators were!"

"I know it is very late, but the Newsome's are there now with a flood light of sorts, you know Mr Bear like builders use."

"Yes, I know but if you think they are after treasure, you can arrest them for that because, all the treasure found in this country is Treasure Trove," Brown Bear was adamant.

"Yes, I know, Sir," replied the Detective. "Belongs to the Crown!"

"Precisely!" replied Brown Bear.

"You see, Sir! It is more than that, those above Superintendent Harding are thinking of reopening the Mortimer case, but it is all very hush hush," DS Cooper was now close to Brown Bear keeping his voice low. "It has come to light that Professor Mortimer handed over a series of threatening letters that his wife had received over the years. Very dark threats that began when she was in university and the last one, we have in our possession, was from the time when they lived at Old Mill Cottage in Swallows village, approximately twenty-seven years ago."

"This is all very serious, Detective, but it is too late for these girls to come out in the dark," Brown Bear always put his charges first.

"We are very tired," said Rosie, rubbing her eyes.

"Yes, we are," said Ursula, yawning.

"If you let us have some sleep," Petra pleaded with the Police Officer. "We will get up early and be ready to come with you at first light! Just make sure that Lescott man doesn't take them back to the mainland. Oh! By the way he has a gun!"

"Well, we can charge him for carrying a lethal weapon. What else do you know about him?" retorted the Officer.

Before anyone could answer there was the old familiar howl from the bears.

"What on earth is that noise?" asked Jake.

"That was loud! We will have to investigate. Come on, constable." And with that the two policemen disappeared into the night.

"Now will you lock the door and follow me?" The girls did exactly as Brown Bear instructed and soon the four were back in the room surrounded by bones and fossils.

"Ursula, aren't you worried about the bears?" Rosie asked, surprised that their new friend hadn't wanted to rush to her beloved ursine friends.

"No, I'm not worried, they are very happy. We will all go and see them as soon as we can."

"Right, I'll fetch the shovel," said Brown Bear. "Now girls back to where we were!"

"May I say what I think?" Ursula looked beseechingly at the others.

"Of course!" exclaimed Brown Bear.

Petra and Rosie were silent wondering how their friend would really be feeling at the prospect of exhuming her dead mother. That is if she was buried there.

Ursula saw their doleful looks and gave them a little smile. "Don't worry about me! I have had many years thinking about my mother and now I feel a sense of relief, because with your help, I will know what happened to her at last. We will see if Joanna Newsome has told those men the truth. What a pity Petra that your phone ran out of charge."

"Yes, I know!" Petra replied. "I must find Mali's charger, when I have a spare moment."

Brown Bear had found the oil lamp and had used a match to light it. So, although the room was filled with eerie shadows it was possible to make out the floor clearly.

"Now, young lady, where shall I start?" His gaze was on Ursula, as he lifted the spade, it was a good strong tool, quite sufficient for the task in hand.

"Over the years," said Ursula. "I have been in this cottage talking to my mother many times trying to reach her, I always felt her presence, but I am not sure I have felt her more in this room than anywhere else, but sometimes she would walk with me along the wet sand just as the tide began to ebb."

"Yes, we know!" announced Petra. "One day Brown Bear and I lost Rosie for a while, and then along the sand at the water's edge we found two sets of footprints. Yours and someone else's. We had seen you walking alone earlier and later when we went to look there was only one set of footprints, yours."

"Yes!" that happened a few times, but I felt her presence more when I was inside this cottage"

Brown Bear was standing patiently waiting for a signal from Ursula to begin the excavation when Rosie suddenly remembered something.

"What about the riddle?" said Rosie. "Those criminals must have read it and thought like we did at first, that it referred to the underground castle, but I am certain they are wrong, and Emily Jane is here!"

"I think," Ursula was deep in thought. "That is why the police followed the Newsome's to the ruins, they think that is where my mother is buried."

"Umm, that is too much to assume," Brown Bear concentrated on the job in hand.

Ursula has had years to think about what had happened to her beloved mother and now her heartbeat was racing fast, and her mind was in turmoil. She thought 'I know my mother's spirit is here on the island, should I leave things as they are?'

And then an amazing thing happened! A light shone in the corner of the room, an eerie light that faded in and out, casting a beam that shone with a bluish tinge.

"Wherever is that light coming from?" asked Rosie, quite scared, as she caught hold of her sister's hand. Petra felt Rosie's tension.

Ursula gasped and went over to the far corner of the room. On the floor at this point was a pile of fossils and then the strange light disappeared, and Brown Bear still stood with the spade in hand.

"Are you alright, Ursula?" Brown Bear wanted to hear from the young lady before he began excavating.

"Yes BB, I am ready now! That light was a message from my mother," Ursula went to the corner and took the shovel from Brown Bear. "I would like to move these fossils first. Girls, come and help me. These specimens are not from land animals; I think they are from ancient sea creatures."

"Yes, you are right!" replied Brown Bear. "There is an abundance of ammonite fossils and even pieces of Ichthyosaur bones."

"You are clever, BB," said Rosie. "What else is here?"

"We need more light!" Announced Brown Bear. "I don't suppose, Ursula my dear, you have any more of those candles?"

"You mean the pink ones I try to keep lighted on my mother's Shine?" Ursula shrugged her shoulders. "No, I've used them all, but there is a secret cupboard upstairs where some plain white ones are stored away! I'll go and fetch some!"

"Good girl! Now Petra and Rosie help me move these fossils!" he said, as he leaned the spade against the cottage wall. "Not a sign of rats now, I think we frightened them all away the night we moved in."

"Good job we did because I would not have stayed here!" Petra exclaimed. "There are all kinds of fossils here," she said, as she moved handfuls to another corner of the room. "Do you recognise any more of them, BB?"

"Yes, quite a few!" he replied. "They are mainly ammonites or ammonoids as they are known in the Scientific community, and coral pieces, some Belemnites and Brachiopods, samples from the Jurassic and Cretaceous periods."

"How long ago was that?" Rosie was picking them up individually. "Emily Jane must have been extremely clever to know about all these creatures."

There was a noise on the cottage stairs, Ursula was descending with a bundle of candles.

"Some of these relics go back as far as 140 million years ago! And yes, my mother was extremely clever," exclaimed Ursula. "Look I found some matches too; I hope they are not damp!"

The box of matches was dry and soon the girls set up six candles, set on six saucers around the room. With most of the fossils moved away Brown Bear now had a clear view of the floor.

"It is a wooden floor!" Brown Bear seemed very surprised. "I was rather expecting a rock floor, like in the kitchen."

"Easier for you to dig, I should imagine," said Rosie. "Hey, can someone bring a light nearer to me, please?"

"Why, what is it? What have you found Rosie?" Petra brought the oil lamp over to where her sister was standing.

Ursula joined the girls in the centre of the room. "Well, I had no idea that was there?"

"Let me see," said Brown Bear. He bent down to look closer at their find, "It is a handle set flat in the wooden boards. This is good news girls; I won't have to dig into stone."

The three girls and Brown Bear sighed with relief.

"You mean there is a trapdoor," said Ursula. "I am very surprised!" She gave them a smile.

"Stand back girls I will try and pull it open," Brown Bear used all his strength to pull the handle of the trapdoor out of its socket. The dust from all the shells and sea creatures had impacted on the wood making it difficult to hold, but eventually they all heard a creak from the trapdoor and suddenly it opened under Brown Bear's grip.

The girls gasped and immediately stood back, feeling a little scared. Soon they let their fear subside and made way for Brown Bear to investigate. The first thing he found in the now gaping hole in the floor of the room was a flight of steps, leading down into an abyss of darkness. He began to descend slowly, testing each step with his foot, checking they were all sturdy and could bear his weight.

"It is only a short flight of stairs," he called up to the girls who were waiting patiently.

"Stop, BB, I must come with you!" exclaimed Ursula. "Rosie, pass me your phone. I need the camera."

Rosie found her phone and passed it to Ursula.

"Thank you, Rosie, I know your battery is low. I will be careful! Are you ready, BB?'

"Of course, my dear!" replied Brown Bear.

Petra and Rosie stood near the aperture watching their friends disappear below. Then they heard a muffled scream.

"Oh no! It's Ursula! I hope they haven't found anything too horrid," Rosie was gripping her sister's hand extremely tightly.

"Okay girls! I am taking two photographs for the police using your phone, Rosie."

"Yes, that's alright," Rosie peered down just making out the steps in the limited light.

"Can we come down?" Petra was getting a little impatient.

"No!" said Brown Bear. "We must not contaminate the scene any further."

"You mean it is a crime scene?" said Rosie.

"Yes, I am afraid so!" Brown Bear was very sombre. "I am leaving Ursula down here for a while so that she can pay her respects to her mother!"

"So, BB, have you found Emily Jane?" Rosie's voice was low and hesitant.

"Yes, we have!"

"Can I go to Ursula please, BB?" Petra was upset. "She did show herself to me first, that night in the dark outside the cottage. I need to comfort her."

"Yes, but don't be too long, I must go and find DS Cooper and break the sad news to him," Brown Bear took charge.

"We have accomplished what we set out to do and found the real secret of the island," Petra said thoughtfully. "Emily Jane was in plain sight after all. If only we had known that we have been living so close to her."

"And now, what the police must find out is who shut the trapdoor of this cellar and who tried to cover their crime by covering the floor with antiquities all those years ago?"

37
THE BODY

The wooden steps beneath Petra's feet creaked with age. She held her breath as she gingerly took each tread carefully, she could hear her heart pounding deep within her and could smell a strange odour she felt certain, she had never smelt before.

Brown Bear passed the oil lamp very carefully down to her.

"Thank you, BB, I am sure we won't be long." She looked up and gave him a feeble smile.

"Take as long as you need," said Brown Bear in a soft understanding voice. "I will look after Rosie. I know it is bedtime, but she won't be able to sleep until you both are back with us."

"I know," Petra took the last step and found herself in a cellar, just the right size for the cottage. At the back was a slab of marble placed on four wooden posts, she tried to think why it was there, what it could have been used for in the past, and then the light of her lamp illuminated two oak barrels. 'Must have been used for wine,' she thought.

And then to the side of the stairs, right at the bottom, her eyes found a scene of horror.

"Oh, Ursula, I am so sorry!" Petra sank down to her knees beside Ursula who had knelt mortified for the last few minutes besides her mother's dead body. "Do you want me here?"

"Yes, of course I do!" Ursula whispered. "Look, she is still beautiful. Time has not taken away her beauty."

"You are right!" Petra got closer and was quite amazed at what she saw. "Even Emily Jane's long black hair is lovely. And look! She is still wearing the floral blouse and gilet you said she was wearing the last day you saw her."

"I know!" answered Ursula. "Even her skin on her face isn't too bad."

"I can see she was a beautiful woman," said Petra. "You know, Ursula, you inherited her good looks!"

Petra withdrew a little so her friend could say goodbye to her mother. "Why do you think Emily Jane's body is in such good condition after fourteen years?" Petra was puzzled as she had expected to see bare bones.

"It is no mystery," Ursula replied. "There must be a draught that runs through this cellar, her body has been mummified!"

"Mummified!" Petra exclaimed. "How do you know that?"

"In the short time I was with her, my mother taught me a great deal about everything. She never treated me like a baby, or an infant, as soon as I could talk, she taught me everything she knew. I must have soaked it all up like a sponge."

"You would have had no distractions, not like Rosie and I have. We go to a big school with loads of other students distracting us most days."

"You are both so lucky. I would have loved that, but at the time I knew no other life." Ursula said wistfully.

Petra glanced around at the sad scene in this room under the beach cottage, and now she realised that everything Ursula had ever said about her lost mother was true, even to the clothes Emily Jane had worn on the last day they were together.

She thought she would give her friend a few minutes more and began to examine the walls of the cellar, they consisted of thick rock. Petra moved slowly around the room hoping to find a draught. She came upon a gap in the wall on the south side of the cellar and examined it closely. Petra held up her hand and could feel a cool rush of air passing through. She then climbed back up the steps and examined the trapdoor. In the square piece of beautifully carved oak, she found something very interesting, exactly where the handle was fitted into the groove, there was a gap wide enough for air to pass though.

'So, that's it! That explains how Emily Jane's body was mummified!' Petra was doing a lot of thinking,

'Yes! It is quite possible, because our Nan remembers a case of a 'Mummy in the cupboard,' in Rhyl, back in 1960, when she was fourteen and was living at home with her parents. One sunny day my Great Nan was in their kitchen making their lunch when Taidy, (that was the affectionate Welsh name for our Great-grandfather) came home with the story, apparently the local news had caused quite a stir in Rhyl town.'

A body had been found mummified in a boarding house in the Westend of Rhyl. The landlady was accused of murdering and hiding the body of one of her tenants, in a cupboard on the landing. Twenty years later her son had decided to spruce up the house and started to strip now shabby wallpaper off the walls on the landing. After a while he discovered a hidden door and was shocked to find the remains of an old lady hidden behind it. He informed the Police and later his mother was arrested.

'She was tried in 'Yr Hen Lys' the Old Courthouse in Ruthin at the time but she was found not guilty of murder, but after hearing the landlady's evidence, she had to go to prison for a short time, as she was guilty of hiding her tenant's dead body in a cupboard, and not reporting a natural death to the authorities and taking the victim's pension allowances every week for many years. It was a draught flowing through that cupboard in Rhyl that had mummified the old lady's body.'

Petra blinked in the fading light of the oil lamp and shook her head. 'Why am I remembering all that stuff now?' she questioned herself, 'Of course, because of the draught I have found down here!'

She went back to Ursula who hadn't moved since she had left

her. "Are you okay?"

"Better than I was! At least we have found her."

"That's good then!" Petra touched her friend's shoulder very gently. "Just a couple of minutes more, we are running out of oil for the lamp!"

"Yes! I won't be long. Do you have your phone with you, Petra?"

"Yes, but I don't think there is much charge left."

"I just want to take one photo!"

"Then we will tell BB, and he will tell the police," Petra went to sit on the top step still gathering more thoughts about past references of when she had heard about Mummies!

It was not long before she recalled a visit with her family, to the British Museum, while on holiday in London. It was a sweltering day in the summer of 2018. It was so hot that day even in the usually cool museum, that no one wanted to linger very long. Her memories took her back to seeing many large glass cabinets and within them lay bodies of the ancient Egyptians, who had been embalmed and buried in their elaborate tombs in the deserts of Egypt. Then thousands of years later the tombs had been excavated and then the remains were discovered. She had read somewhere when the warm desert winds blew in a draught over the bodies as they lay in the tombs, the warm draughts of air mummified all the dead! Or something like that!'

Suddenly Petra was brought back to reality.

"I think we had better go," Petra stood up suddenly, back in the present day and remembering the task in hand!

"Yes!" replied Ursula. "Did you notice the wound on the side of her head?"

"I did," Petra took her friend's hand.

"I think her neck was broken too." Ursula began to cry silently teardrops soaking her cheeks.

"You didn't touch her, did you?" Petra realised the Forensic team would be called in by the police to examine and move Emily Jane's body.

"No, I didn't touch her!" Ursula wiped away her tears. "I longed too, but no! I didn't."

"Good girl come on," said Petra. "Rosie and BB will be wondering why we are taking so long."

Suddenly there were loud noises above. "Quick, there is something going on!"

The two girls climbed the stairs and were immediately back in the eerie room in the cottage.

They expected to see Brown Bear and Rosie hovering over the open trapdoor but there was no sign of either, but someone was blocking the doorway to the outside.

"Oh! what are you doing here?" asked Petra in surprise.

Jake, the young policeman DS Cooper had introduced them to earlier, was standing on guard near the stout front door. It was wide open, and the officer stood silhouetted by the light of the moon.

"What are you doing?" cried Ursula. "Whatever is all that noise?"

"Please tell us," begged Petra. "Where is my sister and Mr Bear?"

"Don't worry, girls, they went upstairs to get a better view!" said Jake. His voice was very calming. "It all suddenly took off and it seemed everything happened at once."

"Whatever do you mean, Jake?" said Ursula. "We have something to report to DS Cooper. Where is he?"

"He's overseeing this operation. They had a breakthrough, back at the station and everyone has had to move fast." Jake ushered the girls outside.

It was well after midnight and the silver moon shone down, making everywhere look like broad daylight. The tide was high and on it they could see two other motorboats, led by Lucas' shiny red craft gliding over the white tipped waves and racing to the island.

"Extra boats!" exclaimed Brown Bear, as he joined them on the rocks. "Something important is happening!"

Jake turned to the girls and asked if they were alright. Petra nodded to him, and Ursula managed a smile. "Yes! Just about."

Then suddenly they all heard a low droning noise coming nearer and nearer to the island. The moon was bright, and the night sky was clear. Within minutes two helicopters were landing, one on the cliff top and the other on the shingle of the North shore.

"What's going on?" said Rosie. "BB, where are you?"

"I'm here! I'll go and find out what's happening! Rosie, stay close to Petra and Ursula! I am going to meet Lucas at the jetty and try to discover what is happening." Brown Bear rushed off to meet his old friend.

Ursula slipped back inside the cottage, she wanted to close the trapdoor so her mother's privacy could last a little longer. Jake however had been given orders by DS Cooper to stay close to the young lady. Her attempted kidnap was still very fresh in everyone's mind.

"What is the matter?" Jake asked, following the young girl inside the cottage. "Can I help you?" He smiled and Ursula nodded. "I understand the next few hours will be an ordeal for you!"

"Yes," she replied. "Will you come with me down these steps and be the first policeman to witness my mother's dead body?"

"Oh!" Jake was surprised with her request and kept close to Ursula, who led him down the wooden steps. He gasped as he saw a woman's body at the bottom of the stairs.

After a while, they returned upstairs and she let him help her close the trapdoor. When it was shut tight, she looked straight into his blue eyes and said, "As you can see, officer, I am no stranger to ordeals."

"I understand you have lived alone on this island since you were a child." Jake was not quite sure what he made of this girl, but he knew he liked her, and in the line of duty would do anything to help her get through this difficult time.

"I will help you with anything, just ask." He took her hand and held it briefly before Ursula pulled away.

"Yes, thank you, I appreciate your offer, I will ask if needs be. You are kind, just like these wonderful people who came to the island and found me. Well actually, I found them. They have been so generous with their friendship and understanding."

"Does that include the big bear?" he smiled at her with twinkling blue eyes.

"Of course, it does!" Ursula exclaimed. "He's amazing! So, knowledgeable! And so very caring, he guards Petra and Rosie with his life."

Jake was about to ask her some more questions but there wasn't time, as all hell seemed to break loose.

"I'm sorry, miss, I will have to go!" Jake gave her a wave as he rushed away along the sand.

Minutes later the three girls stood together on the rocks outside the cottage trying to imagine what was going on down at the jetty. There was such a commotion with police officers swarming the island, some on the cliff tops, some scouring the North Beach and some of them were armed, as Rosie pointed out.

"I am just thinking," said Petra. "Why is the scale of this operation so intense?"

"It is massive," replied Rosie.

"Well!" exclaimed Ursula. "There are lots of men working for this Newsome woman. There were two trying to kidnap Starlight and me, of course, I could hear them shouting, one was called Marcus and the other Rick, and this one here on the island, this Lescott man, and there are others, who knows how many villains she has employed for so many police to be involved?" She hesitated. "For what reason is that awful woman so bitter?"

Petra and Rosie knew why, but they both realised at this point that it wasn't their place to tell Ursula.

The rest of the night was occupied with flashing lights and police officers scouting the North shore caves for villains linked to Joanna Newsome. As dawn was breaking in the east the girls witnessed the three motorboats being loaded with prisoners. Les Lescott was struggling to get away, but the burly officers of the Sea Patrol had him well and truly secured on their vessel.

"Look!" shouted Rosie, as she pointed out to sea. "That trawler is all lit up now."

"Yes, of course," said Brown Bear. "We know the Newsomes have links with that trawler. Whoever owns it must be in with the gang. Come on now, girls, you must get some sleep tonight. It looks as if we'll have another busy day with the constabulary tomorrow."

Only when dawn broke with a golden glow that shimmered in elongated pink clouds across the Eastern horizon was the island quiet once again.

38
REVELATIONS

Brown Bear was waiting patiently on the beach, while Lucas was securing his motorboat to old iron loops on the side of the jetty. The dawn was breaking and just offshore he could see at least three other craft anchored in the bay. Soon Lucas joined him looking a bit anxious.

"Hey, Lucas, old mate tell me what on earth is going on and more to the point what warrants all these Coppers running around this island?"

"Well!" exclaimed Lucas. "More to the point! old mate! now that I've acquired this shiny new speed boat isn't it time you got rid of these rusty old moorings."

Brown Bear gave his head a quick scratch, as was his custom when he found himself in a bit of a quandary.

"Ah well!" replied Brown Bear. "The next time these girls find another adventure, I'll be sure to pack a few stainless-steel hooks just so you can moor your boat!"

"Aye! that be fine," grinned Lucas. "Now have they found them?"

"Who?" asked Brown Bear.

"That smuggling gang!" Lucas jumped down on the sand. "Les Lescott's gang of course!"

"But" said Brown Bear. "We thought it was Joanna Newsome who had a gang doing her bidding. They all seemed in it together when that attempted kidnap was taking place."

"You are right!" Lucas looked back at his boat making sure it was safe. "I should have put a stern line on her."

"What's that?" Asked Brown Bear, as the two commenced their walk up the beach and around the headland.

"Just a line to keep her straight when there are heavy waves rolling in," answered the fisherman. "But it isn't too bad this morning. Now what do you want to know?"

The early morning sky was now a light shade of azure. With the headland behind them there was a good view of the beach and the cottage. They were surprised to see the white tent being erected once again in readiness for Senior Police officers to use as an incident room.

"Oh dear! quick! I must find the girls." Brown Bear raced ahead.

"Where are my girls? Are they safe?" He panted as he was met by DS Cooper and Jake.

"They are fine! WPC Denton is talking to them right now," said the Detective. "I believe it is of a delicate nature."

"Oh! That doesn't sound good," said Brown Bear.

"If you two would take your places in our makeshift room, all will be revealed very soon," DS Cooper ushered them under the white canopy.

"Oh! there you are girls; did you get any sleep?" asked Brown Bear.

"Hardly any," answered Petra.

"Not much!" said Rosie.

"None at all!" replied Ursula.

Brown Bear looked at her with a puzzled expression and then he looked at the WPC.

"What have I missed?"

"There have been developments," the officer said.

"Now, Officer," said Brown Bear. "Please be kind enough to put us in the picture and explain the reason why all these officers have been on the island."

At that moment WPC Denton turned to greet a stranger to the scene. "Now, everyone, let me introduce you to our new SIO."

"Yes! That's me, Detective Chief Inspector Bronwen Jones. I am the Senior Investigating Officer on this case now."

Brown Bear made moves to stand up, but this very efficient lady held up her hand.

"No formalities! I want this meeting to be informal and relaxed as possible under the circumstances."

Everyone under the canopy let out big sighs of relief. There was a bit of a kerfuffle as DS Cooper and Jake Oliver joined them.

From the moment Detective Chief Inspector Jones began to talk no one moved a muscle, so intense, yet compassionate was her deliverance.

"Now listen up, folks. We are dealing with two separate cases on this island today one is solved, and we are dealing with the culprits right now but the other remains a mystery."

Petra and Ursula knew what that mystery was, they looked at each other both feeling guilty for not yet telling anyone about Emily Jane's dead body, still lying on the floor in the cellar. Ursula remembered the young police officer helping her close the trapdoor, she was quite confident that Jake seemed more interested in her, than looking down a dark hole in the floor. The words of the Detective were just skimming over their heads, so intense were the images now cast forever on their young minds. They both gathered from the SIO that all the villains had been arrested. Then Chief Inspector Jones's attention was on her audience.

"Now let me get this clear, Mr Bear, you have been staying on this island with Rosie, Petra and Ursula, for a holiday before the girls must start a new term at their school in September. Is that correct?"

"Correct!" replied Brown Bear. "Except we met Ursula here on the island. She got on so well with the girls that we have stayed together exploring the island."

"I see," continued the SIO. "Now before we discuss the mystery of the disappearing wife. I want you all to be silent and then I will put you in the picture."

The Welsh accent was familiar to the girls. Petra and Rosie's school was in the heart of Wales and Ursula could remember the soft sing-song voice of her Welsh mother.

"Now, I will tell you what my colleagues have found out about the Newsome's gang."

"But Detective, I have something to tell you." Ursula stood up, her voice was shaking, and Petra caught hold of her hand.

"Now! Just be patient, young lady." The Chief Inspector stopped Ursula in her tracks. "I said I will talk about the criminals we have rounded up, first."

Ursula sat down; Petra noticed tears in her friend's eyes. "OK! I can wait," she said as she sat down again, with a strong feeling of uncertainty welling up inside her.

"Now without any further ado I will continue!" Bronwen Jones the SIO stood in front of our group and began.

"I expect you were aware of a helicopter landing on this island a few days ago," she continued.

"Yes, we heard it," said Rosie.

"Well, we landed two officers on the island late one night, to find out where the Newsome's were camping, and to locate any hidden stashes of drugs," the senior officer continued.

"Drugs!" exclaimed Petra. "We had no idea they were smuggling drugs!"

"No, you wouldn't, very cagey that woman was. Been bitter and twisted for years," continued the SIO. "You will be pleased to know that Joanna Newsome and her brother Frederick plus all their associates are now in custody!"

Brown Bear fidgeted a bit before he raised his hand to catch the officer's attention.

"I am so sorry to interrupt you Chief Inspector, but how safe will they be now? You have already had the Newsome's in custody and then you let them out on Bail. Why was that? And will it be different this time?" Brown Bear was studying all the officers very closely.

"Of course, it will be different!" the SIO's voice and stance were adamant.

"How so?" Brown Bear wouldn't give up. The girls looked at him with worry on their faces.

"Because Sir, this time we have evidence to keep Joanna Newsome in prison for the rest of her life." The senior police woman gave a huge smile that beamed at everyone present. "And as for Leslie Lescott, Rick Harewood and Marcus Morris, with the evidence we found of actual drugs hidden in one of the caves on the North shore, and not forgetting Dan Withers the trawlerman, who has made a fortune being involved in their racket. Well, I am delighted to say we caught them all, a nice chunky haul"

"How can that happen on this island?" Petra inquired. "It is a very small island compared to some others!"

"Yes, you are right! It is a small island" Chief Inspector Bronwen Jones was looking very pleased. "But in a case like this, size doesn't matter. So long as these drug smugglers have a supplier, somewhere remote to hide the goods, and then a distributor, they are off to make a fortune by wrecking the lives of the young people who become addicted at the end of the chain."

"And once addicted will keep going back for more," Petra seemed deeply concerned.

"Precisely!" the Senior Investigating Officer nodded in agreement

"But why did Joanna Newsome get involved in narcotics and the like?" Brown Bear inquired. "We believe she had a far more disturbing motive than drug dealing on this island."

"I believe it was just chance, but we have her in custody for a much greater charge!

Now, DS Cooper, will you fill in the rest?" She turned to Detective Sergeant Cooper, who immediately stood up and gave everyone a smile. "After all DS Cooper it was you, who had the pleasure of arresting the woman."

"Yes, I did, quite evil she is! couldn't get rid of an old grudge, I believe." DS Cooper looked very pleased. "Now there is one of you here whom we, the police force, owe a great deal of thanks."

Everyone sitting in the makeshift incident room looked around at each other, with an expectant look on their faces."

The Officer continued, "Now, is one of you here called Petra?" The Detective's question rang out and a cloud of apprehension overshadowed Petra's beautiful face.

"I am Petra!" She stood up a little bewildered.

"If you just answer my questions then I will get straight to the point! Constable Jake Oliver, will you take down notes?"

"Yes, Sir I will!" Jake took a notebook and pen out of his uniform jacket.

"Now, Miss Petra, do you own a mobile?" DS Cooper's voice sounded very serious.

"Yes, I do!"

"And are you in possession of that said phone here on the island?"

"Yes, I am but the battery has run out now!"

"And" continued DS Cooper. "Have you been in a cave on the north shore of this island where you witnessed a confession when Joanna Newsome admitted to her gang of co; conspirator's that she had crept up behind Emily Jane Mortimer and attacked her?"

Petra couldn't stand much more of this severe questioning, and she couldn't help it, but she burst out crying.

"That is quite enough! Exploded Brown Bear, fiercely raising his voice to the offending officer "Sir, can't you see how upset you have made my charge, young Petra here?"

"I am sorry about that," said DS Cooper. "But I have to establish that a message received by the Officer at the desk in Swallows Police station on the 27th August 2021 was from Petra's mobile phone."

"Well, have you, Sir?" Brown Bear was cross.

"Yes, I have!" he exclaimed. "All I need now is for Miss Petra to verify her mobile telephone number, so I can be certain the message was sent from her phone." He turned to Petra, "Now, if you will tell me your mobile phone details."

Petra obliged and told the officer her private number.

"And is it relevant?" Brown Bear looked on closely.

"Indeed, it is Sir!" exclaimed the officer.

"How so?"

"Because the message Petra sent to our headquarters was a recorded message of Joanna Newsome's voice telling her henchmen how she had killed Emily Jane Mortimer here on this island and she was delighted to having got rid of her love rival."

A gasp of disbelief encircled the occupants of the tent.

"When did you do that, Petra?" Rosie was totally surprised. "Why didn't you tell us you were sending a message to the police station?"

"I didn't mention it," replied Petra. "Because although I pressed the send button, I didn't think it would work, as I believed the battery was very low. But obviously not! Thanks to our brother Mali's supercharger."

"But" said the Detective. "Joanna Newsome has not mentioned where her victim's body might be. That remains a mystery and without a body it is very hard to make a charge of that nature, stick."

At that point in the proceedings Ursula stood up and looked directly at the SIO and DS Cooper. Rosie didn't understand all that was happening, but Petra did!

"May I speak now please, it is very urgent," said Ursula, tossing her black hair out of her eyes. This morning a west wind was blowing hard and the noise from the tent flaps was annoying and making it difficult for the police officers to hear the young lady, who now stood in front of them.

"Could you speak up, young lady?" said DS Cooper. "Now what is your name and your address? Jake, will you take notes?"

"Yes Sir," replied the young officer. He looked at Ursula and gave her a reassuring smile, of which the young girl reciprocated.

"Now, young lady, this is your chance to tell us all you know." DS Cooper's tone was now softer and more encouraging.

Ursula looked at everyone in that make: shift room, thinking how lonely she had been in the days on the island without her beloved mother. And now she could hardly believe how many eyes were upon her at this moment.

"I want to report the whereabouts of my mother's body! My address is this island. I have never lived anywhere else."

A loud gasp was heard among everyone present, except for Petra who at that point bore witness to Ursula's statement. She stood up and moved to stand besides Ursula. All eyes seemed to be on her but in that moment, she felt it was time to be truthful with everyone and tell the police everything they knew.

"Yes," said Petra." Ursula is telling the truth. I was with her when she found her mother's body. And Brown Bear, Rosie, and I believe that Emily Jane's husband was none other than Ursula's father."

There was an air of total surprise and disbelief and none more than from Ursula.

"I think they are right! I have had time of late to reflect on it," exclaimed Ursula. She met the gaze of the police officers.

"And where is your mother's body?" asked Chief Inspector Bronwen Jones. "You must show us straight away, because back in the late '90s, every police officer we deployed at the time to find

Mrs Mortimer alive drew a blank. They found no evidence that there was any human life on the island at all. She was presumed dead and must have been washed away by the sea."

"That was because," Ursula began in earnest. "My mother was trapped in caves underground! She and Larry, that's what she called him, came to the island to excavate the castle on the hill. They were living in this cottage," She pointed behind her. "And then Larry was called back to Oxford, he worked in the university. But my mother had discovered some rare ursine bones in caves underground, and she wanted to stay on the island to study them for a few more days."

"And then the landslide hit?" announced DS Cooper.

"Yes!" replied Ursula. "And my mother was trapped."

"So that was the summer of 1999?" reflected SIO Jones. Chief Inspector Jones

"I think so." Ursula replied.

"So, this means Mrs Mortimer was pregnant when she went missing," Chief Inspector Jones was thinking hard." So, Ursula, you must be 20 years old."

"Am I?" said Ursula, looking perplexed. She turned to the two sisters to see if they agreed, when suddenly Rosie exclaimed!

"That's it! That's it!"

"What?" retorted the two police officers, Petra, and Brown Bear, all together.

"That is what Emily Jane wrote in her letter to Larry," remarked Rosie. The letter Petra found in the briefcase in the cave and copied it on her phone."

"Yes! I had to give my phone to DS Cooper so that he could pass it on to forensics," said Petra. "But I see what you mean, Rosie. Of course, Emily Jane had written to tell her husband and that was what she meant when she wrote she had some wonderful news for him, and that she knew he would be as thrilled as she was!"

"Of course, that was what she would be telling him when he returned from Oxford," Petra felt excited that they were solving one puzzle at least.

"Yes! Emily Jane was expecting their baby. This is all so sad because Ursula that baby was you, and there is no doubt that Professor Lawrence B Mortimer is definitely your father!"

Ursula swooned and was about to lose her balance when Brown Bear caught her in his big strong arms.

39
DEPARTURE

The rest of that day was chaotic. To start with Petra and Ursula were coaxed gently by Chief Inspector Jones and DS Cooper to show them where Emily Jane's dead body was lying at the foot of the stairs in the newly discovered cellar. Another helicopter had landed on the island and a team of forensic scientists had been called in by Superintendent Harding who was still senior officer on this case. There was nothing more for DS Cooper and Chief Inspector Bronwen Jones to do now, except write up their reports once back at Headquarters on the mainland.

No one had been able to sleep well the night before and emotions were high. It was the kind officer WPC Denton who accompanied Rosie and Petra to identify Joanna and Frederick Newsome as the two they had seen in the cave, where Petra had secretly used her iphone to record Jo Newsome's confession of her attack on Emily Jane.

Ursula and the girls were nervous about coming face to face with a murderer. They didn't have to go too near the criminals as WPC Denton took them to bear witness just before the two detainees climbed the steps into the helicopter that would soon be taking the criminals to cells in the police station of the nearest big town.

"Right, let's go now!" said Ursula, with a quiver in her voice. "Can we go?" she looked at the policewoman, who nodded.

"Yes, you won't be needed again," she replied. "I am going back to the mainland by boat, I need to see the rocks that lurk around the island. Well, I don't have too, but they may give me an idea as to how determined Joanna Newsome was, when she came back to the island alone all those years ago! My colleagues feel the plan to kill Mrs Mortimer was all her own idea. We think she just used her brother for support." The policewoman began to collect all her belongings together and packed them in a large holdall.

"I have an appointment at the coroner's office first thing in the morning. So, I must leave now! Your associate Mr Lucas Oliver is taking me back to the mainland. I will be calling on your mother in Swallows Village to put her in the picture, as to how you all got involved in such a high-profile case."

"What does high profile mean, BB?" Rosie asked Brown Bear in a low voice.

WPC Denton heard Rosie's whisper. "High profile means that this is a very important case! Not just that it is a murder case, but because Professor Mortimer is a very well-known Archaeologist, extraordinarily clever in his field and so was his wife."

"They both were, by all accounts," said Brown Bear. Then he turned to Officer Denton. "Can we send a message to Petra and Rosie's Mum in Swallows village?"

"Of course!" she replied.

Petra took charge, "Please ask Lucas to tell Mum that we are fine, but please could she ask Lucas to come back tomorrow with enough food for three more days."

"Oh! and," said Rosie. "Tell her we know that school is looming far too quickly, but after so much excitement, we would be ever so, ever so grateful, if we can have a little more time on the island to enjoy the rest of our holiday."

"It has been rather a tense time," remarked Brown Bear to the police officer.

"Yes, I know it has, Mr Bear. But you have all coped extremely well under the sad circumstances." Then she turned to the girls.

'Petra and Rosie, I will give your mum your message," replied

WPC Denton. "Now I must make tracks. Nice to meet you Mr Bear."

"Likewise, Ma'am," He nodded to the officer.

Petra thought Brown Bear seemed a bit edgy. She knew him well and began to think he had a plan he was keeping to himself, for some reason.

Then he said, "I'm going to go on ahead, I can hear Lucas' boat. I will wait for him on the jetty. I want to ask Lucas what he knows about the underground castle! Girls, I have been going through the only papers belonging to the Professor that we brought with us to the island. Do you remember we photographed all the rest onto your iphone Petra?"

"Yes, I do! But the police took my phone, as you know that Newsome woman confessed to Emily Jane's murder and the recording is on my phone. It will be used as evidence when the case goes to trial."

'Yes, I know that!" exclaimed Brown Bear. "Lucas has been coming to this island over the years, I just want to know exactly what he knows about the underground castle's history. He's quite a buff on history, you know!"

"Is he?" asked Rosie in surprise.

"Yes he is, young Rosie," replied Brown Bear.

WPC Denton faced Petra and Rosie. "And, I will make your request to your mother. I am sure she will let you stay a bit longer, especially when I tell her how you helped solve our case." The Officer gave them all a big smile. "I am leaving Jake here, just in case there are any more problems."

"Oh!" exclaimed Rosie. "We don't want any more problems."

Petra had heard the motorboat engine. She was a bit mystified, as she thought she could hear the fisherman's engine coming into the small harbour from a different direction. And she thought BB was being a bit shifty. Petra was very astute and just had the feeling that something was going on that he was keeping from them.

The girls walked down the beach, they could hear Lucas and Brown Bear talking together and then an outburst of loud laughter.

Petra and Rosie ran to meet their old friend Lucas, who had shared some of their last adventure on the island. Ursula was a little way behind them, as she had decided to walk with the Policewoman helping her carry her holdall and a briefcase full of documents.

"Are you sure you will be alright, Ursula?" asked WPC Denton.

"Yes, I am fine, I won't be lonely anymore," replied Ursula. "I have made some wonderful friends, and now I know what happened to my mother, I can get on with my life." Ursula handed the briefcase to the officer.

"Thank you, Ursula, will you stay on the island?" The officer noticed what a beauty this strange girl appeared to be with her piercing forget-me -not blue eyes and long black silken hair.

"I will for a little while," Ursula replied. "And then I hope to study for a degree and then eventually earn my own living and obviously stay in touch with my new friends," Ursula shrugged her shoulders. "I will have to see what happens."

A few minutes later Ursula and the WPC joined everyone near the jetty. The tide had turned, and Petra thought to herself, 'that Lucas had steered his boat to land on the island, from another direction other than his usual approach. But why? She felt sure he had come around the headland, where Ursula's home cave was situated, and all the other secrets they had discovered on the eastern shores of the island, the fallen castle, the lagoon, the lake and the forest. Not to mention prehistoric bears!'

"Hullo," said Lucas. "I'm in a rush, I'm not coming ashore now, as I will be back early in the morning." Then he notices the police officer, "Ah! WPC Denton, I presume?"

"Yes, you may, I am she," she replied. "I am leaving PC Jake

Oliver on guard at the cottage for tonight. Oh! your nephew of course."

Lucas nodded to the officer," Yes, he's a good lad."

"Now, Mister Oliver, my bags?"

"Aar! Yes, I'll get them now!"

WPC Denton focused on the three girls. "There has been a delay in moving Emily Jane's body. I am not quite sure why, but I must obey orders. PC Jake will guard the cottage and will see that the cellar is not disturbed."

Lucas loaded the officer's luggage onto his vessel, at last the policewoman was on board the motorboat and the end of her assignment was in sight. She gave a big sigh and turned to Lucas.

"The young ladies have a request for their mother. They need more food."

Lucas stood tall with his silver fox hair catching the sunlight and looked at the little group. "Don't tell me that the load of goodies I brought over with you has all gone?"

"Yes, nearly," replied Rosie. "You see, Lucas it's the fault of the island!" she proclaimed.

"Is that so?" Lucas gave her a wry smile.

"Yes, it just makes us eat far more than when we are at home!"

Everyone laughed and then WPC Denton felt she ought to keep everyone in the loop.

"I will be going to see Mrs Williamson anyway, at her home in Swallows village, I need to sort out a few formalities with her," she looked directly at the fisherman.

"When you return to pick up my constable in the morning, make sure you have PC Oliver back on time, I will be expecting him at headquarters at 2pm tomorrow afternoon, on the dot!"

Lucas saluted the officer, "Aye, Aye, Madam, he'll be there!" Then he started the engine of his shiny new vessel. The three girls waved goodbye, as they stifled their giggles. Rosie the biggest giggler said, "Lucas always makes us laugh! doesn't he."

"Yes, he does," agreed Petra.

With great relief, the three girls ran hand in hand back up the beach to Brown Bear, who had said something to Lucas and gone on ahead. As they clambered over the rocks, the girls were just in time to see two pathologists exit the cottage and make their way to a waiting helicopter. The pilot had started the engine ready to leave the island and Jake was standing on guard outside the cottage door.

"What a loud noise these choppers make," Brown Bear yelled, trying to cover his ears. "And the draught they send down is worse than a hurricane. Come on, girls, let's get out of the way of this whirlwind, those rotor blades really stir up a storm."

Jake held his post at the cottage door and asked if anyone minded if he took off his dark blue jumper that was part of his police uniform. No one minded of course!

"Why have you been wearing it?" asked Ursula. "The sun is stifling hot at midday! Here give it to me. I'll take it inside for you."

"It is part of my uniform," stated Jake, passing his garment to the young lady. "Yes, thank you, I appreciate that." He couldn't help noticing Ursula's blue eyes and ebony black hair. He gave her a smile and she reciprocated. She felt surprised as she realised she liked his attention.

Then the last of the helicopters took off with a roar and headed out across the Bay to the mainland.

"BB," said Ursula "Why do you think the authorities have not taken my mother's body away to the morgue?"

"I really don't know, my dear," he replied. "Mark my words, they undoubtedly will have a jolly good reason for the delay."

The island was quiet with not even a seagull in sight. It was early afternoon and the hot sun soared in a cloudless azure sky. There wasn't even a whisper of a breeze. The girls were without their flip-flops and the hot sand was burning their feet.

"Ouch!" exclaimed Rosie. "The sand is scorching!"

"Come on!" yelled Petra. "Let's all go for a swim; the tide is just right now."

"Yes, let's!" came delighted squeals from Rosie and Ursula.

"Come on, BB, race you to the sea," yelled Rosie. "Hey girls, let's just go in the water in our shorts and T-shirts, we can get dressed into clean clothes when we get back to the cottage."

"Listen, girls, count me out!" Brown Bear had a very serious look on his face. "I have remembered something I need to do, it's too hot for me! Remember I can't take my coat off, can I? I'm going somewhere cooler for the afternoon. I will be back for supper."

"Oh, BB!" Rosie ran to his side. "I was looking forward to swimming with you, but I do understand, we'll see you later," she reached up to give him a hug. "Phew! it is even too hot for hugs." The little girl ran off to join Ursula and Petra, who were already splashing about in the shallows.

"Come on, let's go in deeper and have a game of chase." Rosie swam out strongly.

It was over an hour later when the girls decided they had enough of the sea, only because all this use of energy was making them feel tired. Reluctantly they left the water and flopped down on the sand, two metres up the beach. They lay there listening to the roar of the waves that were now gaining momentum with a stiff breeze behind them driving in the tide.

"I've got a good game to play," said Rosie eventually.

'What's that?" asked Ursula.

"One, my Nan told me she used to play when she was younger than we are now," replied Rosie. "Nan and her sister and their friends would spend summers on the beach near where they lived in Rhyl. In the summer holidays they would all go swimming when the tide was coming in. Then after a while they would all come out of the water for a rest and lie down on the sand waiting for a big wave to reach their toes. They would all squeal because the sea there was cold, then all the friends would run further up the beach, and again would lie and wait for that inevitable wave."

"That really does sound like a lot of fun!" exclaimed Ursula. "I want the waves to catch my toes."

"What happens if we run out of beach?" Petra was a bit sceptical, as the tide was now coming in fast.

"We won't for ages!" yelled a gleeful Rosie. "Come on, it will be amazing."

"OK! It does sound fun!" Petra was first in the sea again with Ursula close behind her.

With the golden sand and the rushing waves stretching out before them they couldn't resist. After a 'catch me if you can' splash about the three girls were soon lying flat out on the dry sand, waiting for the next big wave to catch them. And when it did, they would run up the beach again and lie down again and do it over again until there was no beach left.

"In my Nan's case it was concrete steps and a high sea wall to stop them," Rosie was enjoying this game very much.

"Oooo and we have rocks and a shingle beach under the cliff," said a delighted Ursula. "I have never had anyone to play with me like this before."

"What about the bears?" Rosie asked. "Do they ever come in the sea?"

"No, they prefer the lake or the lagoon."

"Well, I am so pleased Petra and Ursula that you are enjoying my Nan's game," Rosie squealed as the cold sea caught her toes.

It was over an hour later when the girls were so tired, they had to stop their game. The tide was very high and the last place they could rest was on the shale under the cliff.

"We had better stop now, look how low the sun is getting in

the sky," remarked Petra. "Is there anything cool we could have to eat, Rosie? Nothing heavy as BB said he would be back for supper later."

"I'll go into the cottage and look in the cupboard," she replied. "BB should be back by now. He's late! I bet he's fallen asleep on the big bed upstairs."

It was cool inside the cottage. Rosie found some tins of fruit and a large can of evaporated milk at the back of the kitchen cupboard. She had reached her hand in just to see what else was there and, as luck would have it, her fingers clasped around a packet of chocolate digestives. She put everything on the special tray with E and J's initials entwined upon it.

'What else do we need?' she thought. She found a large jug and filled it with ice cold water from the old kitchen tap.

'This will cool everyone down,' she thought. 'I'll just pop upstairs to wake BB.

but she had a shock when she realised he wasn't there!

Rosie ran as fast as she could to find Petra and Ursula. She found them cooling off in a rock pool, "There you are! I am really worried, BB has gone!"

"Gone where?"

"I don't know? He said he would be back at supper time. You know it is late August and it will be dark by 8.30. Where has he got to?"

"He won't be long," said Petra. Then she tried to reassure her sister but, deep inside she did feel a bit anxious. We had better find our torches. Then if he doesn't return, we will go and look for him."

"BB should have told us where he was going! Now he's missing!' yelled Ursula.

"That is strange PC Jake is missing too, and I know he had strict orders to guard my mother's body.

"We had better search for them!" Rosie was upset, she idolised Brown Bear. "Listen, I can hear something or someone crashing about in the forest. Ursula, how far are we from your bears?"

"About two kilometres over the headland," Ursula answered, she looked very worried now. "But it's much quicker underground the way I took you at first. Now the police have left the island I hope no one else is trying to take my bears!"

"Right! Let's get into jeans and T-shirts and maybe a jacket or something warm, it can get quite cold down there!" suggested Petra.

That summer day ended abruptly. In late August night can come on suddenly, the sun had set over the western horizon earlier and now long black clouds tinged with turquoise closed in over the island, and then it happened again.

"That noise! It is the bears, someone must be disturbing them," said Petra.

"Oh, No! I'm scared," Rosie sounded as if she was going to cry.

"We've got to go now," yelled Ursula. "We can take the shortcut underground for safety."

"No, I don't think we should leave here," said Petra. "If BB comes back and finds us missing, he will be worried. We will get some rest now and if BB isn't back by daybreak, then we will make sensible plans! Anyway, listen, the bears are quiet now."

"I think Jake and BB are together!" Rosie felt sure. "Perhaps something cropped up and they had to go. Oh! I remember now. BB, said he was going somewhere cool out of the sun."

"But Jake wouldn't have left his post guarding my mother, unless something really important had presented itself," remarked Ursula.

"Yes, you are right! And BB, is never late for supper," Petra replied.

"No, he isn't," agreed Rosie. "I don't know why, but I just feel someone or something else is on the island now."

"I think you are right Rosie," Ursula was thoughtful. "It must be someone or something important to take Jake away from his duty of guarding my mother's body."

The girls called Jake's name but there was no reply. Petra and Ursula entered the room with the trapdoor but all they found was tape blocking their way. On the tape, printed in bold letters were the words:

POLICE. DO NOT ENTER. CRIME SCENE.

40
A STRANGER

After that scorching hot day the onset of the evening had covered the sky in dark ominous clouds and an early mist was forming in the air. They waited outside the cottage but there was no sign of Jake or Brown Bear. The noise from the forest continued a while and then silence, a jarring unnerving silence.

"What's happened?" said Rosie, in the lowest voice she could muster.

"I don't know," Petra replied, trying to see Ursula's face in the sudden gloaming. "What do you think, Ursula?"

"Well, the only thing I am certain of is that something must have disturbed the bears," said Ursula. "And now I feel they are settled."

"How can you tell?" Rosie asked.

"Because when they are frightened, they have a call that I have learnt to understand over the years." Ursula looked confident. "You know, I think it may be BB and probably Jake too looking for something."

"Or someone," Petra replied. "Yes! You are probably right! I know that BB has a secret, and I think Jake and Lucas are in on it too. What are we going to do about it?"

"Nothing now, it is far too dark outside. I think we should eat some supper and then go to bed," Ursula gave a yawn. "I am tired out after our game this afternoon."

Everyone agreed that they were all very tired. Rosie rustled up a quick supper of cheese and biscuits and then they climbed the old oak stairs and all three were soon in bed.

That evening the wind got up speed and howled around the old weather-worn chimney pot, on the cottage roof. The noise kept Rosie awake for a while as she lay listening for any other sounds she recognised, but all she could hear was the outgoing tide with the angry wind buffeting along behind it. Eventually she managed to sleep but in her worried mind her dreams took her to searching the wild dark forest alone looking for BB.

However, Brown Bear was not in the woods that night, he had spent the afternoon in the old, ruined castle high in the centre of the island and later he spent the night with a stranger in Ursula's home cave. Prior to that it had been so hot that afternoon he felt drained of energy, so he had spent quite a lot of time in search of somewhere cool.

After leaving the girls playing their game of 'escape the waves' on the beach, he went inside their cottage to re-examine the few hard copies of the Professor's notes they had found in one of the mahogany chests. He and Petra had the contents of both chests in their possession for safe keeping. Old Mill Cottage was not a safe place to leave them, as the Professor was in hospital and they had witnessed intruders getting inside the cottage in the dead of night, a man and a woman who had arrived in a black BMW car. So, earlier that afternoon Brown Bear had poured over the hard copies for a while thankful he had saved the documents.

'And a good job I kept them safe,' he thought, as all the other documents he and the girls had discovered in the mahogany chests, one of which had been in open view in the study on the first evening they had made a visit to the Professor's home. The other chest they had located in the sooty cellar under an iron grating, at the side of 'Old Mill Cottage,' and both the documentation contents were copied to Petra's iPhone, and now her mobile is in the hands of the police.

"There is no air inside here either, I really must get outside." Brown Bear was getting hotter and hotter. The cottage was usually cool inside, but today Brown Bear found it stifling.

He nodded to Jake as he made his way out of the cottage.

"Are you aware of what is happening, young man?"

"Yes! I am, Sir," replied Jake. "In fact, I must go now to make contact!"

"Very good! By the way did Lucas give you any information?"

"Yes, all under control sir," replied Jake, with an air of confidence. "How long have I got?"

"In your own time," replied Brown Bear. "But mind you leave the door unlocked for the girls. Make sure you are back on duty, as tomorrow is going to be a big day!"

Brown Bear scrambled over the rocks to find the steep path that led up to the castle on the hill. As he approached the fortress, he disturbed a flock of sitting gulls that soared into the air with loud squawks, as they flew out over the bay.

It was cool in the castle courtyard and a gentle sea breeze blew the long tufts of marram grass that grew between the flagstones. Brown Bear sat for a while on one of the large stones that had once fallen from the battlements, but alas, he was still too hot.

He felt very sleepy but knew he must find somewhere cooler for a snooze. Slowly he descended the stone steps into the cool cellar under the castle, where he, Petra and Rosie had shared their first adventure together. He remembered it was a few years ago when the girls had been with him and in danger too! How fast those two have grown! Quite young ladies now, and as for Ursula, I wonder what she will do when term time begins, and I must take the girls home to Swallows village and school.

He reached the bottom step of the stone stairs and could feel at once the cold dampness that surrounded him. 'Arr! Very pleasant,' he thought. 'After being exposed to that sweltering sunshine outside anywhere cool will do. I am going to sit on this step and have a short snooze.' Well, that was it he felt so tired, and with the cool air caressing his face he soon drifted off to sleep. It must have been well over two hours before he woke up.

He knew from experience these cellars, or dungeons as the girls used to call them, stretched out under the island like a complex labyrinth. He felt deep into his holdall for the small torch he always carried on him, "Well, ever since I have been involved with these two adventurous girls," he said out loud, and the old familiar echo took up his words, girls 'irls 'irls 'irls' rebounding them from the thick musty walls.

Then suddenly he heard another noise deep in these cellars and couldn't resist going deeper and deeper along the passage to find whatever it was that he had heard. After a steep descent he could hear voices.

'Surely not those scoundrels again!' he thought.

And just as he turned a bend in the dingy passageway he bumped into Jake and another person, who Brown Bear had never seen before.

"Oh! Mr Bear, I wasn't expecting to see you down here, what are you doing?" Jake's loud voice reverberated all around the cellar.

"Hey, steady on Constable!" exclaimed Brown Bear. "Will you please take that bright flashlight out of my eyes?"

"Sorry Sir, I had no idea that anyone would be in these tunnels!" replied Jake.

"And who is your companion?" Brown Bear couldn't see very well in the darkness that hung around them like a large black cloak.

"I am not allowed to say, Sir!" answered Jake in his official capacity.

"Jake, you need to get back on your sentry duty." Brown Bear's voice reverberated all around.

"I know but a most important matter came up and I have to

obey orders," replied PC Oliver.

"I see." Brown Bear was curious.

"What is back there?" asked Jake, pointing to the tunnel behind Brown Bear. "Did you see anything unusual?"

"No, I didn't!" exclaimed Brown Bear. "All I wanted to do was get out of the hot sun!" He was getting a bit cross and he wanted answers. "Can I ask why you are here on your way to the hill castle?"

"Oh! I didn't realise this way led to another castle," said Jake. "But Sir," he turned to his companion "Did you know that?"

"No, I didn't know that for sure," replied the stranger, in a calm, well-spoken voice. "But I had always suspected both fortresses would have had a connecting passage of some sort."

Brown Bear had expected a meeting of some sort with a certain person, but not down here in the castle dungeons. He had expected a much more formal encounter.

"So, you have come from the fallen underground castle?" Brown Bear was getting interested in what was happening. "It wasn't always underground, was it?"

"No!" exclaimed the stranger. "It was built on the eastern cliffs at roughly the same time as the hill fortress, but the fallen castle was built as a storehouse for the residents of the main castle. It had been built within the cliff itself and survived until it fell during the minor earthquake that hit the island in the mid-nineties." The voice of Jake's companion echoed around the passageway.

"Sir, do you know when both castles were built?" Brown Bear was delighted because here was someone he could converse with. He was hoping for a deep conversation with this person, he longed for a profound intellectual debate. Not that he didn't enjoy the chitter- chatter of the girls of course.

The well-spoken gentleman obliged.

"The high defending castle was first constructed in stone in the early thirteenth century, built by a Welsh Prince, to protect his lands and keep the English at bay. The fallen castle would have been built a little later, most probably to store provisions and a certain amount of weaponry." replied the stranger. "But there are no references in history to confirm my theory. You are interested in history; I presume?"

"Indeed, I am and so are the girls!"

"Girls?" questioned the new arrival.

"Yes! Petra, Rosie and their new friend, Ursula, who we all met here on the island. Now, she is a fountain of knowledge!" replied Brown Bear.

"Yes, Ursula! That makes sense. Ursula of course!" The stranger exclaimed as his mind seemed to drift away to somewhere else. He was about to say more when Jake gave a little cough to draw their attention.

"Jake's voice was suddenly echoing around the tunnel, "I'm sorry to interrupt Sir, but I must get back to my post," Jake sounded worried.

"Yes, of course you get back! I will stay a while with my new acquaintance," said the gentleman.

"Here is my torch, I have a spare," Jake handed a torch to the stranger, and without much ado he was gone.

"Now shall we follow and get out of here," said the gentleman, who Brown Bear couldn't see properly in the dim passage.

"I was wondering," asked Brown Bear. "Are you the person we are expecting? We were told by the Police that you wanted to arrive on the island somewhat covertly. Unless you are an undercover officer who has been left behind by your squad?"

"No indeed I am not!" exclaimed the stranger. "I have delicate issues I must attend to. Superintendent Harding has made me aware of certain matters."

"That is good to hear. Well, can I be of assistance?" offered Brown Bear. "I am well acquainted with this island!"

"You can indeed! Now, I don't think I could make it up the hill to the castle, we will go back past the fallen castle ruins and on to the caves near the Lagoon."

"Oh! You know about the lagoon!" Brown Bear noticed the stranger had a significant limp; he caught a glimpse in the torchlight.

"Not before today I didn't," answered the stranger. "The police officer was helping me find a hidden cave. I have a copy of the route on a small piece of parchment that belonged to my wife but alas, we couldn't find the cave."

"The girls and I know where most of the caves are!" exclaimed Brown Bear.

"That's good. I only arrived this morning, an old friend ferried me over early, he said he had to come to pick someone up and take them back to the mainland."

"Do you mean WPC Denton?" queried Brown Bear.

"Yes, I think that was her name. I hope they all treated you well, it must have been an irritation at times."

"Certainly not! They were wonderful. All I wanted was to keep my girls safe and do my best for Ursula and that's what the officers wanted too."

"Ah, yes, I am pleased to hear that. Look, ahead I see daylight."

Very soon they were out of the tunnel and on the beach where Rosie had once followed a baby rabbit into the cave, she had been lost for a whole afternoon.

Brown Bear could see the stranger clearly for the first time. His new companion was a good-looking gentleman in his early sixties, with silver grey hair with long strands escaping out from under a faded sun hat. Brown Bear noticed he was wearing well-worn blue jeans, a check shirt and a tweed jacket. Then he saw him point towards some smooth boulders scattered about amongst the soft white sand.

"Come, let us sit on those rocks over there." The newcomer to the island made the request as he pointed using a stick. "It will be sheltered over there, and you can tell me all about the girls."

It was only then that Brown Bear noticed his walking aid, and in that moment, he knew exactly who this gentleman with a limp was. There was no doubt at all! It was the eminent professor himself.

Brown Bear told him everything he knew about Ursula and her strange life on the island. His listener was most attentive to all the details, as to how old she was, the colour of her hair, even to the colour of her eyes.

"Now there I draw a line, Sir. I don't go looking into girl's eyes. I don't even know what colour my own eyes are!" Brown Bear was a bit perplexed.

"I assure you! Your eyes are the darkest brown I have ever seen!" reciprocated the stranger.

"Well, er, I wouldn't know that I don't go looking in mirrors. In fact, I have never owned one." At that moment Brown Bear felt a little self-conscious.

"I am glad to hear that!" The newcomer retorted with a smile. "Now this island seems to be a maze of caves and tunnels."

"Indeed, it is!" stated Brown Bear "Have you a ride home tonight?"

"No, I haven't, not until tomorrow when Lucas, you must know Lucas Oliver! Chap from the village, he is coming over to collect me. I had thought I would be able to spend the night in the cottage, but I realise now that it is somewhat occupied."

"Yes, with three girls!" Brown Bear was enjoying the company of this gentleman.

"Um, I really want to see my rescuers again," replied the gentleman. "And to ask if they have accomplished the task that I imposed on them back in July."

"Task," asked Brown Bear. "What task?"

"To find the secrets of the island," he gave an impatient sigh.

"Surely you know who I am by now?"

"Indeed, I do. You are none other than Professor Lawrence Butler Mortimer, the famous archaeologist!" exclaimed Brown Bear.

"Indeed! I am he," replied the Professor. "Then you probably will know, as I was incapacitated on that evening I moved into my cottage in Swallows village, I asked the two girls who so kindly helped me, if they could find some of the secrets of the island?" He paused for breath. "You see I had fallen down the wretched step in my kitchen. And broken my ankle. Very kind and thoughtful the girls were, even called the ambulance for me."

"The girls are named Petra and Rosie and have found some secrets of the island!"

Brown Bear hesitated, he didn't want to blurt out everything they had found, he thought better of it. Ursula should be the one to tell her father about everything they had discovered on the island.

But even then, when they meet, what if the Professor wouldn't accept the fact that he is Ursula's true father. Brown Bear's thoughts were in turmoil and worse still, what if Ursula refutes it herself!

As the day progressed Brown bear realised he needn't have worried, for here was a true gentleman courteous and charismatic. The two got along so well until early evening. They were discussing many topics as well as Ursula and her bears. And how devastated he had been when his wife had gone missing. He told Brown Bear how he had enjoyed living in Swallows Village. They had moved into Old Mill Cottage when he and Emily Jane were first married, and how welcoming the villagers were towards him and his young bride.

"We kept our flat in Oxford, as I still worked part time at the university. But what a contrast the village life was for us. Emily

Jane would sometimes go to Aberystwyth, to lecture at the university on her favourite subject, extinct European brown bears and to visit her parents, but most of the time we just settled into village life."

"Yes, it is very peaceful, except when the girls have music on far too loud or occasionally have a bit of a tiff."

Brown Bear shivered even though his coat was warm and thick.

"It has gone quite cold now that the sun has gone behind the headland."

The evening had come too soon, and he started worrying about the girls alone in the cottage but there was nothing he could do about it now.

"Come, I will show you the cave that Ursula calls home. I'm sure she won't mind if we stay there tonight."

"Can you help me up?" The gentleman held his hand out to his new companion. "I'm not supposed to do too much walking, I broke the darn ankle the first evening back in Mill Cottage!"

"Yes Sir, I know all about that! Come on, I'll help you inside. There's a big shelf in there with blankets and cushions from the cottage that make a cosy bed."

It didn't take them long to find the cave with the chiselled away hole, in the middle of the wall. There was little trace of fallen masonry now.

"The police have put me in the picture." Professor Mortimer turned to Brown Bear with moisture welling in his eyes, "So, is this where my wife lived for over six years?"

"Yes!" According to information that Ursula relayed to the girls, Mrs Mortimer had been ecstatic because she had followed directions she had found on an old map, and it led her here, not far from the bears. She had found and made friends with two cave bears. She found their ancestry dated back to prehistoric,

Eurasian Cave Bears that lived in the forest across the lake, where their species had survived here for millenia, living on plant shoots and berries and fish from the lake. I believe there are large caves somewhere in that direction, but the girls and I never had time to explore them."

"Amazing, quite amazing! Now the map she had in her possession at the time must have been the original and she sent me a copy, but she was an outstanding person in her field. And to survive living down here all those years well, until…"

"No, don't go there, Sir. Just wait until you meet Ursula. You will be surprised how accomplished a young lady she is." Brown Bear showed the Professor the rocky bed that Ursula had made into a comfortable resting place.

"Oh, I see! some of the bedding I bought for my darling wife, to make her stay comfortable on the island. But if she was trapped here all those years, how did they come to be down here in the first place?"

Brown Bear gave his head a quick scratch, he was puzzled. "I am not sure," he said. "All I know from what Ursula has told the girls and I is that this is where Emily Jane is…" Brown Bear tailed off his sentence, then said, "Do you mind me calling her Emily Jane?"

"No, of course not, that is what I always called her," he replied.

Brown Bear continued telling the professor all he knew.

"This cave is where Ursula was born," continued Brown Bear. "Apparently the female bear helped Emily Jane in her hour of need."

"Good Lord! How remarkable," exclaimed the Professor. "Now, what do I call you?"

"BB, Sir, that is what the girls call me."

"How original," mumbled the Professor. "You see, the day I was called away to Oxford and left my wife on the island, I had no idea she was pregnant!"

"I know! It must have been hard for you when you did find out," Brown Bear's voice was sympathetic.

"I never did find out for certain. I guessed she might have been pregnant but only found out from a letter she had sent me from the island, delivered to Old Mill Cottage by Lucas back in 1999. I put it away safely in my briefcase. But the problem I was called away for took longer to solve than expected, and, regrettably, I never saw my wife again."

"Oh dear!" Brown Bear sighed. "I am so sorry, Sir. So when did you read her letter?"

"Weeks later and even then she only hinted that she had some wonderful news for me. But she didn't mention the fact she was carrying my child. It would have been marvellous! We lost a child once! Because Joanna Newsome broke into the cottage one night when I was away, and terrified my wife and unfortunately Emily Jane miscarried our baby."

"Oh! how awful for you both," Brown Bear felt a deep anger inside for what this couple had suffered at the hands of that evil woman, Joanna Newsome.

"Well, we both were young then and we put the horror behind us, we both threw ourselves into our work. But my deepest regret is leaving her here alone on the island. I had intended to come back to her in a couple of days." By now the Professor could not control the tears that were welling up in his eyes.

After a while he composed himself and carried on with his narrative.

"It was soon after that I heard about the landslide on the island," the Professor sighed. "After the dust settled, I came over by boat and a massive hunt was conducted by the authorities. Air ambulance, Lifeboat and the whole of Swallows town police force, even villagers offered their help to search for Emily Jane!"

"She was well loved!"

"Indeed, she was! But for me it was the not knowing what had happened to her. That was the part that got to me most."

"Oh! You, poor man," said Brown Bear. "What you must have gone through."

"That is why I never actually sold Old Mill Cottage. I was going to but, in the end I decided to leave it with an agent. Just hoped she would come home one day."

"And then this summer you decided to come back," Brown Bear reminded Professor Mortimer.

"Yes, I did, because I had a dream about my wife and in that dream she was asking me to return to Old Mill Cottage."

"That would be her spirit calling you," said Brown Bear. "She's still here on the island."

The Professor was very quiet, deep in thought, "Do you think so?"

"Indeed, I have felt her presence and so have my girls. She wanted to be found!"

"I am surprised! We scientists don't believe in that sort of thing, but you seem to be earnest."

"I too have been sceptical about such things," said Brown Bear. "But I can't deny the strange occurrences that have happened since we arrived here, even Rosie felt something strange the day she encountered Emily Jane, when she was hiding from the Newsome's, who were quarrelling near the Shrine Ursula had made for her mother, deep in the caves near here."

"What shrine?" exclaimed the Professor. "You are going too fast for me."

"Well, I do not want to overstep the mark but, I have said too much. It is Ursula's place to show and tell you the rest."

"You mean there is more?"

"Yes, much more," responded Brown Bear. "Now we must get some sleep. By the way, have you any food with you, Sir? I am starving!"

Luckily the Professor had some rather flattened sandwiches in his bag which the two hurriedly consumed.

"Tomorrow you will meet your daughter, Sir."

"What if she doesn't like me?"

For all his knowledge and all his public esteem, Professor Lawrence B Mortimer felt at his most vulnerable that night.

41
DISTURBANCE

Next morning the girls were fast asleep in the ornate bedroom in the beach cottage. The sun rose in the eastern sky and then, as the light streamed into the room it woke Rosie. She listened hard to a sound that she could hear getting nearer and nearer to the island. Then she heard voices too, making a disturbance on the rocks below their bedroom window. Rosie scrambled out of bed and rushed to the window to see what was going on outside. She opened the window wide and could see a watery mist hanging low over the sea.

"Whatever is going on?" called Petra, from the warm comfort of her bed.

"What is that commotion?" Ursula leapt out of bed and pushed Rosie aside so she could see what was going on below. "Are Jake and BB back? Jake should never have left my mother alone!"

"I haven't seen BB, but before you pushed me out of the way, I could see Jake talking to two men in black suits," answered a sleepy Rosie.

"And the police are back!" Petra quickly got dressed in dark blue jeans and a long sleeved, white T-shirt. "And I can see one of their helicopters landing on the shale below the cliff."

"Oh dear!" sighed Ursula. "Those pathologists have returned too. Why haven't I been told? I told WPC Denton I didn't want my mother moved yet!" The young girl became overcome with grief. She could not control floods of tears streaming from her eyes.

"Please don't cry," said Rosie, putting her arms round Ursula's waist.

"No, don't cry Ursula," Petra comforted their friend. "I'm going to find BB, I must find him now, as he has never left Rosie and I alone for this length of time, ever before!"

"Not unless he's on a mission," remarked Rosie. "Can you remember where he was when we last saw him yesterday?"

"He was here near the cottage, and he wouldn't come to watch us play on the beach!" remembered Petra. "He was complaining he was too hot and was going to find somewhere cool."

Rosie had tears in her eyes now. "Where could he have gone? And Jake went missing too!"

"Yes, it is a bit of a mystery. BB is devoted to you two girls," Ursula did her best to cheer up a little.

"And I will tell you what else is a mystery," Petra lowered her voice. "Do you remember yesterday morning when Lucas arrived to take policewoman Denton back to the mainland?"

"Yes, of course we do!" exclaimed Ursula and Rosie in unison.

"I don't suppose you noticed anything strange about the way Lucas had moored his boat," Petra asked in earnest.

"No, I didn't," replied Ursula.

"Nor did I!" exclaimed Rosie. "Should we have?"

"Not really, but I noticed yesterday that his boat was facing seaward, every other time he faces his boat leeward," Petra scrutinised their faces for a hint of knowledge, but there was none.

"I don't really know what you mean Sis."

"Never mind, I just felt he may have landed something on the island around the headland, out of sight from our view, before he moored his motorboat. And where's BB? I felt he knew something was up when he went ahead of us to talk to Lucas at the jetty yesterday morning!"

At that moment there was a loud knock at the door, and a flurry of voices outside the cottage.

"It's Jake!" exclaimed Rosie. "We had better go down."

"Don't forget to get dressed, you two." Petra went down the stairs to open the door to the constable.

"What time is it, Ursula?" asked Rosie, pulling on her jeans.

"About 7.30. Come on, let's see what's happening."

Within minutes the three girls were out on the rocks confronting a group of officials. They looked for BB, but he wasn't there. Rose's heart sank, as she loved BB dearly.

"What do you all want?" Ursula asked, tenaciously. Deep down she knew what was happening but deep in her heart she was afraid she wouldn't be able to bear it if they took her mother's body away from the island.

"Can we help?" Petra sounded a little more polite than her friend.

"You are not taking my mother!" interrupted Ursula, in a voice that was tinged with hysteria. At that moment both girls felt extremely angry.

The two men in dark suits stepped closer to the front door. One of the men, the older one seemed to be in charge and the other was much younger and just stood as if waiting for his orders.

"Forgive me, miss, but I have been instructed by a higher authority to attend at this residence. I am James Ely Cuthbert, head undertaker at the firm of Cuthbert and Sons, at your service and this is Jethro, my son, who is my apprentice, so to speak!" he said, "You know, learning the trade as it were!"

"Well, I don't know!" Ursula exclaimed. "And there is no way you are taking my mother's body away from here".

"Miss, we have orders," came the reply from the older man.

"No way! Not like that! I want notice, I need to get my head around all this." Ursula was adamant. "I have spent years alone on this island looking for my mother, and thanks to my new friends here," she nodded towards Petra and Rosie. "We found her in plain sight, a place where we should have looked first, but there were so many animal bones scattered about on the floor from historic times, that we thought were just her collection but now we think that wicked Newsome woman had them layered there to cover her felony. You see," she looked directly at the undertaker, "My mother's passion was archaeology of ancient bones. We felt they belonged to her and should be left untouched for the time being. I just can't let her go with you!"

The young woman looked round at the girls with grief and bewilderment in her beautiful sad blue eyes. In her distress Ursula ran to block the entrance of the cottage with her arms outstretched, "You cannot take her. I won't let you!"

Petra and Rosie were finding their friends outburst extremely upsetting.

Petra slipped her arms around Ursula's slim waist, as her friend stood blocking the doorway, "I think that you will have to let her go with these gentlemen, the funeral directors," said Petra in a calming voice. "But I agree you should have been approached first. You *are* her next of kin."

Rosie had tears trickling down her face, "I think it will be alright," she said, but her voice wasn't very convincing. She knew exactly how their new friend was feeling and she understood what it had meant to Ursula, to at last find out what had happened to her Mum. It must have been heartbreaking to find out that her body had been lying in the cellar, cold yet still beautiful under the cottage, where they all had been staying.

It was one of the pathologists, a woman, who managed to calm Ursula down after many minutes of her distress.

"I am Doctor Erin Barnett," she said as she joined Ursula at the door of the cottage.

"My colleague Andy Jensen and I have been asked to re-examine your mother, as some evidence was overlooked by the forensics officers, who were here on Wednesday."

"What evidence?" demanded Ursula. "What was overlooked?"

"I am so sorry I have to do this," said Erin, the lady pathologist. "I know how stressful it must be for you, but the people who were here before stated that, oh dear I am so sorry."

"Stated what?" cried Ursula. "What fact was overlooked? All I want is for my mother to be at peace and no one will let her be!"

The forensic doctor had no time to reply because at that moment Jake stood to attention and saluted Brown Bear, and the eminent Professor, who were strolling up the beach towards the intrusion.

"Come on, Sir!" exclaimed Brown Bear. "What's this commotion? I think we are needed here. Are you alright with your stick or do you need my arm?"

"I am fine," replied Professor Mortimer. "Oh! Look, the girls I met at 'Old Mill Cottage are here. How splendid!"

Petra and Rosie ran to the Professor and shook hands with him, he was delighted to see them again. Brown Bear received a big hug from the girls, while Ursula stood silent in the doorway observing the scene.

'Who is that man?' she thought.

The Professor had a quick word with the forensic doctors and the smartly dressed undertakers. "Give us a few minutes? Will you please."

Brown Bear took charge.

"Girls go inside and find a rug for the Professor. We'll sit on the rocks. I think we need a catchup?"

"Yes, we do!" exclaimed Rosie, "Where have you been all night?"

"We have been worried. Have you been with PC Jake?" asked Petra.

"Yes, we have proved there is a secret passage from the tumble-down castle underground to the Castle on the hill!" said Brown Bear. "Isn't that right, Sir?"

"Indeed, it is!" replied the gentleman. Who Rosie now thought that he seemed to be a good friend of their much-loved BB.

The Professor looked Ursula in the face.

"My word, you are as beautiful as your mother!" He wiped away an escaping tear.

"Did you know my mother?" Ursula studied his features, quite unaware who the stranger was. She noticed it was a well-worn suntanned face, maybe the result of his life as an archaeologist. Most of her mother's friends had been archaeologists!

She had been made aware of her mother's life many times before the landslide. Ursula grew up quickly listening to her mother's stories of her digs around the world. Ursula was waiting patiently for this man to produce a reply to her question. She still studied his face. 'Probably rugged after many hours troweling away at foreign soils, under the burning rays of a tropical sun.'

"Yes! I met your mother when she was eighteen years old, and I grew to love her more every day I was with her. And you, my dear, look exactly as she did on that first day when I set eyes on her," Then he smiled, and Ursula softened, she liked this man.

"We studied archaeology together for three years, and then I studied for a higher degree and your mother studied for her Masters. Emily Jane changed my life for the better!"

"Emily Jane is my mother's name," said Ursula, trying to put all the facts together. "You mean you are Larry?"

At that moment the dawn broke for Ursula. A new dawn when the early morning mists that hung low over the land allowed only the leafy tops of the highest trees to appear in the sky. Like the morning of the first day, when milky white clouds poised in suspension, waiting in the haze of a new sun. And then the sky emerged out of the mists of time leaving the sky a brilliant blue, and the sun shone on everything, and everything was going to be alright. Ursula swooned in realisation that this man who stood before her was her father. He was Larry, the man that her mother adored.

"Yes, I am Larry, only Emily Jane dared to call me Larry," he smiled, a smile that lit up his face. "I was always known as Lawrence by my parents and even by teachers at school." He looked closely at everyone. "Now it is over twenty years since I heard Emily Jane call me Larry, her voice as light as the breeze with that familiar, sing-song Welsh accent." He looked at Brown Bear, Petra, and Rosie.

"Thank you for finding my daughter. I had no idea I had a daughter, until the Superindendant put me in the picture. And Mr. Bear confirmed it last night."

"Last night!" exclaimed Rosie. "So, you two met up and spent the night putting in the missing pieces. Where did you sleep?"

"Well, Rosie, I was in the castle dungeons trying to escape the hot sun yesterday," retorted Brown Bear. "I was following the passage down and down and then I heard voices and I followed the sound and eventually I bumped into Jake and the Professor. Mind you, I didn't know who the stranger was then. He and Jake had found the underground castle and discovered a secret passage up to the castle on the hill."

"Well, I think we should all go and explore that secret way tomorrow," Rosie was feeling excited at the prospect.

"Sorry girls, we have business to attend to," said Professor Mortimer. "And Ursula, my dear, I think we need to let the pathologists do their job now, and then later we will deal with the undertakers." His remarks were direct and to the point but even so, his voice was kind. After all his years of dealing with the students he had taught over the years, the predicament in front of him now was of uncertainty. He thought he was good at coping with young people but as he looked at his daughter he wondered if he had enough skill to deal with this rather delicate situation sympathetically.

"Yes! You are right!" exclaimed Ursula. "My mother must come first; I have been naive thinking I can keep her here. Of course she must have a funeral and I must let these people help."

All persons present there on this sunny early morning were astounded with Ursula's sudden change of heart. And then Ursula surprised everyone.

"Father! Would you like to see my mother now? We can say goodbye to her together, I know she would like that." A stunned silence prevailed, and even the seagulls ceased to squawk in the sky overhead.

"Yes, that will please me very much!" replied the Professor, who immediately reached out for his daughter's hand.

Brown Bear was overjoyed at Ursula's reaction towards her father. "And now Petra and Rosie come with me and let us give our friends some privacy."

The two girls followed Brown Bear dutifully. He led them in the direction of the jetty. "I have a surprise to show you!"

"I hope it is a good one," Rosie skipped along by his side. "What is it, BB? I can't wait."

"Come on BB, tell us. We need something nice to happen after all the stress we have shared the last few days.

"I don't need to tell you, just look at the end of the jetty," their best friend replied.

"Oh! BB, Is it what I think it is?"

The two girls climbed up on the jetty and ran to the end, "It's a waterproof box!"

"Well, look inside," said Brown Bear, catching up to them.

"Oh, fantastic! One of Mum's hampers," yelled Rosie, "BB, how did it get here?"

"Lucas must have dropped it off when he brought the undertakers over early this morning." Brown Bear replied.

"Do you think he brought the forensic people too?" asked Rosie.

"No, Rosie, I think they came by helicopter, the one that has landed on the shale, at the top of the beach." Brown Bear picked up the heavy hamper and made it look like a marshmallow as he placed it on his shoulder.

"Now, listen girls! I've decided with Professor Mortimer to meet late this afternoon near the Lagoon. That is if all goes well between him and his daughter!"

"Why shouldn't it, BB?" queried Petra. "I think there was a rapport between them."

"Yes of course, but Ursula was a bit feisty to start with." said Rosie, remembering how obstinate Ursula had been in front of the officials earlier this morning.

"Yes," remarked Petra. "I know, but she had a lot to deal with. Can you just think of it?" Petra was rational in her synopsis of her new friend's ordeal. "From six years old she was alone on this island! Then fourteen years later she found us! That was wonderful and thanks to her mother she had become extremely knowledgeable, but she found solace in her mother's great find, the bears. Would she have survived without them?"

"Maybe not," BB shrugged his shoulders, forgetting he was carrying a fair-sized load.

"Yes, and now although she was pleased to find her missing mother," continued Petra. "What a shock for Ursula to learn that her mother had been murdered, by a jealous rival, someone from the past who wouldn't let go of her father's imaginary affection for her."

"Oh, dear what a mess," sighed Rosie. "But at least they both seemed pleased to meet at last. Ursula calmed down very quickly once her father spoke directly to her, did you see?"

"Yes, she did!" exclaimed Petra, feeling very grateful that she and Rosie had always known their own Dad."

"Right, girls, let's find a spot near the lagoon for a picnic and see what goodies your Mum has sent for us this morning."

It didn't take long to find the blue lagoon, its crystal waters beckoning them to jump in and splash about, but the girls seemed rather subdued today, Brown Bear thought. He didn't say anything because he knew they would both be thinking of Ursula and her meeting with her father.

Very soon Petra had managed to open the hamper, she and Rosie couldn't wait to see inside.

"Oh Look!" cried Rosie." A big pack of croissants and a jar of orange marmalade."

"Come on, BB, come and eat some breakfast," Petra started unpacking the hamper.

They were all excited at the prospect of more food, as their rations had become a little scarce. Brown Bear was delighted to see his two girls happy again.

They sat munching away at breakfast with their toes dipped in the warm rippling waters.

"This is bliss," said Rosie. "Anything more to eat?" She looked in the hamper.

There were plenty of groceries like cheese and crisps and two punnets of strawberries and their Mum's famous cherry and almond cake. Also among the items was a letter. Rosie didn't really think anything of the white envelope to start with but after a while took it to Brown Bear and Petra, who was still dangling her feet in the blue lagoon.

"Here is a message from Mum." Petra grabbed it first and read the letter out loud.

> Hi Petra, Hi Rosie,
> I am getting worried about you on that island. A policewoman came to see me yesterday telling me about your involvement with criminals and what is most worrying Petra, you may be called as a witness for the prosecution when the case the police are working on goes to court. Unless you have a good reason to stay on the island your

Dad and I think you must come home at once. I feel Mr Bear is not looking after you two as well as he should. As soon as I find Lucas, I will ask him to fetch you back immediately.
Love Mum XX

An air of gloom descended on all the pals.

"BB! How can Mum say that about you? You always care for us first." cried Rosie.

"Nothing to do with you, BB, but maybe Mum is right," intercepted Petra. "This adventure we are in the middle of, far outweighs our two previous escapades on this island."

"Look, girls," said Brown Bear. "Don't worry about my feelings! Your Mum is right. I have been caught up in everything just like you two have been. But I do owe your Mum and Dad an explanation for my conduct," explained Brown Bear. "If there is a little juice left in your phone Rosie, I will ring her now, to explain everything and how important it all is to the Professor. Remember, girls, he is your Mum's new neighbour!"

"Yes of course, BB, you can explain to Mum much better than we could. Tell her we want to stay until the very last minute before we must come back to school." Rosie was a bit short of breath but managed to tell BB that Mali's charger was in the cottage.

"Right, give me your phone, Rosie. I won't be long but stay here in case the Professor and Ursula are on their way." Brown Bear took hold of Rosie's phone, "Now keep some food for our guests. Tonight, if the officials leave, we might just have the island to ourselves."

"By the way, BB, how did the Professor come to the island?" asked Petra.

Brown Bear looked a little surprised at her question.

"Lucas had already landed him on the island around the eastern headland early yesterday morning, and then we all met Lucas at the jetty. By then he was ready to take WPC Denton back to the mainland." Brown Bear was about to set off to the cottage when Petra remembered something.

"BB, you knew he was coming, and you didn't tell us!" exclaimed Petra." Why?"

"Because Professor Mortimer asked Lucas to inform me of his intentions but to keep it secret."

"Oh! I was right Rosie, I told you BB and Lucas were up to something! And I noticed Lucas had come to land at the jetty from a different direction."

"Yes, you did, Sis," agreed Rosie.

"OK, you are right," interrupted Brown Bear. "But the Doc didn't want to upset things, because he had learnt a little from the police and well, he just wanted his meeting with Ursula to be as easy as possible."

"And what was all that noise coming from the woods last night? Was it you and Jake and the Professor?" asked Rosie.

"No, actually it wasn't, but eventually I think Ursula is the one to reveal all," he said, turning to go. "Right, I'm off to find Mali's magic charger and convince your Mum everything is alright on the island!"

"What on earth does he mean, Ursula will reveal all?" said a puzzled Rosie.

Petra shook her head, "I've no idea!"

42

BONDING

When Ursula and her father stood together on the rocks outside the cottage alone for the very first time, they both felt an unnerving silence, a silence that was only broken by cries of distant gulls and the constant murmur of the sea.

Ursula could hardly believe that this man who stood beside her was Larry, the person her mother had constantly mentioned, always with the warmest affection. Now she knew he was her father, there was no doubt, as she remembered how BB, and the girls had worked it out a while ago. An autumnal breeze sprung up suddenly and Ursula could feel it gently tugging at her hair as confusing thoughts flashed through her mind. Oh dear! So many lost years, precious time she could have spent getting to know this man.

Professor Lawrence B. Mortimer also stood silent as he reflected on his marriage to Emily Jane. His memories of a sunny morning in an Oxford churchyard surrounded by all their university friends and Welsh family members, proved to be one of the happiest days of his life. He had travelled the world as an Archaeologist out in the field when he was young, and a lecturer in the subject for the latter years. But no day to him was as happy as the one, when Emily Jane became his wife. He remembered looking at her when her bridesmaids lifted her veil, and he saw her beautiful face looking adoringly at him.

He shuddered as he remembered a darker moment when Jo Newsome, his previous girlfriend had threatened him, and vowed she would do everything in her power to drive a wedge between him and Emily Jane. In the years since his wife had been missing his ex-had approached him many times to rekindle their previous relationship, but he had always sensed a sinister side of Joanna and as he thought wisely, he would avoid her at all costs.

Ursula remained silent besides him, he looked her way, but her gaze was fixed on the white capped waves out in the bay.

'Her father! I am this beautiful girl's father,' he thought. 'But surely Emily Jane would have told me if she had become pregnant again! Ah yes! Now, I understand. He suddenly realised why his wife had not told him, it was because of the miscarriage! She probably thought it too soon to get excited. Of course, he remembered soon after they moved into Old Mill Cottage, he had received an urgent call asking him to go back to Oxford immediately, he hadn't wanted to leave his wife, but she assured him that she would be fine.

The reason he had to go was because his office at the university had been broken into the previous night, and many of his books had been pulled off the shelves and tossed on the floor of his study. His secretary wasn't yet sure if any important manuscripts had been stolen.

Of course, he had immediately realised that the perpetrator must have been Joanna Newsome, she had made sure he would have been called away, leaving Emily Jane alone and vulnerable in the cottage. She had many villains at her beck and call and any of them could disrupt the security at the college and have found a way into his private quarters.

So vindictive was Jo Newsome that he proved later that on that occasion, it was she who had forced entry into Old Mill Cottage and terrorised his wife.

The next day Emily Jane miscarried the child they were longing for. 'A baby to seal our love, how happy we all could have been.'

Lawrence Mortimer was standing there with his daughter, as

they were about to say their goodbyes to the woman they both loved, when suddenly, he was tortured by numerous regrets.

He regretted leaving his wife alone on the island in August 1999. He regretted taking a call on his mobile phone earlier that morning. It was from one of his students who was having 'a nervous breakdown' over his thesis, begging for his tutor's help. The Professor remembered telling Emily Jane that he would be returning the next evening. He hadn't wanted to leave her alone, but she reassured him that she would be fine.

"I'm a big girl now," Emily Jane had told him, with that impish twinkle in her eyes that had made him smile. She had told him that she intended to follow directions from an old map, to find some 'Bear caves.'

"As if, on this island!" They both had laughed.

'I remember now,' he thought. 'It was I myself who found a screwed-up piece of material in the cellar of the castle on the hill during one of my digs. I had thought little of it and had taken it home back to Old Mill Cottage, and that map was placed with a load of other things inside one of my old mahogany chests. Did my wife find it? Or was there another map? I will never know.'

The Professor recalled how back in 1999 Lucas had arrived on the island with the message from one of his students. He was waiting while the Professor collected a few things together.

He remembered how Lucas started his engine to take him back to the mainland. He could never forget the last image he had of Emily Jane, who stood smiling on the jetty waving.

Lucas manoeuvred his craft into the deeper waters, well away from the treacherous rocks that surrounded the island. 'The last thing I remember doing was to blow her a kiss. And Emily Jane blew one back to me. How I adored her.' He shivered. 'If only I had known what was about to happen.'

'After hearing the bad news about the landslide, the next day, I returned from Oxford, and I made it to the island by evening. I remember the sun had set and it was too dark to start our search. I slept in the cottage and Lucas slept on his boat. Early the next morning we began to search the island. We were desperately searching for Emily Jane and over the next few days the island became awash with Police officers searching every inch of the island. But alas we found no trace of her. My heart was breaking!'

'Then my biggest regret was accepting what the police told me a few weeks later. I had been requested to call in at Swallows town Police station. I can't remember which officer was in charge back then, but I remember what he said precisely.

"It is with regret that the search for your wife has been called off." The Superintendent patted my shoulder, and I remember well what he said at the time.

"Emily Jane Mortimer was assumed drowned and most probably has been washed out to sea."

In the days and months that followed he remembered how he searched the National News every chance he could get, hoping to hear something that would give him hope! But there was no body having been found, washed upon a faraway shore.

In all the years he had not forgotten his beautiful wife. And his worst regret was not knowing his daughter even existed. It was only recently when he was told by the police. He was also informed about the attempted kidnapping of Ursula at the hands of Jo Newsome and her gang, and more remarkably Brown Bear, Petra, and Rosie had worked out the fact that Emily Jane's friend Larry was none other than Ursula's father. Me, Professor Lawrence Mortimer!'

He swooned a little as his now saturated mind was filled with more and more details, and he could feel they all made sense.

"Are you all right?" Ursula's soft voice brought him back to reality.

The Professor remembered where he was and looked at his

daughter, hoping she didn't mind his long silence.

"Yes, I think so. I think I am alright!" He reached out for his daughter's hand. "Come on. Let's do this."

Ursula smiled at her father and took his hand.

Jake was still on guard outside the cottage door. He stepped aside for the Professor and his daughter to enter. Ursula could now see into the room that had frightened the girls on their first night on the island. The room with piles of fossils, rocks, rats and a thunder storm. A room that had held a secret for over fourteen years. The trapdoor was visible now with its flattened handle in view amidst the oak lid. No one would ever have guessed that below were steps that led to an old forgotten cellar.

"This room looks so different now!" exclaimed Ursula. "Where have all the bones and relics gone?"

"I gave the police permission to take them for examination," replied the Professor.

"I thought they were your mother's treasures. But it turns out after Emily Jane was pushed down these stairs and …" he hesitated and looked straight into his daughter's eyes, "My dear, your mother died when her neck was broken. That cruel callous woman closed the trapdoor and forced her brother to collect fossils and rocks from the beach and caves nearby, to be scattered on this floor to hide their crime. I was informed by Superintendent Harding himself."

"Oh! Father, what a wicked woman, I hate her!" Ursula held back her tears. "I always thought this room was where my mother had stored her ancient finds."

Ursula felt anger at this personal tragedy, even though it was years since the day she had worried in their home cave, when her mother failed to return.

"I am so glad I have found you," said Ursula.

"So am I," replied her father.

In that moment she realised how comfortable she felt talking to this man, and by his demeanour she knew he felt the same.

"My mother was so intelligent she taught me about archaeology and oh yes! The cave bears of Northern Europe. That was her favourite subject. There is a cave in Kent that she visited once. Isn't that so, Father?"

"Yes," he replied. He was delighted to hear himself being addressed as *father*. "We both travelled a great deal with our respective careers and working for the college we were very privileged to see numerous historical sites. The work at the university has taken Emily Jane all over Europe in search of her precious cave bear fossils, *Ursa Spelaeus*, their bones are mainly found in caves, the European brown bears, however, only used caves for hibernation. Oh, my dear, am I boring you?"

"Certainly not!" replied Ursula. "I hope to follow my mother's lead one day. That is if I ever have the courage to leave this island!"

"That is a splendid idea! I can help you if you want to go to university." he said, smiling down at her. "Mind you! You will have to get some A levels under your belt first."

"I feel I could pass examinations," Ursula looked up at the Professor. "Emily Jane was an expert at many of her favourite subjects, she taught me in detail. When I was three, she pretended she was my teacher in a schoolroom and a year later when I was four years old, I could read everything she put in front of me. Sometimes she would scratch words on some of the rocks or when the weather was warmer, we would sit by the lake, and she would continue our game of school by scraping letters in the sand. She said I soaked up all her knowledge like a sponge! So, for years she crammed my head with all kinds of facts, especially historical ones, while we were trapped in the cave, it passed the time."

"But you could get out of the cave to go to a lake?" her father looked puzzled.

"Not to start with when I was a baby but later the bears showed us the lake to wash in and to catch fish and we would all swim together. They were amazing. After a while mother used to find weak spots in cave walls and every day, she would use another sharp rock to chisel away until there was a hole big enough for her to go out. One day she brought lots of things back from the beach cottage to make our home more comfortable."

The Professor was finding it difficult to take on board all that his daughter was telling him.

"My dear, one day soon you must tell me everything, every detail!" he was very happy to be in the company of his newly found offspring. He took a step towards the trapdoor.

"Now, Ursula, are you ready?"

"Yes, I am. Father, I am so glad you are here with me. I was rather dreading saying goodbye on my own, but Petra was amazing she found the draught that caused the mummification. The day my mother did not return, I knew at once that I would never see her alive again. She loved me too much to leave me for any other reason. I just can't imagine how difficult it must have been for you, not knowing where your wife was year after year."

"I was in deep remorse when we had news of the landslide because two or three years before there had been a minor earthquake, the damage to the island was minimal and when Emily Jane and I decided to spend some time here we were told that the earthquake had been very low on the Richter magnitude scale and then we were told later, that apparently only the fortress on the East shore was damaged, it disappeared underground but that might have happened years earlier. It has never been excavated.

So, there was the landslide on the day after I was called back to Oxford. When I came here with the police the next day to help in the search, it didn't look as if there was a lot of damage, but of course most of it was subterranean and unfortunately, we had no idea about the caves, where Emily Jane had made your home. How I wish I had known that fact back then, I would have dug her out with my own bare hands," he said passionately.

"I am sure you would!" Ursula squeezed his hand. "I can tell how much you loved her. Come on, she will be happy to know we are together."

Ursula led him down the steps into the cellar helping him a little because his walking stick kept getting in the way.

The room was cool and lit by seven large candles. Emily Jane still looked beautiful in a pale blue velvet lined coffin. Ursula gasped. "She's not as wrinkly as some of those Egyptian mummies I read about."

"No! she's not too bad," replied the Professor. "There's a sufficient draught down here, perfect for mummification. Do you have some of your mother's books on the subject?"

"Yes, when I was old enough to climb out of the cave through the hole in the rubble my mother made, I would come here to this cottage and go up to the bedroom and take some books away to read myself. It passed many a cold or wet afternoon."

"Very resourceful!' The Professor was fascinated by this young lady. "And preparing you for college!"

"Yes, I hope so, mother would be so pleased for me." Ursula replied.

"I hope you don't mind my dear, but I gave the Undertakers Emily Jane's wedding dress, so that she can be buried wearing it." The Professor's voice began to waver, "Oh my dear we three could have had a wonderful life together."

"Yes, to see you and my mother everyday, I would have loved growing up in Swallows village." Ursula's voice was soft and gentle like falling snow.

"Yes, it would have been bliss," he said as he took out a handkerchief and wiped a stray tear from his face.

The young girl was already pleased that she felt a closeness to this man.

"Of course! I don't mind, that would be wonderful," Ursula responded, as she gently caressed the velvet lining of her mother's coffin. "So, you have kept her wedding dress for all these years?"

"Yes, I have treasured all her things, you must have everything one day."

"I would love to see the cottage and the village, Petra and Rosie have told me so much about it all. But Father, I want to ask you one thing."

"And what might that be?" he asked.

"What was it the forensic people overlooked?" said Ursula.

"Oh yes!" He met her steady gaze in the half-light of the candle lit room. "They wanted to know if your mother had possessed a necklace made of sea pearls."

"Oh," exclaimed Ursula. "I never saw one, she didn't have a strong interest in jewellery."

"No, she didn't! I gave her an antique necklace made of sea pearls on our first wedding anniversary. She seemed pleased, but I got the feeling a pair of Levi's and a sturdy trowel would have been appreciated more."

That made Ursula smile in agreement, "Why are the pathologists so interested?"

"Because some of the beads from the necklace were found tightly held in your mother's hand and there was no evidence of her ever wearing it around her neck on the day she was murdered."

"No, there wouldn't have been because a few years after she went missing, I was about ten, I discovered the cottage on the beach. I found all the dishes and stationery and beautiful bedding with her initials on everything, but not a trace of any jewellery."

"Yes, our cottage on the beach!" her father replied. "It was a couple of years after the earthquake that we came to the island to excavate for anything interesting we could find. It was at the time when I bought 'Old Mill cottage'. The house needed a little renovation, so we stayed a couple of weeks here to get out of the way of the decorators. We hadn't been married very long then and everything was exciting."

"And the bedroom?" Ursula was curious.

"I loved her so much and wanted to make her comfortable having to put up with me and my constant digging."

At that moment all the flames on the candles around Emily Jane's coffin started to act strangely. It was like a gust of strong wind blew around the cellar room and then all seven candles went out, but there was no familiar smell of extinguished wax. The floorboards began to creak as if walked upon, and then all the candles were suddenly aflame again.

"What on earth?" exclaimed the Professor.

"It's mother! She knows we are here together."

"How do you know?"

"Because since the day she disappeared I have at times felt her presence. And I am sure BB, Petra, and Rosie have too! It means she is not at peace, and she is trying to help us all in some way."

"Then in that case, we must say our goodbyes and let her be buried in the church in Swallows village"

"Yes! Father, I agree but you didn't finish telling me about the pearl necklace you gave my mother. What happened to that necklace?"

"The night Joanna Newsome broke into Old Mill Cottage and terrified my wife, not only were her actions fatal to our child, but days later Emily Jane found that her necklace had been stolen."

The candle flames flickered in the holders once again.

"So, father, what is the necklace to do with the forensic experts?"

"Because the beads found screwed tightly in your mother's fingers belong to a necklace found broken in Jo Newsome's jewel box in her flat, and that is the necklace I gave your mother all those years ago! They could distinguish it was the same by the jeweller's mark."

"Wow!" Ursula gasped.

"Yes, absolute proof she was here on the island," continued her father. "On the day Emily Jane was attacked it looks like Jo Newsome was wearing your mother's stolen necklace while she was forcing her down this stairwell. Even though she was injured Emily Jane fought back and broke the necklace by pulling it off her attacker's neck, obviously before Newsome could shut the trapdoor," Professor Mortimer gave a big sigh. He wondered to himself how much more he could take of this delicate matter. He could feel his heart weighing very heavily at that moment.

"Yes of course! When the chain snapped it would have released some of the beads to fly all over this room," Ursula wished she had her torch with her so they could scrutinise the rocky floor.

"The precise reason," said her father, "why we must let the forensic team in to finish their job!"

"Father, before we say our farewells can I ask you one more question?" Ursula looked at her father in the candlelight. "Did the police tell you her gang almost kidnapped me? I was puzzled that they knew I would be your concern as I had lived alone?"

"Lucas told me that according to the coast guard that woman came to the island on numerous occasions."

"But why father?"

"When she was questioned about the attempted kidnap, last week she let slip to the police that she knew there was a young girl on the island, and because Emily Jane was begging her at the time of the murder not to lock her in this cellar, because she had a young child living in the caves. Newsome put two and two together and she realised the girl must be you. My dear, that you were *my* daughter! She confessed to all the charges brought against her and added more evidence without even being asked."

"Oh Father, my mother would have begged for her life. She would have been distraught at the thought of being taken away from me, a six-year-old left to fend for herself."

At that moment a howling wind could be heard swirling around the cellar. The candles were blown out and Ursula grabbed her father's hand.

"It is Emily Jane! She is very angry with that woman," said Ursula. "Father, you must shout out to her! Tell her we have found each other, and no one will ever come between us. Tell your wife that the wicked woman is going to pay for what she has done to your family. Please, Father, do tell mother that Joanna Newsome is going to prison forever!"

Her father did not shout, he was too refined for that, but he did speak to his wife's spirit in a calm and positive voice. He said everything Ursula had wanted him to say.

As father and daughter knelt in the semi-darkness beside Emily Jane's body, the howling wind ceased, and the candles flickered into flame once again. They said their farewells to their beloved wife and mother and the equilibrium was restored once again. As father and daughter climbed the cellar steps they both felt the atmosphere had changed, something dark and sinister was lifted and now serene peace surrounded them. Both were ready to face the imminent future.

43
THE LAST SUNSET AND A FINAL SECRET

After their lunch Petra and Rosie had wanted to swim in the lagoon but Brown Bear had stopped them. "No! you should wait at least an hour before you go in the water, it gives your body time for your food to go down."

"What a load of rubbish," retorted Rosie laughing.

"No, it is not actually." Petra stood up suddenly. "Hey listen! I can hear a helicopter landing on the island."

It was now mid afternoon. A few hours had passed since Brown Bear had led them away from the cottage. He was very aware that the Professor and his daughter needed some time alone to get to know one another.

Rosie had looked back. "No one is talking, I hope this goes well," she said as she skipped along beside Brown Bear as they strolled towards the jetty.

"We must give them some space," Brown Bear replied. "I feel all will be well."

They watched until they saw the helicopter fly over the island on its way back to the mainland. As soon as the noise died away, they could all hear a motorboat chugging into the bay. And at that moment Ursula appeared. She looked like a different girl; her face was radiant as she approached them.

"Hey! We've got to be quick?" she said.

"Why? What is happening?" Petra replied.

"Lucas and the undertakers are going to take my mother's body to the mainland. So she can lie for a while in the Chapel of Rest."

Ursula looked very happy to be talking about such a sad subject.

"Are you sure that's what you want?" Rosie felt concerned. "You were so upset this morning."

"I know! I was, but now I have got to know my father, well a little. But I am so happy to know him, and I feel it is the right thing to do, and he is so nice, and we have lots of catching up to do……." Ursula didn't even stop for breath. She was so happy and excited.

"Hey! Steady on Ursula, what's the rush?" Petra was so pleased to see her friend happy at last.

"Quick, they want to catch the tide. And wait until you see what they have done to Lucas' boat." Ursula paused. "Anyway, I want you three to come to see them off at the jetty, and I really want you to meet my father."

"But we have met him!" exclaimed Rosie.

"Yes, we have," agreed Petra. "Rosie and I met him the day he moved back into his cottage in our village. It was fortunate that we went to greet him because he had already fallen in the kitchen before we arrived, and it was us who called the ambulance."

"It was the Professor," interrupted Brown Bear. "Who suggested the girls come to the island in search of its secrets. And By Jove, they have found lots of them!"

"Like what? What secrets have we found?" asked Rosie, teasing her sister.

"You know," Petra reeled off a list. "We found a rather strange girl to start with."

"So, that is how you see me?" Ursula smiled.

"We did at first but not now," Petra reciprocated her smile. "Secret number two was discovered when we followed the Professor's notes and found the sunken castle, with its secret passage to the castle on the hill. Well, I know we haven't been there yet but!"

"Yes!" exclaimed Rosie," We should be exploring that right

now!"

"Oh! and the cave bears, they are a big secret too, and don't forget the criminals, safely locked away in custody," remarked Petra.

"What about the ghost?" Rosie lowered her voice and looked all around.

"The ghost of my mother, you mean. Once she is buried in Swallows Village near to my father's cottage, I feel sure she will find peace." Ursula was so calm she amazed them all. "Oh, listen, Lucas is ringing the bell on his boat, we must hurry!"

In a while they were making their way down the cliff path to the beach near the cottage.

"That's a quicker way to reach the lagoon. The first journey we made following Ursula seemed to take ages," Petra yelled as she raced to the jetty.

"That's always the way!" remarked Brown Bear. "Wherever you go in life, it always seems much quicker coming back."

"Yes, I know what you mean, BB, let's hurry now they are waiting to sail," Ursula was first to reach the motorboat and greet her father. He was about to help her aboard. "No Father, I think it better for you to go alone, you know, time to yourselves."

"Thank you, Ursula," replied her father. "I will make all the arrangements. There are a few things I must resolve with the Senior Investigating Officer first, but then I have an appointment with the vicar so I hope you will all come to Emily Jane's funeral in St Germain's Church in Swallows village!"

The Professor looked relieved to have found his missing wife and after all the lost years he looked deliriously happy to have found his daughter too.

Lucas had a quick word with Brown Bear, and then he made ready to start his vessel. He was very proud of his shiny new motorboat and was ever thankful to his sister who had persuaded him to buy a lottery ticket from Sally in the paper shop.

"If we go now, we'll be higher in the water than those treacherous rocks that surround the island." He looked around to see if he could see his nephew. "Ah! There, you are, Jake. I think it best you stay one more night on the island to see my friends don't get into any more danger."

"Yes, Uncle, I am already under orders to stay."

"Oh! Aye," Lucas turned to the girls. "Your Mum says I am to pick you up at eleven o'clock sharp tomorrow morning." The fisherman felt the pain the girls were trying to hide in that moment of disappointment.

"Oh no, only one more night on the island," said Rosie, stifling some tears. "It's just not fair?"

"Don't cry, I have something very exciting to show you later on." Ursula took Rosie's hand.

"What is it?" Rosie wiped her eyes.

"Wait, and see? I will show you at sunset." There was promise in the young woman's voice. "Now we must wave goodbye to my mother and father. I never thought I would ever say that in context."

"Your mother and father together," said Petra. "I know what you mean."

They were now all standing on the jetty looking down into the boat to say their farewells to Professor Mortimer.

Ursula blew a kiss to her father, and he likewise responded.

And then they were all silent as they stood on the jetty and looking down, they witnessed the coffin of Emily Jane.

Lucas had transformed his motorboat into a carriage of beauty. The seats inside the boat were now covered in crimson cloth and the coffin itself was draped in a pall of purple velvet. On top of the velvet was a huge display of white flowers, carnations, lilies and roses, and on the casket itself was a simple plaque with words from the Professor to his wife.

'Lost, found and loved forever.'

Tears streamed down Ursula's face as she read her father's sentiments. Rosie held on to her hand so very tightly, as she fought back her own tears.

Petra slipped her arm around Ursula's waist, "Everything will be fine from now on!"

Brown Bear, Jake, still wearing his uniform, and the three girls watched as Lucas steered his boat away from the island. The sun was still high in the early September sky. A cool gust blew windswept strands of their long hair across the girl's faces. Their eyes were glued to the sad scene before them, and Lucas, suntanned and tall, stood at the helm with the Professor at his side. Brown Bear and the girls watched in silence until the vessel disappeared over the horizon.

"Your Dad is very handsome," remarked Petra.

"He is," replied Ursula. "With a kind heart too. Now come with me I have something amazing to show you all."

"Right then!' exclaimed Brown Bear. "We had better go into the cottage for some provisions."

"Of course, you are right, BB," said Ursula. "Bring loads of food as we might be up all night?"

"What?" Rosie exclaimed.

"Wait and see! I have a lovely surprise for you all."

Petra thought that she had never seen Ursula so happy. It was now late afternoon and BB thought it a good idea to hurry up a bit.

They reached the lake in time to see the most wonderful sunset they had ever seen. The waters were still, not even a ripple, and the dark green of the nearby forest was reflected in the sun-gold lake. It was an enchanted scene.

"Why are we here?" asked Rosie.

"Listen!" Ursula put her finger to her mouth. "Keep very quiet.

Let us sit on these rocks and later you will see why I have brought you here."

"You are very mysterious, Ursula," remarked Jake. "Is it okay if I join you all?"

"Jake! For goodness's sake take off your jacket and relax. Rosie, do we have enough food for supper?" They were all surprised to hear Ursula being dominant for a change.

"Yes, we have loads of food thanks to Mum. She knows what big appetites we have. I will set out our supper on that flat rock over there," Rosie pointed to an outcrop of smooth rocks under the canopy of a large old tree.

"Now, Jake!" Brown Bear exclaimed. "Do you feel there is enough evidence to convict the Newsome's and their gang? Come sit here and we can collaborate our thoughts."

"Well, actually BB, I have other plans for Jake," Ursula proclaimed positively.

"Oooo," said Rosie, and Petra gave her new friend a knowing look.

Ursula took Jake's hand and led him away from the others. He accompanied her dutifully as she led him towards some rocks on the shore of the lake.

"I think he likes her," Rosie kept her voice to a whisper. "Do you, Sis'?"

"They definitely have an affinity between them," Petra looked over to where Jake and Ursula were now chatting enthusiastically. "It is nice that they like each other. Remember Ursula has never had any friends before us."

"Well, I am happy for them," sighed Rosie. "But she did have the three bears as companions. I suppose it wasn't the same as human company though. What do you think, BB?"

Brown Bear gave a little cough. "Well, I only had bears for company as I grew up. I never longed for company from another species."

"But" said Petra, "I bet you wouldn't like to be without us now."

"No, I wouldn't!" he exclaimed. "Hey, look over there! Whatever is going on?"

The evening sun was now low on the horizon spreading a pink and gold display of glowing clouds across the sky. And then they all heard the crashing sounds of the night before.

"Petra, Rosie, BB, come and see what is happening." Ursula's voice was filled with excitement.

They all obeyed and stood together at the edge of the lake. Parts of the waters glowed burnished gold, with splashes of muted red reflections moving amongst the ripples. There was now an eerie silence that only Ursula understood. The others were watching with anticipation, and then it happened.

Bushes and shrubs were being trampled on with speed, even young trees establishing themselves on the forest floor stood no chance. Then out of the forest appeared a young furry animal.

Petra and Roses caught hold of Brown Bear, fear had gripped them as everything was happening so fast. But soon they realised it was Starlight who had dived into the water with wild abandon.

"Look!" exclaimed Ursula. "He is so excited, happier than I have even seen him before."

"Wow!" said Rosie. "He's having such a good time."

"Now, I can see his parents. Kent, his father and his mother, Moonlight," said Ursula. "Look, they are coming sedately out of the trees and Starlight is showing off for them."

Brown Bear was certainly enjoying the spectacle, watching Starlight splashing about in the water with sweet abandon.

"He is growing fast and will soon be as big as his father."

They all watched the scene while standing on the shore of the lake, and everyone, even Jake started to laugh at the young bear's antics.

"That little bear is so funny," said Rosie. "But wait. Look! There is movement at the edge of the water." They all looked to see what was happening.

No one had noticed but the day had ended, and the golden sunset was no more. In the west the sun had disappeared below the horizon leaving the darkening sky filling with myriads of silver stars.

"It was on a night like this," interrupted Ursula. "When that rascal in the water was born but only the other day, I found out something very exciting had happened on the island!" Ursula led them nearer the tree lined edge of the lake. "Now, please be very quiet and just watch."

Everyone obeyed and waited with bated breath wondering what could have happened. It was obviously something to make Ursula and the bears very happy. Even Starlight ceased his activities and swam to his parents.

"What's going to happen?" whispered Rosie.

"Shush!" said Ursula putting her finger to her mouth.

After a while Brown Bear picked Rosie up, "See, what you can make out in the shadows?" They all waited quietly. Starlight had now joined his parents and all that could be heard was a gentle lapping at the water's edge. The silvery moon was rising, casting a soft gentle light that shimmered over the scene.

And then the moment they had all waited patiently for was upon them with such a frightening speed. Out of the woods rushed two small young bear cubs. They had a play fight with their older brother and then threw themselves into the lake.

"Twins! A boy and a girl!" exclaimed a delighted Ursula. "It happened when Jake and BB disappeared, the night they met my father. I went to see what was happening in the woods, remember?"

All eyes were on the lake watching Starlight teaching the cubs to swim. This was the reason for his excitement, he will have a brother and sister to play with.

"No need to teach them," said Brown Bear stoically. "Their species can swim from birth."

"Yes, but what species are they?" Jake asked. He was becoming very interested in Ursula's life on the island. "Are they really descended from ancient bears?"

"Indeed, they are!" exclaimed Brown Bear. "*Ursa Spelaeus*, the cave bear!"

"Do you mean there are prehistoric bears breeding on this island?" Jake was amazed. "Is it the same as Jurassic Park?"

"Not exactly," replied Ursula. "But there are large caves here that are subterranean and we don't know what's in them."

"Wow!" exclaimed Rosie.

"Listen, everyone!" Ursula's voice was serious. "This is the biggest secret of the island, and it must never be told on the mainland."

"Quite so," Brown Bear agreed.

"But where are the bear caves?" asked Rosie.

"About a kilometre into the forest the terrain changes and becomes very rocky," explained Ursula. "The first large cave is there and that is where my bears hibernate in the winter but deeper into the system the caves go lower, and some reach out under the sea."

"Oh!" exclaimed Rosie. "You mean like the sea caves we once found on the South coast."

"No," replied Ursula. "Those caves are tidal."

"And the ones you are telling us about go deep into the bedrock!" said Brown Bear.

"Precisely!" Ursula made a gesture and pointed in the direction of the forest. "In fact, that is where my mother first found the bones of *Ursa Spelaeus*. And some of the bones that were on the floor in the first room in the cottage came from there." Then her attention focused on the lake.

"Just look how happy they all are. Come and let me introduce the cubs to you."

It was a magical scene. The sky was aglow with myriads of shining stars ascending the heavens. Ursula stood at the water's edge and called to her five ursine friends. The babies stopped all the frolicking and followed their parents, and soon all five bears were on the shore.

"Well, Starlight is none the worse from the kidnap attempt," said Rosie. "Oh, look how friendly the cubs are." She reached out her hand to stroke one. "Oh, their fur is so soft."

"As they are only days old, it will stiffen up soon enough," said Ursula.

So it was decided that Brown Bear and the girls would go back to the cottage and Ursula would go with the family of bears to their cave.

Ursula looked at the young constable and asked, "Jake, will you come with me please?"

"Of course," he replied.

"They know the way of course," she informed Jake. "I am only fussing because the cubs are so young."

"I see," replied Jake and they both set off on the way to the caves.

"Since the failed kidnap attempt I have not felt at ease with them," Ursula sighed. "Please understand, Jake, they are the only family I have ever known."

"Yes, of course I understand," Jake pondered. "I have two brothers and two sisters."

"How wonderful! I will never have any siblings. But Rosie and Petra are like sisters to me now, I love them to bits."

"My uncle Lucas tell's me they are great kids," he replied.

"Yes they are," remarked Ursula. "Lucas told me they had adventures on this island when they were much younger. Did you know that, Jake? I think once he rescued them from aliens." Ursula smiled and looked into Jake's blue eyes.

"My uncle is quite shy. I think he would be embarrassed to tell me something like that," Jake was fascinated with this girl. He took hold of her hand and this time she didn't pull away.

By now they were approaching the far end of the lake. Dusk was all around them, but because of Jake's large police issued torch he could see as clearly as Ursula, who was used to the dark.

"Over the years I have often wandered about in the dark. In fact that was how I met Petra in the first place. Come this way there's a sort of grotto at the end of the lake."

They approached a rocky area with low shrubs entwined in ivy.

"Where have the bears gone? It is very quiet now." Jake looked all around.

"Some nights they rampage the forest and other nights they sleep in large caves that in parts go under the sea," replied Ursula. "Look, we are here, my secret grotto!"

Jake stood besides the girl trying to take in everything Ursula was showing him.

"Oh dear! You are so tall! Can you manage to bend double and squeeze inside?" Ursula let go of Jake's hand. "It will be worth it, I promise you!"

After a bit of a struggle Jake was inside Ursula's enchanting portion of Paradise.

"Wow, this is unbelievable," Jake was quite amazed at what he could see inside. "Have you shown here to Mr Bear and the girls?"

"No Not yet. It's amazing isn't it." She beckoned Jake to sit on some smooth flat rocks at the edge of a pool of deep blue water.

"We don't need my torch in here," the young constable was totally amazed. "There is a sort of reflected light shimmering from the cave walls. Do you know what causes it?"

"Not really. Could be phosphorous?" Ursula had just accepted the light and not really thought what was causing it. "I don't even know what is making the pool water so blue either."

"I have never seen anything like this before," Jake was mesmerised. He reached out for Ursula's hand again. "How long ago did you find this grotto?"

"I found it many years ago and whenever I wanted to sit quietly and remember my lost mother, I would come here and reflect on our short time together."

"You are a remarkable young woman, Ursula," he said tightening his grip of her hand. "You know I have often looked across the bay from the mainland and wondered what was over here but nowhere in my mind could I have envisaged anywhere like this. So peaceful. Thank you for bringing me here."

"The problem is I always forget time when I come here, I have been so wrapped up with the girls and their secrets, this is the first time I have been here in ages."

Jake looked at his wristwatch. "Oh goodness, we must go!" he exclaimed. "I am supposed to be guarding the jetty near the cottage tonight."

"Right then we must go! I hope one day I can bring you back here."

"Yes, I would like that very much. When this case is over I am due for some time off."

They walked back to the jetty with the lit up cottage in view. Jake kissed his new friend goodnight.

Ursula returned to join our three adventurers. Rosie had made supper with the last of Mum's food.

"Suppose it's a good thing we are going home tomorrow," she said wistfully. "I haven't even kept anything for breakfast."

"BB, what time is Lucas coming to collect us?" asked Petra.

"He will be here with the high tide." Groans could be heard from Petra and Rosie, they both loved the island very much and would really like to stay forever, but of course the new school term beckoned.

"Right!" Jake looked at his watch. "I'll have to go, I have to guard the jetty tonight." The policeman said goodnight at the doorway.

Ursula rushed past him onto the rocks.

"I need to ask if you will be at my mother's funeral?"

While Ursula had been away Brown Bear had been a bit worried that she had been out so long and had spoken to Petra of his concern. Brown Bear had an anxious look on his furry face.

"Oh! BB, stop worrying about Ursula!" exclaimed Petra. "She has grown up into a responsible young woman. After all she has survived alone on this island since the loss of her mother, fought off kidnappers, and goodness knows what else she has had to deal with."

"I know about all that, but I care about you all, and now Ursula seems to have become one of the family," Brown Bear took hold of the girls' hands. "Yes! you are right, and I am sure Jake will look after her. He seems like a nice lad with a certain amount of authority. Come, let's have one last night in the cottage."

They all agreed and soon Petra and Rosie were tucked up in the big ornate bed the Professor had provided for the comfort of his much-loved wife. Brown Bear decided to sleep downstairs and keep guard.

'Now what am I expecting?' he thought. 'Surely I can relax now. There are no more criminals or ghosts for that matter anywhere on the island, and the girls have found all the secrets for the Professor, so what am I worried about?' All the recent events they had shared rushed through his mind but eventually Brown Bear fell asleep quite exhausted.

44
REST IN PEACE

It was early October before the coroner released Emily Jane's body for burial. Petra and Rosie were both back at the High School. The Professor had arranged for his daughter to attend a nearby sixth form college, as a mature student. After he had explained the unusual circumstances, the school was pleased to be of assistance in Ursula's education.

Most of the residents of Swallows Village welcomed Professor Mortimer back to 'Old Mill Cottage' with open arms. They felt deeply for his loss but were relieved that his wife had been found after all these years. They were delighted to know about Ursula. And those who saw her would agree she was the image of her beautiful mother, Emily Jane.

It also was a shock for the locals to learn that criminals had been in operation on the island, there was a lot of gossip in the village shop. The post office was awash with speculation too! It seems that everyone was inviting themselves to the funeral, now set for three weeks Tuesday when the girls would be home for half term.

Professor Lawrence Mortimer didn't mind the gossip at all, he remembered how the whole village had welcomed him and his wife when they first moved in as newlyweds all those years ago.

Petra and Rosie's worried Mum had been reassured by WPC Denton that Petra would not be required to give evidence against the Newsome's in court. Joanna Newsome's confession had been thought to be enough but now that it had been established that

Emily Jane's stolen necklace was worn by Newsome on the day she murdered her love-rival. The new evidence proved that the beads clasped tightly in Emily Jane's hand and the rest of the pearls had been cast around the cellar room, when Emily Jane reached out and pulled at the necklace trying to defend herself against the evil Joanna Newsome. The pearl beads that were examined by the Forensic team proved that Newsome had committed the crime as her DNA was found on all of them. The police and coroner agreed that would be quite sufficient for a jury to return a guilty verdict.

While the Professor had been convalescing with his friend Eustace in the South of England, he had paid for some refurbishment to be undertaken at Old Mill Cottage. He had been quite aware that nothing had been done to the property in the intervening years and now he had reason to make it suitable for entertaining and make a welcoming home for his daughter.

The day of Emily Jane's Funeral arrived. It was only a short walk through the village for Petra, Rosie and their Mum and Dad. The foliage on the village trees was a glorious sight, the colours looked spectacular with hues of copper, burnished reds and endless golds all shimmering in the morning sunshine. The girls noticed the laden chestnut tree in the grounds of their old primary school. Rosie felt she would like to climb the branches and pick some, but then as she saw the shiny black hearse arrive at St Germaine's church she reached for her Mum's hand.

The church was packed with villagers all smartly dressed in black. The church warden had saved the front rows for family and close friends. Brown Bear had made excuses not to come.

"I will be with you in spirit," he had said to Rosie after breakfast. "But you girls must go without me!"

"Okay," Rosie had said with a large tear trickling down her cheek. "But what will you do, BB?"

"I will plan something nice to do for the rest of the week, as it is half term," he exclaimed. "There is also something I must check out with Lucas. Anyway! I will see you later at the Wake."

Tuesday had soon come around and the old grey stone church with its tall, sturdy spire looked majestic in the morning sunshine.

Rosie, Petra and their parents were sitting in the pews at the front of the church near the choir stalls. Two seats remained vacant awaiting Ursula and her father for after they had escorted Emily Jane to the front of the church, where her funeral service will commence. There was a murmured buzz of expectancy within the congregation with many turning their heads watching the entrance, hoping for some sign of movement.

Professor Mortimer and Ursula were lone figures in the porch at the back of the church waiting for the Vicar and the coffin carrying their loved one. The Professor dressed in a smart dark grey suit, his silver-grey hair looking slightly less unruly as he smiled at Ursula who was standing beside him wearing a black dress that Petra had helped her choose.

Everyone waited in silence, only the light footsteps of the churchwarden could be heard ushering some late comers to their seats. Silent anticipation grew within the mourners, all here to say their goodbyes to a much admired and loved neighbour who had been missing without a trace, for a very long time.

Suddenly the great door of the church was opened letting in beams of sunshine carrying within them swirls of rainbow coloured dust particles, captured, circling within the colourful rays of light.

Then to everyone's relief recorded choral music was heard being played in the background. The Professor had chosen 'Jesu Joy of Man's Desiring,' written by Johann Sebastian Bach, as it was one of his wife's favourites. Organist Mrs Maggie Jones, who lived at a nearby farm, fidgeted a little waiting for her turn to play the chosen hymns to accompany the funeral service. Everyone in this village had waited a long time for news of the Professor's wife and now were all gathered here to pay their respects to Emily Jane.

James Ely Cuthbert, the funeral director, lead the small cortage in to the church. Emily Jane's coffin was followed by the Professor, Ursula, and Eustace, an old family friend. There was a low murmer from the congregation and then a hushed silence as the vicar began his special service for Emily Jane.

Petra and Rosie squeezed their Mum and Dad's hands tightly at this special moment.

As the first notes of the hymn 'Lord of All Hopefulness' resounded around the church, everyone stood up to sing.

All eyes were turned to the coffin that stood at the front of the aisle. The stained glass windows lit up with the morning sunshine and Rosie could see colours of red, blue and yellow dancing on the smooth surface of the coffin.

Later that morning in the cemetery gardens outside the church where many village souls had been laid to rest over the years, close friends of the Professor gathered. Even his old university friend Eustace had made the journey from Dorset to be present at this special burial of Emily Jane. Everyone said what a wonderful heart-warming service the vicar had led, and Maggie's rendition of some age-old funeral hymns deserved the highest praise.

The Professor was quite overwhelmed by the sincere wishes he received from all his neighbours. He agreed to meet them all in the public house later, after a private graveside service with the vicar.

Laying his beloved wife to rest he wanted to be alone with only his daughter, his oldest friend Eustace and Petra and Rosie.

He was slightly disappointed that Eustace had to leave to catch the Plymouth train at one o'clock.

"My wife is returning home from another dig. Egypt, again! That country certainly captivates all us archaeologists, don't you think, Larry? Her flight gets in this evening," his friend informed him. "Be in trouble if I'm not there to greet her."

"Of course! I understand," the grieving widower replied. "Come and visit and bring Geraldine in the New Year. I want you both as my oldest friends to get to know Ursula, my long, lost daughter. Well, I was unaware that I have a daughter until these amazing girls found her on the island."

"Yes, indeed we will visit in January, and I have been hearing all about how your daughter was discovered, from one of your neighbours," replied Eustace. "I look forward to getting to know Ursula." Eustace put his hand on the Professor's arm. "Larry, she is the image of Emily Jane, but of course you know that!" Professor Mortimer nodded in agreement to his old friend.

"Now you take care, old chap, I will ring you next week." Even Eustace had tears in his eyes, as he patted the Professor on the shoulder and took his leave.

Professor Lawrence Mortimer had selected for Emily Jane a grave near the wall that edged the village boundary, and under a spreading Willow tree that draped its branches like a canopy of protection over the piece of consecrated ground he had chosen, as a final resting place for his wife.

So, Emily Jane was laid to rest amid a sea of flowers, given with love from everyone in the village. Many a tear was shed that day.

Later all the villagers gathered in the local pub. In the back room was a magnificent spread, prepared by Jenny, the landlord's wife, at the Professor's request. To start with, all were in a sombre mood, until they witnessed how the Professor and Ursula were so happy together. Then all the villagers relaxed and started to tuck into the country fare. There was an enormous choice from hot sausage rolls and homemade pasties, to a side of ham waiting to be carved and numerous salads and various sandwiches. Rosie spotted a trolley laden with deserts. "Ooo tiramisu," she was delighted.

"Well!" exclaimed one of the guests. "The Doc' certainly knows how to treat his neighbours. Here's to you, Sir!" Old Hugh Llewelyn lifted his glass, and everyone joined in with the toast.

"And here is to your courageous and charming daughter, who undoubtedly has inherited her mother's beautiful looks," said Mrs Jones the organist, also raising her small glass of Sherry to the Professor.

There had been great sadness hanging over the village ever since the news had spread about Mrs Mortimer being missing on the island. But the heartache of the last twenty years was nowhere to be seen or felt today. Instead, there was joy, relief and a very warm welcome to their neighbours in 'Old Mill Cottage'. Everyone in Swallows Village was happy that day.

But alas, that happiness wasn't to last long.

It was getting dark outside the public house when most of the mourners decided to leave and go to their own homes in the village. Petra noticed the Professor gave a discreet sigh, as he stood by the door with Mick the landlord, shaking hands with all his guests as they left.

'It must have been a harrowing day for him,' she thought. Her Mum and Dad had left while it was still light so they could take the family's pet dog for a walk. But the Professor had stayed to the end and had been very congenial with all his neighbours.

Ursula, with an anxious look on her face, had persuaded Petra and Rosie to stay behind, after everyone else had gone.

"What is it, Ursula? I can see something is bothering you!" Petra was apprehensive. 'Whatever could be wrong?' She thought to herself. 'Especially as everything had gone so smoothly all day.'

Ursula looked drained and tired. "I overheard some people talking, they were sitting at the table by the window."

"Oh!" said Rosie. "They were some of the Griffith-Rowen family. Why? What was said?"

Petra nodded, "Yes, farmer Ivor Griffith-Rowen and his wife and two sons. Why Ursula, what has worried you?"

"I heard the farmer tell his family that he had received an offer for the island! Does he mean our island?"

"Yes! Ursula, he does. He is the biggest landowner in these parts," replied Petra. "But I didn't know anyone owned the island! I always thought it was in the hands of the Welsh Trust."

The three girls sat round a table looking extremely concerned. They looked across the room and saw Ursula's father standing at the bar, paying his bill.

"Should we tell the Doc'? Maybe he has heard something?" asked Rosie.

"Well," replied Ursula. "I feel sure he won't like it, because it would affect his work. I know he wants to excavate both castles soon," she sounded extremely anxious.

"I wonder why farmer Griffith-Rowen wants to sell the island now?" Petra was puzzled.

"I can tell you that," said Rosie, surprisingly. "You couldn't help but hear what they were saying, the boys have loud voices."

"What did you hear them say, Rosie?" Petra and Ursula pulled their chairs nearer to the little girl. "Come on, tell us."

"They talked about how nice it was for the Doc to have a daughter and the lady said that the Doc' has been on the TV a few times."

"And?"

"They talked a lot about Les Lescott, and all those criminals using the island for kidnapping and smuggling, and God knows what? Those were Mrs Griffith-Rowen's actual words." Rosie took a deep breath and continued. "She was most upset, to the extent that Farmer Ivor patted her on her knee to comfort her."

"Oh Rosie!" said Ursula. "I never thought of you as an eavesdropper. But I am so glad you are. I am worried sick about my bears, other people on the island would never understand how important it is to leave them alone and undisturbed."

Petra stood up. "We must find out who has made the offer," she looked around, but everyone had left the Wake, and only Professor Mortimer remained. He was still talking to the landlord at the Bar.

"Father," said Ursula. "I am so sorry to interrupt," she looked at the landlord. "I am very sorry, but it is important. We just need to know who had made an offer to Farmer Ivor Griffith-Rowen to buy the island."

Mick looked blank, "I don't know anything about it, hang on, my wife might know."

At that moment a pretty, dark-haired woman came in carrying a tray of clean glasses.

"Hey! Jenny, have you heard any rumours about someone wanting to buy the island out in the bay?" Mick's wife put the tray down on the bar and turned to the girls.

"Only what I heard here earlier," Jenny had a serious look on her face. "It's a disgrace, I think! Ruining a lovely haven like that. All those seabirds that live there will have nowhere to nest in the future!"

She caught everyone's attention including the Professor's and two old local men playing Dominoes, at a table in a corner of the room.

"Come on, Jen, tell the young ladies what you have heard." Mick looked uneasy.

Jenny looked around the room to see how many guests had remained. When she saw it was only the girls and Mr Mortimer, she relaxed. Sam and Jim in the corner were concentrating on their game, she knew they wouldn't be interested in what she had to say.

"I heard him tell his wife and sons that a conglomerate wants to buy the island."

"What's a conglomerate?" asked Rosie in horror. Whatever it was, she didn't like the sound of it.

"I don't know!" exclaimed Jenny. "But they talked about building a hotel over there, with a golf course, a diving school and turning the castle on the hill into a museum!"

"That is outrageous!" Lawrence Mortimer looked angry. "I and my team of college students have much more work planned for next season. And the sunken castle has had no work done on it at all since its collapse."

The three girls looked horrified, "That would mean we could never go to the island again!" Rosie was on the verge of tears but somehow, she managed to hold them back.

"What did the farmer say?" asked the Professor. "What is his name? Griffith, is it?"

"Ivor Griffith-Rowen," replied Mick, the landlord. "They don't need the money. The richest farming family in these parts. Hey Jen!" he turned to his wife. "Did you hear what Ivor said?"

"Well, come to think of it, he said he had been a bit shocked when the company approached him, but his sons seemed in favour of the deal," continued Jenny. "He said that the island and most of the land they owned had been in their family's possession for hundreds of years, and as for selling he would have to give it serious thought."

Jenny placed all the glasses on a shelf behind the bar and picked up the empty tray. "Now that is all I know. I have a kitchen to clean. Mick, give us a hand when you have finished here."

"Aye right. I'll just see if Sam and Jim want another pint and I'm all yours." Mick asked the Professor if he wanted anything else.

"No, thank you, we are fine now. He thanked his host for an exceptionally good afternoon. "Come on Rosie and Petra, I will walk you home!"

"But Father! I need my friends tonight. We have a lot to discuss about the island!"

"If it is alright," said Petra. "Ursula could come and spend the night with us, it is half-term, after all."

"Well, I don't mind, shall I ring your mother, Petra?"

"No need we often have friends to stay over," said Rosie, holding back an enormous yawn.

"All right then all come over for breakfast, I have a new housekeeper now!" Mr Mortimer turned to go when Ursula caught him and gave him a huge hug, "We will be there for breakfast," then she hesitated. "Father, I do hope you have checked out your new housekeeper."

"I've done the usual checks," responded Professor Mortimer. "Why?"

"Well," said Petra. "We thought Joanna Newsome was your housekeeper when she came nosing round your cottage, after you were taken into hospital, and look what happened there."

"I didn't know that fact, Petra!" The Professor exclaimed, looking thoughtful. "Tomorrow night you must come to dinner and tell me everything! Especially how you came to find my daughter. And don't worry it was Mrs Lewis who cleans the church, who answered my advertisement for a housekeeper."

"Oh, she is very nice, very trustworthy," remarked Rosie.

"Yes, she is!" agreed Petra. "Good night then, and don't worry about Ursula. We'll look after her."

"So long as your mother won't mind,"

"No, of course she won't mind, she never minds when our other friends stay over."

Then suddenly Rosie had a serious thought.

"But Doc,'" Rosie called after the Professor. "Perhaps we should persuade Ursula to stay with you tonight, in case you are sad and lonely."

"That is very kind of you Rosie, but I need to go online tonight and find out all I can about this conglomerate who has plans to buy the island."

"Goodnight Doc'" called Rosie. She couldn't help calling him Doc, the name most of the village called him with great affection.

The Professor turned into Old Mill Lane thinking, with a smile on his face, "We are home. At last, we are home!"

45
PANIC IN THE VILLAGE

Petra and Rosie's Mum didn't mind a bit having Ursula to stay that night, it had been a sad and stressful day for the village, and she agreed it would be nice for the girls to be together.

"Where's your bear, Rosie? He is not on your bed and nowhere in the house! I thought you might have had him with you." Their mum seemed surprised that they didn't know the whereabouts of Brown Bear.

"Right then you girls can put up the camp bed for Ursula in your room. It is in the cupboard on the landing, better do it now as it is getting late."

Then their mum spoke to Ursula. "That was a very special day for you, I know. It went without a hitch, and it is good to see your dad's ankle recovering so well. Ursula, you are very welcome to stay with the girls whenever you like."

"Thank you, I will love this village I know. People have been so kind to me."

"There isn't anyone local who hasn't wondered what had happened to your mother. And I am so glad my girls helped you solve the mystery……" Mrs Williamson was running out of what to say to Ursula on the day of her mother's funeral when suddenly the family dog started barking. Their pet started licking Ursula›s hands who then bent down to give their canine friend a fuss.

"She is gorgeous, so friendly. What's her name?'

"Candy," replied Petra and Rosie together.

Later, the girls waited till Mum and Dad had gone to bed and the house was quiet before they talked about this huge worry that was hanging over them.

"If this conglomerate person buys the island, then we can never go there again!" exclaimed Rosie. She felt angry but did her best to keep her voice low.

"Rosie, darling, a conglomerate isn't one person," whispered Ursula. "It is a company made up of several smaller companies engaged in diverse or unrelated business all working for the same end."

"Like spoiling our island," Rosie couldn't help blurting out.

"Shush!"

"Shush, Rosie."

"I'm sorry, I want BB!" Rosie snuggled down under her Duvet.

"I feel the same as you do Rosie," whispered Ursula. "If someone else goes to the island with noisy building machinery, like a monstrous bulldozer, or anything like drills that would upset my bears I would be so worried," Ursula gave a distressed sigh. "They had a happy life with my mother and me. They trusted us. If anything noisy were to disturb them I know what they would do."

"What would they do?" Petra was intrigued.

"I am sure the older bears would round up the cubs and they would disappear deep into the caves to die. I explored the caves once, they go deep under the sea. I found skeletons down there." By now Ursula was smitten with grief, imagining the fate of her beloved bears at the hands of the destructive conglomerate. "Whatever can we do?"

Petra, who was the one chosen to sleep on a camp bed on the floor, climbed up into the top bunk where Ursula was tonight.

"Listen," she said, "as soon as it is light, we'll go and find BB, he always knows what to do."

"I am very worried about him." Rosie's muffled voice came from under her duvet. "He said he would see us in the pub, but he never showed up."

At last, all three girls slept, but they were dreaming of chaos on the island. The lovely beach cottage would be pulled down, a featureless hotel built on the cliff top, kiosks selling ice cream or potted shrimp, all acceptable in a large seaside town but not on the island.

In the morning their mum woke the three girls.

"Your Dad is on the house phone Ursula, here take it." Their mother passed the mainline phone over to the young girl.

Petra and Rosie were wide awake now, they listened to their new friend talk to her father.

"Oh no!' exclaimed Ursula. "Please Father say that is not true. Oh! I can't believe that it has happened so quickly. Yes of course, we will meet you on the quay. How did you hear about it? Yes, Father, of course I will!"

Petra and Rosie knew from the tone of Ursula's voice that it was bad news. "What's happened?"

"The island has been sold! The farmer has sold it! I just can't believe it!" The girls had never seen Ursula so upset before. "Father heard it on the local radio at seven this morning."

"I'll look it up on the internet," said Rosie, trying to be helpful. She reached for her mobile phone.

"Father said he was going to meet with a group of protesters on the quay."

So that was it. They scrambled to get dressed and then they all hurried down to Swallows Quay, where about thirty protesters had gathered already. Mick and Jenny from the pub were there.

They both looked very worried indeed, "A hotel over on the island will take away all our business," announced Mick.

"It's a bit of a struggle now, even without competition," sighed Jenny. There were many other worried faces gathering on Swallows Quay.

The weather that morning was not at all clement, a grey overcast sky threatened worse weather to come. There was already a fine drizzle wetting everyone. October was not the best time of year to meet on the quay, but the irate group of protesters injected heat into the morning, they were all so angry with Farmer Ivor Griffith-Rowen having sold the island to a big corporation.

A few minutes later the Vicar arrived with Maggie Jones the church organist, and just as they reached the group of protesters, a large car drew up and in it was Sam Lewis the reporter from the Coastal Recorder, the local newspaper.

"Now who is going to give me the story?" he said to the crowd, as he got out of his vehicle. "And who knows the name of this multinational company that has bought the island?"

The crowd surrounded him with negativity, "We don't want a giant company, coming to these parts setting up business on our doorstep!" Mr and Mrs Hughes from Rose Cottage had the first say, and then everyone joined in making their protests known, loudly.

"Anyway! Sam, how have you got to know so quickly?" Mr Jessop from the stables asked the reporter.

"My boss texted me early saying I must cover the bit of trouble surrounding the sale of a nearby island," replied Sam Lewis.

"Bit of trouble!" exclaimed another resident. "Don't you be sarcastic now. It's big trouble to us folk who live here, and if you don't report it properly, none of us are going to talk to you at all!"

Petra and Rosie could not believe how much this news was causing such a debacle.

"I wish BB was here," said Rosie. "He would know what to do, I am really worried about him."

"When did you last see him?" asked Ursula.

"Yesterday morning before Emily Jane's funeral," replied Rosie.

"I thought he was coming to the service," said Ursula.

"So did I!" exclaimed Petra. "We must find him!"

But something stopped them. Just as the protest was getting out of hand, they all heard a familiar noise, the deep thud, thud of a motorboat engine chugging into the harbour.

"Hey look!" cried Rosie, pointing at the boat and jumping up and down for joy. "It's Lucas and BB too."

Minutes later, Professor Mortimer stood by his daughter as the Lucas pulled alongside the jetty. Rosie was very excited, "And Jake is with them too."

All the villagers rushed towards the new arrivals, pleased to see Lucas, Brown Bear and Jake, who stood tall and handsome in his uniform.

"Now we have the law on our side," called Mick, being a little presumptive.

Everyone in the crowd knew Lucas and were pleased to see him, but Mrs Maggie Jones had noticed he hadn't been in church yesterday.

"Not like Lucas to miss a wake! Where do you think the three of them have been?"

Ursula called the girls aside. "Something is going on. Jake had assured me he would come to the funeral but as you know he didn't turn up either, I was a bit hurt."

"That is the downside of dating a police officer," said Petra.

"What do you mean, Petra?"

"Well," said Petra. "To be honest they always have to put their work first."

"Humm, I know that, but I have never had a date in my life," Ursula flashed her deep blue eyes. Then there was a slight disturbance.

"I think we had better do something about that!" Jake had jumped down from the boat and now stood by Ursula, he had overheard what she said... He smiled down at her.

"How about dinner on Saturday night?" Jake smiled apprehensively at Ursula waiting for an answer.

How could she refuse this charming man. She hesitated and then took hold of Jake's hand.

"I will have to ask my father," she answered, with a twinkle in her eyes.

"No, you don't! My dear," Suddenly, the Professor appeared out of the crowd of protesters and gazed down at his daughter. "If you have survived all the ups and downs on the island, then I will trust you to make your own decisions."

"Thank you, Father, I appreciate you saying that, but I will never leave you. I love this place and all these energetic people who know when something is not right." Ursula smiled.

Lucas secured his boat by tying up alongside the jetty and helped Brown Bear to alight the vessel. "Whatever is all this fuss for?"

"Haven't you heard the news, BB?" cried Rosie. "A conglomerate has bought the island, and everything will change from now on." She was so eager to tell him all they had gathered. "They are building a hotel and a restaurant like McDonalds, and a diving school that will frighten all the fish, and a golf course!" The little girl explained everything at great speed. How Rosie didn't cry was a miracle! Because upset and near to tears was the way all the locals were feeling at this moment in time.

"Where have you been, BB? I have been so worried," said Rosie.

"And you two, Jake and Lucas, all missed the service for Emily Jane!" exclaimed Ursula. "We would have liked you to be there, wouldn't we, father?"

"Yes, we would. But I feel certain the three of you have a perfectly good explanation why you didn't attend," said Professor Mortimer.

"Indeed! we have. Can we find shelter? It has started to rain heavily. Look old Jack has opened the Lifeboat station, we can go in there." Jake in his official capacity took charge of the situation.

"Aye you can do that!" Jack, one of the retired lifeguards ushered everybody inside, out of the rain. It was a bit of a squash, but everyone was anxious to hear the reason why the three had been missing for over 24 hours.

There was a raised area at the front of the building and Jake encouraged his uncle to climb onto it. Brown Bear and Jake stood aside.

"Uncle Lucas, tell them all where we have been."

Lucas was usually a very shy person never liking being the centre of attention, but today was different. The crowd of protesters were silent. In fact, you could have heard a pin drop, so was the tension in that building.

"Well, aye, we've been in my boat along the coast to the big Port," he hesitated. "See, I am not used to this public speaking but today, I do have something to say as you are all worried about the island."

A loud murmur spread round the room.

Then Mick from the Pub said, "Yes, we are very worried, on the news this morning the local radio station announced that Farmer Ivor Griffith-Rowen sold his island to a conglomerate."

Lucas Oliver stood tall amongst these frustrated villagers who were so concerned about losing the island to entrepreneurs.

"Well! I can tell you all for certain, that if that's what you've heard? Well, that is fake news!" Lucas stood tall as another murmur went round the crowd.

"How can it be fake? It was on the radio!" called out young Johnny from the stables.

"Yes, it is fake news!" exclaimed Lucas. "Because Farmer Ivor did not sell his island to a conglomerate, or any corporation. In fact, he sold it to me!"

At first there was a stunned silence, followed by a barrage of questions from all present.

"Listen, I will explain!" announced Lucas. "I heard a few

months ago that the island belonged to the Griffith-Rowen family. Well, to be honest it was because I overheard one of my regular customers, who comes with me on my fishing trips telling one of his mates what a good place it would be as a holiday destination. One day we were speeding along out to sea when he said he wanted to buy the island to expand his hotel business."

"Come on, Lucas!" A man at the back called out. "Pull the other one, how can you afford to compete with these conglomerate people."

The girls had been amid all the goings on and suddenly Rosie pulled at Petra's arm.

"What's the matter, Sis?"

"It's that word again," said Rosie. "I love it! It keeps going round and round in my head. Con-glom-er-ate. Con-glom-er-ate."

"I know what you mean. I have had words that do that." Petra put her finger to her lips. "Now shush Rosie, we might miss something."

"Well," said Lucas. "I certainly do not want to compete with anyone, certainly not a conglomerate!"

Rosie giggled and Petra gave her a gentle nudge.

"But" Lucas continued, "I did want to buy the island for the girls, Petra and Rosie and Ursula, who has been living alone on the island for years, who stayed to be close to her mother who, we now know was murdered at the hands of Jo Newsome," Lucas hesitated to wipe a tear from his eye. He looked round the lifeboat station at all his friends and neighbours. "I bought it because I want us villagers to be united, I certainly won't be taking bulldozers or anything like that to the island. I want the Doc to carry on with his excavating and my old friend Mr Bear and Petra and Rosie to be able to go there whenever they want!"

Everyone present, joined in with a hearty round of applause for Lucas.

Then Sam Lewis, the reporter from the local newspaper, raised his hand to ask a question that everyone else was dying to know.

"Mr Oliver, may I ask how much you paid for the Island?"

"No! you may not!" Lucas exclaimed. "That is Ivor's business, and mine."

"Sorry Sir, but it is my job to ask," replied Sam Lewis.

"I will tell you all this," continued Lucas. "I am sure you all want to know, the same way I bought my shiny red motorboat."

"Was it with your lottery win?" Rosie was the only one to challenge the fisherman. She didn't seem at all shy speaking in front of the whole village.

"Yes, little Rosie, you are right," he answered, with a very generous smile.

Everyone present felt very relieved and again gave Lucas a huge round of applause. They were all delighted that no conglomerate would ever have access to Swallows Island now or in the future.

Professor Mortimer said a few words of appreciation and thanked Mister Bear, Petra and Rosie for finding his daughter and their persistence and bravery when it came to finding evidence against Joanna Newsome.

At the end of that day everyone in the village was very happy indeed.

"There is just one last thing I want to do before winter weather sets in," said a very serious Lucas.

Everyone looked directly at him, but no one had any idea what he meant.

46
ONE LAST TRIP

It was the end of October and pleasantly warm for the time of year. Lucas had brought the girls and BB to the island for one last visit before the Christmas term began. This was the one thing he had wanted to do when he bought the island. He knew how much the girls loved the challenge of being able to stay with BB in this beautiful place whenever they could make time from their busy school schedules. When he had signed the deal with farmer Ivor Griffith-Rowen, Lucas felt he wanted to give the girls a break on the island without any of the horrors they had recently endured.

As they had approached the only safe harbour on the island, Petra was pleased to read out aloud a large sign nailed to the jetty.
'PRIVATE ISLAND. Unauthorised Visitors Will be Prosecuted.' She gave Ursula a big smile.
"Wow!" exclaimed Rosie. "That's telling them!"
Brown Bear nodded his head in approval. The tide was high, and they all got their feet wet as they climbed down from the jetty. The water was warm so, nobody cared as they were all deliriously happy to be back on their beloved island.
"I will pick you up Sunday afternoon. The tide will be high at two-thirty. Now look after yourselves, and no more adventures! That's an order!" Lucas called to them with a mischievous sparkle in his eyes. He started the engine of his motorboat, gave them a wave with his weathered brown hand and within minutes he safely passed the dangerous rocks, and was well on his way to the

mainland.

"It's amazing how Lucas could buy the island," said Petra, giving the fisherman one last wave.

"Very lucky for us, and we are lucky with the weather too," replied Rosie.

"Yes, we are," agreed Brown Bear. "I cannot believe an old friend of mine could afford to buy this piece of paradise." He picked up all their bags from the jetty, and then the little group made their way up the beach towards the cottage.

"My Nan said it is an Indian summer," remarked Rosie. "To have hot weather in October."

"We had better make the most of it," remarked Ursula. "Where shall we sleep tonight, Petra?"

"I don't think I would feel comfortable staying in the cottage, so soon after…" Petra hesitated.

Ursula interjected, "So soon after, knowing that was where my mother's body was hidden all along. Look girls! Please, no pussyfooting around my feelings, I am just relieved Mother is safe now. In fact, I would love to stay in the cottage."

"Of course, you have been very brave and somewhat stoical my dear," Brown Bear gave Ursula an understanding glance. "Right! here we are now," he unlocked the door to the Professor's cottage and placed all their belongings down on the floor in the first room.

"Oh girls! I forgot to tell you, the police have secured all the windows and the door with new locks."

"Oh! Yes, I forgot to tell you!" Ursula exclaimed. "Father arranged for everywhere to be cleaned thoroughly and for all the animal bones and fossils to be taken to the university to be analysed."

"That's the right thing to have done," replied Petra. "We should have some lovely days here now without any worries."

"And it will be just us alone, and no conglomerate to worry

about," stated a joyful Rosie.

"Yes, all we want is a little peace," said Ursula. "Now let's go upstairs and unpack a few warm hoodies and sweaters, it's Autumn and it surely will get very cold tonight."

Petra found what she needed quickly and sat on the big ornate bed waiting for Ursula and Rosie to decide what they wanted.

She sat quietly remembering all the tense times they had endured this summer. Come to think of it, she had always felt a presence in this room, and when BB had told her about the rolled-up piece of material he had found, and he mentioned hearing the swishing of a dress swirling on this floor, she hadn't been a bit surprised.

She closed her eyes as she remembered the whiffs of perfume that wafted round the room, especially after dark. Now with hindsight it was obvious that Emily Jane was trying her best with only her ghostly existence, to make them all aware that she wasn't at peace.

"Are you girls ready yet? I have been waiting for ages!" Brown Bear's booming voice hollered up the stairs.

"We are on our way, BB," Rosie called down to him. "Ursula wants to show us the caves where all the bears hibernate."

Moments later they all agreed that is what they would do first. Rosie had retrieved the picnic basket from inside the front room and given it to Brown Bear to carry.

"The weight of this feels very acceptable!" He exclaimed, as he gave Rosie an appreciative look. "I think we had better go the underground way, as the beach is under water right now, the high tide makes surrounding the headland on foot impossible!"

It didn't take them long to reach the lagoon. The late morning sun shone down on the enchanting stretch of water, making the blue ripples sparkle in the reflected sunlight. All was quiet, not even a squawk of a seagull disturbed the tranquil air. They soon found a place to sit on some smooth rocks.

"This is like heaven!" Petra lay back wiggling her toes in the fine white sand.

"Well, it would be if I wasn't feeling so worried!" exclaimed Ursula.

"Why?" asked Rosie.

"Because there are no signs of the bears," Ursula's voice was almost breaking. "I am puzzled, they always come to greet me."

"Not even their howls," replied Petra realising how quiet it was.

"Well, let us have a bite to eat and then we should go to find them," Brown Bear passed Rosie their provisions box.

"It really is quiet. I would have thought they would have heard us by now," declared Ursula, as she took a sandwich from the pack Rosie handed her.

"Thank you, Rosie. As soon as we have eaten our lunch, we will make our way to the lake," Ursula was thinking it strange that her ursine friends had not come to greet her, but then she had been away for the past few weeks, settling into her father's cottage and starting a new life at the sixth form college.

"I hope they don't think I have deserted them," she uttered solemnly.

"Okay then!" Brown Bear bellowed, making the girls jump. "We will go and find them right away!" Then he said in a lower tone, "Ursula, they could be fretting, because you have been away for so long."

The girls knew that when Brown Bear decided something, he would always stick to it whatever it might be. He never changed his mind or reneged on anything!

They all ate their food in silence. Rosie spoke first.

"BB, can you close this picnic box, I can't do it for some reason."

"Now let me, see! There you are Rosie, all done," Brown Bear stood up and picked up the hamper. "Are you all ready?" He asked. "Then we are off to the lake, and the forest beyond. Will you please lead the way, young lady?" Ursula gladly led the way.

The journey from the lagoon through to the rocky area at the edge of the forest didn't take them long, as everyone was anxious to see the bears again. At last, they stood on the shores of the lake. The waters looked murky today, and a fine autumnal mist was slowly rising into the air above. There was a smell of damp foliage wafting on a breeze that was blowing softly around them, its gusts skimmed the lake making ripples on the water.

"It is so quiet," said Rosie in a whisper.

"No sounds of the bears at all, I am so worried." Ursula and the girls clung together for a moment; they too felt the agony that Ursula was feeling right now.

"I will lead the way through the forest!" announced Brown Bear. "And then Ursula, my dear," he stopped. "Will you show us the caves where your friends hibernate for the winter?" Brown Bear was in charge.

The forest had been growing in thick abundance in August, when they had last been here. The floor was lush and thriving back then, even though the young bear Starlight was constantly playing and trampling down the undergrowth. Today, they all were knee deep in a carpet of fallen leaves, scattered around in shades of browns and rusty reds lying under the many deciduous trees. However, the Conifers, Scotch Pine, and the Hollies, already with orange berries pushing through, were still standing proudly in verdant green, as they reached up tall for the canopy and the sky beyond.

After a while they came to a halt. Ursula stood still and took stock of the situation.

"All I can think of is that they have taken the little ones deep into the undersea caves, preparing for winter. The first winter when I was alone here, they tried to coax me down there for safety."

"Did you go with them?" asked Petra.

"I thanked them for their consideration, but I refused, because at that time I still expected my mother to return. But of course, she never did."

"Oh! my dear you have suffered," said Brown Bear.

"Yes, I have, but once I find Kent and Moonlight, I will be fine. Now follow me. Have you got your phones? It can be very dark in the caves, some at the entrance have skylights, though, like the one in my home cave."

"That sounds good, but we have plenty of lights. I am carrying two torches and the oil lamp," Brown Bear sounded very confident.

"You seem to be prepared for a long journey, BB," remarked Petra.

There was no reply from Brown Bear.

So, Ursula led them into the Cave bear's retreat. These caves were larger and not wet and slippery like the sea caves they knew from another adventure they had endured on this island. Today the floor beneath their feet was smooth and well worn.

"How much further, Ursula?"

"Not far now, just keep behind me." After a while Ursula stopped.

"Can you see, to the side of this cave there is a big drop. Be careful if you look down you will see the sea raging down below."

"Oooo! That looks frightening," gasped Rosie, getting a little too close to the edge.

"BB, come and look, the waves are far down below us washing in and out over the rocks. It does look very rough down there. Do come and see, BB?"

"Will you please come away from there, little one," Brown Bear was urgent in his request. "That looks very dangerous! Now, you hold on to me, Rosie, and don't look down."

Rosie's face was ashen as she hadn't realised what peril she had been in. She took his arm, as he led her to safety.

Suddenly, the cave they were in widened out into one large cave with a long low shelf of bedrock on one side. Brown Bear sat down immediately and beckoned to Rosie to do the same. "I am sure these caves are prehistoric. Look there are Petroglyphs, up there," he pointed to some etchings carved out of the rock face."

"Does that mean that early man once lived here?" Petra reached up to touch the carvings high above her head.

"Yes, I am certain of it," replied Brown Bear. "Neanderthals were known for capturing the cave bears as they woke from hibernation, docile then, you see."

At that moment Ursula became impatient, "I really must go on!" she exclaimed. "I think I will go on alone to see what is happening."

"No, don't, we are all coming now," said Brown Bear, as he stood up. "I will lead the way."

Then suddenly from somewhere nearby came a familiar roar. Brown Bear, Petra and Rosie were glued to the spot, not moving a muscle. Then unexpectedly the two adult bears Kent and Moonlight followed by Starlight, who was now half the size of his father, trundled into the cave. They were followed by the twin cubs, their latest offspring.

There was such joy and happiness amongst this ursine family. As soon as they saw Ursula, they greeted her with huge hugs. The two baby cubs who had grown a lot in the last few weeks, climbed up onto the rocky seat beside her wanting to show their affection too.

It was amazing how Ursula communicated with the bears. Rosie, who was always alert with almost everything, had noticed it was because Ursula could make a low-pitched gravelly sound deep in her throat.

"How did you learn to make that noise?" Rosie asked her

friend.

"My mother taught me. She told me that when Moonlight had helped her in her confinement, you know girls, when she was in labour with me, Moonlight had taught her how to recreate the same sound and not only that, but she also gave my mother some herbs that helped her with the pain."

"This is the most incredible story I have heard since I left the forests of Northern Europe!" exclaimed Brown Bear.

"Yes, I think it is," retorted Ursula. "But in my first English class a few weeks ago, we were asked to write a brief history of our lives so far, and I wrote all I could remember about my solitary life here on this island."

"I bet you wrote a very accurate account, my dear!" Brown bear looked very pleased that Ursula could put her experiences into words.

"I told the absolute truth in my nine-page essay, but not one of the other students believed me."

"Umm," Brown Bear was deep in thought. "It is the case that seeing is believing!"

For a while it was like a social event, Ursula was telling Kent and Moonlight all about her new life and they were telling her of their difficulties of rearing three cubs instead of one.

Then the youngsters started a bit of bored shuffling, touching their parents as if to say, "Come on, let's get going."

After a while, Moonlight took Ursula to one side and after a moment of communication came over to Brown Bear and the girls.

"They want us all to go deeper into the caves," announced Ursula. "To see how they have everything they need ready for a cosy winter."

"We would love to come," replied Petra.

"Oh, yes!" exclaimed Rosie. "I want to see where they sleep.

Come on BB, let's go?"

But Brown Bear's reply stunned them all. He stood in front of them and blocked the way.

"No! I don't want Petra and Rosie to go any further!" Brown Bear had decided.

"But BB! Why not?" Rosie persisted. "Why can't we go? Ursula, please tell BB, how much we want to go and see where the bears live?"

The girls were dumbfounded because they had never seen their bear being so adamant before.

Then moments later there was a little relief. Brown Bear was being greeted by Kent, the patriarch of the group, in fact they became deep in conversation, and Moonlight appeared to be communicating with Ursula, while the young ones were trying to get Rosie to play a game with them.

Eventually all became clear. Brown Bear asked the girls to come back and sit on the long seat of rock, as he had something very special to tell Petra and Rosie.

"What is it, BB?" asked Rosie.

"You sound very serious, BB" remarked Petra. "Whatever is the matter?"

Ursula didn't question Brown Bear, and the girls felt at that moment that she already knew what he was going to tell theme. Instead, she sat on the rocky ledge and let the twin cubs play with her feet.

Now Brown Bear was ready to tell the girls his plan.

"Petra, you are such a grown-up young lady, and I know you will understand how important it is that now you are both young adults and no longer need me as your chaperone bear," he hesitated, waiting closely for her response.

"What are you saying, BB?" Petra answered, deep in thought.

"Well, er, argh!" he was awkward in his response. "I am getting older, and I have been devoted to you and Rosie ever since I was rescued from a recycling bin by your dad!"

"Oh! BB, we thought you had forgotten all about that!" Petra felt embarrassed remembering the trauma. "That was a mistake, BB, you know what Mum is like."

"Yes! to be honest I do, but we won't go into that right now!" he took a deep breath.

"I forgave your Mum and ever since that incident I have loved her dearly."

"Thank goodness for that!" exclaimed Petra. "So, what is your problem?"

"Rosie, come close too," he beckoned to her. "I think my news will upset you the most." He put his big furry arms around both his girl's. "I want you to be very brave because it has taken me a while to decide my future."

Both girls felt apprehensive.

"So! what have you decided, BB?" Petra felt sick, she realised BB's decision would affect them all.

"I hope you are not going to upset me BB, you know how much I love you." Rosie's voice was fading, as she finished her plea.

"My dear Rosie, please try and understand," he pulled the girls closer. "You need to let me go. And I need to realise how grown up you both have become, and that you don't really need me sleeping at the bottom of your bed every night anymore." Brown Bear looked so sad that Rosie was convinced he had tears welling up in his big brown eyes. Her heart was aching so much she could feel pain deep in her chest.

"But BB, where will you go?" asked Petra. "If you leave us, we may never see you ever again!"

"And" continued Rosie. "I think you should stay with us, especially now that Lucas owns the Island. He will bring us all here whenever we want to come."

"That is precisely why now is the right time!" remarked Brown Bear. "You both will be leaving school next year and concentrating on further education for your futures." At that moment the two baby bears started pulling at his fur, wanting him to play.

"BB, I won't be able to survive, if I didn't see you every day!" Tears that Rosie had kept in check were now rolling down her cheeks.

Petra put her arm around her sister and hugged her tight. "Listen Rosie, I think BB is right!"

"No! he can't be, I do love him, and I will miss him terribly, Petra you know I will!" Tears now streamed down her face, as she cried uncontrollably.

Petra let go of her sister and stood looking deep into Brown Bear's eyes. "This could be catastrophic for us. Where exactly are you planning to go, BB?"

"Just here on the Island!" he exclaimed. "The bears want me to spend the winter with them and maybe stay forever."

"Oh no! BB, please come back home," begged Rosie.

"Ursula seemed to be in favour of Brown Bear staying on the island. "I think it is a good idea, I will know these cubs grow up, polite and well behaved then."

"Yes," agreed Petra. "And Lucas is very kind. I am sure he will bring us here, whenever he can."

"Come here, Rosie. Sit by me, and I will explain myself to you!" Brown Bear patted the rocky seat beside him.

Rosie did her best to stop crying and did what her beloved BB told her to do. She sat so close to him he couldn't help saying,

"Rosie dear you are so close to me; you remind me of a limpet!"

"Yes, I suppose I am clinging on tight, but it's because I don't want to let you go!" she exclaimed. She was still shuddering a little, as she coped with her tears. She took some deep breaths, and she did her best to calm herself.

"Okay! BB, tell me what has made you want to stay on the island," Rosie's glum face looked at her hero.

Brown Bear was feeling very emotional himself, "I have been

so very happy looking after you and Petra all these years, but seeing the other bears has made me realise who I really am." His tone was gentle and calming and he could see Rosie was beginning to understand him. "Because you, my sweetest Rosie, Petra and I have had a comfortable home life, with exciting adventures to contend with, I had really forgotten I was of Ursine stock!"

"What's stock?" Rosie asked.

"You know, relatives, family," he was extremely patient with this young lady. He knew he loved her too, and life would be hard without her and Petra, and of course their mum, dad, and Mali, their brother, who had once rescued them from a horrific ordeal some years ago. Brown Bear knew his life was about to change drastically.

"Okay! I think I understand," said Rosie eventually. "I wish I could stay here with you and all the bears. But you see, BB, my life is getting exciting now. I am going to college and next year I want a summer job too."

"Well, there you are my dear! That's the spirit. You see we must all follow our dreams, whatever they are." Brown Bear felt very relieved with Rosie's positive attitude.

"It will be alright!" said Rosie. "Now the island belongs to Lucas, your old friend. I'm sure he will bring us to visit you whenever we ask him."

"Undoubtedly he will. Now girls, let us enjoy our last couple of days together, before Lucas returns." Brown Bear could feel a lump in his throat. He was just as sad to leave the girls as they were to let him go.

The girls agreed to his plans, and Ursula convinced Rosie that Brown Bear would enjoy helping the adult bears bring up their three cubs. The new babies were already very boisterous and quite a handful for Moonlight their mother to cope with.

It was almost dusk when the girls and Ursula reached Professor

Mortimer's cottage on the beach. They had made their way out of the caves and promised to meet the bears at the Lagoon tomorrow.

Ursula, Petra and Rosie were going to sleep in the upper bedroom as before, but Brown Bear said he was too excited to sleep and would keep watch, outside on the beach.

However, when the girls went to find him in the morning, he was fast asleep on the rocks outside the front door. Rosie hugged him tight, and Petra handed him a huge picnic basket to carry.

"Come on BB, do wake up. It is a beautiful day for October, and we have been up since six making special sandwiches for our picnic."

"Right ho! I'm coming, where are we going?" He brushed some sand off his fur, and stood tall, towering over the three girls.

"To swim in the lagoon." Rosie's eyes were red, she had been crying again this morning, but realised this would be their last full day with BB, on the island and she wasn't going to be sad for one minute of it.

"Won't it be too cold to swim there at this time of year?" he asked.

"No, it will be fine!" announced Ursula. "There are some hot springs that rise from below. The water flows from deep underground and that is why the lagoon is warm all year round!"

"That is fantastic!" Petra exclaimed. "This island is quite amazing! From sea caves to castles and resident bears! No wonder you want to live here permanently, BB!"

"Right then let us be off," said Brown Bear, stifling his own feelings.

Deep in their hearts the girls were sad knowing BB's decision to leave the comfort of their family home and remain on the island.

Ursula however wasn't sad at all; she was pleased to know her beloved bears will have a companion who will care about them all, as she has done all her life.

Well, their penultimate day was all they expected it to be. To start with they left all their belongings on the sand and jumped into the blue waters. Ursula was right! The water was very warm, and they swam around playing chase and laughing a great deal of the time.

"I don't suppose the bears will join us today?" remarked Brown Bear. "They all were looking a bit sleepy yesterday ready for their hibernation!" And before he could finish his sentence all three cubs appeared at the edge of the water.

"Come on in, you scallywags," called Ursula.

That was the beginning of lots more fun and antics. The three cubs played with Ursula and the girls for ages. Brown Bear had left the young ones in the water and had gone over to sit with Kent and Moonlight, who had just arrived to supervise their cubs. From their body language, Petra could see how well Brown Bear was merging into his new life with his ursine relations.

Later as they all ate supper on the shore of the Lagoon, they decided to spend their last night here, and sleep on the soft sand. It was such a warm pleasant evening, and it would prolong the little time they had left with BB, their dearest friend.

Next morning, they all woke suddenly wondering where they were. There was no tide in the lagoon, no noisy waves washing in and out, the waters were always still and remained the same level, unless occasionally in mid-winter when a storm at sea sends high waves crashing over the natural sand bank into the tranquil waters with a great force to upset the symmetry.

"I have thought things through," Rosie said suddenly. "It won't be too bad without you, BB."

"I am glad to know you will accept the situation, my dear Rosie. I dare say Lucas will always bring you to visit me next summer," said Brown Bear, hurriedly wiping away some tears of his own.

High tide was due early afternoon, that is when they expected Lucas to steer his motorboat around the headland towards the jetty. There was no sign of the bears this morning. The girls decided to have one last swim and get into dry clothes ready for the journey home. Anyway, they had all said their goodbyes last evening.

"Come on, girls. I will come with you to the jetty and wave you off," said Brown Bear.

It took them a while to reach the cottage and collect all their belongings. Brown Bear pulled the door shut and after locking it securely, handed the key to Ursula.

"Please give this to Professor Mortimer, uuh, I mean your father, when you are home. And thank him very much," he handed her the new shiny key.

"Thank you, BB," she said, giving him a huge hug. "I am so glad you all came to the island and found me. I know I was a bit strange at first, but you can all see now, how I was afraid of strangers, especially after what happened to my mother!"

Petra and Rosie gave her a hug. "Yes!" Petra replied. "We did think you were a bit strange at first, but we are so pleased we got to know you."

"I am so happy Father decided to live in Swallows Village again!"

"Yes," joined in Rosie. "We will be able to get together whenever we like."

At precisely two o' clock they heard the chug-chug of a motorboat engine, and as usual, exactly on time, they saw Lucas steering his craft into the bay and alongside the jetty.

"Oh, look, Ursula. Jake is with him."

Petra noticed that the young woman was blushing as her eyes met Jake's. Lucas, oblivious to all that, was occupied fastening his boat to the moorings.

Rosie ran down the beach to greet their visitors. "Look, Petra, why do you think Jake is wearing his police uniform?"

Brown Bear interrupted. "He must be here in his official capacity I should think, but goodness knows what that might be?"

"Perhaps he thinks we are trespassing?" Rosie said, looking very worried. "You know because of that sign."

"No, that can't be the reason," Petra exclaimed. "Look Rosie, they know we are not trespassers, they know exactly who we are. Anyway, they are both smiling. They are pleased to see us!"

Once the vessel was secured both men jumped down from the boat onto sand below the jetty. Jake ran towards Ursula and gave her a hug and a kiss.

"Sorry, I shouldn't have done that as I am on duty, but I couldn't resist, as I have really missed you, Ursula," said Jake.

"I have missed you too," Ursula smiled back at this tall, handsome officer.

Eventually they all were standing on the sand dodging the incoming waves.

"Would you mind coming higher up the beach to sit on the rocks for a minute or two?" said Brown Bear. "I have some news for you, Lucas!"

"Aye, old mate, and what news be that now?" Lucas sat on the rocks with a bit of a groan. "I am getting too old to be sitting on low rocks nowadays. So, what be your news?"

Brown Bear seemed to be a little apprehensive which was unusual for him; he was always very self-assured.

"I have decided that now that Petra and Rosie are growing up, too quickly I might add! They don't need my protection anymore, and I know them well enough to know they will make the right choices in life!" Brown Bear took a deep breath.

Petra and Rosie drew closer so that they could hear the conversation.

"He's right!" Petra said in a whisper. "Our present friends accept that BB has been with us since we were small. But our new college friends won't understand, will they Rosie? They will think we are nutty."

"Yes, I know." Rosie nodded to her sister. "Anyway, I am sure Lucas will bring him to visit us sometimes." Then suddenly they heard a roar of laughter from Lucas.

"You are going to do *what*?" said Lucas to the bear.

Brown Bear was a bit upset that his old mate wasn't taking his decision to stay and live with the bears seriously.

"I'll give you 'til Christmas! Then you will be home with the girls toasting your toes on their radiator."

"No!" proclaimed Brown Bear. "I will stay with my own kind until the end of my days. I have such a lot to catch up with my relatives."

"What will you live on?" Lucas was beginning to believe his old friend. He knew that whatever Brown Bear stated he would never renege on.

"Well, that will not be a worry," replied Brown Bear, his oldest friend. "These cave bears, *Ursa Spelaesus*, who have lived on this island since the Pleistocene era and have survived because of abundant supplies of freshwater fish in the lake. And today I was shown their undersea caves with access to the ocean far below. Not only that, but they have told me about a dry cave that is full of berries from the forest. In Spring and Autumn, they collect enormous loads of fruit and berries, and herbs to dry and keep all winter."

Rosie looked on amazed. "There is one thing you won't be able to have, and I know you will miss it."

"Now what will that be, young Rosie?"

"BB, a nice cup of tea!" gushed Rosie.

"I will have herbal tea, herbs from the forest floor," he answered. "Made with water from the hot springs in the lagoon!"

"I give up! BB, you have it all planned." Rosie gave her bear a huge hug and smiled round at everyone. "Now Jake, why are you here wearing your police uniform?"

Jake, who had been close to Ursula all this time, let go of her hand and took hold of a briefcase that Lucas handed to him.

The late October sun shone down with a triumphant bust of brightness at that moment, as the high tide crashed onto the shore. A flock of raucous gulls flew over the scene making the loudest cries that Rosie had ever heard. She was getting impatient. 'Why is Jake here looking so, very official in his police uniform?'

Suddenly they all had to run out of the way of a huge wave that was about to deposit a massive foam-capped wave on the beach.

"Quick this way! Jump aside everyone!" Lucas had spotted it coming.

After running from the relentless sea, they had ended up the beach near the cottage once again.

"Now shall we get down to business?" said Lucas seriously.

"What is going on, Lucas, old mate?" Brown Bear was beginning to worry. "It's nothing to do with that conglomerate, is it?"

Rosie nudged Petra and giggled.

"Shush, Rosie, I think this is serious," Petra couldn't help feeling worried too. Her thoughts were running wild. After all, were they going to tell them that the conglomerate was still coming to spoil the island? In her mind's eye she could see the purpose-built hotel on the cliff top, and tourists leaving cigarette ends and ice cream wrappings, littering the beautiful, unspoilt beaches.

Jake stood aside and fumbled in his briefcase.

"I am instructed to give you three girls two documents," he said, loud and precisely. "In my capacity as a police officer, I bear witness to these transactions."

He formally handed Ursula a sealed letter, which she immediately opened and read.

"Oh! How amazing! Father has given me the ownership of the beach cottage! How wonderful!" Ursula was full of joy. "How can I ever thank him enough?"

Then Jake seriously handed Petra and Rosie the other document. The two girls stood hesitantly.

"Go on, do take it." he said.

Petra reached out with a trembling hand and took hold of the very official looking envelope. She opened the seal and gasped, then she smiled in delight.

"Come and see, Rosie. It is only the deeds to the island!"

Rosie read the document. "I can't believe it! How wonderful!"

Lucas was delighted to see how happy all three girls were at that moment.

"Yes, girls, I have no need of the island. I bought it to stop the conglomerate taking possession!" With a broad, happy beam on his face, he said, "Old Bear can live out his days in peace and I will bring you over here whenever you girls want to visit. So, from now on, Petra and Rosie, this mysterious island with all its secrets, belongs to you!"

THE END

Printed in Great Britain
by Amazon